Intimacies

Nelda Jo,

Enjoy the Book!

Mary . Drechsel

Sissy Marlyn

3/06

Intimacies

SISSY MARLYN

Copyediting by Robert Richie

WASTELAND PRESS
Louisville, KY

Wasteland Press
Shelbyville, KY
www.wastelandpress.net

Intimacies
By Sissy Marlyn

Copyright © 2004 Mary C. Drechsel
& Faye Lynn Woods
ALL RIGHTS RESERVED

Cover design by Wasteland Press
Copyediting by Robert Richie
Second Printing – August 2005
ISBN: 1-932852-58-1

Printed in the U.S.A.

CHAPTER ONE

THE WEDDING

"Flora Isabelle Dawson, do you take Jacob Alan Roberts to be your lawfully wedded husband? To love, honor and cherish, in sickness and in health, forsaking all others, till death do you part?" the minister inquired, with a slight grin.

"I do," she responded in a whisper, gazing into the adoring eyes of the man she dearly loved.

"Jacob Alan Roberts, do you take Flora Isabelle Dawson to be your lawfully wedded wife? To love, honor and cherish, in sickness and in health, forsaking all others, till death do you part?" the minister asked Jacob.

"I most certainly do," he resolutely proclaimed, giving Flora a wide, appreciative, confident smile, his steady hands holding her trembling ones.

"Then by the powers vested in me, I now pronounce you man and wife. You may kiss your bride, Jacob," the minister directed.

The minister waited patiently for the two to conclude their passionate embrace before announcing to the congregation, "I'd like to introduce Mr. and Mrs. Jacob Roberts."

The newly married couple briefly glanced and smiled at the well-wishing assembly gathered in the church. Then Jacob clutched Flora's hand, possessively leading, practically dragging, her down the aisle and hurriedly out of the church.

* * * *

This was the second marriage for both Flora and Jacob. Flora's first husband, Anthony, had died of acute leukemia five years ago. Anthony had been diagnosed with the illness shortly after they had wed. For that reason, he and Flora had agreed not to have children.

Jacob's first wife, Elizabeth, on the other hand, had given him a son. Unfortunately, when Jonathan, Jacob's son, was still fairly young – eight years old – his mother had died of a cerebral hemorrhage. So Jacob, and a caring nanny, had been left with the task of raising the boy.

Jonathan, being the flamboyant playboy he was, had not been available to make it to his father's wedding. He was out of town on a cruise to the Caribbean with his current flame. At thirty-four, he unmistakably intended to remain a carefree bachelor his entire life, at any expense. It was not as if his dad had given Jonathan a lot of notice prior to the wedding date. Three days had hardly been sufficient warning to change his plans.

* * * *

Jacob and Flora's wedding reception was being held at Crescent Meadows, an elegant and exceedingly expensive country club on the outskirts of town. Since Jacob was a highly respected cardiovascular surgeon, he could afford to foot the bill for such a lavish affair.

At the age of fifty-five, Jacob persisted in being a stunningly handsome man. He was tall – six-foot-four – with a sturdy chest, and robust arms and legs. His skin was innately bronze, and he had a magnificent smile that showcased perfectly straight, sparkling white teeth.

Jacob's hair, other than a touch of gray at the temples, was a wavy glistening black. In striking contrast, his eyes were the most attractive, alluring shade of sky blue. They instantly captured rapt attention. Flora frequently noticed women longingly appreciating him.

Sometimes Flora wondered why Jacob had chosen to marry *her*. At the age of forty, she was an appealing lady, but unquestionably no fashion model. Flora considered herself short and thickset, standing merely five-feet-three and weighing 125 pounds. In Flora's opinion, this made her hips and upper thighs heavier than she preferred.

If only I was able to move this additional fullness to my bust line, she whimsically contemplated. Flora's breasts were on the small side but *thankfully* firm.

Regardless, Jacob constantly flattered, "In my eyes, you have a perfect woman's body."

He's positively fallen head over heals in love with me, Flora noted with slight amusement and utmost delight.

Shoulder length, permed, short, loose curls softly framed Flora's face. Her hair would have been mostly gray had she not kept it colored its natural, light mousy brown. She had a fair complexion, her skin nearly ivory in places, and she did not tan easily.

Flora's most attractive feature was her deep chocolate brown eyes. They were large and captivating and immediately conveyed warmth to those who beheld them. As did her lovely full lips, often curved into an illuminating smile since the first moment she set eyes on Jacob.

Jacob first met Flora when he retained her services as an attorney to represent him in a malpractice suit. After several months of grueling legal battles, Flora won the case for him. To celebrate, Jacob insisted on treating her to an extravagant dinner at one of the finest, most expensive restaurants in town. Hesitantly, Flora assented, and a very passionate, whirlwind courtship followed.

Jacob and Flora had been romantically involved for less than six months when he had proposed, and she uncharacteristically accepted his proposal without a second thought. He had begged her not to force him into suffering through a lengthy engagement.

"I see no sense in it," Jacob maintained.

He expeditiously persuaded Flora, with his charm and sexual prowess, to marry him as soon as possible. It had taken

Jacob merely a week to make the arrangements for a small, but elaborate, ceremony in a local church, with a chosen group of his associates and Flora's close friends attending. Since he was already an affluent member of the country club, they had been delighted to have been chosen to host the wedding reception, even if it was an awfully short notice.

After having an abundance of wedding photographs taken at the church, Jacob and Flora united with their guests at the country club. "Jacob! Good show. Congratulations!" Dr. Norris approached him, as soon as they had walked in the door. Dr. Michaels, another friend, slapped him on the back, "Glad you finally did it again, Jacob! It's about time!" Three more doctor friends rushed forward as well. He suddenly found himself surrounded by them and distracted by their loud and boisterous well wishes. Jacob looked over a few shoulders at Flora, smiled and shrugged, as if to say, 'sorry'. She gave him a glorious, understanding nod and smile. Then Flora turned and began to search for her two dearest friends, Jackie Lynn Forrester and Mary Julia Walters. She spotted them right away and hurried in their direction.

She had known both these women for many years – Jackie Lynn a few extra, having met and roomed with her in college. After graduating from law school and passing the Bar, she and Jackie Lynn joined separate legal firms. Mary Julia was a partner in the same firm as Jackie Lynn.

Jackie Lynn and Flora often met for lunch. Flora became acquainted with Mary Julia when Jackie Lynn brought her along to lunch one day. Flora instantly hit it off with this younger woman, so Mary Julia also became a close friend of hers.

Flora had been opposite both these ladies in a larger amount of cases than any of them cared to count. Nonetheless, crossing swords in the courtroom had never shaken their deep friendships. They were careful to separate business from their private lives. They never discussed pending briefs or any settlements away from the courtroom.

Flora had shared many delightful occasions with these two women. She had also shared some excruciatingly sad ones as well – the death of both her parents and the death of her beloved first husband. During these despairing events, the constant, unwavering support of these two special women had been a beacon of hope and strength for Flora.

Flora truly believed that she would have never overcome her grief if it had not been for the vital support and companionship of Jackie Lynn and Mary Julia. She had been an only child, but in Flora's heart, Jackie Lynn and Mary Julia were her sisters. Even though Flora considered these two women kindred sisters, no one would have ever mistaken them as such.

The differences in their appearances were distinct. Jackie Lynn was the tallest, being almost five-foot-eight, with a flattering breast line, a narrow waist and long slender legs. Her luminous, straight, jet-black hair hung well past the center of her back when she let it down.

Today, Jackie Lynn had styled it with soft, feathery curls, pinned up with sparkling butterfly clips. A floor length, tangerine dress clung loosely to her body, with a scoop neck and drastically low cut back. Her deep-set eyes were a guarded, yet seductive, emerald green, ideally highlighted by the most appealing, long, curled eyelashes. Her skin tone was inherently dark and she had a wide, radiant smile. She was a lovely lady.

Mary Julia was a ravishing woman. She was nearly as tall as Jackie Lynn. She had a tiny waist, long sleek legs, and voluptuous breasts, giving her body a distinct hourglass shape. Mary Julia's long, flowing hair was a flashy, naturally wavy, golden blond. She had big, dreamy, sapphire blue eyes and the most enticing, fullest, soft pink lips. Her eyes shone even brighter considering Mary Julia carefully kept her skin tanned a golden brown, either from the sun or tanning beds.

Away from her professional life, Mary Julia dressed in ways that emphasized her shapely body. The formal, periwinkle, strapless, form fitting gown she had chosen to wear for this occasion was no exception, with a slit up one side practically to the hip. The string of pearls she donned brought greater attention than necessary to her exposed cleavage.

"Congratulations, Flora," Jackie Lynn uttered, stepping forward to give her a tight embrace. "You look absolutely beautiful!"

Jacob had insisted upon buying his wife-to-be a traditional wedding gown. The three women had taken an entire day and flown to New York, in a private jet chartered by Jacob, in search of the perfect dress. Jacob emphasized they spare no expense.

By the end of an exhausting trip, they had chosen the finest from Sachs Fifth Avenue – a white satin dress, floor length, with an empire waist. The top half of the gown was inlaid with tiny divine pearls. Soft chiffon covered the lower half, and the impressive train was in excess of ten feet in length.

Flora's accompanying veil was a halo adorned with dainty pink and white roses. Chiffon lace was attached across the back with a small portion across the front to drape her face. Her bouquet had large white roses, intertwined with tiny pink ones, white ribbons trailing beneath it.

"Thanks, Jackie Lynn," Flora replied with an ecstatic grin. "I haven't been this happy in many years."

"I can tell," Mary Julia cordially chimed in with a warm smile, also initiating an affectionate hug. "You're glowing."

"I'm going to miss both of you," she wistfully admitted. "We'll have to get together often for dinner. Maybe I might even drive into the city and have lunch with the two of you on occasion."

"Definitely," Jackie Lynn concurred as Mary Julia vigorously nodded. "The practice of law won't be the same without you to fight."

When Flora had accepted Jacob's proposal, she had elected to depart from her law firm. Jacob owned a spacious residence in a small town two hours from the city, and his wish was for her to join him there after their weeklong honeymoon in the Cayman Islands. Flora intended to set up a modest, private law practice closer to her new home, even though she did not expect to be overly busy. She was so exclusively in love with Jacob she was willing to make the sacrifice.

"So here is where you've run off to," Flora heard Jacob say. He stepped behind her and covetously circled her waist with his arms. "Some of our other guests are waiting to be introduced to my lovely bride."

"Hey, they dragged you away from me," Flora teased, turning in her new husband's arms and giving him a brief, reassuring kiss.

"Well, I'll have to make sure this doesn't come to pass anymore. I can't stand not having you by my side for one second now that you are Mrs. Jacob Roberts," he stated, giving her one more kiss before grasping her hand to sweep her away.

"I'll talk to you later," Flora informed Jackie Lynn and Mary Julia with a broad, agreeable smile, light-heartedly permitting herself to be whisked in the opposite direction.

"I'm thrilled Flora is so happy," Jackie Lynn confessed. She and Mary Julia headed toward the buffet line, an impressive arrangement of gourmet food.

"Me too," Mary Julia conceded. "She was devastated when Anthony died. I didn't imagine she would ever love again."

"I'm going to miss her though," Jackie Lynn acknowledged.

"I will as well," Mary Julia seconded. "Even though we still have each other."

"Yeah, until you find someone special and walk down that ol' wedding aisle too," she teased.

"Hey, I'm only thirty-five. You're the one turning the *big* 4 O later this year. You're the next one who should settle down. I'm having way too much fun playing the field. See that waiter standing at the end of the buffet?" She pointed, leering suggestively at the young, handsome Mexican. "I may either give him my telephone number or get his before this soiree is over."

"You're incorrigible," Jackie Lynn playfully reprimanded.

Mary Julia undeniably *did* play the field. She rarely dated the same guy twice, and her indiscriminate wildness sometimes worried Jackie Lynn. However, Jackie Lynn had no lasting relationships with the opposite sex either. She was content having many, occasional, short lived romances. So, in some ways, she and Mary Julia were remarkably alike.

"Ma'am, would you prefer Prime Rib or Filet Mignon?" She heard the server at the buffet question, as she refocused her attention on the reception.

* * * *

Mary Julia did not wait until after the wedding reception to acquaint herself with the inviting Mexican waiter. That he barely spoke English mattered little. She was not interested in his personality. She was solely interested in getting him alone somewhere, to discover if the parts of his body obscured by clothing were as desirable as those showing. She quietly sneaked from the table she was sharing with Jackie Lynn.

Jackie Lynn saw Mary Julia leave and figured she was heading to the ladies' restroom. When Mary Julia did reappeared within a reasonable interval, Jackie Lynn went to check on her. Finding the bathroom empty, she apprehensively wondered where her friend might be.

Perhaps she is in the dining room, mingling in the crowd, and I overlooked her, she theorized.

Jackie Lynn reentered the dining room, headed toward their table and thoroughly scanned the vast hall, but she glimpsed no sign of Mary Julia. *That's odd,* she thought.

A massive golf course and some beautiful grounds surrounded the country club, but it was absolutely sweltering outside. So Jackie Lynn could not imagine why Mary Julia might have ventured outdoors. As she had prepared to abandon her search and be seated, Jackie Lynn spotted Mary Julia coming through the kitchen doors.

The Mexican waiter Mary Julia had pointed to earlier was behind her. Jackie Lynn watched Mary Julia turn toward the fellow with a wicked grin and brazenly point downward toward his pants. Mirroring her lewd grin, the Mexican reached down to zip his trousers. Mary Julia straightened her dress. Jackie Lynn hoped her perception of the situation was faulty. *This man is a virtual stranger. Surely Mary Julia hasn't just.... No! There must be some other logical explanation.* Jackie Lynn urgently tried to convince herself.

CHAPTER TWO

DISCOVERIES

Despite her nagging worry, Jackie Lynn chose not to confront Mary Julia concerning what had transpired with the Mexican waiter. *Does she do this sort of thing often with total strangers? Surely not! But if not, why engage in such distasteful behavior at Flora's wedding reception of all places?*

The whole incident sickened her. If she witnessed it happening anymore, she would have to speak to Mary Julia. Her erratic conduct could get her into serious trouble or even *God forbid* killed. She could meet up with some psycho or catch AIDS.

"Jackie Lynn," Mary Julia addressed, interrupting her deep reflection. "Which defense should we use?"

They were sitting in a conference room, researching past legal cases in search of the proper defense for the wrongful death suit they were currently representing. Jackie Lynn studied this younger lady's intelligent face. *For God sakes, she's a professional lawyer, and skillful at her career,* she acknowledged. She decided to disregard the silly occurrence at Flora's reception. *Mary Julia's fine. She's promiscuous, but I don't suffer in that area either.*

"Um…we should use this one," Jackie Lynn answered. She pointed to a specific legal decision and handed her partner the supporting written documentation to read.

* * * *

That evening after work, Mary Julia persuaded Jackie Lynn to go to a nearby, popular bar. *I may meet somebody new*, Jackie Lynn reflected. *Regardless, we always have a lot of fun when we go out together.*

They followed virtually the same routine every time. They had a few drinks – Jackie Lynn preferred Cuervo Gold Tequila or Miller Lite Beer; Mary Julia mostly stuck to mixed drinks: Strawberry Daiquiris, Pina Coladas, or Whiskey Sour. They danced until they practically dropped, and they always ended either giving out their phone numbers or accepting a telephone number from at least one guy. Jackie Lynn did not always date these men. She even sometimes gave a fictitious phone number if she wished not to receive a call from the man.

It was a big game to her, and playing the game was always fun. Jackie Lynn assumed playing this courting game with men was merely fun for Mary Julia as well. The notion that her sidekick might actually be entertaining every male she accepted numbers from or gave numbers to never occurred to her.

* * * *

The ladies were accomplished lawyers, but even the best legal teams are incapable of winning every case. After an especially grueling morning in court, the two women returned to the firm exhausted and disappointed. They had dedicated countless hours to preparing for their latest case – a civil suit against a sexual offender, who had been found innocent in criminal court. Yet, they had lost.

To lighten the mood, Jackie Lynn suggested, "Why don't we take an early lunch?"

"Um… I can't. I have an important meeting with a prospective client," Mary Julia enlightened her. "Hopefully, they didn't hear about our recent loss, or they may not show."

"You're familiar with the saying 'you win some; you lose some'. But *damn*, I was sure we would win. I feel as if

I've been bled out, they clobbered us so severely," Jackie Lynn shared in despair.

"Me too," her partner commiserated, staring discontentedly down at her feet.

"Well, I'm going to lunch and have a stiff drink to settle myself down. See you later."

"Bye," Mary Julia absently responded.

Her mind was already deeply preoccupied by a secret plan to elevate her own mood. Mary Julia waited until she was certain Jackie Lynn had left. Then she telephoned a male associate who worked for a nearby opposing legal firm. She was not calling to discuss a case.

* * * *

Jackie Lynn returned to the office half an hour later. She did not have much appetite, so she had patronized a small, but decent, nearby bar, snacked on some pretzels, had one drink and left. She had also stopped at a fast food restaurant, purchasing a couple of sodas and sandwiches, for herself and for Mary Julia.

Perhaps I might persuade my hardworking partner to share lunch with me when she is finished with her client, she conceived.

As she passed by the receptionist, she questioned, "Is Mary Julia's client still in her office?"

"You mean Sam Meadows? I'd hardly regard him as a client, and the activity being engaged in behind *that* closed door is *barely* even legal." The receptionist snickered. "They got somewhat loud, but they've quieted down. Guess it was simply a quickie. Rather good for a fellow his age."

Sam Meadows? The receptionist's assumption must be incorrect, Jackie Lynn loyally theorized. *Mary Julia doesn't even like Sam Meadows. She considers him an egotistical jerk. Worse yet, he's quite a bit older than she is. Mary Julia is half his age.*

She gave the receptionist a stern, disapproving grimace and scurried down the hall past Mary Julia's office. She was about to enter her own office when she heard Mary Julia's door opening. Sam Meadows emerged into the hallway. Fortunately, he was busy smoothing down his perfectly white hair, neatly straightening his tie and checking his other clothing, so he did not notice her watching him.

* * * *

Jackie Lynn sought momentary refuge in her own office. She wearily took a seat behind her desk, allowing her perplexed brain to run wild. *First, the stranger at Flora's wedding reception! Now, Sam Meadows! What in the world is going on?! Am I crazy?! Am I imagining things that aren't actually happening?!*

She sensibly accepted that confronting Mary Julia was the only way to unravel her suspicions. *How do I even raise the issue?*

It would be bad enough if her friend was dating and sleeping with multiple men. Mary Julia was known to behave in such a manor from time to time. *But a stranger and a significantly older man, who this woman had never hidden her dislike of?*

Jackie Lynn's racing concerns were giving her a dreadful headache. She reached in a drawer, located a container of Tylenol, popped two pills in her mouth and washed them down with some of her soft drink.

I've got to speak to Mary Julia about this, and fast!

Jackie Lynn dashed from her office and determinedly charged, without knocking, into her partner's office. She whisked the door shut behind her, slamming it in the process. Substantially startled by the noisy, unanticipated interruption, Mary Julia shuddered in her chair.

"What on earth is going on, Jackie Lynn?!"

"Funny you should ask that. That's exactly what *I'm* wondering," she initiated. "What the hell was Sam Meadows doing here?! Pardon my French, but you absolutely loathe him!"

"When did you see him?" Mary Julia evasively questioned. Her eyes were serious, and she squirmed in her chair.

"He was leaving your office, appearing strangely to be redressing. The receptionist swore it sounded as if the two of you were having a hell of a soiree in here!" Jackie Lynn disclosed, not mincing any words.

Mary Julia's mouth flew open. She stared at Jackie Lynn in astonished disbelief for a few moments. Then she unexpectedly burst into tears.

"There… there's no logical explanation why I did it," she said through her sobs. "It was something I had to do. Will you please be a good friend, and get off my back. There's no harm done. I ran into him the other day and…well… he was flirting, and suggested the two of us get together for lunch. I told you I was meeting with a client because I knew you might think I was crazy after the nasty things I say about him. Although…he's a lot better at this sort of activity than he is at being an attorney."

"Mary Julia, lunch with him is one thing. You had sex with him in your office. That's extreme!" Jackie Lynn persisted. She took a seat in front of Mary Julia's desk, apprehensively studying her friend.

"You're right," Mary Julia concurred. She pulled a tissue from a box on her desk, blew her nose, and dried her eyes and cheeks. "I appreciate your worry since I know you care. Except your worry isn't necessary. It won't happen again. It's just…we've been working so hard for so long. Still we lost the case. I needed something totally out of the ordinary to occur."

Mary Julia paused, adding with a slight giggle, "It was nuts! Especially when the true cure for what ails me would be getting out and having some fun. Why don't we plan a girl's night out this Saturday? We'll call Flora and persuade her to join us. What do you say?! Come on! It will do us *all* some good. Do you realize how long it's been since the three of us have had some real, down to earth fun?!"

Jackie Lynn had to admit it had been an exceedingly long while since they had done anything fun. It had been over

14

a month since the two of them had even stopped by a nearby bar after work. They had been so busy lately neither had taken the opportunity for any enjoyment; yet they had lost the case today anyway.

Maybe that's it. Perhaps Mary Julia's simply overworked. If she cuts loose, she'll be alright. "Okay," Jackie Lynn conceded, rashly deciding it would be delightful dressing down – *not in our prim and proper attorneys' wardrobes* – and having some well-deserved fun for a change. *I haven't even been on a date in months*, she recognized.

"Great! You won't regret this!" Mary Julia was exuberant.

I hope not, Jackie Lynn thought. She vowed to keep a close watch on her younger friend.

* * * *

The idea of getting together with the two of them excited Flora. She had talked to her friends a few times on the phone, but she had not seen either of them since the wedding. Jacob would be away for the weekend on business, as he frequently was, and Flora had discovered it could be very lonely in his mansion when he was gone. Plus, she greatly missed seeing these women anyway.

Flora agreed to meet Mary Julia at her apartment, and the two would ride together to Snippets Saturday night. Snippets was their favorite club. It was downtown in the heart of the city. Jackie Lynn intended to join her friends there.

The club was housed in a large, old, restored brick building. There was a huge, wooden dance floor with spectacular strobe lighting all around it. There was a stage behind the dance floor for either the DJ or the live band. Music from the seventies was always booming from speakers from one of these two sources. A well-worn, large mahogany bar was along the other side. The same friendly bar staff and bouncers had been there for years, so the girls always felt relaxed coming to Snippets – either as a group or on their own. In fact, they knew the bartenders and bouncers by name, and vice versa, the bartenders and bouncers also knew them. There were several tables with chairs around them. The walls of the bar were decorated with framed, heartthrob, pinup posters and pictures from popular television shows and movies from the seventies.

When Jackie Lynn arrived at Snippets, twenty minutes after her friends, Mary Julia was already nursing her third drink, had left Flora's side and was vivaciously flirting with a loud and rowdy group of males near the bar.

Flora hastened to share her uneasiness concerning their friend with Jackie Lynn. It was not merely the fact that Mary Julia was drinking amply and flirting with so many men so early which bothered Flora. It was much, much more.

It was the crazy way Mary Julia had styled her hair. Flora had never seen it picked so full and sticking out in so many wild directions. It was the abundant makeup she had applied. Mary Julia's eyes were heavily outlined with deep black eyeliner and gobs of mascara. Her cheekbones were rather unattractively emphasized by tons of red blush, and she had applied a vivid scarlet red lipstick.

Yet, the worst was Mary Julia's choice of wardrobe. She had on a skin tight, barely below the hips, shimmering, bright red dress. The neckline was cut so low it practically flaunted half of her bare breasts in the open.

To Flora, Mary Julia did not look herself. On the contrary, she looked quite cheap. Nevertheless, Jackie Lynn reassured Flora that it was altogether in fun, "Like the old days when we would tease the boys and leave them at the doorstep. Mary Julia just needs to loosen up a little tonight. It's been a rough week."

Hence, as the evening moved into night, the ladies – except Flora, who was purely a cheerful observer – drank, laughed, and teased. At one point, Mary Julia and Jackie Lynn simultaneously rose from their small table, impulsively accepting two men's dance invitations.

When Jackie Lynn reappeared, she inquired, "Where'd Mary Julia go?"

Flora told her Mary Julia had gone outside for some fresh air and would return shortly. *Shortly* wound up being over half an hour, and when their friend reemerged, she was a mess. Her clothes were peculiarly disheveled and her hair was frazzled.

Jackie Lynn had intended to interrogate Mary Julia about her odd appearance, but Mary Julia did not give either of her friends the opportunity. Instead, she headed directly to the bar and mingled briefly with a group of men standing there, before she nabbed one of them to dance.

Mary Julia eventually revisited their table, but it was simply to declare, "Well, girls, I'm in lust. I'm splitting with my new honey."

"Yeah, right!" Jackie Lynn exclaimed with an amused chuckle. She thought Mary Julia was merely teasing.

"Flora, take care. Jackie Lynn, I'll see you Monday," she established and raced toward the leering male who impatiently waited near the exit. The unknown man pulled her tautly alongside him, ushering her out the door.

"Is she alright?" Flora probed apprehensively.

"I'm not sure," Jackie Lynn admitted. She had been convinced a fun girl's night out would throw Mary Julia back on track. *Did I really believe that? Or was I avoiding facing that there is a problem?* Jackie Lynn had to wonder.

Regardless, the woman had left with yet another stranger. "Listen, it's late. Why don't you come to my apartment, stay tonight and I'll fill you in on what's been happening with Mary Julia lately. Maybe we can put our heads together and decide what to do. Then tomorrow, when I drive you to your car at Mary Julia's, perhaps we might reason with her."

"Sounds like a winning plan," Flora hastened to agree. Jacob was not supposed to return until tomorrow evening, so she was free.

The ladies left the bar and headed to Jackie Lynn's for the night.

* * * *

17

Flora was shocked and unsettled when Jackie Lynn relayed Mary Julia's bizarre, troubling encounters with a waiter at her wedding reception and with Sam Meadows at the firm. She loved the girl and was very concerned about her also.

Early the next morning, Jackie Lynn drove her to Mary Julia's, but they did not find her at home. Flora parted from Jackie Lynn then, headed to her house in the country, but she was intent on returning to the city that afternoon for their essential conversation with Mary Julia.

Flora wanted a fresh change of clothes. Hers smelled highly of smoke from the bar, and Flora could not borrow any of Jackie Lynn's due to the enormous differences in their heights and body shapes. She also wanted to make sure the house was in order for Jacob's arrival that evening.

* * * *

Two hours later, as Flora pulled into her driveway, she was surprised to discover Jacob's Porsche there. *He must have returned early for some reason*, she happily accepted.

Flora rushed inside with a delighted, expectant grin. She missed Jacob immeasurably when he went away on business, which was much too often. "Jacob?!" she joyfully howled, sprinting into the great room.

He was sitting on the couch with a drink in his hand. "Where have you been?!" he interrogated, his face locked in a dark scowl.

"I spent the night with Jackie Lynn," Flora clarified, apprehensively wondering why Jacob appeared solemn and annoyed. "The girls persuaded me to go out with them last night. It was so late afterwards that I stayed in the city."

"Don't lie to me, Flora!" Jacob unexpectedly shouted. He slammed his drink on the table so hard that the liquid within splattered across the black walnut tabletop. Jacob then sprang to his feet, grabbing Flora's elbow. "Who were you really with?! Tell me the truth!"

"Jacob, you're hurting me!" Flora exclaimed in utmost surprise. "What on earth's the matter?! I really was with Jackie Lynn. Call her if you don't trust my word."

As if Jacob's cutting words and his painful vice grip on her arm were not bad enough, Flora was shaken to the core by what happened next. With lightening speed, Jacob struck her. His hand met Flora's cheek with such deafening force that she stumbled backwards, landing awkwardly on the couch.

"How stupid do you presume I am?!" Jacob demanded to know. "I recognize friends cover for friends. You bitch! You're cheating on me, aren't you? Come on! Admit it! You spent the night with another man!"

Jacob climbed on top of Flora, pinning her to the sofa. She could smell the strong stench of brandy on his breath. He senselessly ripped open her blouse. In stunned bewilderment, Flora pleaded for him to stop.

"Shut up, you whore!" Jacob yelled, squeezing below her cheekbones so hard that Flora genuinely wondered if her teeth might be crushed.

Is that blood I'm tasting?!

"You're *my* wife! I may take from you whatever I desire! You *won't* stop me! Especially considering you've broken our vows and freely given it to somebody else."

Jacob jerked Flora upright onto unsteady feet and spun her around. With repeated uncompromising thrusts of his open palm to the middle of her back, he shoved her from the room. When she toppled in weakened shock at the foot of the stairs, Jacob cold-heartedly dragged Flora up each and every marble step leading to their bedroom on her knees. Had it not been for her jeans, the hard stairs would have easily torn all of the flesh on her knees and the bottom of her legs to shreds. As it was, it still agonizingly cut and bruised her.

Once behind the closed door, Jacob heaved Flora to her feet. He flung her across the room as if she were a rag doll. She fell with a loud thud by the bed, narrowly escaping striking her head on the bedside table. Jacob walked over to the bed and hoisted the bedcovers back.

He yanked Flora from the floor, unzipped her tattered jeans, and pushed these and her panties down to her ankles. Shoving her into a sitting position on the side of the bed, he stooped to fully discard her jeans and panties. Jacob completely disregarded the injuries to her legs that he had so cruelly inflicted.

Jacob peeled the torn blouse from Flora's body and unhooked her bra and removed it, so that she was totally naked. He tossed these items of clothing on the floor with her jeans and panties. Flora began to silently cry fearing that Jacob was about to rape her.

"Get into bed, you lying, cheating bitch!" Jacob hatefully commanded as Flora shuddered in response. "You *will* sleep in the arms of your husband. As it should always be! As you vowed it *would* always be! As it shall be from now on. You will *not* ever cheat on me again! I'll see you dead first!"

Flora weakly pulled her legs off of the floor. She hurriedly slid beneath the bedcovers, pulling the sheet, blanket and comforter all the way up to her neck. She lie flat on her back trembling, terrified of what Jacob might do next.

Jacob unbuttoned his shirt and pushed it from his body. Then he hastily removed his jeans and underwear, pushing them to the floor. He went around to the other side of the bed and slid his nude body under the bedcovers beside his horrified wife.

Jacob turned Flora toward him and possessively slid her into his arms. Flora squeezed her eyes shut and uncontrollably cried and shivered. "You are *mine*, Flora. Now and forever! You will not *ever* forget that again!" he sternly warned. He pressed her bruised body much too tightly against his own body.

* * * *

Hours later, Flora awoke from an uneasy sleep. *Had I actually been sleeping or did I pass out from the shock?*

Thankfully, she was alone in the bed. As Flora allowed herself to fully regain consciousness, memories of the ghastly ordeal from earlier materialized with vivid clarity. She wished it had all been a terrible nightmare, but she knew it had not been.

Further proof that Jacob's unthinkable assault had genuinely occurred was the throbbing pain from head to toe that now coursed through Flora's body. She felt as if she had been pounded by a sledgehammer.

Tears trickled down her cheeks once more. In fear, she pulled the bedcovers to her neck again to cover her entire naked, battered body. She began to wail, yet sensibly muffled her noisy sobs by placing her battered face deep into the pillow.

As her brain replayed the whole horrifying incident, she prayed Jacob had left, gone somewhere far away. A noise at the door alerted her that her prayer was not to be answered. When the door opened, Flora pretended to be asleep – a move she felt wise.

Jacob advanced slowly and quietly to the bed. He observed the fresh wet places on the pillow near his wife's head. Without pause, he dropped to his knees and began to cry.

He adamantly professed in a whisper, "I adore you, Flora. I never intended to harm you. It was the liquor. This won't ever happen again. I promise. I'm begging for your forgiveness!" Jacob gently stroked Flora's hair as she inconsolably wept. "Please don't cry. I'm *so* sorry, my love," he further maintained.

Flora hesitantly rolled to face him. *Who is this man I have the misfortune to love with all my heart? Why'd he marry me?*

"Jacob, do I really know you? How could you be so violent? Why did you marry me? How could you have ever…ever thought that I might have…have cheated on you? I love you more than…than I can possibly put into words," she ranted between sobs.

"Oh, my darling, Flora! I know!" he exclaimed. He took her hand in both of his and kissed it. "I was a fool! Such a beast! I can't stand the way I've hurt you." He burrowed his face into the mattress, brokenheartedly weeping.

21

Flora's profound love for Jacob propelled her to reach out to him despite the monster he had been hours before. She caressed the back of his head, tears streaming down her own cheeks as well. Jacob raised his head and torso, gathering Flora in his arms with care.

They remained embracing and weeping for nearly an hour. "Flora, will you forgive me? May we put this dreadful incident behind us and never mention it?" he pleaded. He pulled his chin off her shoulder and studied her bloodshot eyes.

"Jacob, I have to be honest with you," she hesitantly began. "I'll never forget the horrible things you did to me. I don't understand how you are capable of such...such...awful violence."

"It's not who I am, Flora," he maintained. "You know the real me. You married the real me. I went totally crazy. My first wife couldn't handle how much I had to be gone with my career. She was constantly running around on me. When I got home early this morning and found our bed unslept in, I drank myself into a furious jealous stupor. When you sauntered in with that blissful innocent smile, something within me snapped. Elizabeth used to lie with a smile after she had been with other men. The memories of her betrayal and the fear that I might be losing you to another man as well were unbearable for me. That's no excuse for hurting you, but please try to understand. I won't allow it to happen again."

"Did you hit Elizabeth too?" She dared to suggest.

"Wha..what? Of course not!" He professed. "Oh my God! Do you regard me as a monster now?! It was just this once! I promise my actions will *never* be repeated! You said you went out with the girls. It was quite late afterwards so you stayed in the city with Jackie Lynn. Where did you go with the girls? To a bar? Are you telling me you didn't go there to look and dance with other men? If you persist in doing this, eventually it would be too easy to spend the night with another man whenever I'm away. Don't you realize this? Flora, it's a necessity that I trust you. I must be convinced you won't betray me and break my heart like Elizabeth did."

Flora was suddenly struck with guilt, despite the fact that going out with the girls had been completely innocent on her part. If Jacob had been wronged by his first wife, it was reasonable he might be insanely jealous if he deduced she was with other men when he was not at home. *When the cat's away, the mice will play.*

"I apologize, Jacob. If you'd told me of your insecurities before, I wouldn't have gone with the girls. Even though I wasn't flirting with other men or dancing with them. You consumed my mind the entire night. I don't have the desire to so much as look at another male. I adore you!"

"I adore you with my whole heart too, Flora! I couldn't stand it if I lost you. Life wouldn't be worth living," he vowed, hugging her.

Flora winced in pain. Her side was extremely sore where she had fallen when he had hurled her across their bedroom. Jacob immediately noticed her discomfort.

"Darling, it's essential you remove the covers and permit me to examine you," he informed her, his eyes relaying his concern and regret. "I'll get my medical bag."

When Jacob left, Flora laid there actively thinking. *What else don't I understand about Jacob? In fact, how much do I really know about him? He'd been drinking. Maybe it was the alcohol that caused his drastic change in demeanor. He's kind and caring now. I love him deeply. Don't I owe him one more chance?*

Jacob reentered the bedroom. He carefully peeled the bedcovers away, fully exposing his wife's naked body. He began to expertly care for the injuries he had so brutally imposed. His eyes held such pain and remorse they broke Flora's heart.

I'll give Jacob one more chance. Perhaps I do truly understand what I need to about him. Surely, he'll never hurt me again. Flora was convinced.

23

CHAPTER THREE

ACCEPTANCE

Flora telephoned Jackie Lynn late that afternoon. "I'm sorry, Jackie Lynn," she apologized. "Jacob came home unexpectedly. Moreover, since we've been apart, it seems like forever since we've had the opportunity to be alone together."

"You don't have to apologize or explain to me," she stated with an envious chuckle. "You two lovebirds enjoy being together. I'm capable of confronting Mary Julia by myself."

"Tell her I'm concerned too," Flora requested. Guilt washed over her because she could not be there for these two dear women.

There was no way she was capable of joining Jackie Lynn with Mary Julia this afternoon. She was severely bruised from head to toe, and Flora had promised Jacob she would never divulge the appalling things he had done to her.

It is to be our secret.

Desperately endeavoring to atone for his unforgivable actions, Jacob had gently made love to Flora an hour before. She had tried in every way to respond to his lovemaking as she had before, but the unbearable memories from his brutal attack had kept reemerging and forbidding her to do so.

Jacob entered the study as Flora was hanging up the telephone. "Who were you talking to?" He was calm, genuinely interested.

Flora hesitantly responded, "I was talking Jackie Lynn. Mary Julia's having some major problems. Jackie Lynn and I had intended to get together again today at Mary Julia's apartment and attempt to reason with her."

Jacob walked to the sofa, sat down beside Flora and gently placed an arm around her shoulder. He raised her hair and affectionately kissed her neck. "You're not going, are you?" he probed with some concern.

"No, Jacob," Flora assured him, as tears welled. "I told you no one would ever find out what transpired. I meant that. I *am* worried about my friends though."

"Of course you are. You're an exceedingly caring person. But do you have to remain *so* involved in their lives? They have each other to lean on in their troubles. You have me. After all, they are single. You are married," he reminded Flora, briefly kissing her lips before she had a chance to respond.

"I need for you to show me I'm indispensable in your life, Flora. I need for you to stay here in this house. Not merely when I'm here, but when I'm gone. It would mean a great deal to me. I'll never have to wonder where you are or who you're with. You'll always be here to greet me as soon as I walk through the front door or answer my calls when I'm away. If you promise to abide by this *small* request, it would enormously ease my mind," Jacob enlightened her.

Flora incessantly studied his eyes, considering Jacob's request and the terrible insecurities his first wife had instilled. Very slowly, barely above a whisper, she replied, "Jacob, I love you! I *can* do this for you. I'll be here to greet you when you return and speak with you when you are far away. I promise."

Jacob adoringly laid his head on her lap. In a low soft voice he responded, "Flora, there aren't words to express how much that means to me. When I'm not home, I long to be with you. I miss you profusely. To hear your voice on the other end of the phone will give me unfathomable comfort. To behold your beautiful smiling face first thing when I enter shall make me happier than you might imagine. Knowing you'll always be here will make it substantially easier for me."

Flora smiled down into Jacob's face and bent to kiss his forehead, as if he were a child. *I'll remain in his house and be here exclusively for him. I'll convince him of my complete, unwavering devotion to him and he will soon doubtlessly trust me. That awful insecurity that caused him to be so uncharacteristically violent shall be eliminated. I'll make certain of this.*

* * * *

Jackie Lynn rang her friend's doorbell and waited. When Mary Julia did not answer after several minutes, she held in on the bell and loudly clapped the knocker. A few more seconds passed before she heard the chain rattling on the other side of the door.

When the door opened, she was shocked to find herself face-to-face with a long, greasy haired guy she had never seen before. Jackie Lynn warily backed up a step or two, glancing around in the hallway, bewildered, wondering if she perchance had somehow approached the wrong residence.

"What can I do for you, babe?" The derelict questioned, leering at her suggestively and rubbing his bare chest.

"Is..Is..Mary Julia at home?" Jackie Lynn stuttered in a shaky voice, noticing how badly he smelled. He reeked of body odor and bad breath.

"She's busy with a buddy of mine. Why don't you come in and wait, pretty lady. Or you can join in on the fun yourself. Or sit and watch," he offered with a sinister grin, reaching for her hand as if to draw her within.

Jackie Lynn instinctively pulled away from his repulsive touch, staring at him in disbelief. Her stomach churned and a frightened chill ran up and down her spine. *Surely Mary Julia hadn't slept with this vagabond and was currently having sex with somebody else. There must be some terrible mistake!* Her brain could not possibly conceive of this latest atrocity.

"If you aren't coming in, baby, I'm closing the door in your pretty face. They're waiting on me...or probably not. Most likely already going at it hot and heavy. But we planned a threesome and I'm not missing that. You are welcome to join us and make it a foursome," he propositioned.

The leech surveyed her body, especially her chest. A wide smile revealed yellow, almost green, teeth. Jackie Lynn spun around, scampering down the hall toward the stairs leading to the exit. "It's your loss," she heard the scraggly beast shout as he closed the door.

Oh my God! He's going back to her! she discerned in horror. *It's essential I do something. But what?*

Jackie Lynn recognized that she could not barge into Mary Julia's apartment and drag her out of the middle of two men. She herself might likely get raped in the process. *Something's seriously wrong with Mary Julia! I've got to help her!*

Jackie Lynn raced from the building, got in her car, and locked the doors behind her. With trembling hands, she reached in the glove box and retrieved her cell phone, dialing 9-1-1. She ingeniously pretended to live in the building, telling the operator, "I heard several screams for help from a neighbor's apartment...I think someone's being assaulted!" She gave them Mary Julia's unit number.

When the police show up and demand the door opened, I'll rush in and shake some sense into Mary Julia. She sat impatiently, straining her ears to hear the police sirens. *It's taking much too long! Where in the world are they!* Jackie Lynn anxiously wondered. In actuality, it had only been a few moments, but in Jackie Lynn's mind, it was taking an eternity for the police to arrive.

Finally! she thought with relief, as she heard the siren getting louder and louder. *Thank God!*

The police cruiser skidded to a halt in the parking space beside her car, and two officers sprang from their vehicle and rushed toward the building entrance. Jackie Lynn decided she could not wait any longer. She leapt from her automobile, stumbling over the curb in a hasty attempt to get through the door with the gentlemen in uniform.

The policemen were already climbing the steps. When she arrived on the third floor, they were emphatically pounding on Mary Julia's door. The police officers were becoming irritated by their hampered effort to end the violent episode inside. Faint moaning sounds came from within.

After several persistent knocks and shouts of 'Police! Open the door this minute!' the larger officer motioned for the smaller one to step aside.

The larger policeman planted a foot in the thin door, breaking the flimsy lock and sending it crashing open alongside the wall. The police officers stormed inside, guns drawn in preparation for being confronted by a violent criminal. Upon the sight of the guns, Jackie Lynn became frightened and she followed them inside, screaming in alarm, "Please don't hurt her! She doesn't realize what she's doing! Mary Julia, where are you?!"

The smaller officer turned and caught sight of Jackie Lynn jogging wildly toward them. He grabbed her by the waist and roughly flattened her alongside the closest wall. "What the hell do you think you're doing, lady?" he barked.

Then the officer sternly ordered, "Stay where you are!" and left Jackie Lynn, racing to assist his partner in the other room – Mary Julia's bedroom.

For the next few moments, Jackie Lynn heard much yelling. The police were commanding somebody to desist and put their hands above their head. She heard additional shouts – protests from the riffraff Mary Julia had been fooling around with. She was startled when she heard a noisy racket that sounded as if someone was fiercely struggling, and simultaneously heard Mary Julia wailing.

My God! What have I done?

Jackie Lynn could linger in the living room no longer. She dashed into her friend's bedroom, stopping abrupt when she came face-to-face with a sheer nightmare. The foul smell was nearly unbearable. Mary Julia was crouched on the floor completely naked. Red handprints were visible up and down her back and bottom side.

She was hysterically crying and screaming, "Get out! What is wrong with you? They weren't hurting me! It was voluntary. Stop it!"

The policemen ignored her. They had already handcuffed one of the highly offensive culprits. The other, after foolishly striving to fight off the larger policeman, had been shoved facedown on the floor near Mary Julia. In the foulest of language, he was cursing and spitting, furiously attempting an escape. Luckily, this vile animal was no match for the policeman. He was swiftly handcuffed too.

The two men safely under control, Jackie Lynn ran to Mary Julia's aid. However, she did not receive the warmhearted welcome she had naively expected. Mary Julia gaped at her in shock, questioning, "You did this?! You called the police? What's wrong with you?! Have you gone totally nuts?!"

Jackie Lynn watched in astonishment as, without concern or shame, Mary Julia stood and strutted seductively to the big policeman. Openly flaunting her nakedness in front of him, she questioned, "So, considering you've rudely interrupted my fun, are *you* planning on finishing the job they started?"

Jackie Lynn grabbed the bedspread, sprung forward and hastily wrapped it around Mary Julia's lewdly exposed body. Hoping to clarify, she pleaded, "Please don't pay any attention to her, officer! She hasn't been well! She's reacting strange to the trauma of today's events."

Mary Julia, enraged, struggled with Jackie Lynn, attempting to rip herself free from the concealing blanket. "Let go of me! Who do you suddenly assume you are?! My mother?!"

"Ladies," the policeman addressed, directing his partner to remove the two men. "I'm unclear as to what transpired here, but I have an excellent guess. I'm assuming it won't be necessary to place rape charges against those two men we are removing."

"Hell no!" Mary Julia screamed in defiance, her eyes glaring with hate at Jackie Lynn. "This lunatic is obviously mistaken. I was a *very* willing participant. And as I said, if you'd like to stay…"

Jackie Lynn seized a handful of Mary Julia's hair, yanking it in a desperate attempt to shut her up. "Ouch! Damn it! That hurt! You've thoroughly lost your mind!" she protested, staring at Jackie Lynn with fiery fighting eyes.

"Enough!" the police officer conceded, throwing his arms in front of him in surrender. "You two ladies are the ones who have a few things to settle. I have a job to perform so I'm leaving. If we are sent here again, the both of you will be the ones we'll take into custody. Understood?" he warned. His eyes studied Mary Julia oddly as he made his way from the room.

"Jackie Lynn! Get off me!" she growled through gritted teeth after the police officer had gone.

Reluctantly, Jackie Lynn released her. Mary Julia spun around and glowered at Jackie Lynn. "What on earth were you thinking?!"

"What was I thinking?! You're kidding, right?! What in the hell have *you* been thinking?!" she challenged. "What gutter did you drag those slimeballs from?!"

"Let's get something straight. Who I have sex with is none of your damn business. Like whoever you choose to be with is none of mine. Ah…maybe that's the problem here! You meddle in my life too much because you obviously don't have a sex life of your own lately. Why don't you go get some good fucks and leave *me* alone!"

Jackie Lynn was stunned, but more upset, by Mary Julia's unanticipated and vicious tirade. *If that's the way she honestly feels, I'm leaving.*

Embarrassed, as tears welled, Jackie Lynn turned and took long quick strides toward the door. She began crying, and it was difficult to escape the apartment without fully breaking down. She was barely outside the door when Mary Julia attempted to slam the door, not realizing the officers had broken it. It bounced back at her and almost hit her in the face.

She carefully pushed her broken door shut as best she could. *I need to get maintenance to fix the door ASAP*, she made a quick mental note.

Her vision clouded by tears, Jackie Lynn stumbled to the stairs. Weary, she collapsed on the top step, weeping uncontrollably. Overcome by raw emotion, she started idiotically verbalizing her tortured thoughts, "How could this have gotten so messed up? I was simply trying to help her. She doesn't even recognize how severely she needs my help or how sick she must be."

When she regained her senses, she noticed an old woman standing on the landing below. With obvious concern, the lady explored, "Honey, you alright? Could I call somebody for you?"

Jackie Lynn was so upset she was unable to speak clearly. She merely turned her head side to side, mumbling, "N..no...N..no."

Clutching the rail, Jackie Lynn dragged herself to her feet. Dejected, she continued the rest of the way down the stairs, outside the building, and to her car. Shaking, she fumbled to unlock the door. She climbed inside the automobile, tiredly draped her fingers over the top of the steering wheel, and managed to compose herself. Starting the vehicle, she absently glanced up at Mary Julia's front window.

Jackie Lynn caught a glimpse of her friend – *at least someone who* was *my friend* – but then the drapes slapped together. She looked away, shifting the vehicle into reverse and backing from her parking space. Jackie Lynn remained in a confused, depressed daze the entire drive home. She maddeningly replayed the whole incident over and over in her mind as if that might somehow enable her to change anything. Nothing helped her accept the way the sordid event had ended.

Things should be different. How will I possibly make this friend of mine - Oh God! She is my friend! - admit her actions are horrible. Something terrible is liable to happen to Mary Julia if I'm unable to get through to her.

Jackie Lynn's deep concern for Mary Julia instilled such overwhelming fear – *so unbearably familiar* – she would not be able to contain it for long. *I have to find a way to save Mary Julia. I simply must!*

* * * *

Several times that evening, Jackie Lynn picked up the phone, dialed a few digits of Mary Julia's number, and then set the receiver back in its cradle. Eventually, she decided to get some sleep, but this did not work either. She kept waking with the ghastly image of the scene in Mary Julia's bedroom, and she kept wondering what her friend was doing or what she might have done. Jackie Lynn prayed continually during the night that her treasured friend would be safe.

After analyzing Mary Julia's spiteful words, Jackie Lynn arrived at the conclusion that Mary Julia had been purposely trying to hurt her to force her to leave matters alone. *But I'm not going to leave matters alone!* she decided. *I'll go to Mary Julia's office first thing tomorrow and we'll discuss the appalling things I've seen her doing.*

* * * *

Jackie Lynn rushed down the hall to Mary Julia's office, but was disappointed to find it empty. After checking the restroom, she headed to the receptionist's desk, asking her if she had any idea where her partner could be. Noticing Jackie Lynn's obvious distress, she responded, "She called saying she wouldn't be in. I guess she's sick. Are you alright?"

Jackie Lynn ignored her concerned question, as her mind automatically raced in despair, *Sick is correct! No telling where Mary Julia could be going or what she might be planning to do!* Mary Julia was no doubt welcoming new trouble.

Discouraged, Jackie Lynn went into her own office, taking a seat at her desk. Frustrated, she tried to establish what her next step should be. It was obvious Mary Julia was determined to fight her assistance. She was avidly denying there was a problem.

It suddenly dawned on Jackie Lynn that dealing with Mary Julia was similar to dealing with somebody with some sort of addiction. *Is that the problem? Is Mary Julia addicted to sex?*

Somewhere, she vaguely remembered reading some article or watching some television documentary on sex addiction. The disorder was real, but Jackie Lynn understood nothing about it. *Granted, as Mary Julia hatefully reminded me, I've had my own share of affairs, but I've never picked a stranger off the street.*

Jackie Lynn reached into a lower drawer, retrieving the Yellow Pages. She searched under Mental Health and scanned the ads for hospitals in the area. One particular ad jumped out at her. It read, 'Is someone you care about completely out of control? Is their behavior a threat to themselves? Call today. We'll explain how we can help.'

She jotted down the number, not caring that it was long distance. Glancing at the address, she noted that the hospital was located in a county a few hours from the city. *That would be perfect!* she ascertained. *Mary Julia would be far from the city. Her problem was capable of being easily hidden from rivals who might seek to destroy her reputation with it.*

With renewed hope, Jackie Lynn snatched the telephone and dialed the number, anxious to receive some professional advice. After a lengthy discussion with a psychiatrist who dealt exclusively with sexual disorders, Jackie Lynn left her office optimistic. She merely told the receptionist she would be gone for the rest of the day.

Jackie Lynn was going to Mary Julia's. The doctor had advised Jackie Lynn to confront her without delay, face-to-face, with everything she had witnessed. He instructed, "No matter how defiant she gets, keep assuring her you love her and that she needs help. It may get ugly since she *won't* easily admit she has a problem. You *must* do everything in your power to convince her that she does."

The doctor was frank, "Hospitalization will likely be in order. Here, we can fully enlighten her that there are many others who have the exact same disorder. That she *isn't* an awful person. Bring her here as soon as possible."

Jackie Lynn prayed she would be able to reach Mary Julia. She was so nervous about confronting Mary Julia again that her hands shook as she gripped the steering wheel. Her stomach had nervous butterflies as she arrived at Mary Julia's apartment complex.

Even though Mary Julia's car was in the parking lot, repeated knocks on her door went unanswered. Jackie Lynn had cleverly stood to the side of the peephole so Mary Julia could not detect who was knocking, but if the woman was there, she evidently wished to not be bothered. Jackie Lynn then turned the doorknob in hopes the lock was still broken, but it had been fixed.

Lord, I hope she doesn't have another weirdo in there and that's why she isn't answering, she could not refrain from worrying. *Mary Julia won't be able to avoid me forever. She'll have to come into the firm tomorrow...I'll simply have to wait the rest of the day and tonight. Or I'll possibly catch her here later.*

The waiting would be excruciating. Jackie Lynn had hoped to promptly initiate this dreaded confrontation. Mary Julia's life might well depend on it. She had just opened the outside door to step into the parking lot when she caught a welcome glimpse of Mary Julia coming around the corner.

Mary Julia's appearance was less than becoming. She was dressed in ratty sweats and sneakers. Her hair had been pulled back into an unruly ponytail, and she donned a baseball cap. Mary Julia did not normally go out dressed in this manner.

Maybe she's been jogging.

Jackie Lynn stepped out of sight, inside the building, to wait for her. She was going to intervene no matter what – *What's the worst that can happen? Mary Julia might kill me.*

Jackie Lynn was shocked when Mary Julia opened the door and entered the building. Her right cheek was severely scraped, and several bloody cuts were visible. Her clothing was tattered on the same side. Bloody spots showed through the various rips and tears. It appeared that Mary Julia had been drug along the pavement.

Emerging from the shadows, Jackie Lynn probed with stunned concern, "My God, Mary Julia! What's happened to you?!"

This abrupt, unanticipated encounter caused Mary Julia to jump and gasp in fright. Quickly recovering from her shock, she snarled, "Why don't you leave me the hell alone?! Why do you insist on tormenting me?! I told you to mind your own business and stay out of mine! Didn't I make myself clear?!"

While Mary Julia was shouting, she inched further away from Jackie Lynn. She was distinctly contemplating making a mad dash up the stairs and leaving Jackie Lynn far behind, but Jackie Lynn grabbed Mary Julia's arm to prevent her from fleeing. Mary Julia was badly limping from her unexplained injuries.

"I don't care what you said yesterday, or what you say today. We need to talk! And we are going to talk! I'm not leaving until you have heard me out!" Jackie Lynn was firm.

She started toward the stairway and pulled Mary Julia along. She did *not* want to have this conversation in the hallway. Yet she would if Mary Julia forced her. Her friend winced as she silently climbed the steps beside Jackie Lynn. The bloodied leg was evidently painful.

"Lean against me. I'll help you up the stairs," Jackie Lynn offered, a sorrowful knot forming in her throat.

The doctor had advised, "If tears threaten during your confrontation, permit them to flow freely. The greater your friend beholds how deeply you care, the better likelihood you might have of convincing this stubborn lady to seek vital help."

Regardless, Jackie Lynn stifled the pitying sob threatening to escape. *It's essential I remain strong for as long as I possibly can. Otherwise, Mary Julia might manage to wear me down. I can't allow that. Getting Mary Julia help is too critical.*

Reaching Mary Julia's residence after the difficult climb, Jackie Lynn strongly demanded, "Give me your key! I'll let us *both* in."

Mary Julia was unusually sedate. Jackie Lynn was surprised when she surrendered her key without a fight. She eagerly unlocked the door, carefully helping her friend inside and to the sofa. "Tell me what in the world happened to you!" Jackie Lynn demanded. She had a seat in the chair directly across from Mary Julia.

"You don't want to know," Mary Julia evasively responded, tears filling her eyes. Jackie Lynn's kindness in helping her climb the stairs and into her apartment had touched her even though she had not wanted it to.

"God, Jackie Lynn! My life is out of control! Why'd you have to find out? No one was supposed to find out what I'm really like, especially my friends. I realize I'm disgusting! Is that what you want to hear?! I can tell by the way you are looking at me that this is how you regard me. You're looking at me the same way my mama used to. Go ahead. Say it."

Jackie Lynn vacated her chair to rush toward the friend she dearly loved. She yearned to hug Mary Julia, but she was afraid she might hurt her. More wisely, she sat down beside her, gently placing a supportive arm around her shoulders.

"I would never, *ever*, call you disgusting no matter what you have done," she pledged, staring with compassion into Mary Julia's troubled eyes. "You have a serious illness. You need help. Please allow me to help you."

"You *can't* help me!" Mary Julia proclaimed, sounding as if she had regained her strength and was angry. She shoved Jackie Lynn's arm from her body. "You're the wrong sex. If you were a guy…"

"Then you would have me take you to bed," she bluntly finished. "That's the way you deal with your self-disgust, isn't it? You have sex! With whatever male is most readily available! When did it begin, Mary Julia? Were you abused as a child or something?" she interrogated.

"That's none of your damn business!" Mary Julia shouted, becoming defensive. "Where do you get off lately, constantly interfering in my life?! Who asked you to?!"

"I'm *interfering* in your life because I love you," Jackie Lynn confessed, choking up, failing in her resolve not to cry.

"You're one of my dearest friends. Friendships as treasured as ours don't arise every day. I don't want to lose you. Tell me what happened to you. Were you thrown from a car by one of your sex buddies? You're damn lucky today, but what next? Do you keep on until you get yourself killed – either violently or by AIDS? You *can't* keep living this way, Mary Julia!!"

Jackie Lynn broke into sobs. Mary Julia started crying as well and with defeat, slumped alongside her. Jackie Lynn wrapped an arm around her shoulder, and they hugged and cried for quite a while.

"I'm sorry, Jackie Lynn," Mary Julia declared. "I'll do better. I promise."

Jackie Lynn remembered the doctor's statement, "The troubled person will be deceptive, promising to change even though they won't, actually *can't*."

"You won't," Jackie Lynn challenged. "Not unless you receive help. I spoke to a doctor at a hospital outside the city. He says they will be able to help you. His opinion is that you're addicted to sex. If that's the case, you'll be unable to stop letting yourself be abused."

"That...that's the most absurd thing I've ever heard!" she denied. Mary Julia pushed Jackie Lynn aside. "Where in the world did you arrive at something so stupid?!"

"You've been picking up total strangers. I saw you with the Mexican waiter at Flora's wedding, *old* Sam Meadows, who you don't even like, the stranger at the bar, the scumbags yesterday and evidently some maniac who tried to kill you today. How in the world do you logically explain this?" Jackie Lynn grilled.

"I don't have to explain any of that to you!" Mary Julia argued, standing and stumbling away. "Get out! I don't want you here! First, you claim you're my friend and you love me, and next, you come off with such bullshit as me being addicted to sex. Plus, you talked to some nutty shrink about me without my permission! Naturally, he wants you to admit me to this hospital! He's probably drumming up business for his nut clinic! How big a fool are you?!"

You're intent on making the fight to save you difficult. You won't win, Mary Julia! I won't permit it! Jackie Lynn resolved. *I'm not giving up no matter what. Nothing terrible is going to happen!*

Jackie Lynn's heart raced, and a wave of nausea overtook her as painful memories from her past threatened to resurface. *No! Concentrate solely on Mary Julia! The past is the past and you had no control over that. Mary Julia's situation is totally different!* she convinced herself.

Jackie Lynn clutched Mary Julia's shoulder and shoved her towards the sofa. Due to Mary Julia's injuries, her friend's rough treatment inadvertently caused her physical pain. Mary Julia gasped and winced. Responsive tears formed in her eyes, as she warily sat down.

"I'm not going anywhere. And you *will* sit there until you are ready to admit you need help," Jackie Lynn bossed.

Mary Julia eyeballed Jackie Lynn with stunned, tear-filled eyes for a second. Then she broke down and cried without restraint. Her shoulders heaved, and she shook so violently it almost appeared she was having some sort of seizure. Jackie Lynn patiently waited, permitting her to gain some measure of control, at which point she hoped she might listen.

Standing directly in front of Mary Julia, Jackie Lynn spoke in a soft, level voice. She diligently tried to persuade Mary Julia that the appropriate road to travel would be checking herself into the hospital. "Mary Julia, you're breaking my heart! Please think about what I've said. Take a while to decide. It's not as if you must make the decision to go to the hospital this very minute. But you do need to admit you need help of some kind."

Mary Julia finally raised her head. Her despondent facial expression twisted Jackie Lynn's heart in a tight knot. "You don't understand. You have no idea. I'm unable to delay making any kind of decision because if I do, I'll be precisely where I've always been," she admitted.

Mary Julia grabbed Jackie Lynn's elbow, pleading in desperation, "Sit down, my dear friend" and tugged her down onto the sofa. "It's time you learn the real story about my life." She was silent for a long while, attempting to compose herself so she could relate the appalling details of her past.

Despite her glazed and haunted eyes, when Mary Julia eventually spoke, her voice was surprisingly clear, "It began when I was very young. I was seven when the first man touched me...not like my daddy meant to do anything wrong. He just loved me so much. At least that's what he said. In a strange sort of way, despite it being wrong, it made me happy. He would play games with me and hug me and kiss me. It wasn't totally bad. Then my mom came home early one day."

Tears steadily ran down Mary Julia's cheeks and dripped off her chin, but she was oblivious to them. She took a slow, deep breath and continued, "Mama was furious with me. She screamed, calling me names I had never heard before…And the way she looked at me, like I was this filthy disgusting creature. I'll never forget her tone of voice, or that look. You used that same tone a second ago when you pushed me down on the couch – you gave me that look too."

That explains why she suddenly broke down. Jackie Lynn noted. She felt guilty but relieved that she had penetrated Mary Julia's obstinate shell.

"My mama divorced my daddy soon after. It was obvious she hated me, and I understood why. I never saw my dad again after the divorce. To this day, I'm uncertain if he's dead or alive. Then when I was ten, things seemed to be looking up. My mama got remarried and was considerably happier. I vowed I wouldn't mess things up. I kept my distance from my stepfather, but he kept trying to convince me to like him. Eventually, my mama told me that I *simply must* give him the chance to love me. It was essential to him. So I decided to trust him, and everything seemed fine. I finally had the nice family I had always dreamed of. A few years later, the night of my thirteenth birthday, things changed. My step- dad sneaked into my bedroom. He informed me it was time I became a woman. He covered my mouth with his hand, telling me to be very quiet. He whispered in my ear that he was tired of waiting, watching me sashay around in my T-shirts that were too tight, shorts that were too short and most of all, my much too revealing nightgowns. He ran his tongue across my lips, forcing me to open my mouth. Then he darted his tongue so far in I gagged, but this didn't stop him. He unzipped his jeans, yanked down my panties, and shoved himself deep inside me, tearing my untouched flesh to shreds. Afterwards, I laid there crying into my pillow. I knew if mama found out, she would never forgive me. After that first night, he came to my room often."

Mary Julia's distressing, candid disclosures and the unbearable pain in her eyes tore Jackie Lynn's heart to shreds. She loved Mary Julia greatly, and hated the pain she had suffered as a child. Jackie Lynn took Mary Julia's icy hand into her own.

How could parents do such intolerable things to their children? Jackie Lynn angrily wondered, contemplating her own childhood as well. *At least I was never sexually abused.*

"I'm sorry," she crooned, comforting Mary Julia with a heartfelt embrace and sympathetically weeping. "It's going to be okay," she promised, trying to reassure herself as well.

* * * *

Before her courage dissipated and she changed her mind, Mary Julia gradually rose to change clothes and to pack for the hospital. One of her dearest friends knew the sordid details of her past and her secrets from the present. Her life had to change.

Truth be told, Mary Julia had desperately desired her life be different, but she had lacked the strength to seek help by herself. *I'll be able to with Jackie Lynn's support.*

* * * *

"God, Jackie Lynn! What if they're unable to help me?" Mary Julia fearfully moaned. She closed her suitcase after packing a week's worth of clothing. Jackie Lynn suspected Mary Julia might be in the hospital significantly longer, but she did not share her contemplation.

"They will. They have to," she reassured. She pulled Mary Julia's suitcase off the bed and placed her other arm staunchly around her to guide her from the room.

It'll be hard to leave Mary Julia behind at that hospital. "You'll leave the hospital a brand new woman." *Oh, how I hope this is true. I remember too well this isn't always the case.*

"I hope. I strongly dislike who I've become," Mary Julia remorsefully admitted. She allowed herself to be led across her living room. "Despite the fact that I might have been killed today, it won't cease. I'll do it over and over. I hate myself afterwards, but I keep doing it to deal with my disgust. I'm a wreck! Are there actually others as bad as me?"

"First, you aren't bad or disgusting. You had horrible things done to you as a child that you had no control over. According to the doctor I spoke with, there are many others who were hurt as greatly as a child. You'll come through," Jackie Lynn affirmed. She was endeavoring to be optimistic. She opened the front door and ushered a very uncertain Mary Julia from her residence.

* * * *

Leaving Mary Julia at the sanitarium was a harrowing experience for Jackie Lynn. She helplessly watched two seemingly cold nurses lead Mary Julia away, through a door that locked loudly behind them. It had taken every ounce of her strength not to break down. It vividly brought back terrible memories of when her stepfather had admitted her mother to a similar asylum, many, many years ago.

Jackie Lynn sought refuge in her car in the hospital parking lot. She permitted her emotions to overcome her. She dropped her face into her hands and cried and shook for a long, long while. She was weeping for poor Mary Julia but also for her own unwelcome, troubled memories.

INTIMACIES

My friend will receive help here, she reassured herself.
I'm helping save Mary Julia's life. I am.

CHAPTER FOUR

BETRAYAL

Jackie Lynn phoned Flora as soon as she got home. She urgently needed to speak to another friend to settle her haywire emotions regarding Mary Julia's hospitalization. She could always count on Flora to stabilize her.

It's possible I'd be as messed up as Mary Julia if I hadn't constantly had Flora's unwavering, wise guidance to assist me along my path.

They had become close friends long ago, when they had roomed together in college. She missed seeing Flora each day, and when she went into the firm tomorrow, Mary Julia would be gone as well. An almost unbearable loneliness suddenly engulfed Jackie Lynn.

"Roberts residence. May I help you?" a strange gentleman's voice answered.

"Um…I was trying to reach Flora," Jackie Lynn replied, thrown by the private answering service.

"I'll find out if Mrs. Roberts is available. May I inform her who is calling?" the man very properly inquired.

"Please tell her it's Jackie Lynn. I'm a good friend of hers," she responded, smiling with satisfaction. She was delighted for Flora. Her handsome husband was treating her like royalty. If they had not been dear friends, she might have been jealous.

She patiently waited for several minutes before she heard, "Hello."

"I'm not interrupting your massage or anything, am I?" Jackie Lynn teased, overjoyed to hear her voice.

"No. I was in the garden. It's a pretty day, and the grounds are beautiful. You and Mary Julia have to stop by soon," she offered. "Speaking of Mary Julia, how is she? How did your conversation with her go? I'm sorry I didn't get to accompany you, but Jacob monopolized my day. Not that I'm complaining. He's on another trip and I miss him already."

"I'm glad you're happy. Mary Julia isn't faring nearly as well. Confronting her was difficult. She was in total denial. After a great deal of persuasion, she eventually agreed to check into a hospital," Jackie Lynn gingerly broke the news, fighting not to choke up.

I can't possibly have any tears left after that spell I had in the car.

"A hospital?! What happened?!! Was she hurt by some stranger carrying on the way she was?!" Flora probed in heightened alarm, extremely concerned.

"Actually, she *was* injured by a stranger. Though not severely. I didn't take her to a medical institution. I took her to a mental one. They are going to treat her for sex addiction. Flora, the horror stories Mary Julia told me concerning her childhood are unbelievable. My heart is absolutely breaking for her," she confessed. She was grateful to have someone she was able to trust to share her heartbreak with.

Jackie Lynn remained on the phone with Flora for in excess of an hour telling her the dreadful details of Mary Julia's pitiful life. Flora was overwrought by the tragic news. Her heart ached for Mary Julia's agonizing pain. She loved these two women immeasurably. Flora missed sharing in their lives, despite having Jacob. She could not break her promise to him though.

I have to show Jacob I'm different from his first wife. When he recognizes I'm worthy of his trust, I'll be allowed to leave the house and join my friends sometimes.

"When can we visit Mary Julia?" Flora inquired as their conversation was drawing to a close.

I'll speak with Jacob. He shouldn't have a problem with me calling upon a friend in distress. This shouldn't threaten him in any way. And if he's home, maybe I might persuade him to go along with us.

"I'm not sure. I'd guess it would be at least a week," Jackie Lynn acknowledged. *"Sometimes it's considerably longer,"* she absently verbalized her recollection.

Jackie Lynn's voice sounded unusually haunted. "I gave the sanitarium my number at home and at the firm. They're supposed to contact me in the next few days with some details."

"Call me as soon as you hear anything. Perhaps you could stop by here and have dinner, and afterwards we'll make a trip to the hospital together," Flora offered.

"That's a delightful idea," Jackie Lynn affirmed. "Take care. I'll be talking to you soon. Tell Jacob I said hi."

"Will do. You take care too," she concluded, reluctantly hanging up the receiver. A strong tinge of guilt overcame Flora.

I should have been by Jackie Lynn's side when she confronted Mary Julia. What an awful thing for her to have had to face by herself. Flora was still intensely contemplating both her friends when the telephone rang, causing her to jump.

"Hello," she answered, completely disregarding Jacob's rule to wait for the house manager to answer the phone.

"Who in the world were you talking to for so long?!" Jacob's voice barked, sounding exasperated. "Of greater importance, who were you expecting to telephone you, to have snatched up the receiver so eagerly? Why'd you bypass the service? Is there some reason you don't want them to be aware of who is calling?"

Flora disliked the tone of his voice and the insinuating interrogation. A cord of fear raced up her backbone, unsettling memories resurfacing. *Settle his insecurities.*

"I apologize, Jacob. I had no idea I'd been on the phone for so long. Jackie Lynn called to share that Mary Julia had been hospitalized. While she was filling me in on the details, the minutes just flew by. I'm sorry it kept you from getting through. I'm glad to hear your voice. I miss you greatly."

"The few moments I had to converse with you have passed," he snapped, thoughtlessly showing no concern in respect to Flora's dear friend. "I have surgery to perform. I'll be home for dinner. Have the cook fix something special."

"Alright," she consented, stunned by his abruptness.

He's concentrating on the surgery he's about to perform, she assured herself.

"I love you," Flora added. She doubted he heard, because Jacob abruptly hung up without saying one more word.

* * * *

Jacob was expected about 6:00 p.m. This was the time they usually dined together when he was in town, if an emergency at the hospital did not detain him. Flora attentively watched the driveway for his car at 5:45. Jacob arrived twenty minutes later.

She stood near the front door, under the sparkling, four-tier, crystal chandelier, intending to greet him with open, welcoming arms and a cheery grin as soon as he entered. *As Jacob prefers.*

"I'm glad you were able to make it for dinner, darling. I've missed you," Flora gushed, after warmly kissing his lips.

"You had the cook prepare a special dinner as I requested?" Jacob questioned rather gruffly, with no trace of a smile.

He must be tired from the surgery and the long drive home, Flora theorized.

"Of course, sweetheart. The cook is fixing your favorite. Why don't you relax on the sofa, and I'll find out if it's ready. Would you like anything to drink?" she fawned, affectionately hooking her arm through Jacob's and guiding him toward their spacious great room.

"Fix me a bourbon and coke. Heavy on the bourbon," he ordered, unsettling Flora. He plopped down on the black leather couch. This faced the four-story palladium of windows that looked out upon an impressive rose garden. Hybrid roses, in a brilliant array of colors – bright pink, orange, red, and yellow, just to name a few – made for a colorful view.

Something's wrong. Jacob's definitely upset. Although it couldn't possibly have anything to do with me.

"I'll be back," she pledged. Flora rushed over to the wet bar to procure his drink and speak to the cook, so she could return to his side and discover what might be bothering him.

Maybe he had needed to discuss something troubling earlier but hadn't had the chance since I was on the phone with Jackie Lynn for so long. She was besieged with guilt.

Flora reappeared minutes later, carrying Jacob's drink. She handed it to him and took a seat on the couch by his side. "Jacob, honey, is everything alright?" she probed. Flora apprehensively noticed that he was staring up at the high, post & beam ceiling overhead. His face was drawn.

He took a large swallow from his glass, plastered on an exaggerated grin and answered with heavy sarcasm, "Everything is chummy, my pet. I lost a patient a short while ago. How can things be any better?"

Flora watched Jacob gulp more of his drink. His alcohol consumption, combined with the sharp tone of his voice, sent chills up and down her spine. *No!* she denied despite her better judgment. *There's nothing to be scared of. He's not upset with me. He won't hurt me. He's simply troubled due to the dreadful day he's had. Be there for him as a good wife should be.*

"Oh, Jacob, sweetheart, I'm *so* sorry," Flora moaned. She reached to squeeze his hand. "Do you want to talk about it? Tell me what happened. I'm here for you. I love you."

"What happened? That's a superb question. Especially coming from you," he oddly retorted. He emptied the contents of his glass down his throat and handed Flora his glass. Then he stood and walked over to the elaborate granite fireplace. Leaning against the ornately carved, black walnut mantel, he said, "Get me another drink. I'll apprise you of the details, my sweet. *You* should be enlightened."

"Um…Jacob…shouldn't we eat some dinner first?" she warily suggested. She was getting scared by the tone of his voice, the glare in his eyes.

Flora painfully remembered what had transpired the last time he looked at her this way. *Put that out of your mind! That isn't going to happen. Jacob has a justifiable right to be distressed and to have a few drinks if he's lost one of his patients. That merely reveals what a caring individual he is.*

"You're right. We should eat first. The cook is awaiting us. We'll discuss this later in the privacy of our bedroom," he stated. He sounded more chipper, chivalrously offering his arm to whisk her toward the dining room to be served their dinner.

Flora was relieved by this upswing in his demeanor. After dinner, they would take refuge in their bedroom, make love and discuss his distressing experience. *I will help him deal with this painful trauma. I'll prove to him I am capable of being the perfect wife.*

* * * *

They had a quiet dinner, although Jacob uttered a few cross words concerning his Prime Rib, claiming it was tough. "Inform the cook I expect the finest cuts of meat served to me!" he snapped at Lolita, their server and housemaid. "Bring me some wine! Pronto!"

"Yes sir, Mr. Roberts. So sorry, sir," she respectfully uttered. She rushed from the room to tend to his needs.

Lolita was a sweet girl. Flora hated when Jacob behaved nasty to her. However, she figured he was inappropriately taking out the stress of the day.

He'll be fine after we've made love and talked.

Flora wished Jacob had not requested additional wine. He had already had two glasses. Plus, he had consumed the drink before dinner. He usually did not drink this much. And when he did, it worried her.

Quit being a worrywart! Everything is going to be fine. Allow him to work the pain out of his system even if he does have a greater amount to drink than you prefer.

Jacob drank three more glasses of wine before he finally informed Lolita he was through. She expeditiously cleared the table. Jacob staggered when he stood; Flora rushed to his side.

"I could use your strong arm around my shoulder as we climb the stairway to our bedroom," she suggested with a deceptive grin. She wanted to assist him without insulting him.

Jacob wrapped his arm around Flora's shoulders. He clenched her to his side too tightly. *He's had too much to drink. He doesn't realize he's squeezing so hard.*

It was a difficult climb up the two flights of marble stairs. Jacob was dead weight as he leaned on her. Nonetheless, Flora did not complain.

As soon as they entered their room, to her relief, he released Flora. Jacob shut and locked the door behind them. "Dress exceedingly sexy for me," he requested in a slurred voice, leering at her suggestively.

"What's your pleasure, sir?" she playfully probed, wearing an agreeable smile.

Jacob staggered to her spacious walk-in closet. He slid open the doors and rooted through her dresses – many of which he had bought her during their courtship. "Honey, aren't you in the wrong spot? My negligees are in these drawers," Flora relayed, pointing to her dresser.

Jacob turned, pulling forth a bright red, sparkly, formal gown. "Put this on," he demanded, holding the dress outward. "Simply this. Nothing else. No underwear."

"Okay," she conceded, eager to please. She walked toward him, took the dress, and went into the bathroom to change.

Confusing game my husband's playing, but if it makes him happy for me to act out some strange fantasy, I'll do it.

She emerged from the bathroom a few minutes later, in only the gown. "Come here," he ordered, directing her to her

49

makeup vanity. Flora smiled at him and strolled seductively across the room.

"Sit down," Jacob instructed.

Flora obediently followed directions. The moment she was seated, he proceeded to pick up some blush, brushing too much on her cheeks. He handed her some bright red lipstick, telling her to apply it. Lastly, he made her cake on tons of mascara.

Bizarre game, she silently acknowledged but kept acting as directed.

When Jacob was finally satisfied with Flora, he stood her up, placed an expensive, long, pearl necklace he had bought her around her neck and led her to the full-length mirror by the bathroom. "Take a good, long, hard look at yourself. What do you see?" he quizzed, his voice sounding strange.

"What am I supposed to see?" she asked in confusion, chuckling slightly at the absurdity of what was happening. *I think I look like a clown with all this makeup on.*

"Oh, I beg your pardon. Naturally, you wouldn't see it," Jacob acceded, placing his hand in the back of her hair. "Because you are too damn stupid to see it!!"

No sooner had the hateful snarling words registered, than Flora's forehead struck the mirror in front of her with such overpowering force that the mirror cracked. Blood trickled down her forehead. Immediately afterwards, Jacob grabbed her necklace from behind, strangling her as he hauled her toward the bed. "You ignorant whore! I've given you everything! What do you do?! You cause me to mess up and kill a patient!!"

"Jacob! Wha...what?! What are you talking about?!" She gasped as he released his stranglehold. He tossed her atop the mattress.

*Oh, my Lord! This can't be happening **again**!* Flora desperately denied. She was seeing stars and her head throbbed in pain. For a fleeting moment, she wondered if he had cracked open her skull.

"Don't play stupid with me, bitch!" Jacob screamed.

He fell to a sitting position on the side of the bed. He grabbed a fist full of Flora's hair and furiously jerked her head so her eyes met his. "You weren't on the telephone that long with some female friend. You always conveniently use Jackie Lynn's name. You were talking to another man, weren't you?! Admit it!"

"Oh, God, Jacob! *No!!* I'm begging you not to do this!" Flora pleaded. "It *was* Jackie Lynn. Ask the house manager. He answered her call."

"I refuse to listen to any more of your damn lies!" Jacob declared.

He sealed a hand firmly over her mouth, and he straddled Flora on the bed. With his free hand, Jacob reached down to grasp the bottom of her dress and hurled it up over her hips. Then, to Flora's horror, he unfastened his pants. He removed his hand from her mouth for a moment to use both hands to hastily heave his pants and his underwear down. Jacob ignored Flora's revolted screams and protests. He barbarously shoved himself within her, taking her against her will.

When he finished his inconceivable sexual assault, Jacob lay very still on top of Flora for several long moments. Her body uncontrollably shuddered beneath him in fear and repulsion. The strong odor of wine and bourbon on his breath and deviating from his pores turned her stomach. Finally, Jacob pushed himself up on his arms a slight bit and stared down into his wife's petrified face.

"Damn! Damn you!" Jacob cursed. He gave her hair a conclusive, forceful yank before he released her.

He stood and paced beside the bed. Flora watched him in terror, wondering if Jacob might viciously pounce on her again. "I went to surgery fearing you had been expecting another man's call. I couldn't focus. A patient died due to that! Do you grasp the damage you have caused?! You promised me you would put me first. That you would *always* be here to receive my calls. Instead, you permitted a mere friend's needs to come before mine. Do you have any idea how this makes me feel? Look what you have made me do to you.

You can't make me angry this way, Flora. I thought you understood this."

Sitting down, with remorse, Jacob reached to gently touch the cut, red swollen whelp on Flora's forehead. She shivered at his touch. He compassionately turned, reached and grabbed the bedside telephone, dialing the kitchen.

"Bring some ice, *at once*!! Mrs. Roberts has slipped and struck her head!" he briefly explained and then placed the phone in its cradle. "They'll be here in a second, darling. You'll be okay. You won't even need stitches. It's already stopped bleeding. I didn't intend to hurt you. My career used to be indispensable to me. Yet I couldn't concentrate on being a surgeon today, because I was certain I might be losing you. You're what's most vital in this world to me. Convince me that I'm the most important person in your world too. Put me first. I need that. You said you would. Will you do that for me or not?"

I thought I was, Flora miserably distinguished.

She had given up her profession and constantly stayed around the house unless Jacob took her somewhere else. Granted, her conversation with Jackie Lynn had been lengthy, but it had been important, not idle chitchat. *Is Jacob proposing I totally give up my friends as well? Undoubtedly I've put him first. But why isn't it possible for me to have Jackie Lynn and Mary Julia in my life as well?*

There was a knock on the door, and Jacob went to retrieve a bucket of ice from the servant. He raced into the bathroom, preparing an icepack. Returning to the bedroom, he gently scooped Flora's trembling body into his strong arms, lifting her from the bed. He turned and sat on the side of the mattress. He cradled Flora, as he carefully held the icepack to her injury.

"Flora, darling, promise me you're entirely devoted to me. That I'm the most important person in your life. Let me hear you profess these words. Please!" he pleaded, hoarse with emotion.

Flora fearfully stammered, "Jacob, I am *completely* devoted to you and you are the most important person in my life." Inside, she recognized though, *I can't live like this.*

CHAPTER FIVE

BEGINNINGS

Two weeks passed without any more violent outbursts from Jacob. Meager relief to Flora, considering most of these days he had spent out of town on business. Oddly, it had also been that long since she had last heard a word from Jackie Lynn.

Why hasn't she called me? She's bound to know something in respect to Mary Julia by now. I'll call Jackie Lynn tonight when she gets home from work and ask her what the story is, she maintained, as she dragged her lazy torso upright in bed.

Flora had slept a bit late this morning, since Jacob was out of town. She hardly slept when Jacob was home. Flora dreaded going to bed due to his intense interrogations concerning her movements each day. She knew what might ensue if she answered any of his questions incorrectly.

Her life had become devastatingly sad. She was afraid to speak to the people at the grocery store, the old fellow who drove the truck that picked up their dry cleaning, or even the young paperboy. After a while, Flora became mindful that any of the hired help she befriended were promptly fired, with somebody new expeditiously hired to replace them. She was trapped in a living prison, her life a sheer nightmare.

* * * *

That evening, Flora telephoned Jackie Lynn as she had resolved to do. She caught her as she was walking in the door from work. "Yes?" Jackie Lynn responded.

Flora laughed in response. "Is that how you've started answering your telephone? No preliminaries, simply a *yes*?" Still chuckling, she kept teasing, "I guess that's getting right down to business. Yes, I'll be there. Yes, I'll do it. Yes, I want it...Yes, I need it. Yes really works, doesn't it? Except, I'll pay a dating service to call you, and the answer shall be, of course, *Yes!*"

They both succumbed to a fit of boisterous laughter. It had been awhile since either of them had spontaneously laughed. When their cozy merriment subsided, Jackie Lynn asked, "Why haven't you returned any of my calls?? I have tried for two weeks to contact you. I had hoped you might accompany me to visit Mary Julia."

Flora was taken aback. She had not gotten any messages that anyone had called her. Had she known, she would have promptly returned Jackie Lynn's call. "I apologize. I have been...well...a little out....No, not out...oh, you can imagine how it is," she rambled, unsuccessfully endeavoring to concoct a feasible excuse.

"I most assuredly can *not* imagine how it is," Jackie Lynn replied, sounding confused. "Why don't you fill me in with all the details? All's not well, is it?? I knew it wasn't like you not to return calls. When this strange voice answered two days ago, I honestly thought I had the wrong number. As a matter of fact, you guys must not be able to hire decent help. The last two people I spoke to were new. They weren't even certain how to address the calls. They gave me a 'Well, the Mrs. is busy, and we'll inform Mr. Roberts you telephoned'. I told them I wasn't calling Mr. Roberts. So they assured me you would receive my message."

Flora was intently listening and fitting the pieces of the puzzle together. *Jacob isn't letting anyone give me telephone messages. He purposely isn't telling me either.*

"I'm on the line now. Tell me what's happening with Mary Julia," Flora prodded.

Jackie Lynn was glad to finally hear from Flora, but she was not going to be brushed off so easily. She was determined to uncover exactly what was amiss with her friend's life. "Explain to me what the deal with your phone service is first. Why am I unable to get a message through to you? What if anything horrible had happened to Mary Julia? God, she may have become suicidal."

Nearly as soon as the awful, untruthful words had left her mouth, Jackie Lynn instantly regretted them. Her heart sank in distress. "No! I didn't mean that! Mary Julia is not in *any way* suicidal. It's just…well…to be honest, Flora, I miss talking to one of my best friends…. Forget it…I'm making a mountain out of a molehill. Please forgive me."

Jackie Lynn's uncustomary tirade worried Flora. She struggled for a fitting response. Jackie Lynn seemed slightly lost, even lonely. She wished this special lady would meet a decent man to share her life.

Then again, hadn't I found a decent man to settle down with? Look at the mess my life has become. It doesn't have to be exactly the same as my situation though. There are truly good men out there.

To lighten Jackie Lynn's dismal mood, Flora helpfully added, "You should have somebody to talk to about what's happening in your life other than me and Mary Julia. If you would involve yourself with a good man, you would have a constant source of support in your life. Have you ever considered calling a dating service for real?"

Jackie Lynn was swiftly beside herself with forceful laughter at Flora's endearing persistence, "No, no, no!! I am not interested in a dating service! Can we stay on track here? The reason I called *and left messages* was to invite you to go and see Mary Julia with me. The doctor has kept in close contact with me. He tells me she's ready for visitors. He assured me she is making steady progress and seeing caring friends would be exactly what she needs. He says time and patience will be a necessity, but you and I will stand by her in this. Which night would you prefer to make the trip together?"

Flora was at a loss for words. There was no way she was able to accompany Jackie Lynn anywhere. There was too much likelihood it would incite Jacob's insane fury, but she was unable to reveal her situation to her friend. Flora had to fabricate some probable excuse. She hated this because she had never lied to Jackie Lynn before.

"Jackie Lynn, I wish I could come with you, but this is such short notice...and I...well...I have plans to join Jacob for a couple of days of alone time. Please understand. I am *truly* concerned about Mary Julia, but in reality, it might be a little much for her to have two visitors this soon. Why don't you go by yourself, and next visit, I'll come along."

Jackie Lynn did not know how to take this. Flora had always been the one to insist, 'We all stick together'. She had always used that funny saying from the Three Musketeers – *All for one and one for all.* "That's us, girls," she would customarily profess.

But now, Jackie Lynn detected a new tone to her voice, as if she were not being honest. *That can't possibly be what I note in Flora's voice. We never lie to each other.*

"It *is* essential you keep that husband of yours satisfied and content. I'll visit Mary Julia, and when I leave, I'll assure her we will *both* be coming again soon. Tell Jacob I said hello. And to hire some decent help. Mention the messages you never got. I'm gonna run. Miss you, love you."

Flora responded, "I miss and love you too. Reassure Mary Julia she is in my thoughts and that I love her as well. I'll keep you both in my prayers."

"See you soon," Jackie Lynn persuasively added.

I hope, Flora yearned. She stared at the telephone as she slowly placed the receiver in its cradle. *I've got to persuade Jacob to permit me to go speak with Mary Julia...at least once...so she knows how much I care.*

* * * *

Jackie Lynn made a trip to the hospital Friday. She did not have court today, so she left work early, with plans to spend the full visiting period with Mary Julia. Walking through the entranceway to the asylum, her stomach anxiously knotted. Bad childhood memories haunted her.

No, I'm not thinking about that. I'm here for Mary Julia. They're helping her.

Jackie Lynn stared straight ahead and attempted to disregard that she was in a hospital. She walked very quickly down the long, straight corridor, ignoring the humming of the fluorescent lights overhead, the gleam from the too white, polished floor, the patients and nurses in the hallway, and the many rooms she rushed past.

She was extremely relieved when she found Mary Julia waiting in the hallway for her. She did not want to go into her room. All hospital rooms looked alike in these places – tiny confined spaces, with a bed, chairs, and a standard bathroom, except the sink had no stopper. She remembered these details more vividly than she would have liked.

Mary Julia was delighted to have Jackie Lynn's company and greeted her with a wide grin and a tight embrace. "It's great to see you! I miss not seeing and laughing with you each day," she admitted. "I was hoping Flora would drop in on me as well. Did you tell her I'm allowed visitors?"

"Yeah. I spoke to her yesterday," Jackie Lynn divulged, intentionally adding, "She said to pass on that she is thinking about you, loves you and you are in her prayers. She's with Jacob. They had made plans they couldn't change. She promised to stop by with me soon."

"Good. I miss her too, but I'm glad she's found happiness. Thanks to you, I may too soon," Mary Julia proclaimed with an appreciative grin. She guided Jackie Lynn down the hall toward the recreation room, a nice place to sit and chat.

"I'm *so* thrilled to hear that," Jackie Lynn shared, mirroring her smile.

They had a cozy seat, side by side, in two chairs near a huge picture window. The window overlooked a beautiful glistening stream that ran down through the green grassy hills. "I mean it," she affirmed. "For the first time in my life, my past behavior is beginning to make sense to me rather than make me hate myself. Thank you, my friend, for bringing me here."

"I wish I was able to claim it was my pleasure," Jackie Lynn teased with a slight chuckle, lightening the mood before she got overly emotional. "The scenery here is breathtaking though," she added after glancing out the window.

Mary Julia cackled in response. She was exhilarated to be sharing in wholesome laughter again with her cherished friend. Jackie Lynn enjoyed being graced by Mary Julia's vivacity once more as well. They discussed the therapy Mary Julia was thoroughly embracing.

Jackie Lynn remained until 9:00 p.m., when the hospital announced visiting hours had ended. "Time flies when you're having fun," Mary Julia commented. She gradually walked Jackie Lynn out. "Come again soon. Bring Flora please."

"You may count on that!" She enthusiastically promised. Jackie Lynn gave Mary Julia one more reassuring hug. "I'm glad you're doing well!"

"Thanks. See you soon," she replied, reluctantly releasing Jackie Lynn. Mary Julia flashed her a bittersweet grin and waved goodbye.

Jackie Lynn smiled widely at the nurses at the front desk before she exited the sanitarium. She headed to her nearby car. *Mary Julia is going to be okay.* This newfound confidence in Mary Julia's recovery made her ecstatic.

Mary Julia might need the aid of friends when she leaves this awful place, but Flora and I will provide the support necessary. I'm certain of this. I'll call Flora as soon as I get home to relay the favorable news concerning Mary Julia.

She cranked up the car stereo, listening to a CD with various rock hits from the seventies, and she headed out on the three-hour drive home. An hour into the journey, on a desolate stretch of country highway, and without warning, her engine died. "What the…." Jackie Lynn commented out loud. She steered the automobile to the side of the road, struggling with the somewhat useless power steering and brakes to bring the vehicle to a halt.

Jackie Lynn attempted to restart the automobile a few times. With frustration, she found it would not turn over. She opened the glove compartment, located a tiny flashlight, and popped the hood.

"Unbelievable! And naturally, I forgot to bring the cell phone!" she stated aloud, shaking her head in disbelief as she climbed from her Toyota Camry.

Jackie Lynn was walking around to the front of the vehicle when a pickup truck slowed down. The vehicle pulled to the side of the road just past her. "Great! Who's this?" she mumbled under her breath. She fumbled for the mace she had in her purse – *just in case*.

Jackie Lynn switched her flashlight on. She shined it toward a tall male stranger who was nearing her. "Having a problem, ma'am?" His voice seemed friendly.

"My engine stopped for some reason," she revealed.

She backed away as this guy approached the front of her car. He had a substantially bigger flashlight in his hand. "Well, I know a little about cars; let's take a look." He bent over the open hood, lighting her entire engine. "Uh oh," he commented. "Your main drive belt has snapped in two. The engine won't do anything without that. You aren't going anywhere in this automobile. You'll need a wrecker."

"Are you a mechanic?" Jackie Lynn suspiciously scrutinized. She shined her flashlight in his direction, so she might somewhat discern his face. He appeared to be handsome from what she was able to tell. It was dark on this stretch of highway, and getting darker by the minute.

"Not professionally," he answered with a smile. *A nice one*, Jackie Lynn noted. "I dabble a little with engines. I can show you what I'm talking about if you'd like," he offered. He gestured for her to move closer to him.

"No, that's okay," Jackie Lynn responded. She folded her arms and glanced up and down the highway.

As far as the workings of an auto went, she understood little. She merely drove them. Jackie Lynn was unconcerned about how they worked, but she was concerned when they failed to work, like tonight. "How close is the nearest service station?"

"About five miles up the road," he replied.

"Would you mind heading there and sending a wrecker back for me?" she suggested.

"Not at all. Nevertheless, I'd rather not abandon you here by yourself in the dark. There's plenty of room for you in my truck," he offered, adding, "I know that it's hard to trust people nowadays, but you *can* trust me."

Right! And the check is in the mail, Jackie Lynn sarcastically compared. She was absently listening as he continued, "If I leave you here alone, I'll be worrying about you until I send someone back. Why don't you put both of our minds at ease and ride with me to the garage?"

Jackie Lynn was not prone to *trusting* strangers. In fact, she had significant trouble trusting the male species in general. Nevertheless, she did not relish the idea of sitting alone in her car on this dark desolate stretch. The very concept made Jackie Lynn's skin crawl and her stomach roll.

She absolutely hated sitting in dark, confined places. Images of a chilling past event made Jackie Lynn's spine tingle uncomfortably. *Quit!* she chastised. *You're not a kid. You're capable of handling this. On the other hand, what if this guy is some sort of maniac and he heads off on some side road?*

"I'll be fine here by myself," Jackie Lynn assured him after an extended pause. She was surprised to hear how shaky her voice sounded. Her legs were also quivering.

"Why don't we do this...I'll give you the keys to my pickup. You may drive. I'll show you the contents of my pants' pockets. You can even investigate my glove box," he proposed.

He was resolutely trying to convince this frightened lady she *could* trust him. "My name's Abraham Greathouse." He reached in his back pocket and pulled forth his wallet, showing her his license. I'm not some nutcase. It simply goes against my grain to abandon a woman in trouble. Will you please do me a favor and drive us both to the garage?"

Jackie Lynn hesitated for a second longer. This man genuinely seemed to be a nice guy. *Yet so had Ted Bundy. Can I really trust him?*

The alternative, sitting in the tiny dark space of her car, lingering by herself, bothered Jackie Lynn far worse than chancing a ride with this individual. *I'll keep my mace handy, and if threatened in any way, I'll blast this guy in the eyes. And, if need be, I'll pound him with the heel of my shoe. I'm capable of protecting myself.*

"Okay, Mr. Greathouse," she consented. He eagerly held his truck keys outward. "That's alright. If I'm agreeing to trust you, I'll trust you to drive too."

"Okay," he assented. He walked beside her as she headed for the passenger door. Being a gentleman, he opened it and helped her into the vehicle.

He clutched Jackie Lynn's hand with his own. His hand was large, warm and surprisingly soft. She consciously noted she liked the touch of that big masculine hand. She also noted that he was not wearing a wedding band.

Jeez! Flora's right! I need to start actively dating! she admitted, troubled by her ridiculous, slightly childish notions.

As the truck ambled down the road, Mr. Greathouse engaged in idle conversation. "If you don't mind me asking, how is it you are out here in the middle of nowhere? You look like you just came from some office in the city."

"You're very observant," she stated. *He checked out how I am dressed. Stop it, Jackie Lynn!* she admonished.

"I did come from the city. I'm a law partner there at Grayson & Associates. My name's Jackie Lynn Forrester, by the way."

"Pleasure to meet you, Jackie Lynn. And you may call me Abraham, instead of Mr. Greathouse," he teased, referring to the way she had addressed him earlier. "Don't tell me you are here in the country ambulance chasing legal cases."

"Not hardly. I work for a respectable law firm," she proudly assured him. "If somebody wants my services, they retain me. Not the other way around."

"I'm glad to hear that," Abraham said with a chuckle. "What brings you way out here straight from the office?"

"I was visiting a friend who's in a hospital about an hour from here," she confessed. She started to relax for some reason.

"Oh, I hope it's nothing serious," he replied. He knew of only one hospital around these parts. It was not a medical facility.

"She's going to be fine," Jackie Lynn confidently answered. "I take it you live around here?"

"Yeah. A couple of miles from the garage I'm taking you to. The owner is a buddy of mine. He'll take excellent care of you," he attested.

They rounded a bend. The bright sign of a service station on the side of the road came into view. "There's the garage," Abraham announced. He pointed through the windshield as they drew closer.

He parked his pickup close to the office and leapt from the truck. He also circled around to the other side to assist his pretty female passenger with her departure. *I get to touch this man's wonderful hand again*, she accepted. *What is wrong with me?! It must be the heat!* she concluded in embarrassment.

Yet, Jackie Lynn held on longer than necessary. Abraham directed her inside the office. A scrawny fellow in greasy coveralls scurried from the rear when he heard the bell on the door jingle.

"Hey, Long Wolf," he greeted, waving to the guy beside Jackie Lynn.

Long Wolf? she noted.

Some facial expression must have relayed Jackie Lynn's confusion, because he immediately clarified, "I'm half Indian. Folks around here are acquainted with me as Long Wolf, my tribal name." Attending to the business at hand, he directed his full attention to the mechanic then. He explained to him about Jackie Lynn's car.

"The main drive belt, huh?" The mechanic repeated, speaking exclusively to Long Wolf. "I'll drive my truck up the road and tow the automobile here, but there's no way I'm able to put another drive belt on tonight. Could you put this charming lady up at your place for the night? I can get her another drive belt as soon as the auto parts' place opens tomorrow at 10:00 a.m. I'll have her vehicle ready for her by noon."

"Tomorrow? By noon? 12 noon?!" Jackie Lynn anxiously restated.

What does the mechanic mean by asking this other man if he would put me up at his place for the night? This was getting weird and uncomfortable.

"Yes, ma'am," the mechanic responded. "The parts shop closed five hours ago. Won't open again 'til 10:00 a.m. Long Wolf here is a good guy. I've known him for years. He enjoys saving damsels in distress. He's worthy of your trust."

"Thanks for that vote of confidence, Otis," Long Wolf uttered with an amused grin.

Jackie Lynn was studying them both curiously. She had a clear view of Abraham *Long Wolf* in this bright office. *I was correct about him being handsome.*

Abraham *Long Wolf* had the darker coloring of an Indian and short, thick, shiny black hair. His alluring, golden brown eyes instantly caught and held your attention, and his charming smile was heartwarming. He was a large man, considerably taller than Jackie Lynn, with an expansive, hairy chest. It was impossible to miss the abundant black hair curling from the top of his slightly unbuttoned shirt. The dark masculine hair also carpeted his rugged, sinewy arms.

Oh, I bet it's wonderful to snuggle in that hair, her mind betrayed. *There's no way I'm spending the night at this guy's house!! When I get home, I may call a dating service as Flora suggested though, because I'm losing it.*

As she caught Long Wolf gazing into her eyes and feared he may have noticed her yearning stare, she nervously grilled both men, "Um…how far is the closest motel?"

Otis and Long Wolf shared a hearty laugh. "You're in the middle of nowhere, missy," Otis relayed. "There ain't no motel. Take her to your place, Long Wolf. I'll see you both in the morning. Can I have your keys, missy?"

Jackie Lynn glanced from one person to the other, feeling trapped. *What alternative do I have but to go with this mysterious man?* She hesitantly reached in her purse, handing the mechanic her keys.

"Don't worry. Long Wolf is a good guy," Otis assured. He headed from the shop then, holding the door open for them to follow.

When they vacated the office, Otis locked the door. He placed a sign in the window that read, 'Be back in a few minutes'. He unmistakably was the only one there.

Jackie Lynn was exasperated that her car had broken down in a tiny secluded town. *Is this fellow even intelligent enough to fix my car?*

Long Wolf somehow read her mind, because he assured her, "Don't worry. Otis is a good old country boy, but he is also an excellent mechanic. He'll have you on your way as soon as he's able to. You'll be perfectly fine at my place. I live in a fair sized cabin. Have I given you any reason to distrust me?"

There's that trust *word again*, she anxiously acknowledged.

"No. But, I don't really know you. For instance, what might I call you? Abraham or Long Wolf?" she grumbled with aggravation.

"Whichever you like," he replied. He opened the door to his truck, offering a hand to help her inside.

"I can get in by myself," she snapped, not wanting him to touch her again. Notwithstanding, Jackie Lynn recognized how rude she was being. "I'm sorry," she apologized.

"It's alright," he replied. He left her then, strolled around the vehicle, and climbed into his side of the pickup. "All I wish is for you to be comfortable. It has to be frustrating to have your automobile break down and discover you're stuck with some strange man for the night. Though I'll enjoy having the company for a change. Please relax. Make the best of this."

Turning to face him, Jackie Lynn discovered Long Wolf's golden brown eyes intently boring into her. *The way a wolf intensely studies a stranger*, she noted. The name Long Wolf suddenly fit him nicely.

"Okay, Long Wolf," she agreed, cooperating. "Thank you for being kind and putting me up for the night."

"My pleasure," he stated. He started the truck and headed down the road.

They arrived at his home shortly thereafter. It appeared nice. It was a secluded, decent sized, log cabin.

"Do you have company often?" Jackie Lynn questioned, as she climbed the steps leading onto his lengthy front porch. She noted that the porch had a roomy swing at the end and a few wooden rockers placed here and there.

"Friends, yes. Women, not in a long time," Long Wolf answered surprisingly.

Jackie Lynn wondered why. *I can't imagine why he might have any problem luring a female here. Quit!* She tried not to stare at him as he unlocked the door, switched the light on inside, and ushered her past him.

"This is nice," Jackie Lynn commented as she permitted her eyes a sweeping survey of her surroundings.

There was a spacious living room with an enormous cultured stone fireplace, a cushy Futon sofa, two recliners and a television. There was a small, cozy kitchen directly to the side. She assumed the other two doors that were closed must be bedrooms.

Surely there's a bathroom here somewhere too! Or maybe there's an outhouse hidden out back, she humorously conjectured.

"It suits my needs well," Long Wolf told her.

He shut the front door and started across the room. Long Wolf opened the door to one of the other rooms, and he switched on the light. "This is the bathroom. I'll get you one of my T-shirts to sleep in, if that's okay. Would you care for anything to drink? I have soft drinks, tea, orange juice, milk or water."

"No thanks. I'm fine," she informed him, making her way toward the couch.

"Okay. Be right back," Long Wolf shared. He hastened to open the door and disappear into the only other room.

When he reemerged, he was carrying a pillow, a sheet and one of his T-shirts. "Here," he offered, handing her the shirt. The pillow and sheet he placed at the end of the Futon couch. "You can sleep in my bed. I'll bunk on the sofa."

"I can't do that," Jackie Lynn argued. "I'll be fine on this couch."

"Nonsense," he adamantly disagreed. "You wouldn't have any privacy. If you take my bed, you'll be able to shut the door. I insist. You are my guest and I want you to feel at ease while you're here. It's late. You could go in the bathroom and prepare for bed. Oh, there's a toothbrush that hasn't been opened in the medicine cabinet. Help yourself. I'll sit on the porch so you can have some additional privacy. When you're through, switch off the light in the living room. I'll take that as my cue it's alright to come back in."

Jackie Lynn was awed by the graciousness of this handsome stranger. He was definitely going out of his way to make her feel at ease. *I've never met a guy quite like him. Is this for real? Or have I somehow unexpectedly entered the infamous* Twilight Zone?

"Jackie Lynn, are you okay?" Long Wolf scrutinized with concern after she stared at him in silence for a few minutes. She liked the sound of her name on his lips.

Definitely bedtime!

"Yeah. I appreciate how kind you're being. I figured you might have had a guestroom, considering you were so quick to invite me to stay. I hate to put you out," she answered.

"Don't worry about it. It's refreshing to have the company for a change. I'll be outside on the porch," he explained with an attractive glistening smile. He made quick strides for the exit.

Jackie Lynn scampered into the safety of his bathroom, shutting the door. She headed directly to the sink and turned the cold water on. *Let it run a few seconds. I want it to be very cold!* She vigorously splashed her cheeks and chin.

This is what happens when I don't date for a while, Jackie Lynn told herself in frustration.

She finished washing her face and brushed her teeth. When she pulled Long Wolf's T-shirt on after discarding her clothes, she turned the cold water back on, splashing her cheeks anew.

It's simply a shirt. Because it's his shouldn't be making me crazy!

She neatly hung her suit on an empty hanger and placed it on a peg on the outside of the closet door. She crept through the living room, with her undergarments in hand, switched off the light, rushed into Long Wolf's bedroom, and closed the door. A second later, as she sat on the side of his bed, she heard the water running in the bathroom, so she knew he had come in.

Everything's fine. Climb in this bed, relax and go to sleep. Morning shall soon arrive.

Jackie Lynn peeled back the bedspread, cover and sheet. It was too hot for any of them. *Or at least I'm hot!* She lay down on her side.

No sooner had her cheek touched the pillow, then she smelled this wonderful masculine smell. It was *his* scent. *It's merely saturated in the pillow,* Jackie Lynn reasoned. She irrationally tossed the pillow to the floor.

Lying her head flat on the sheet, she discovered the whole bed was saturated with his desirable scent. *Ignore it!* she ordered.

Jackie Lynn rolled onto her back, attempting to concentrate on other things. *Flora would get a big kick out of this. So might Mary Julia. No, Mary Julia would have already humped Long Wolf in his truck. What in the world am I thinking?!*

She sat up on the side of the bed in angry frustration. *When I get home, I have got to start dating regularly again. This is ridiculous! I'm acting like some teenager.*

Jackie Lynn rose and advanced to the window. She unlocked it, carefully sliding it all the way up. *The cool air from outside will clear my mind. I'm getting in that bed, ignoring* his *smell, and going to sleep,* she tried to stubbornly persuade herself.

She stood in front of the window, enjoying the breeze for half an hour or so before she returned to the bed. She left the window raised. Jackie Lynn reluctantly lay down. She attempted to focus her brain on anything other than that wonderful smell and the man it belonged to – *just on the other side of that door.* She tossed and tumbled in frustration.

I'm barely acquainted with this guy. Why am I so powerfully attracted to him? It has to be because I haven't been with someone in a while, even though Long Wolf is very handsome and a nice man.

Jackie Lynn rose to her feet in exasperation. *Maybe if I sit on the porch for a bit, I'll relax enough to get a little shut eye.*

She quietly turned the doorknob. She was endeavoring to be careful so as to not wake Long Wolf, if he was already sleeping. Creeping out, Jackie Lynn glanced toward the Futon couch. She was not prepared for the glorious sight she naughtily beheld.

Moonlight was brilliantly streaming through the tall, wide, front window. Directly beneath its vibrant glow was the magnificent, completely naked, male body of Long Wolf. He was sound asleep on the Futon couch. Evidently, he did not sleep clothed. As Jackie Lynn indecently stared, her body stirred with longing.

Get out of this room immediately! her mind frantically registered.

Jackie Lynn rushed back into the bedroom, softly closed the door, turned, and leaned wearily against it. *Oh great! Just what I needed!*

She could not expel the image of that nearly perfect, male body from her memory. *You're a grown woman. You've seen lots of naked men's bodies before. But you knew those men. Not so with this guy. Calm down!*

Jackie Lynn scurried to the open window. She dared to stick her whole torso outside. She grabbed Long Wolf's shirt, hoisting it over her head. She was too hot to have anything touching her skin. He had the right idea. She maintained this posture for an eternity, letting the breeze caress, cool and calm her unclothed body.

* * * *

Long Wolf awoke rather late the next morning. He was surprised he had slept so soundly. When he had first laid down on the Futon, his sole focus had been the fact that he had a lovely lady sleeping in his bed.

He had angrily chastised himself for such ideas. *Jackie Lynn appears to be a sweet lady.*

Long Wolf yearned to become better acquainted with her while they awaited her car being repaired. *Perhaps I might get her telephone number and call her sometime soon.*

He wondered if she was awake and was merely waiting for him to make some noise so she could arise. He had not intended to sleep so late. Long Wolf arose, scooped his jeans from a nearby chair where he had left them the night before, and slipped them on.

He was glad Jackie Lynn had not ventured from the bedroom. He had carefully covered his unclothed pelvis with a sheet last night, but he must have accidentally kicked it off after he fell asleep.

He gradually made his way to her door, listening for any sound of movement. *I'll quietly open it and see if she's still asleep,* he speculated, turning the knob.

The sight that invitingly met his eyes was stunning. Jackie Lynn was lying on her side, facing him, completely naked. Long Wolf decently hastened to close the door. Nonetheless, as he ambled toward the kitchen, he could not help but notice the instant hardness in his lower region. *Down boy!* he playfully instructed.

Long Wolf opened the refrigerator, retrieved a jug of milk, poured himself a tall glass, and gulped the ice cold fluid down. *I would undeniably enjoy becoming much more familiar with that lovely lady.*

Grabbing pots and pans, he intentionally clanged them together. He also whistled a tune, hoping Jackie Lynn might soon hear the racket and arise. His plan worked, because a few minutes later, she slowly emerged.

"Good morning, sleepyhead," Long Wolf greeted with an enormous grin.

He was trying not to stare at her body. Thankfully, she was now clothed by his shirt, which easily hung down to her knees. He could not refrain from glancing at Jackie Lynn though. *She looks remarkably sexy in my oversized T-shirt also*, he could not help but notice.

Long Wolf turned, fighting his strong desires. "How do eggs, bacon and toast sound for breakfast?"

"Fine," she brusquely answered. Then she disappeared behind the bathroom door.

Lord, I'm glad I put my bra and underwear on before I left his room. This shirt is thin, and with the way he was just studying me, he would have been able to see straight through, Jackie Lynn thought with a sigh of relief.

When she emerged from the bathroom, Long Wolf had breakfast prepared. After they had eaten, he suggested they take a stroll in the woods. "Otis will call when your car is ready. I have a message machine. I'm not totally technology free here. We might as well enjoy this beautiful day until we hear from him. What do you say?"

"I'd say I'm not exactly dressed for it," Jackie Lynn replied. She pointed to her body and the suit, blouse, pantyhose and dress shoes she donned once more. She had not had any other clothing to put on.

"I'm capable of fixing that. I could give you some drawstring shorts to throw on and another T-shirt. You'll look adorable," Long Wolf inadvertently commented, his gaze too admiring. "Come on. Say yes. The woods around here are very pleasant to walk in," he persuaded. He deliberately glanced aside so she did not notice his obvious attraction to her.

Long Wolf's lingering eyes had not escaped Jackie Lynn's attention though. *I'd be delighted to walk through the woods with this gorgeous, tall, Indian*, her mind conceived.

"Give me the clothes and a second to change," she impulsively assented with a wide eager grin.

This guy is interesting, she concluded as she curiously followed Long Wolf to his bedroom.

Jackie Lynn stood in the doorway as he retrieved some clothing for both of them from some drawers. Long Wolf joined her in the doorway – *so noticeably close* – and handed her the clothes. An overwhelming yearning for this man caused Jackie Lynn's blood to rush and her breath to catch in her throat.

"Um...I'll be in the bathroom, changing my own clothes," he established.

He moved aside. Long Wolf was fighting his tremendous urge to gather Jackie Lynn in his arms and passionately kiss her tempting lips. *Not now*, Long Wolf adamantly decreed. *Yet I'm definitely planning to familiarize myself better with Jackie Lynn.*

Jackie Lynn inhaled with relief as she watched him disappear behind the bathroom door. *Thank God!*

* * * *

Long Wolf's knit shorts looked downright hilarious on Jackie Lynn. With the pull string tightened as much as possible, they were still quite baggy. Fortunately, Jackie Lynn had a pair of tennis shoes and some socks in her bag from work – decent footwear for walking in the woods with this magnetic male.

At least the shorts will be comfortable to stroll in. That is, if they don't work their way loose and fall off somewhere along the trail, she somewhat comically visualized.

Long Wolf's T-shirt was also enormous on her. It hung loosely from both shoulders and almost entirely covered her shorts. Hence, Jackie Lynn neatly tied it at her waist, slightly exposing her flat stomach.

Long Wolf studied her with an appreciative grin as she emerged. "Gee, those clothes never looked – *The word flashing in my brain like a neon sign is sexy* – um…they don't look the same on you."

"Let's hope not," Jackie Lynn stated, laughing wholeheartedly.

He walked to the front door and opened it. He reached out to pull an intricately carved walking stick from a stand by the door. He had carved the stick himself – a talent taught to him by some of his Indian ancestors. "Well, shall we hike?" Long Wolf suggested. He waved his arm for Jackie Lynn to proceed to the great outdoors.

She followed his lead, heading across the room and through the doorway. Stepping off the porch, Jackie Lynn surveyed her surroundings in the light of day. There were many, tall, beautiful trees and colorful bushes. *A wilderness refuge*, she noted, an unusual comfort overtaking her. *There's no logic why. I'm a city girl through and through.* She also inhaled a deep breath of the fresh country air.

"You picked a nice spot to call home," she commented. "Did you build the cabin yourself?"

"Uh huh. With assistance from friends," Long Wolf replied.

He placed his palm in the middle of her back to prod her forward toward the footpath leading through the woods. This caused pleasurable tingles to run up and down Jackie Lynn's spine. She could not help but like the feel of this guy's big, strong, yet remarkably gentle hands touching her body.

Oh, don't start! Jackie Lynn sternly warned herself. *He's a kind man, who's also remarkably handsome and appealing. But you most likely shall never spend time with him again after today.* She scurried for the trail, purposely separating her back from his tantalizing touch.

"You cleared this path too?" Jackie Lynn whimsically questioned. She briefly glanced at Long Wolf as they continued along it, strolling side by side.

"I did," she was amazed to hear. She was impressed. It was a nice established, wide path.

73

Jackie Lynn could not refrain from wondering, *Why doesn't he have a female by his side to share this? Then again, who am I to judge?*

"It's the Indian in me. I cherish being outdoors surrounded by nature," Long Wolf shared.

Then, as if he had been reading Jackie Lynn's mind, he rather eerily added, "It's the perfect spot to be alone. Fortunately, I prefer it that way."

"I understand exactly what you mean," she mumbled, staring down at the ground. They came to a clearing in the trees, and directly ahead of them was a fair sized, shimmering, round body of water.

"Welcome to my pond," Long Wolf stated with a proud grin. "It's not overly large but good for fishing. I've had some decent fish dinners, and it makes a great swimming hole. Especially on warm sunny days like today."

His pond? Surely he isn't suggesting he owns the land we just hiked across and this pond.

"Darn. I forgot to bring my bathing suit," Jackie Lynn teased.

"I don't usually wear a bathing suit. I usually swim all natural," he mischievously divulged, his eyes twinkling devilishly.

Sleeping isn't the only thing this guy prefers to experience totally naked, she unchastely noted. She strived to dissipate the torturing picturesque memory of Long Wolf lying on his Futon, in the revealing moonlight.

Jackie Lynn walked closer to the stream. There was a small wooden dock – *probably where this man sits and fishes* – directly ahead. *I'll sit there and stick my feet in the cool water for a few moments*, she wisely considered, suddenly quite heated. Jackie Lynn discarded her shoes and socks.

"What are you doing?" she heard Long Wolf inquire. She glanced at him and discovered he was curiously studying her. It was then that it occurred to Jackie Lynn that Long Wolf mistakenly surmised she was preparing to skinny-dip.

"I'm only taking my shoes off. I was planning to stick my feet in the water for a second," she clarified, surprised by how hot her cheeks had grown.

Good gosh! I'm actually blushing! Jackie Lynn evasively turned from his view, strutted to the dock, and sat down, dangling her feet in the cool refreshing water.

Long Wolf had not intended to embarrass her, but Jackie Lynn's flushed checks managed to endear her even greater to him. When she had removed her footwear, right after he had mentioned skinny-dipping, he had consequentially, yet incorrectly, assumed she meant to swim as such. Recalling the beautiful, slumbering, nude body he had accidentally happened upon, he would have greatly enjoyed skinny-dipping with this lady.

No, Long Wolf! he reprimanded himself. *Take it slow. You don't want to scare her away. She produces the most overwhelming desire in me.*

He approached the dock. Long Wolf intentionally sat with his back to Jackie Lynn, even though he could have sat beside her. He needed a second to compose himself. Long Wolf discarded his shoes and socks and placed his feet in the chilly pond as well. He also cupped some of the water in his hands and abruptly lowered his head, sufficiently cooling his face and neck.

After silently swirling her feet in the *thankfully very cold* water for several moments, Jackie Lynn logically inquired, "Shouldn't we be getting back to the cabin? My car might be ready. I should be returning to the city. I have some things I'd like to accomplish today, if possible."

The actual, slightly panicked thought running through her brain was: *It would be best if I separate from this Indian I'm finding myself naturally drawn to for some reason.*

"I suppose," he agreed with some regret.

Jackie Lynn had splashed her own cheeks with cold water, after she had seen Long Wolf do it out of the corner of her eye. Even though he had his back to her, his body in such close proximity was significantly disturbing Jackie Lynn.

Long Wolf's broad shoulders are appealing. Wonder how it might feel to massage them? Good Grief! Separate from this guy ASAP! The lack of passion in my life must be causing my hormones to rush uncontrollably.

Long Wolf glanced down at his watch. It was almost noon. Considering Otis was not overrun with business, he probably was already finished with the vehicle. Nevertheless, Long Wolf hated for his opportunity to be alone with Jackie Lynn to end. There was no way he would allow her departure without getting her phone number so he was capable of calling her in the near future.

He gathered his walking stick, shoes and socks, rose, and gallantly offered Jackie Lynn his free hand, helping her rise. They were standing face-to-face – temptingly near one another. Jackie Lynn was stunned by how severe her desire was to touch her eager lips to this man's. She slid her fingers from Long Wolf's firm grasp, whirled, and sprinted toward her nearby abandoned footwear. She could not stop unless she distanced herself from this individual.

Long Wolf watched her with an amused smile. Jackie Lynn was hopping from foot to foot, nearly tripping, as she struggled to pull her socks onto her damp feet. As she lowered to push her shoes on and tie them, he slipped his own footwear back into place.

Long Wolf purposely trailed behind Jackie Lynn on the return trip to the cabin. He was so overwhelmed by his fierce desires he did not trust himself to draw too close to this captivating lady in front of him. *The view from this vantage point is excellent. She has pretty, shapely legs*, he could not avoid noticing.

* * * *

The message light on Long Wolf's machine *was* blinking when they entered the cabin. Unfortunately, it bore a message from Otis saying the automobile was ready whenever, "the damsel in distress might like to pick it up."

"I should change into my own clothes," Jackie Lynn observed. She instinctively began heading toward Long Wolf's bedroom.

"No. Don't do that," Long Wolf oddly disagreed. He stepped in front of her to block her way. "There's no reason for you to go to that trouble. It's not as if I'm going to miss those shorts and t-shirt. You can wear them home. I work in the city every day myself, so if you would give me your telephone number and address, I could stop by and pick the clothes up one evening next week."

This is the chance I've been waiting for, he eagerly anticipated. He awaited her important reply. *If Jackie Lynn rejects this offer, I'll find another way to obtain her phone number. I haven't been this interested in acquainting myself with a woman in quite a while.*

"You work in the city?" Jackie Lynn asked. She had assumed he was a good ol' country boy, who lived and worked far from the city. She could not picture him working there.

"Yeah, at a construction company," he responded. His desire was not to talk about himself. He yearned to get this pretty, enticing lady's address and telephone number. *I haven't wished so badly for additional time with a woman in ages.*

He's a construction worker, she noted. *That definitely explains the prominent muscles in his arms, chest and legs. Although, his soft, smooth hands surprise me, and I always figured most construction workers were usually younger men. I'd guess Long Wolf to be at least forty, if not a little older.*

Jackie Lynn realized she was staring at him. "Um…I don't want to put you out any greater than I already have by taking your clothes," she replied.

"You truly have *not* put me out. I had a good time." Long Wolf admitted. He found he was gazing at her more yearningly than he had planned.

He deliberately glanced away, adding, "Besides, you'll get away quicker if you don't change. I'll get you some hangers for your blouse and suit if you'd like. Didn't you tell me you'd prefer to return to the city as soon as possible since you had some things to take care of?"

"You, sir, should be a lawyer," Jackie Lynn teased with an amused chuckle. "You argue a case very well. Okay. You provide the hangers, and I'll give you my phone number so we can arrange to meet one evening next week."

Yes! he cheered. Long Wolf turned and headed into his bedroom to retrieve some hangers from his closet.

Jackie Lynn followed him into the room. When he opened his roomy closet, the many expensive looking suits neatly hanging there surprised her. *Why does a construction worker need such fancy clothes?* she could not help but wonder.

Jackie Lynn's facial expression must have betrayed her confusion, because when Long Wolf turned with the hangers in his hands, he asked, "What's wrong?"

I'm being ridiculous. I have no right to be cross-examining this man in respect to his clothing, she concluded.

"Uh...nothing. Why?" she lied.

Averting her eyes, Jackie Lynn took the hangers. She attached her suit to them. "Ready when you are." she informed Long Wolf. She snatching her purse and bag from the floor and threw them over a shoulder.

"Okay," he agreed. "Let's be off. I'll get your telephone number at Otis' garage."

"I'll do you one better. I'll write it down for you on the way there on my business card," Jackie Lynn promised. She strutted past him toward the front door, eager to get to the garage, get her car, and be on her way.

Last night and today have been too overwhelming for me.

CHAPTER SIX

HEALING

Sunday night, Jacob returned from his latest surgical tour. Flora enthusiastically greeted him with a hug and a kiss, brought him bourbon and coke, and sat down to listen to him recount his tiring, but successful, work week. She was especially attentive, since it was imperative he be extremely relaxed and comfortable. She needed to somehow raise the subject of the phone messages she was *not* receiving and her essential visit with Mary Julia.

Flora arranged for the cook to serve Jacob's favorite dinner and enticed him into a few glasses of wine. When they went upstairs to their room, she dressed in a tiny, sexy negligee, luridly tantalizing him. She dreaded what would follow. Flora could not describe sex with Jacob as making love anymore. It was no longer in any way pleasurable for her to be intimate with this incredibly selfish man.

Jacob had ceased to care about satisfying her anymore. He fulfilled only his own needs and rolled over, falling into a fast sleep. He did not even attempt to lovingly cuddle Flora in his arms afterwards anymore, and she did not pursue this, for fear that he would become angry and cruel.

If Flora dared to claim that she was tired or did not feel well, Jacob would shame her, claiming she was being unthoughtful to his needs. "Are you unable to grasp how important normal relations are with my wife, especially after a grueling trip?!" he would bark. "Can't you even behave like a good wife and put forth the effort to make love to your husband? After all, you should be very well rested after the lifestyle that I have provided for you. Why are you unable to appreciate the multitude of things I give you, Flora? Your shallowness never ceases to amaze me."

How had he been so gentle, caring and loving once? she still wondered from time to time. *It plainly had been some sick act to entice me into his web, but why? With his money and great looks, he could have easily had a younger, more willing mate. He's similar to a black widow; but they kill their mates. Only a black widow would be quick in respect to it, not like Jacob, with his slow torture. This creature is gradually killing me a little day by day.*

Jacob had his way with Flora that night and rolled off, eager to fall into a contented post-coital sleep. She snuggled alongside his back, purring softly in his ear, "Jacob. Honey, can I talk to you? Please?"

He slowly rolled to face her. "When you ask me so nicely, how can I possibly say no?" he answered with a silly satisfied smile. "What is it, my pet?"

Be careful, she warned herself before responding. The combination of the alcohol and the satisfying sex – *at least it had been satisfying for him* – had settled Jacob into a relaxed, agreeable state. But that might easily change in the blink of an eye.

"Well, it's just...I called Jackie Lynn Thursday to check on Mary Julia. She told me she had phoned and left a message for me on a couple of different occasions. Our answering service never gave me any messages. Could you please speak to them for me, Jacob? It's important to me that I'm aware of how things are proceeding with Mary Julia. Even though I won't remain involved in their lives, I would like to follow through with this. It sounds as if she is significantly improving. Jackie Lynn said she's allowed visitors. Would you take me to the hospital she is in sometime soon? Or if you are too tired...and I accept that you could be, darling...may I possibly go this once with Jackie Lynn?"

Jacob was silent for several, long, tense moments. Flora nervously held her breath. She intently watched for signs of an unexpected burst of anger. "Flora, you totally baffle me," he stated, an unmistakable edge coming into his voice. "Haven't I given you everything a woman could want? A huge expensive house to live in, beautiful expensive clothing, people to take care of your every whim. I *was* beginning to deduce I was being put first in your life. Now…"

Before he was capable of finishing his sentence, Flora swiftly interrupted him. She sickeningly *and quite untruthfully* gushed, "No darling, I appreciate all you have given me. Really I do! It's more than I could ever desire!"

She rushed on, "I'm pleading with you, Jacob, not to be angry with me. You come first in my life. You are my life! Yet the girls have depended on me for so long, and Mary Julia is in trouble. Will you try to understand? Once Mary Julia is well, if you want for me to break all ties with her and Jackie Lynn, of course I will. I'd do anything for you. Don't you know that? I cherish you greater than life itself."

Flora hoped her act was convincing. *The person I'd like to break ties with is you, Jacob. However, I have to be clever concerning how I rid my life of you.* She had no doubt that Jacob would not hesitate to kill her if he even had an inkling she planned to leave him.

"What exactly are you saying?" He questioned, propping his head up on a wobbly elbow. "If I permit you to receive calls from Jackie Lynn, these shall *only* be regarding Mary Julia? And afterwards, *one* get together with Mary Julia and chummy friend Jackie Lynn and you'll agree to cease fraternizing altogether with these two?"

"If that's your wish, of course I will." Flora consented. She affectionately caressed Jacob's cheek. "It's asking a lot after everything else you have given me and done for me. But will you grant me this final reunion with my friends? I'll make it my last. I swear I will, Jacob," she pleaded.

Flora wanted to dash into the bathroom and vomit. She was sickened by her sugary sweet arguments. Nonetheless, she recognized that lowering herself to this level was the only likelihood she had of getting to speak with Jackie Lynn and visiting Mary Julia. These special ladies were worth the sacrifice to her.

"That's a definite promise?" Jacob further intimidated.

"I *definitely* promise," Flora vowed. She brought her lips to his for a lengthy – *hopefully convincing* – kiss.

"If that's what it takes for you to no longer need anyone in your life other than me, I'll grant your wish. I'll talk to the answering service. I'll direct them to put Jackie Lynn's calls through to you. Plus you may visit Mary Julia. *Once!* And only *once!* Does that make you happy?" he scrutinized with an expectant smile.

"*You* make me happy," she further lied. She put her arms around Jacob's neck and lavishly devoured his mouth. Flora was determined to do everything she was capable of to insure he would not change his mind.

* * * *

Monday, after she got home from work, Jackie Lynn telephoned Flora. She hoped her friend was not still gone with that irresistible husband of hers. She also hoped that Flora had spoken to Jacob concerning their answering service being so poor.

"Roberts' residence," another strange voice answered.

"Hello. Is Flora there? This is her friend Jackie Lynn," she divulged. She crossed her fingers that Flora might be there, or she would at least receive her phone message.

"One moment please," the service politely replied. "I'll inform Mrs. Roberts that Jackie Lynn has telephoned."

She is *home. Furthermore, I'm going to be able to speak to her on the* first *try,* Jackie Lynn was amazed to discover. Hopefully, this meant she would no longer have trouble getting through to Flora.

"Hello, Jackie Lynn," Flora greeted.

Jacob is *keeping his promise and letting me receive Jackie Lynn's calls, or at least this time. Surely he'll allow me to see Mary Julia as well.* "Tell me everything. How was Mary Julia?"

"She's doing well," Jackie Lynn eagerly shared. "She asked about you. I informed her you would be coming to the hospital soon. When would you prefer to get together to make a trip there? How was your Shanghai weekend with Jacob, by the way?"

"It was fine," Flora curtly responded, then added, "Would Wednesday night be good for you? I'm free almost anytime."

"Of course, Mrs. Socialite," Jackie Lynn teased. "You're free, except for the hours you spend with that handsome husband of yours. I take it you enlightened him about the trouble with your answering service. I'm amazed I got through to you."

So am I, Flora noted. *It's essential I set a definite date with Jackie Lynn to visit Mary Julia, so I may obtain Jacob's permission. My life is so insane.*

"How about it? Shall we plan on Wednesday being the day?" Flora inquired too seriously.

Jackie Lynn was surprised. She had given Flora two decent chances to talk about Jacob. She had ignored both. *This is odd. Flora used to continuously gush about the new love of her life.*

Jackie Lynn worried there might be something up between Flora and Jacob. However, she did not probe. If there was a problem, Flora did not seem to wish to discuss it. If it was anything serious, she was confident Flora would eventually confide in her. They had shared considerable turmoil in one another's lives over the years.

"Wednesday sounds great!" Jackie Lynn assented. "Where'd you want to meet? You're on my way, if you would like me to stop by your un-humble abode. It would be delightful to see it. It sounds wonderful."

Flora expected Jacob to be out of town, but she believed inviting Jackie Lynn to the house would be a definite mistake. It was likely Jacob would somehow discover that Jackie Lynn had been there. Flora was being overly cautious not to do a single thing that would ignite his fury.

"Um…I'd love to have you come to the house soon, but may I give you a rain check?" she nervously asked. "Can we get together somewhere for dinner first instead and visit Mary Julia after?"

"Of course," Jackie Lynn warily acceded. Something in Flora's voice definitely bothered her. She had sensed it when they had last spoken. If they went to dinner, she could possibly persuade her to confide what the problem might be. "Name the place."

"Why don't I have our driver bring me into the city, we'll pick you up and we'll eat at Gregory's? We haven't been there in ages. I can taste their wonderful dishes. Can't you?" Flora happily reminisced.

She sounded more like her old self now. *Maybe I'm imagining there's a problem since I've missed her so much.*

"That sounds terrific," Jackie Lynn concurred. "Except..why don't I join you at the restaurant rather than you picking me up at my apartment? You could send your chauffeur back, and I'll drive us to the sanitarium and drop you at your house on our return trip. That way I at least know where your place is located. Even if I don't get the chance to come in."

"Okay," Flora conceded.

I have to somehow convince Jacob to agree to this. I dread his next call.

"I'll meet you at Gregory's Wednesday. Is 4:00 too early? Travel time from the city is three hours to the hospital, isn't it? I figure if we have an early dinner, we might have a longer stay with Mary Julia. But when do visiting hours end? Around 9:00 p.m. or so? That will make you getting home fairly late…."

"Don't worry about that. Meeting at 4:00 sounds like to a winning plan to me. I'm looking forward to meeting with you," Jackie Lynn acknowledged.

Although she was concerned by the way Flora had been rambling, Jackie Lynn ended their call. *Something's wrong, but I'll get to the bottom of it when we meet.*

Jackie Lynn had just lowered the receiver when the telephone rang. "What did you forget?" she said with a chuckle, as she snatched the phone back to her ear. She naturally assumed it was Flora phoning her again for some reason.

"Well, it certainly wasn't you," Long Wolf's voice unexpectedly answered. Then, with an amused laugh, he stated, "I take it you were expecting somebody else?"

"Yes. I was just talking to a friend. I figured it was her calling back for some reason," she shared. "I guess you are calling about your clothes," Jackie Lynn idiotically established, unnaturally nervous.

Yesterday and today, this Indian man, on and off throughout the day, had totally preoccupied Jackie Lynn's mind. She hated to admit it, but she was glad to hear his voice.

"Yes, I was calling about my clothes" Long Wolf confirmed. "I was wondering if I might stop by Friday evening and pick them up. That is, if you aren't busy."

Is he fishing around to find if I have a date? Jackie Lynn suspiciously wondered.

"I'm not busy. That would be fine," she admitted, her heart rate quickening as if she was some foolish teenager.

What is it about this guy?

"Great!" Long Wolf exclaimed, more enthusiastically than he had intended.

He was already excitedly contemplating the fact that he was to share the company of Jackie Lynn again soon. Long Wolf had almost had to sit on his hands yesterday because he had badly yearned to telephone her and hear her voice. He had waited, so as not to seem overly eager.

Jackie Lynn might easily be frightened off if he came on too strong too soon. Nonetheless, Long Wolf was having trouble containing his delight. "I gather everything is kosher with the car?" he cleverly changed the subject.

"Yes. It's still running, and I haven't had any other problems," she hastened to assure him. "Thank you for your aid and the hospitality. What would I have done if you hadn't happened along?"

"As I've already informed you, it was my pleasure. It must have been fate that brought me along your path in the first place. I'm usually home long before." Long Wolf stated, fully accepting what *genuine* pleasure it had been for him. He hoped for additional pleasure in both their futures. "Since you said you aren't busy Friday and I'm coming by your place to pick up my stuff anyway, why don't you let me treat you to dinner?"

"Oh, I couldn't do that," Jackie Lynn declined, even though part of her desired to say 'Yes'.

This man is dangerous. I sense it. My attraction to him is too great. It's best that we remain apart, she warned herself.

"How come?" he questioned with slight disappointment.

Is it possible I've read the cues inaccurately and this woman isn't interested in me? He sincerely hoped this was not the case.

"It wouldn't be right for me to allow you to buy me dinner after everything you have already done," Jackie Lynn pointed out. Nevertheless, she surprised her own self when she flirtatiously offered, "I can buy you dinner instead. It would be a gesture of my gratitude to you for being kind and putting me up in your cabin. I could at least do that much for you."

"Oh," he laughed in response. "Well, if you insist, how can I possibly refuse such an offer? When shall I pick you up? Or do you intend to pick me up as well? I'll be performing an onsite inspection of our newest construction site Friday evening."

"An onsite inspection? Where is this site located?" She continued to play.

"Right in the heart of downtown. On the corner of Chestnut and Eighth street," Long Wolf shared.

"Aw...isn't that the new Tricon site. I'm impressed," Jackie Lynn continued to tease. "What time do you get off work, sir?"

86

"Any time you wish," he hastened to propose.

That sounds odd, but considering he's probably the head guy at the construction company, he should be able to somewhat set his own hours, Jackie Lynn considered.

She also decided it would be wise to change clothes before leaving her office. After all, Long Wolf was a construction worker. Thus, he would not be dressed nice. They probably would not eat any place too fancy either.

"How does 6:00 sound to you?" she asked.

"Sounds fine. I'll be waiting at 6:00 on the corner, Eighth street side." he agreed.

"Great. I'll see you then," she concluded. "Take care."

"You too. Don't have any other breakdowns," he pestered, hating to hang up. Long Wolf was looking extremely forward to Friday.

* * * *

Flora sat in the study, impatiently awaiting Jacob's phone call. He telephoned every evening, but never consistently. This way, she had to remain in the house the entire night. Otherwise, Flora might accidentally miss his almighty call, and Jacob would have to kill some other, poor, unsuspecting soul.

That isn't fair, she scolded herself. *He doesn't kill people because he's mad at me...or does he? No, don't even think that.*

Flora was startled to reality when the telephone rang. She presumed it was Jacob. She absently grabbed for the receiver. At the last minute she hesitated, remembering she was prohibited from answering the phone.

Flora merely held her hand on top of the receiver in anticipation, without raising it. In the few moments it took for the intercom to chime, her palm was damp with nervous perspiration.

"Mrs. Roberts, Mr. Roberts to speak with you," the answering service announced.

Without replying to the service, she picked up the receiver gushing, "Hello, darling! How was your day?!"

"What do you care? I'm here alone at this revolting hospital in a dingy sleeping room, with damn idiots for interns."

The cruel, disgusted tone of Jacob's voice divulged to Flora that she had started their conversation on the wrong note. Their discussion was doomed to be difficult. Notwithstanding, she was fixated on accomplishing her vital goal.

"Jacob, darling, you sound tired. They should have better consideration for the job you perform and supply you with some decent interns. If they appreciated you as I do, darling, they would provide you with necessary assistance. I pity you, sweetheart. I wish I were there to comfort you. I miss you terribly when you are gone, darling." She deliberately went overboard with mushiness.

The tone of his voice softened, but his words were just as hateful. He replied, "Flora, my sweets, you couldn't possibly begin to deduce what I'm dealing with. The idea of your tiny brain conceiving this is surely amusing though."

Flora hated it when Jacob belittled her. He talked to her as if she had never been an accredited attorney and survived long before he was a part of her life. *A sad part! I'll be free from this bastard's tortures soon. Until this liberation, I'll silently pray for the strength to endure this punishment.*

"Jacob, you are absolutely right. I'm incapable of even attempting to stand in your shoes. Loving the greatest surgeon in the world is enough for me...I adore you, darling. When will you be coming home?" She continued her clever charade.

Jacob laughed in condescension, speculating how stupid she was. He confirmed it when he meanly stated, "I'll be there the same time as usual. You always seem to forget. Perhaps I should have a doctor examine that pea brain of yours, Flora dear. Maybe, just maybe, they might give you some miracle drug to assist you in retaining some memory. It's impossible for me to surmise how you functioned in that miniscule unknown law firm you thoroughly believed hung the moon. With colleagues comparable to you, I can't imagine how they kept the place open."

Flora's resentment of Jacob's hateful taunts was growing overwhelming. *Before I make the mistake of saying the wrong thing and unwittingly inciting Jacob's anger, it's imperative I secure his permission to visit Mary Julia. That's the important thing! Stay focused, Flora!*

"Jacob, darling, I have you to take care of me now. My life before that meant nothing. Let's focus on the present. I would never have survived without meeting you."

She paused for a few minutes to permit her carefully chosen – *entirely untruthful* – words sink through Jacob's egotistically inflated skull. Afterwards, she cleverly added, "Honey, I have recently spoken to Jackie Lynn. She is going to the hospital to visit Mary Julia Wednesday evening. I'd like to join her. If that's alright with you?"

In a slightly angry voice, he stated, "The sooner you get this out of your system, the better our marriage shall be! Perhaps we'll finally have the opportunity to be happy together once and for all!"

After a lengthy, drawn-out sigh, Jacob continued, "Go! With my supreme blessing! Get it over with."

He concluded their conversation with a chilling declaration, "You best be the kind of woman that keeps her word, Flora. I'm completely serious in regard to the deal we've made. No compromising; this one chummy reunion is it. After that, you cut those dangling strings. You are *my* wife. Remember those words you proudly repeated at our wedding, to love, honor, and the most valuable for you to recall, *obey*?!"

Flora had tears in her eyes as she answered, "I remember, Jacob. I'll be true to all of my promises. This will be the last contact I'll have with my friends…my life shall be entirely devoted to you."

She heard the dial tone then. Jacob had hung up without saying goodbye. *Well, that's fine. I got what was necessary. It wasn't that hard. It simply required a little extra effort on my part.*

Nevertheless, as Flora further contemplated her farce, she sadly realized, *My life is terrible! I'm frightened nearly every minute!* She proceeded to cry until she had no tears left to shed.

* * * *

Flora was almost ecstatic when Wednesday finally arrived. *God, it's going to be unbearable coming back to this house!* she sadly accepted as she sat in Jacob's limo and permitted the driver to transport her to the city to join Jackie Lynn.

If only I was capable of rolling back time, to before Jacob, so I could remain in the city and never return to the country and to this lonely place of madness. I'll figure a way out of this soon, she determinedly promised. *At least I'm allowed to be with my friends tonight. I'll fully concentrate on that.*

Jackie Lynn was eagerly awaiting Flora in front of Gregory's Bar and Grill. She greeted her with a broad exhilarated smile and an affectionate hug. "Oh, it's great to see you!" she happily proclaimed. "It seems as if it's been forever."

"Yes. Much too long," Flora declared too seriously, embracing her even tighter.

As she drew back, Jackie Lynn was surprised to observe tears standing in this woman's eyes. "Flora, is everything alright?" she inquired with concern.

"Of course," she deceptively covered. Flora hated the fact that she was lying.

She could not share with Jackie Lynn how unquestionably awful her life was. *It's not as if she's able to help me anyway. I got myself into this mess and I'm the one who has to somehow free myself.*

"I'm overjoyed to see you, that's all. I hadn't appreciated how much I would miss the time we spent together, even if it was merely lunch whenever we might manage and a couple of evenings a week. I miss both you and Mary Julia so much. Why don't we go inside and enjoy a pleasant dinner. After that, we can go visit with our other dear friend."

Flora opened the door to the restaurant and motioned for Jackie Lynn to enter. She was smiling, but Jackie Lynn knew her well enough to recognize when she was covering her emotions. Without a doubt, all was not right in Flora's life, and she intended to uncover the problem before they parted.

Jackie Lynn got started on her important crusade as soon as they were seated. Their server had just disappeared with their drink orders. "So...tell me...how is your law practice coming in the country?" she began the cross-examination. "Do you have many clients?"

"I don't have *any* clients," Flora confessed. She squirmed in her seat and seemed uncomfortable. "I changed my mind about setting up a practice there. My life is full without it. Are things as insane as ever here in the city?" she explored, cleverly reversing the subject to Jackie Lynn.

Jackie Lynn was not about to permit her to accomplish this. Flora delighted in practicing law as much as, *if not greater than*, she did. *How's her life so full without it? Especially since Jacob is gone so often.* Things were not adding up.

"Same crazy pace you were always excited about," she reminded her. "What keeps you so busy if you aren't working?"

Flora was relieved when the waiter brought their drinks. It gave her a second to carefully compose her thoughts. Jackie Lynn was unsettling her with her intense line of questioning. She was unduly suspicious, and Jackie Lynn was an excellent interrogator when she yearned to get to the bottom of something. It was one of the qualities that made her a superb lawyer.

"Are you ready to order?" Flora asked. She glanced from their server and flashed Jackie Lynn a deceptive smile. "I've been looking forward to this meal. I must simply have Gregory's famous chicken and pasta dish. Even if it might be a little heavy."

"Excellent, ma'am," the waiter replied. He studied Jackie Lynn, patiently awaiting her decision.

"Same for me," she swiftly stated. She snapped her menu shut and handed it to their server. She only wished to get rid of him.

"Why didn't you order your favorite dish?" Flora inquired. "Don't tell me you've given up eating steak. We haven't been apart that long, have we?"

"What I eat doesn't matter, Flora," she declared with greater aggravation than intended.

Flora was deliberately attempting to throw her off the subject, and it was beginning to make Jackie Lynn angry. *"You* matter to me. I get the distinct feeling all isn't well with your life. Why don't you cut the crap, and tell me what's going on?!"

"What are you talking about? Everything's kosher with me. Why would you assume otherwise?" Flora adeptly lied, deliberately averting her eyes.

At this moment, I plainly understand what is meant by one lie begets another and another and another....

"Can you look me in the eye and promise me that?" Jackie Lynn cleverly demanded.

Flora reluctantly raised her eyes and fixed them with Jackie Lynn's invasive ones. *Oh no! It's hard to lie to her. But to look her straight in the eyes and lie...*

"Alright. You win. I'm having a few problems. It's part of adjusting to married life," Flora admitted.

"You can tell me anything," Jackie Lynn asserted. She reached across the table to reassuringly pat her hand. Her touch and obvious caring painfully twisted Flora's heart.

Hold it together! I'm capable of handling this! If I could deceive Jacob, I'm capable of surviving this. There's nothing Jackie Lynn can do to help. I can't involve her in this mess. Say something to satisfy her curiosity, quickly!

"You've already guessed. I'm down about my legal practice. There wasn't enough business in the boon docks. You're right, I miss it. I'll be fine though. It will simply take a while. There is no reason for you to, my friend," she attested.

Jackie Lynn could easily accept that Flora was missing being a lawyer. Yet, she sensed something significantly deeper was amiss. *Although, why wouldn't Flora confide in me if that is the case?* They had always shared everything.

"Are you sure that's all it is?" she tried anew, extensively studying Flora's face.

"Of course! May we proceed with the evening and enjoy being together?" she deceptively proclaimed with a slight chuckle. "How about the important reason we are here? Mary Julia is the person you need to be worried about. I have all a woman might ever desire. My only necessity is that I find other ways to spend my days. Will you quit worrying about me? What's been happening with you? Any new men in your life yet?"

That question slightly threw Jackie Lynn. It rattled her when Long Wolf's image uninvitingly popped into her mind and she smiled without meaning to.

"What's that wishful grin for?" Flora hastily converged. "There *is* someone new in your life, isn't there? Who is this? Come on, spill your guts. When and where did you meet? Tell me everything. Seems you're the one keeping secrets!"

"No, no!! It's nothing like that!" Jackie Lynn emphatically denied. "My car broke down Friday night during the drive home after visiting Mary Julia, in the middle of nowhere. This Indian man came to my rescue. He drove me to a service station, helped have the car towed and put me up in his cabin for the night…"

"Uh huh!" Flora interrupted, teasing. "This sounds interesting! He put you up for the night? You spent the night with this gentleman?"

"It's not some big romance," Jackie Lynn assured her. "He's a nice guy whom I'm treating to dinner Friday – to show my appreciation for his kindness."

"That seems a terrific start to me. You smiled when he entered your mind so you are somewhat interested," she pointed out with a wide mischievous grin.

Flora yearned for Jackie Lynn to encounter the love of a good man – *a genuinely good man…not like the one I've ended up with.*

"Some things never change. You love to match make, don't you?" Jackie Lynn accused, laughing and returning her smile. She was glad Flora was smiling and relaxing. "Why don't you tell me about that handsome husband of yours instead?"

Curve ball right between the eyes! Flora unsuccessfully attempted to prevent her facial expression from showing it. It was essential she not talk about Jacob. That would mean she would have to lie to Jackie Lynn, over and over.

"Jacob's fine," she responded, forcing a smile.

Flora picked up her glass of soda – *I wish it was hard alcohol* – taking a large swallow. She motioned to the waiter in the next instant. She informed him, "I could use a refill." "Are you okay on yours?" she questioned Jackie Lynn, glancing at her practically full glass. Flora's glass was not even half-empty. Their server scurried off with Flora's glass to fill it to the top.

Jackie Lynn recognized a brush off when she saw one. However, before she was capable of uttering one more word, her friend playfully charged with a hearty chuckle, "You're trying to change the subject on me, aren't you, you rascal? Give me more details in regard to this mysterious Indian of yours. You're already familiar with all there is concerning Jacob. Everything is the same between us. He still travels; he still operates; and so on."

Jackie Lynn had the oddest feeling this was not true. For some strange reason, it was obvious Flora did not wish to talk about Jacob. This was not at all like her. She was becoming even more worried.

Should I push Flora to confide in me? No, that probably wouldn't be wise. Flora is extremely loyal. That's probably why she's being tight-lipped. I'll quit for now, but I'm planning to stay in close contact with her to give her the opportunity to discuss things if she needs to, Jackie Lynn reflected.

Their server returned with Flora's drink refill, and he also brought them their food. Respecting Flora's privacy, Jackie Lynn allowed her interrogation regarding Jacob to

94

suitably drop. Instead she proceeded to fill her friend in on her escapades with Long Wolf at his cabin. Jackie Lynn carefully omitted having seen him naked, or her staggering attraction to him.

As they comfortably talked with one another, their dinner passed much too quickly. They were too soon leaving the restaurant to begin the long journey to the sanitarium. At least they had the chance to continue chatting on the long drive.

* * * *

Mary Julia was delighted to find Flora had come with Jackie Lynn. She eagerly shared her wonderful progress with both these dear ladies. She divulged it made her stronger being together with the two of them and knowing she had wonderful friends to depend upon.

Mary Julia also relayed that the doctor said she might leave the hospital soon. She also acknowledged how scary this was for her. Both Jackie Lynn and Flora assured her she could depend on their full support whenever this occurred.

I'll find a way to help Mary Julia, Flora resolved.

When they rose to depart, and embraced, Flora clung to Mary Julia. "You take care. Don't forget, no matter what, that I love you," she staunchly, and rather strangely, proclaimed. She gave Mary Julia a farewell kiss on the cheek.

It sounded peculiar to Mary Julia. She stared bewilderingly at Jackie Lynn over Flora's shoulder. Jackie Lynn mirrored her confused gaze, shrugging her shoulders. It sounded as if Flora was saying a final farewell, rather than a brief goodbye until their next gathering. Jackie Lynn was even more worried about her.

"I hope when I leave here we can *all* get together at least once a week. Even though we won't meet at a bar," Mary Julia chuckled. She pulled back from Flora so she was capable of viewing her face. *Are those tears in her eyes?* "It's unnecessary for you to go to a bar anyway, you're not a single woman any longer. In fact, you have a wonderful husband."

"Yeah," Flora dishonestly conceded. She realized it was essential she lighten the mood and gain control. She was way too emotional tonight, and she noticed Mary Julia's eyes looking concerned. "If things progress for Jackie Lynn, she'll have a special guy in her life soon."

Curiously directing her attention to Jackie Lynn instead, Mary Julia investigated with an eager grin, "What is this?"

"It's nothing!" Jackie Lynn firmly denied. She gave Flora an aggravated smirk. "Simply Flora up to her good old match-making. Ignore her. Come on, let's go."

Jackie Lynn grasped Flora's elbow. She pulled her from Mary Julia and began to lead her down the hall. "We love you. We'll come again soon," she uttered over her shoulder.

Flora earnestly wished this could be true. She had the distinct impression it might be a long while before she laid eyes on either of these women again. She had to escape the chaos that had overtaken her life first.

CHAPTER SEVEN

MAGNETISM

Friday, prior to leaving her office and heading for the Tricon construction site, Jackie Lynn changed into comfortable khaki shorts and a white short-sleeved T-shirt. Bearing in mind it was cooler that day, she also slipped on a thin burgundy vest. She freshened her make-up and restyled her hair, tying it back with a burgundy ribbon that matched her attire. So as not to appear too perfectly put together, she carefully pulled a few strands of hair loose around her face and the nape of her neck.

Why am I going to so much trouble? This isn't a date. I'll thank this gentleman for his kindness with a meal tonight. Then the two of us will never see each other again. But what if Long Wolf is interested in seeing me again? Or if I'm interested in seeing him again? Quit, Jackie Lynn! Dating Service, here I come!

She departed the building, got in her car, and drove the few blocks to Long Wolf's construction site. As she rounded the corner onto Eighth Street, Jackie Lynn caught a glimpse of a well dressed, tall, handsome man. He was standing by the chain length fence. Pulling alongside the curb, she was shocked to discover the man she had been admiring was Long Wolf.

He was not clothed like a construction worker. He was attired in what appeared to be an expensively tailored suit. *One of those suits I glimpsed in his closet. Surely he didn't dress up such as this for our dinner,* Jackie Lynn pondered. She suddenly felt foolish and terribly underdressed, as she glanced at her short-clad legs.

Long Wolf opened the passenger side door and climbed into the vehicle. With an enormous, heart melting smile he commented, "You're certainly prompt. It's 6:00 on the nose. And you took the opportunity to change clothes. I should have thought to do that."

He should have thought to change clothes? So he hasn't dressed up merely to go out. He's been clothed that way all day, she concluded with confusion. Her facial expression relayed her obvious bewilderment to Long Wolf.

"Is everything alright, Jackie Lynn?" He gently touched her closest arm.

"Um…sure. I was…I just…I assumed…" She realized she was babbling like an idiot. Long Wolf scrutinized her with his totally captivating, warm, wolf eyes. "Are you a construction worker or not?" she explored, finally managing to put together a concise sentence.

"A construction worker?" Long Wolf repeated and heartily laughed. "I guess I did make it sound that way, didn't I? See that sign by the fence?" he questioned, helpfully pointing it out. He had one of his arms around her shoulders.

It feels delightful. Jackie Lynn followed the direction of his finger and studied the sign. "Greathouse Construction," she read aloud.

It took a second for the name to entirely sink in. She turned her head, gaping at Long Wolf with apparent surprise. "Are you trying to tell me…that's *your* company?"

"It was my dad's company, until he died a few years ago. But, yes, it's mine now. I apologize if I misled you. I'm glad to know you would have accompanied me to dinner even if I was a lowly construction worker."

Long Wolf was teasing her, and Jackie Lynn was enjoying this. *What is it about this man that makes me feel strangely relaxed?*

"That explains the nice suits. I wondered about them when you opened the closet at the cabin to get me some hangers," she confessed.

"Ah...I knew something was up. I couldn't figure out what I had done. Now I understand why you were studying me so peculiarly," he relayed with relief.

"Do you remember every one of my expressions from the time we spent together?" Jackie Lynn quizzed.

She noticed the extraordinary smell of his cologne and liked the closeness of his charming face. *He has nice lips*, she sinfully observed.

I remember every minute of the time we spent together, Long Wolf accepted.

He was gazing into Jackie Lynn's eyes. Long Wolf suddenly became aware of his overpowering desire to hungrily feast on Jackie Lynn's beautiful, supple lips. He pulled his arm from the top of her seat and safely moved his entire body back to the opposite side of the auto.

"I have an excellent memory for things that are important to me," he breathlessly conceded. He peered out the windshield, struggling to gain control. "So where are you taking us for dinner?" He intentionally changed the subject.

Jackie Lynn fixedly stared at Long Wolf for a few seconds. She was shaken by her fierce desire for this man – *this virtual stranger.* "I guess we are going somewhere casual, unless you'd rather I go home and change once more," she informed him, adding with an honest chuckle, "I purposely dressed as such so you'd feel comfortable when I picked you up after work. Following a hard day of laboring at the construction site."

"That was considerate of you," he commented, laughing. "I did have a hard day at the construction site, despite not laboring with my hands. I did start out that way though. My dad made me work my way up from the bottom."

Long Wolf promptly discarded his jacket and yanked his tie from around his neck. He removed his fancy cuff lengths and placed them safely in his pant's pocket. Then he even rolled up both sleeves. He also unbuttoned the top two buttons of his shirt. "Take us someplace casual please."

"What's your pleasure, sir?" she innocently inquired.

Nonetheless, their eyes met and heatedly held. The passionate yearning Jackie Lynn beheld had her heart racing. She averted her eyes, staring straight ahead through the windshield. She gripped the steering wheel so hard her knuckles were turning white. "I'm not significantly acquainted enough with you to know what you enjoy eating," she remarked, reminding herself of this fact. *Cool down, Jackie Lynn!*

No, she doesn't know me well enough, Long Wolf established. He fully intended to rectify this situation though. *I can't move too quickly!*

"Do you like barbecue?" he asked. "There's an awfully good barbecue diner on Fifth street."

"Sonny's?" Jackie Lynn and the girls had walked there for lunch on various occasions. Their barbecue was delicious. Even though the restaurant was a hole in the wall, what space they had was always packed.

"That's the one," Long Wolf concurred. He flashed her another endearing smile.

"Barbecue it is then," she happily assented. Jackie Lynn put the automobile in drive and headed out.

* * * *

Jackie Lynn was surprised by the ease of her conversation with Long Wolf throughout their leisurely dinner. They talked about their careers, family life and friends. Jackie Lynn divulged that she had one stepbrother and one stepsister, who she had no relationship with at all. She shared that she had two dear friends, and these two special women were who she considered to be her family.

Long Wolf disclosed he was an only child. He informed Jackie Lynn that his mom had been raised on an Indian Reservation, and she and his father had taken him there many times when he was a boy. So he felt a definite kinship with many of the people there. He also told Jackie Lynn that his mother now lived at the Reservation, since his dad had passed away five years ago. He thought it odd Jackie Lynn never mentioned her own mother and father.

On the contrary, she intentionally changed the subject after listening to me discuss my mom and dad. Long Wolf gathered that Jackie Lynn must not be close to either of her parents.

They remained at their table, conversing long after they had finished eating. Neither desired their interlude together to end. Ultimately, it became apparent their waitress wished them to vacate their table, as a new stream of customers were rushing in.

Noting there were numerous others waiting by the door to be seated, Long Wolf suggested, "We should pay the check and leave."

"Yeah. You certainly were a cheap date," Jackie Lynn kidded and laughed, glancing at the check and flashing the most radiant smile. Both of their meals, including the tip, were scarcely even twenty dollars. "I should treat you again, to a nice dinner next time."

"No. Next time is on me," Long Wolf maintained. Then he proposed, "How about tomorrow night?"

"Are you asking me out on a date, sir?" Jackie Lynn heckled. They relinquished the table and headed for the cash register, which was practically on top of them.

"Would your answer be yes if I was?" he returned her banter, following closely behind her.

As Jackie Lynn turned around from paying the check and stood face-to-face with Long Wolf, she was startled to recognize, *I don't know if I am capable of denying you anything!*

"I should check my planning calendar first. To confirm I don't already have something scheduled," she continued teasing, despite her elevated cardiovascular rate.

Long Wolf locked eyes with her, a wide and amused smile spreading across his face. "Well, will you do that for me?

If you are available, I'd *very much* appreciate being penciled in for at least a few hours."

"I'll write it in ink, so it can't accidentally be erased," she flirtatiously affirmed. She returned his smile.

Jackie Lynn started past Long Wolf. She worked her way through the crowd and out the door. Walking side by side on the sidewalk toward the car, Long Wolf commented, "Ah...the sky this evening is breathtaking. Might you have time for a stroll by the waterfront?"

I have time for a stroll anywhere *with you!* Jackie Lynn conceded.

"I've entirely cleared my schedule tonight, exclusively for you. So, I'm free for however long you need," she persisted in bantering.

Need? If she was free for however long I might need her, she would have to be free all night. To start out with, Long Wolf recognized. He gazed with desire at her attractive face.

"I guess you better drive us to the waterfront. Because I *need* to spend time walking with you there."

* * * *

Jackie Lynn and Long Wolf cozily meandered by the waterfront for a long while, even though they did not stray far from the car. They walked amidst other couples, and people on bikes and children on skateboards whizzed past them, but they were obvious to them all. They were solely focused on one another. They contentedly beheld a radiant sunset. The water glistened like diamonds and the cityscape of many tall, differently shaped buildings seemed to come alive with color. Long Wolf slipped Jackie Lynn's hand into his. Afterwards, they reluctantly headed to Jackie Lynn's automobile.

I feel so warm and toasty inside. What happened?! Did the sun set within me? she idiotically contemplated.

Yet, Jackie Lynn recognized that the sun was miniscule to how she was feeling. The gentleman walking in pace beside her was the real justification for her warmth and happiness. *I'm remarkably drawn to this man,* she fearfully accepted.

Numerous things about Long Wolf seem to greatly attract me – his appealing smile, caring eyes, the sound of his voice, the touch of his gentle hands. She shivered in response to her scary invasive conclusions.

"Are you cold?" Long Wolf attentively asked, observing her shoulders quivering. He wrapped his big brawny arm around her, pulling her close to his body to provide warmth.

Oh! I don't want you to touch me?! Jackie Lynn mind grasped in panic. Long Wolf's fond touch was making her crazy. *I'm imagining those robust, powerful arms wrapped around my body as we passionately entangle.*

"Um...I'm fine," Jackie Lynn acclaimed. She gently pushed from his alluring embrace.

They climbed into her car a few minutes later. The streetlights had turned on, and there was a soft glow within. Jackie Lynn started the car and focused on the soft hum of the engine. In anticipation of an awkward goodbye, she headed for the construction site to take Long Wolf to his truck. *It's definitely time we part*, she decided. It only took a short while to drive back to the spot where she had picked Long Wolf up on Eighth Street.

"I enjoyed tonight," he revealed. Jackie Lynn could not clearly view Long Wolf because it was beginning to get dark, but she sensed his intent eyes. "How about I pick you up around 7:00 tomorrow. We'll have dinner and see a movie? Casual again, but not quite as casual as today," he laughed.

I should tell this gentleman I'm unable to see him, she noted.

Nevertheless, her betraying mouth responded, "7:00 sounds good." Jackie Lynn was powerless to refuse him. She desired to be with him much too greatly.

"Fantastic! I'll see you then. Have a safe drive home."

Long Wolf affectionately squeezed her hand. It was not what he wished to do. He longed to pull her into his arms and kiss her over and over.

No! I'm not going to do that. I'm determined to take things slow, he sensibly swore. Long Wolf released his grasp, opened the door and vacated the auto.

Jackie Lynn watched him standing there – *he's still watching me too.* She put the automobile back into drive and pulled away. *I should run far from this man and not ever look back.*

Something about Long Wolf told Jackie Lynn that he would not be easy to get rid of, and that was her real specialty, breaking off relationships before they got overly serious. *Be very, very careful with this one!* she warned herself.

Regardless, she glanced in the rearview mirror to see if any truck was pulling out of the construction lot. Jackie Lynn might have stopped her vehicle and waited for him to drive past if she had believed there was a possibility she might catch one final glimpse of Long Wolf.

I need a cold shower and a good night's sleep, she told herself with aggravation. She determinedly focused her eyes forward on the road and drove on toward the safety of her apartment.

* * * *

After changing into a cool, silk nightshirt, Jackie Lynn washed her face, and awash in contentment, slipped between the soft, chilly sheets of her queen-sized bed. As she attempted to gradually drift off to sleep, scenes from the refreshing evening she had just shared with Long Wolf raced through Jackie Lynn's mind. The chaos in her life subsided while she was with this guy. Long Wolf had this special way of putting her totally at ease. It was as if they had known each other for many years.

Jackie Lynn vividly envisioned Long Wolf's attractive face – golden brown skin, his exquisite, dark brown eyes, strong cheekbones, and his appealing, soft, alluring mouth. She pictured the way he had unconsciously licked his lips a few times as he ate dinner. It appeared he was tasting and enjoying the flavor from his meal for the first time.

Much more than he should have, at least in front of me.

Jackie Lynn had caught herself intently staring more than once, and she knew Long Wolf had noticed it. But she had not been able to refrain from scrutinizing him. Presently, lying alone in her room, Jackie Lynn intensely longed for his presence. Keeping her eyes closed tightly, the smell of Long Wolf's cologne lingered in her imagination.

Suddenly, Jackie Lynn could swear that she smelled Long Wolf all around her. Startled, she bolted upright in her bed and spoke out loud as if there was somebody else in the room, "This isn't possible! Yet, even with my eyes open, I can still smell that fine sensual aroma, of body and cologne mixed together."

"*Quit*! Quit *right now*!" she insanely scolded herself. "This will wear off by morning! Go to sleep, Jackie Lynn! Morning shall come all too soon." With that final stubborn order, she lay down, closed her eyes, and her haunting thoughts lulled her into a restless sleep.

CHAPTER EIGHT

REVELATIONS

Saturday morning, Jackie Lynn found herself reflecting on Long Wolf throughout her breakfast. She began to feel very uneasy. *Why is this guy in my thoughts so often? Yes, he is handsome and seems to be a decent individual. That's no reason to totally obsess over him. I shouldn't have agreed to go out with him again this soon. What on earth was I thinking?!*

She finished eating and went directly to the phone. *I'll call and inform him I won't be able to make our date. Maybe I'll telephone Flora and see if she really knows the number of a dating service. If I joined a dating service, I can basically be a friend to Long Wolf. When I wasn't busy with some other guy, then Long Wolf and I could occasionally go out together. My overwhelming attraction to this guy would lessen if I was dating regularly. That has to be why he's on my mind so much. He's simply another guy.* She would telephone a dating service and prove this to herself.

Jackie Lynn picked up the phone, but she dialed only a few numbers before she hung up. *Perhaps I'll call Flora first,* she considered. *No, if I mention Long Wolf, she wouldn't give me a dating service number if she had one. She'll think it's wonderful I'm so intrigued by this guy.*

Jackie Lynn was exceedingly confused and torn. *This is ridiculous! From now on, I will have a minimum of one date a week, or at least the possibility of one.*

Jackie Lynn briefly stared at the phone, deciding what she should do. *Maybe I should see Long Wolf once more tonight.*

Long Wolf had forgotten to take his clothes the previous night. She could give them to him when he came to pick her up. She would telephone a dating service on Monday and set up a date with another eligible bachelor next weekend. That way, should Long Wolf call and ask her out, she could tell him she was busy. She could sincerely tell him there was someone else. He would either merely be her friend or she would no longer hear from him.

Yes, this is what I'll do. I'm not a kid. I'll surely be able to be with this guy two nights in a row without falling head over heels in love with him.

* * * *

Jackie Lynn decided to telephone Flora anyway and find out how she was doing. *This should take my mind off my date with Long Wolf.*

The phone rang once, answered by the always faithful answering service. "The Roberts' residence. May I help you?"

Jackie Lynn hesitated before she asked, "May I speak to Mrs. Roberts, please?"

The voice on the other end paused and then slowly inquired, "May I ask…who is…calling?"

For some reason, Jackie Lynn feared she might get the runaround again. Noticing a box of hair color on the kitchen counter, she cleverly lied. "This is Mrs. Brown, from Revlon Cosmetics, calling. Mrs. Roberts is expecting my call."

Jackie Lynn laughed to herself as the service put her on hold. After another pause, she listened to another receiver being raised. "Hello, this is Flora Roberts."

Jackie Lynn remained silent until she was certain she heard the answering service hang up. Since the pause was too lengthy, Flora stated once more, "This is Mrs. Roberts. Whom did you say was calling?"

Jackie Lynn burst into uncontrollable laughter. "It's me, silly! The lady from Revlon had to get back to the shop."

Flora was surprised *and thrilled* to hear Jackie Lynn's voice. She had expected she would not be speaking to either of her friends for a long while. She whispered, "What's the deal with the pretend name?"

"Oh, I was testing that service of yours. It worked fine. Since they don't intend to allow you to talk to your friends, from now on, you will be heavily involved with a new glamour hobby.

The two ladies proceeded to discuss everything then: the weather, their hair, clothes, current trends in the courtroom, and even men. It was obvious to Jackie Lynn that Flora was starved for communication. She seemed very lonely and sad.

"I am not going to let you off the hook about telling me what the hell is *really* going on in your *perfect* little world!" Jackie Lynn adamantly acknowledged. She was fiercely determined that she was going to get the details soon.

Jackie Lynn had asked her several direct questions about Jacob once more, and Flora had each time quickly changed the subject. Something was unquestionably amiss in her dear friend's life, and Jackie Lynn was very tired of being kept in the dark. Flora eventually, reluctantly admitted she was not very happy with her new life.

"Oh, Jackie Lynn, I should have gotten to know Jacob better. I am always in such a damn hurry! I'm begging you to take a good friend's advice, 'don't ever rush into a relationship'. People aren't always what they seem to be. That is, following marriage. Before, during our courtship, Jacob was a darling, amazing man. He was so attentive and gentle..."

Jackie Lynn did not want Flora to quit talking about her married life, so as Flora hesitantly paused, she promptly probed, "And now? How is he now? Please tell me. I want to be here for you. You can share anything with me; you know that."

108

There was total silence for a bit. Then Jackie Lynn heard something unexpected – Flora sobbing. *Oh God, she's crying. It must be bad.*

"Tell me, Flora. Tell me everything. You've been hiding something. It must be especially bad, because we have always shared everything. You've got to confide in me."

"Oh, Jackie Lynn! I am positively living a nightmare," Flora frightened her by wailing.

She rambled on, "When Jacob's away, all I focus on is the gentleman I met, kind and tender-hearted, that treated me as if I was a princess. He loved me tenderly without any restrictions. Then I hear his voice as he enters the house, the voice of a stranger, cruel and uncaring, demanding my attention, my affection. My blood runs ice cold! The fear he has created, instilled within the very heart of me, is tearing me apart. I have to be so cautious around him. One evening with him is more exhausting than an entire day in court. I second guess each word I utter...will this make him enraged? Or will he ask too many questions, and when I'm unable to furnish answers he expects...?

Flora was sobbing so intensely Jackie Lynn could hardly decipher what she was saying. She wholeheartedly wished she could be there beside this precious friend to hold and comfort her. "Flora? Flora?? Are you alright? I'm sorry I pushed you to reveal this. I detected something was horribly wrong. I believed, if I knew what it was, I'd be able to help you. Now, common sense is telling me to leave this second and rescue you from that place. You can't remain there. Your life with Jacob sounds terrible! I hate to ask this...but I have to know. Is it just verbal abuse Jacob is inflicting, or does he hit you?"

"Oh, Jackie Lynn!" she lamented in a troubled voice, painfully incapable of stopping. "Hit me?! If only it were just that. That he hits me doesn't begin to describe this beast. He doesn't only slap me around a little now and then. No, that's merely the start. I've been beaten, thrown across rooms and down a marble stairway and...and I've...I've been...ra...raped, Jackie Lynn! I consider myself lucky though. So far, I have only been taken to the hospital once, when he slung me down a flight of stairs. The other incidents, he doctored my wounds, all the while telling me how regretful he was, how much he loves me and how he desperately needs me to understand and love him."

Flora fell eerily silent. Jackie Lynn paralyzed with disbelief. She had not imagined something so appalling was happening to Flora. "Dear God!" she instinctively repeated over and over in shock.

Flora listened to these caring words coming from the receiver, and continued, "Speaking of God, each time Jacob leaves I pray he won't return. That he will have some sort of accident and not return home. He has told me he won't ever allow me to go. He'd rather kill me than think of me being with another man. I believe he is capable of murder."

Jackie Lynn could not fathom what she was hearing. *I must be having a terrible nightmare. But I can't be. I'm awake*, she painfully recognized.

"Flora, you *can't* stay there! I'm going to leave *right now* and come get you. He won't hurt you again!" she declared, striving not to cry although she was fiercely overwrought.

"No, Jackie Lynn! You can't do that!" she strongly protested. "I'm not exaggerating when I claim Jacob is capable of murder. I think he harmed one of his patients in a fit of rage over me. He'd find me, and he wouldn't hesitate to harm you. I am going to leave, hopefully soon, but you can't be involved. I'm working on a way."

"But Flora...what is going to prevent him from killing you in the meantime? I can't sit back and do nothing!" she earnestly argued. Jackie Lynn's heart was breaking for her friend. "You're aware of how distressed I was about Mary Julia's life before I took her to the sanitarium. I'm just as frightened, if not more, for you. I know Mary Julia will be okay, but I'm not so sure about you."

"Being able to *finally* talk to someone...to confide all that has happened...helps more than you can know," Flora assured her, sobbing once more. "You and Mary Julia mean the world to me. I'd never forgive myself if anything happened to either one of you because of me."

"How do you think I'll live with myself if that maniac kills you while I stand by and do nothing?" Jackie Lynn argued, her voice cracking with emotion. Her total helplessness made her feel like screaming. She had to find a way to save Flora.

"If you enable me to do this my way, none of us will be harmed. That's what I need to be assured of...that we shall *all* be safe. It's the only way. I won't go with you if you come here," she firmly upheld. "You're aware of how stubborn I can be."

"What exactly is your plan?" Jackie Lynn questioned.

She had to be reassured Flora was somewhat safe. *If that was conceivable. Oh, God! How am I going to sit by and leave her in this horrible situation?!*

"I can't tell you that," Flora maintained. "But I swear I won't be here much longer. In the meantime, I've discovered a way to keep him from becoming brutal. He hasn't beaten me severely in a while. Even though he does an extraordinary job of totally belittling me. I keep reminding myself it won't be much longer. Don't worry, Jackie Lynn. I am careful. Talking to you does help though. I love you and appreciate your concern greater than you could possibly know. But I should be getting off this phone. Jacob calls sporadically. I've tied up the line far too long already. If he has been trying to call, he will be enraged that he hasn't been able to get through. He'll be convinced I have been on the phone with another man."

"I'm going to be checking on you. I plan to call you every day," Jackie Lynn divulged.

"That's not a good idea," she disagreed. "I'll call you. The service reports every single incoming call to Jacob. He'll get suspicious if I receive a lot of strange calls. Things such as this especially set him off. I promise I'll phone you once a week, if I can. I've really got to go. You take care. Bye."

Flora abruptly hung up the telephone. Jackie Lynn reluctantly lowered her receiver. She felt awful. She sat staring at the phone and cried for her friend.

Jackie Lynn began earnestly praying, *God, I'm imploring you to look out for Flora. Please keep her safe. I need my friends in my life. They are all I have. They are my family. Please take care of them.*

* * * *

After her painfully enlightening conversation with Flora, Jackie Lynn's mind was certainly taken off of Long Wolf. Now, practically all her brain could focus on was her imperiled friend. She had felt helpless when she had watched Mary Julia's life falling apart, but dealing with Mary Julia's predicament had not been nearly as awful. Where Flora was concerned, Jackie Lynn would have to basically wait, pray, and have faith that her friend's plan – *whatever that might be* – worked and that she escaped her hell alive.

And what a hell it is! Even if Flora doesn't expect Jacob to kill her, how will her sanity withstand that kind of constant torment? Oh, how I wish Mary Julia wasn't in the hospital with her own serious problems. I need another friend to talk to, Jackie Lynn lamented.

She went in her bathroom to take a refreshing shower. *I need to get out of this place. I'll go nuts if I sit around here all day thinking about this.*

When Jackie Lynn emerged from her lengthy shower, she threw on some leisure clothes and headed out. She had no idea where she was going, but she had to occupy her time some way. Suddenly, she was looking forward to seeing Long Wolf tonight. He would serve as a necessary diversion for a little while.

Jackie Lynn perceptively realized, *until I know Flora is safe, she won't be far from my thoughts, and forever in my fervent prayers.*

* * * *

Jackie Lynn did not return to her apartment until 4:00 that afternoon. She immediately checked her answering

112

machine. With a sigh of relief, she found there were no messages. She had run constantly all day, trying, and somewhat managing to succeed, to put her overbearing apprehensions aside. She put away groceries, clothes, and other items she had purchased during her neurotic shopping frenzy. Then she finally set to the task of getting ready for her date with Long Wolf.

As long as I stay busy, I'll be alright. I have to remain strong for my friends, she reminded herself.

Long Wolf rang her doorbell a little shy of 7:00 p.m. *Fantastic! He's early. I'm ready to get out of here again,* Jackie Lynn thought with relief.

She had finished getting ready a short time ago. Following another prolonged and relaxing shower, she had mechanically dressed in a simple, above the knees, jeans skirt and a pale, rose, silk blouse. She had dried her hair and stuck hot rollers in to set while she applied her makeup – something light and soft. At the last minute, to add more color to her ensemble, she had tied a pretty multi-colored scarf around her shoulders.

Jackie Lynn was still brooding over Flora's horrible dilemma. She had been severely fighting the urge to phone her friend, to attempt once more to persuade Flora to abandon that house immediately. However, she knew her efforts would be futile...and might even prove dangerous. Flora was indeed obstinate. When she thoroughly made up her mind, there was no use attempting to change it.

"Well, shall we go?" Jackie Lynn rudely proposed with a cheesy smile and a nervous chuckle, almost as soon as Long Wolf had stepped through her doorway.

She picked up his clean, folded clothes from her sofa and handed them to him. "You forgot these last night."

"Oh, so I did," Long Wolf remarked with a conniving grin. Jackie Lynn did not reciprocate it. She raced for her door, opened it, stepped out, turned the lock, and started down the hall, without looking to distinguish if he was following.

Something's wrong. Long Wolf arched an eyebrow, watching her scamper ahead of him. *Jackie Lynn seems to be upset about something. I'll have to try to get her to discuss whatever it is. From the small glimpse I got, she certainly looks pretty though.*

Long Wolf anxiously pulled the door shut and followed her down the flight of stairs leading to the exit door. He admired the way Jackie Lynn's skirt naturally complimented her attractive feminine curves. She stopped her urgent dash when she reached the parking lot.

"Where's your truck?" she asked in confusion, scanning the surrounding parking spaces.

"At home in front of my cabin," Long Wolf shared with a chuckle.

He extracted his keys from his pocket and pressed a button on his remote entry control. The lights of a nearby Mercedes Benz Sedan flashed in response, the doors automatically unlocking. "I presumed we might be more comfortable in my *car.* Hope that's okay."

"Sure. That's alright," Jackie Lynn answered rather absently, missing his humor. She approached the automobile and reached for the door.

"Wait a minute!" Long Wolf harshly protested, grabbing her hand. "I'd very much prefer to open your door for you if you don't mind. Sorry, but I was raised to be a gentleman."

Even this carefree banter gained no response from her. *No smile and absolutely no laughter.* Jackie Lynn merely withdrew her hand from the door handle and permitted Long Wolf to open her door. She climbed into the vehicle and waited for him to shut the door.

Yes, I'm positively going to try to get her to reveal what's on her mind, Long Wolf resolved.

He made his way around the car, opened the driver's door, and scrambled in beside her. He was worried about Jackie Lynn. She was with him in body. *And what a body she has,* Long Wolf could not help devilishly noting. However, he could easily tell *she isn't with me in mind.* Jackie Lynn's brain was heavily preoccupied by something other than him.

"How was your day?" Long Wolf investigated in a chipper voice. He started the automobile and headed toward the restaurant he was taking them to for dinner.

"Fine. Busy. I did a lot of shopping and running around," she answered in a near monologue, scarcely looking at him. Being polite, Jackie Lynn inquired, "How was yours?"

"Well, frankly, I spent much of today thinking about being with you again," he confided, briefly glancing from the road to observe her reaction.

She turned her head to give him some attention. Met by his rapt expectant eyes, Jackie Lynn finally realized how aloof she was being. *This guy has driven two hours to go on a date with me. Don't be such a bitch!* she scolded herself.

"That's nice to hear," Jackie Lynn truthfully replied, smiling at him. "I thought about you too."

That is assuredly true. I would have thought about him much more, if my pervasive concern for Flora hadn't thoroughly taken over. Contemplating her dear friend, Jackie Lynn was incapable of keeping up her carefree charade. The smile disappeared from her face, and she averted her eyes.

"Jackie Lynn, what's the matter?" Long Wolf's question took her by surprise. "You're obviously upset about something. I'm an excellent listener if you'd like to confide in someone."

She stared into his warm caring eyes and tears threatened to betray her. Jackie Lynn needed somebody to talk to concerning all that had transpired. But, she barely knew this fellow. *Should I risk divulging something so personal? Will he honestly understand?*

Long Wolf surmised she was struggling to decide whether or not to trust him with whatever was troubling her. He reached across the seat and cupped his hand over the top of Jackie Lynn's. "It's okay, Jackie Lynn. You can trust me. Honestly you can," he reassured her. "I'd like to get to know you better, if you will let me. That includes the bad things too."

As usual, his big soft hand felt wonderful touching hers. As Jackie Lynn gazed appreciatively at Long Wolf's appealing profile, she wished she could crawl into his rugged, safe arms and not come out. "It's been an awful day for me," Jackie Lynn decided to confess. "I told you yesterday about my two dearest girlfriends. One is in the hospital. Well, I recently discovered my other friend is in greater trouble. The man she married not long ago has turned out to be a monster. Today, I found out he horribly abuses her. I'm terribly afraid he might kill her. She won't enable me do anything to help."

As Jackie Lynn finished, her emotions got the best of her, and she started to cry. She turned her head from Long Wolf, toward the side window, desperately fighting to compose herself. He immediately steered his automobile over alongside the curb, released his seatbelt, slid across the seat, and placed his arm around Jackie Lynn's shoulders.

Long Wolf pulled her against his body. Jackie Lynn instinctively laid her head upon his warmhearted, broad chest. *Oh, this feels much too delightful!* she noticed after a few seconds.

Jackie Lynn removed her head from his torso and with a bittersweet smile asserted, "I apologize. I'm okay. This shouldn't ruin our night. You drove too far to listen to me whine."

"Hey," he said, gently raising her chin so he could look into her glistening green eyes. A few remaining tears stubbornly escaped. He tenderly brushed them away with a monogrammed handkerchief he swiftly produced from his pant's pocket.

"Don't ask forgiveness from me for showing your emotions. It shows what a truly caring person you are. It's refreshing to see how much you can love. They are lucky to have you in their lives."

I hope you'll give me the same opportunity. She fits nicely into my arms, he noticed. *It's like she has been sculpted to belong there.* "But, there is only so much you can do for a friend. If she doesn't want your help, or won't accept it, all you can do is be there for her when she does eventually turn to you. I'm sorry I'm unable to be of more comfort."

Oh, what comfort he most assuredly is being! I should pull myself out of his magnificent feeling, secure arms.

Nevertheless, Jackie Lynn did not wish to separate from this magical union. It filled her with the most terrific, reassuring – *and yes, comforting* – warmth. *I should be very, very scared of this guy,* she concluded. *There is something unquestionably special about him.*

Jackie Lynn allowed Long Wolf to hold her for a bit longer. Then she hesitantly moved away. "I apologize for being preoccupied. I promise I'll try to give you my undivided attention," she pledged, forcing another smile. "Thank you for listening. I feel lost not having my friends to talk to. You're a sweet man."

"I wish I could do more. I'd be glad to listen to you anytime," he confessed. Long Wolf slowly slipped back behind the wheel and started the Mercedes up to a purr.

How odd. I barely know this woman, but I long to eliminate her pain, he realized, alertly studying her.

As Long Wolf steered the automobile from the curb and returned his focus to the road, Jackie Lynn took the opportunity to secretly admire him as well. Not only was his body large in build; it seemed his heart was also. The way he had securely held her and the caring way his eyes had gazed directly into hers had managed to deeply touch her.

This greatly frightened Jackie Lynn. It had been years – *when I was a naïve teen* – since she had had any serious involvement with a man. Serious involvement equaled serious heartbreak in Jackie Lynn's book. She had no intention of having her heart severely trampled again.

When our date ends, I'll concoct excuses not to see Long Wolf, at least not for a while. My life is complicated enough at the moment, without adding the risk of a broken heart.

* * * *

Jackie Lynn and Long Wolf rode together in silence, each seeming to be lost in their own deep reflections. Shortly thereafter, they arrived at a restaurant named Cornucopia. It was so named on account of the wide variety of dishes offered there.

It figures. Jackie Lynn smiled in amusement. *Naturally, he picked one of my favorite restaurants. Is this guy psychic or what?*

She was still smiling when Long Wolf opened her car door, gallantly offered his hand, and waited for her to emerge from the vehicle. "Why are you smiling? Not that I'm complaining. You have a lovely smile," Long Wolf noted, a handsome, admiring grin coming to his own face.

Jackie Lynn strangely became quite self conscious at his words of admiration. *Please don't let me blush like an idiot again,* she privately pleaded. She could not explain the effect this fellow had on her. *He's not the first man to inform me that I'm attractive.* Perhaps it's because his comments appeared genuinely sincere.

"Thank you," Jackie Lynn eventually responded.

She slid her hand from his clutch and headed toward the door to the restaurant. When she was certain her embarrassment had passed, Jackie Lynn turned and admitted, "I was smiling because you somehow managed to pick one of my favorite restaurants. Are you positive you haven't been following me? Maybe it wasn't merely a coincidence you pulled up when my car broke down."

"Maybe it wasn't a coincidence at all," Long Wolf submitted. "Perhaps it was fate, and the two of us have been meant to meet all along. Do you believe in fate, Jackie Lynn?" he dared to suggest. They were promptly approached by a hostess, prepared to seat them.

"Oh, come now, do you use that line with all the ladies, or do I appear to be an easy mark?" she surprised him by sarcastically and rather hostilely asking. They were following the young girl to their table.

Jackie Lynn undeniably did not believe in anything as absurd as fate. *Sexual attraction is the only thing that brings a man and woman together. It has nothing to do with any divine intervention. If fate had anything to do with it, couples would be content and remain together forever.* Jackie Lynn knew too well this was not often the case.

Long Wolf waited until they were both seated to adamantly reply, "First, I don't use lines. I'm honest, and I expect the same from other people. Second, I would *never* peg you as an easy mark. You seem to be an intelligent, independent and well-rounded woman."

Most assuredly well-rounded, he caught himself indecently concluding.

"I apologize. I didn't mean to snap at you," Jackie Lynn established. She felt guilty for having offended him. Her attack had been unwarranted. *It's the stress from today. That, and trying fiercely to keep my distance from this guy.*

"I take it you don't believe in fate at all? In two people being soul mates?" Long Wolf began again, studying her.

Jackie Lynn had truly wished he would change the subject. "No," she firmly maintained, meeting his critical eyes with her decisive ones. "I put fate and natural soul mates right up there with fairytales. They are both nice stories, but there is unmistakably no truth to the happily-ever-after endings."

"Ouch!" he responded. "Something tells me you have been badly hurt to be so jaded about love."

"I'm not jaded. Just realistic. I see life for what it is," she proclaimed. Jackie Lynn was relieved to observe their waitress approach the table. She directed her attention from Long Wolf to take a moment to study the menu.

Long Wolf opened his menu as well. Nonetheless, his thoughts were fully captivated by the beautiful, strong willed female across from him. It was obvious some other man *or men* had torn her heart to shreds. If he was going to have a relationship with Jackie Lynn *—and I greatly desire to –* he would have to somehow put that broken heart back together.

Her defensive comment regarding him using lines made sense all at once. Jackie Lynn apparently no longer trusted the male species in general. *I will show her it will be different with me. I'll gain her trust, no matter what it takes.* Long Wolf strongly sensed this woman was worth the patience and duration.

They ordered their dinner, and Long Wolf steered the discussion in a different direction. He asked Jackie Lynn about her work. *It's much too soon for me to expect her to confide former heartbreaks. I have all the time in the world to unearth Jackie Lynn's past. And also to divulge important details in regard to my life.*

Long Wolf wanted this badly. When he genuinely wanted something, he usually got it – no matter how long or diligently he had to strive. *I'm not letting this woman escape.*

* * * *

They went to a movie following dinner. Jackie Lynn was surprised when Long Wolf proposed they see a romantic comedy. "We don't have to do that. There's a James Bond movie playing if you'd rather see it," she thoughtfully offered. Jackie Lynn did not care for action movies, but she was used to having to sit through them on dates. Men seemed to thrive on them.

"I'm not much of a James Bond fan," Long Wolf confessed. "If I'm going to take in a movie with someone, I'd prefer to watch something that bears resemblance to real life. I enjoy fairytales, remember." He smiled mischievously, before he added, "But we can see James Bond if romantic comedies are too offensive for you, Miss Realist."

Jackie Lynn realized he was teasing her. She returned his smile and replied with a snicker, "No. Let's see your fairytale, Prince Charming. Just don't attempt to slip any glass slipper on my foot. Not that it wouldn't fit. I wouldn't enable you to get it close enough to place it on my foot. I'd kick it out of your hand, and it'd crash to the ground."

"Okay, okay. I get your point. You're no Cinderella," Long Wolf chuckled in surrender, shaking his head in disbelief. He stepped to the window to purchase their tickets. Then he placed his hand warmly in the square of her back. He urged Jackie Lynn through the crowd in the lobby toward their theater.

* * * *

In the car, as Long Wolf drove her home, they talked and laughed about *A Twist of Fate* – the movie they had just seen. Both of them had enjoyed it and believed it was good. *Do we have the same sense of humor too?* There had been occasions when the two of them had laughed, in exact unison, when others in the theater did not.

How is it possible I have so much in common with this guy? Well, it doesn't matter. I won't date him for a good while after tonight, Jackie Lynn rigidly promised herself.

She was a mixture of nerves and relief as Long Wolf pulled up in front of her apartment complex. She was nervous he might attempt to kiss her. If he tried, Jackie Lynn would not be able to prevent herself from giving in.

Nonetheless, she was relieved to be home. If Long Wolf kissed her and she spontaneously reciprocated his affections, it would not matter, because she was not far from the safety of her apartment. Jackie Lynn positively was not planning on allowing this fellow to walk her to the door.

"Thank you for another enjoyable evening," Long Wolf said, taking her hand. He grasped it for a few seconds, before he informed her, "I'll walk you to your door."

"No. That's not necessary," Jackie Lynn instantaneously protested. "I'll be alright. There has never been any problem at these apartments."

"I'm pleased to hear that. But I'm walking you to your door," he determinedly upheld. "You may think you are as tough as steel, but regardless, I always make certain a lady gets in safely, and I'm unable to determine that from this parking lot. So stay put. I'll get your door, and we will walk up together." Long Wolf opened his door and vacated the auto, not leaving Jackie Lynn any opportunity to disagree.

Okay. This will be fine. I basically have to make sure he doesn't kiss me! Jackie Lynn wisely discerned. *It would be exceedingly easy, if we get into a passionate embrace, to open my door and foolishly invite this charming gentleman inside...and then....Oh, no! That isn't going to happen! So, it's no big deal if he walks me to my door.*

Her heart was racing from tension and anticipation as Long Wolf helped her from the automobile. To make matters much worse, without invitation, he wrapped his arm around her waist, pulling her close to his side for the climb up the stairway. *He smells delicious, and he is touching my waist.* Jackie Lynn's body uncontrollably stirred in response. She longed to turn her head and kiss the side of Long Wolf's hot neck.

Oh, get a grip on yourself, Jackie Lynn. When you get upstairs, you have to be competent enough to push yourself from his sturdy arms and escape behind that door. Quickly! *Very, very* quickly! *Then close and lock it!*

Her brain was focused entirely on what might come next. Jackie Lynn climbed the stairs beside Long Wolf almost unconsciously. Before she could grasp it, they were standing in front of her door. Long Wolf slipped his other arm around the other side of her waist.

Oh God! I feel so trapped! She was not only trapped by Long Wolf's secure arms, but by her own severe emotional longings. She irrefutably did not wish to separate from him.

"Long Wolf? I...um…" Jackie Lynn wanted to say, '*I need to get inside. Thanks so much for a nice evening. Please take your arms from my body. Oh,* please*!*'

"Jackie Lynn, you're trembling, honey," he pointed out, instantly squeezing her against his heat emitting body.

She isn't trembling due to the fact that she's cold, Long Wolf noted with satisfaction. *She's trembling because she's scared of the overwhelming emotions I'm arousing in her.*

"It's okay," he said in a soft voice, his mouth within inches from her ear. Long Wolf's warm moist breath on Jackie Lynn's face caused her to shudder more.

Damn! I have no control over my own body! she observed in frustration and fear. *I must part from this guy, and stay far from him. He is somehow casting some sort of weird spell over me. He must use Indian magic or something. Lord, help me!*

Jackie Lynn squirmed restlessly in his arms. As she stubbornly removed her head from his shoulder, she found herself gazing directly into Long Wolf's needful eyes and at those scrumptious lips of his. She had never desired to kiss a man so greatly.

She wants me to kiss her. I see it in her eyes. But, no! If I kiss her now, I may not be able to stop there. No. I'll give her one final hug and place an innocent kiss on the cheek. Slow, Long Wolf! Slow!

He drew Jackie Lynn into a tight embrace, and he permitted his fiery lips to linger on her feverish cheek for several moments. Using every ounce of strength he possessed, Long Wolf pushed Jackie Lynn out of his arms. However, he was incapable of completely breaking contact. He retained both her hands, stretching them forward in the gap which safely stood between them.

"You're really something!" he breathlessly professed, displaying a happy, seductive smile. "I'll call you tomorrow."

"Okay," she acknowledged rather dreamily, feeling shaken. *Make your escape! Quick!*

Jackie Lynn removed her hands from Long Wolf's grasp. "Bye. Have a safe drive home," she dismissed him.

"I'll be thinking of you the whole stretch. Talk to you soon," Long Wolf pledged and reluctantly turned. He started down the hall toward the stairway.

Jackie Lynn stuck the key in her door and unlocked it, but she continued to stand in the corridor watching Long Wolf as he strolled down the stairs. Appearing to sense her stare, halfway down, he looked back. Long Wolf flashed Jackie Lynn another heart melting, contented smile. Her heart leapt delightedly in response. She opened the door and scampered inside the safety of her apartment.

Oh God! What in the world have I gotten myself into?!

A crushing disappointment instantaneously washed over Jackie Lynn as she realized, *He didn't try to kiss me.* As Jackie Lynn slowly made her way from the door, she fearfully recognized how much she had wished Long Wolf had.

CHAPTER NINE

NEW START

Late Sunday evening, Flora accompanied Jacob to the airport to see him off on an extended trip overseas. There was an important medical conference being held out of the country, and he had been invited to attend. Jacob was supposed to tour Rome, England and Germany with a large group of surgeons and make several speeches to various assemblies of doctors, demonstrating his expertise.

Jacob was expected to be away for four weeks. Flora had to pretend to be heartbroken about his extended absence. In actuality, she was overjoyed. This would provide a vital opportunity to finish formulating her plan to rid her life of Jacob for good.

"I'll phone you each day," Jacob promised, as they announced for first class passengers to board.

To somebody unfamiliar with the real Jacob, his offer might have seemed sweet. Flora knew it was meant solely as a warning. He intended her to stay put in his home, awaiting his calls.

"I'll be waiting," she promised, giving him one conclusive, drawn-out kiss. Inwardly, her stomach churned. Outwardly, it appeared she loved this fellow very much.

Flora wanted to cheer when Jacob finally disappeared from her sight in the detachable ramp leading into the airplane. She felt freer than she had in ages. *Careful! Keep up your charade of being the ideal loving wife. He could abruptly take a jet back if he suspects anything different.*

She went to the limo and told the driver she was ready to return to the house. Flora avoided calling it home anymore. It was a prison, not a home. When she got back, Flora informed the house staff she was going to bed.

About a half hour later, she quietly sneaked down the steps, in the dark. She crept into the privacy of Jacob's library. It was late, but Flora intended to phone Jackie Lynn anyway. Jacob had removed the telephone from their bedroom, fearing she might call some other lover late at night during his absence.

Jacob had probably directed some, or possibly every one, of their house staff to keep a close eye on her while he was out. If they reported her making a call this late, Jacob would assuredly assume it *must* be to another man. He would undoubtedly cancel the remainder of his trip, fly home, and beat her silly in punishment.

Jackie Lynn answered the phone on the first ring. Nevertheless, she did not sound groggy as if she had been awakened. Flora was baffled. After all, it was past midnight, and tomorrow was a workday for her friend.

"Weren't you sleeping?" Flora scrutinized.

"Flora?!" Jackie Lynn exclaimed happily. With slight apprehension, she immediately questioned, "Is everything okay?!"

"Yes. This is the only chance I've gotten to telephone. I apologize for it being so late. But it doesn't appear that I woke you. You sound wide awake. What's going on?" she anxiously quizzed.

"I just walked in the door about five minutes ago," Jackie Lynn informed her. Then she added, "Mary Julia's doctor telephoned earlier. He asked me to come to the sanitarium to discuss Mary Julia's release. It seems she may be getting out of there Wednesday afternoon. He claimed she needs plenty of support. He suggested she stay with someone for a bit. I guess she'll be staying here with me for a few weeks."

"Will she be returning to work right away?" Flora probed.

"No. She is supposed to gradually ease back into a normal routine," Jackie Lynn divulged.

"She will be by herself all day with nothing to do? That doesn't sound like a good idea to me," Flora warily pointed out.

"Yeah. But the doctor thinks returning to work might be overly stressful after just being released from the hospital. I'll be worried sick about her all day though. I'll phone a million times to check on her," Jackie Lynn admitted. "As I've wanted to do with you. How have you been since we last talked? Where is Jacob?"

"It's only been two days," Flora reminded with a chuckle. "I appreciate your concern. I've been fine. I have excellent news. Jacob is out of the country for nearly a month at a medical conference. Quit worrying about me for a while."

"Great! Why not leave while he is gone? You can stay here also. We'll be a little cramped, but we'll be okay," Jackie Lynn offered.

"Thanks for the offer, my friend. But I can't do that. I hope to be out of here shortly though. I have three weeks or more to seriously concentrate on my plan," she secretively mentioned.

"Could you tell me what you're planning?" Jackie Lynn explored. "Maybe I'm capable of helping somehow."

"You help by listening and caring," Flora asserted. She was touched by the earnest concern she heard in her friend's voice. "I have a much more suitable place for Mary Julia to reside."

"How is that? What do you mean?" Jackie Lynn questioned with confusion.

"Mary Julia needs to be someplace where there is somebody there with her throughout the day. If she came here to live, she wouldn't be alone. And I'll be contributing in helping her for a change. I've badly yearned to be there for her. Jacob has kept me from it. But he's gone right now. Mary Julia could stay during his absence. She could live with you if she needs a companion after that," Flora logically indicated.

"I'd rather you solely focus on your plan for escape, instead of taking on tending to Mary Julia," Jackie Lynn declared. "She'll be alright here."

"You said you'll worry about her constantly if she comes there," Flora argued. "If she comes here, you won't have to worry about either one of us. We'll both be safe as long as Jacob is away. Having Mary Julia here won't hinder me planning my escape. With any luck, the two of us will be leaving about the same time. Come on; let me do this. It would mean a lot to me."

"You sound like the Flora I know and love," Jackie Lynn commented. "Always wanting to look out for everyone else. I simply have to be convinced that includes yourself."

"I assure you it does, Jackie Lynn," she maintained. Flora realized she was taking a supreme risk by having Mary Julia come there to stay, but she did not care. Being able to finally have a part in helping Mary Julia was worth the gamble for Flora.

"Why don't you come here Wednesday afternoon? You could leave the office early. We'll have an early dinner together, and then we'll pick up Mary Julia and bring her here. It will be wonderful to see the two of you again," Flora continued.

Jackie Lynn could not refuse Flora's offer. Her friend sounded so thrilled about having the potential to help. It was terrific to note her sounding happy. If Mary Julia went there, it would provide Flora sorely needed companionship. Jacob had totally cut her off from the rest of the world.

Plus, Jackie Lynn believed what Flora had said. 'We'll both be safe as long as Jacob is away.' It seemed an ideal solution for both of them. "Okay," she conceded. "I'll plan on seeing you Wednesday around 3:00 p.m. I'm looking forward to it."

They said their warm good-byes. Flora was satisfied with the way things had ended. She felt more relaxed and content than she had in ages.

I might be able to have a secure, good night's sleep for a change. She crept out of the library and silently made her way up the stairs toward her bedroom.

* * * *

Wednesday at 3:00 p.m., Jackie Lynn arrived at Jacob's two-story, sprawling mansion – *unfortunately still Flora's residence.* She was greeted by her friend with a fond hug and practically pulled inside. "How have you been?" Flora cheerfully inquired. She led her friend through the large great room into the massive dining room. Salads and ice tea already awaited them.

"How did everything go this weekend with you and your helpful Indian?" she grilled with a hopeful smile. "Have you heard from him since?"

"Whoa, Flora! One question at a time," Jackie Lynn chuckled in amusement, halting the persistent woman's rambling interrogation.

"Sorry," she apologized with an embarrassed and silly grin.

She directed Jackie Lynn to take a seat across from her at the long dining room table. They were sitting at the end. The table sat twelve people. Even though Flora and Jacob had never entertained guests, the dining room was set up to accommodate many others. A fancy lace tablecloth adorned the table, and there was an enormous vase of fresh flowers in the center of the table. A dazzling chandelier hung from the ceiling overhead. A beautiful, solid cherry china cabinet sat against the far wall. It was filled with lovely plates and many, pretty, glistening, crystal pieces.

"I miss not being able to talk to you each day as we always used to. We used to share everything, just as it was happening," Flora spoke again.

"I miss that too," Jackie Lynn confessed. "Hopefully, it won't be much longer before you can speak to me anytime you wish," she added in a soft voice, barely above a whisper. She was intently studying Flora's eyes.

"Jacob won't have a hold over me much longer," Flora reassured her, in an equally quiet voice. Then she persistently demanded in an animated voice, "Don't change the subject. Tell me about your Indian man. How did your date go?"

"Dates." Jackie Lynn corrected. She instinctively smiled in happy reflection. Despite her resolve not to see or speak to him, Jackie Lynn had conversed with Long Wolf the night before.

He had called her Sunday and left a message on her machine. She did not return his first call. Therefore, he had left a second message Monday evening, kindly saying he hoped everything was okay. When he had phoned Tuesday night, Jackie Lynn could not bear to allow his call to roll to her message machine. She had claimed being overwhelmed by an important case as an excuse for having not returned his previous calls.

Simply the sound of his voice had sent her heart racing in exhilarated anticipation, and Jackie Lynn had vividly imagined his striking face. Regardless, when Long Wolf had suggested that they get together that weekend, Jackie Lynn had cleverly lied and professed to be tied up with business matters all three days and nights.

I might talk to him on the telephone, but I'm not going to see this guy face to face for a while, she had cautiously reminded herself.

"Jackie Lynn," Flora addressed, returning her friend's smile. "Where'd you go? Thinking about that handsome man? Judging by that devilish grin on your face and the fact that one date led to another in the same weekend, I'd wager things went well with your Indian gentleman. What's his name?"

"Long Wolf," Jackie Lynn responded with a nervous giggle. She sank a fork deep in her salad. "Yes, things went well. Perhaps too well... I'm going to lie low from this guy for a spell."

"Why?" Flora questioned with visible exasperation, absently pointing her fork prongs in Jackie Lynn's direction. "You always behave this way. I don't understand why. You're obviously *very* interested in Long Wolf, so why are you already trying to put him off. I realize you've been hurt in the past, but you can't go through the rest of your life destroying each relationship before it's begun. You worry me, my friend. You genuinely do."

"I'm fine, Flora. There is no reason for you to worry about me," she reassured her. "You told me the other day what a mistake it is to rush into a relationship, right? I'm basically slowing things down, that's all."

"I was talking about myself, not you. I was referring to rushing into something such as marriage. If you put a halt on a relationship before it's started, it will never take hold. That's precisely your intention. I'd hate to watch you renounce the love of a lifetime," Flora argued.

"I'm glad to discover you are still a true romantic," Jackie Lynn playfully noted. She affectionately patted her friend's hand across the table, before concentrating on her food.

Their server came from the kitchen and asked if they were ready for the main entree. Flora apprised them that they were. Hence, the girl promptly disappeared into the kitchen.

"Look, why don't you direct your concerns to Mary Julia," Jackie Lynn advised. She shoved her salad plate aside so the girl could take it when she came back with the remainder of their food. "I'm alright with the way my life is. I have a fantastic job that I enjoy. I have a nice home, even if it is an apartment. I'm basically a happy, secure person."

"So was Mary Julia," Flora pointed out.

Jackie Lynn grimaced at the comparison. "My life isn't out of control, and I'm not behaving in ways that will harm me," she argued.

"That's debatable," Flora stated with a somber expression. The girl reappeared and sat their plates in front of them. Each held a heaping portion of chicken and pasta with a side of steamed mixed vegetables – broccoli, cauliflower and carrots. "I can tell you want me to change the subject, so I shall. But I want to ask you to do me a favor. Give this Long Wolf fellow a fair shot. Okay?"

"I plan to…in time," Jackie Lynn professed without reservation.

I won't enable anything major to develop, but I might occasionally welcome his presence.

She did not reveal this reflection to Flora. Her friend desperately desired happiness for her, but Jackie Lynn believed her life was fine without a man in it – *at least a relationship that ties me down.*

* * * *

Before they released Mary Julia, Jackie Lynn and Flora had a brief meeting with her doctor. He defined what types of behavior Mary Julia was likely to exhibit throughout the next month and how they should deal with it. He gave them both his telephone number and told them to call anytime, day or night, should a problem arise.

He explained that the next few weeks would be crucial to Mary Julia's full recovery from her sexual addiction. "Once the patient leaves the security of these sanitarium walls, they often suffer a setback. Sometimes, they lose hope of actually recovering. It appears Mary Julia will have plenty of constant support though…what with friends like you, her sponsor, and the group therapy, she will still be attending once a week. Consequently, she should be fine." He proceeded to walk them from his office to their meeting with Mary Julia.

Mary Julia was thrilled to see both of them. She enthusiastically hugged and kissed each one. Nonetheless, it was obvious when she walked out the front door of the hospital, Mary Julia was nervous about leaving. "It's going to be alright," Flora pledged, noticing her friend's anxiousness. She wrapped a reassuring arm around her shoulder and guided her the rest of the way to Jackie Lynn's automobile.

"I'm looking forward to seeing your home, Flora," Mary Julia revealed, when they were settled in the vehicle and heading out of the parking lot.

She was in the front seat with Jackie Lynn, and Flora was in the back. Mary Julia turned her head and concentrated solely on Flora's face as she was speaking to her. She was striving to avoid pondering the fact that she was departing from the hospital grounds.

"It shall be nice having you there," Flora recounted with a cheerful grin. She patted one of her shoulders. "Jacob is in Europe, so we'll have the whole gigantic place completely to ourselves."

This appeared to relax their young friend. *Being with Flora won't be much different than being at the sanitarium. There won't be any pressure, and Flora has always been supportive. It's going to be okay.*

Mary Julia forced herself to look out the windshield. It was a beautiful evening. The sun was setting and everything seemed perfect. She felt free all at once.

I'm capable of being a normal person. I won't have any ugliness in my life anymore, she proudly concluded.

"What's that smile for?" Jackie Lynn investigated, noticing a satisfied grin on Mary Julia's face.

"For having such amazing friends and being able to be *out* with them again," she warmly answered, the smile deliberately widening.

"We're delighted to be with you too," Jackie Lynn confirmed, returning her smile. "You've been missed. What would you prefer to do first, now that you're a free woman?"

"Honestly? I'd like to go to Flora's and begin settling in. Pretty pathetic, huh?" she acknowledged with a nervous snicker, glancing from one woman to the other.

"That sounds like an excellent plan to me. For now," Jackie Lynn consented. "The weekend is only a few days away. I can get together with the two of you then. We could all see a movie together or something."

"That sounds terrific!" Flora agreed. "It shall be nice for us all to go out somewhere fun together."

"Sure it will," Mary Julia concurred. It would be disturbing to venture from Flora's. But Mary Julia genuinely believed that with the aid and strength of her friends, she could accomplish the feat. She thanked God for allowing her to have these special people in her life to help her find her way. She relaxed, engaging in comfortable small talk with both Flora and Jackie Lynn for the remainder of the ride.

CHAPTER TEN

AWAKENINGS

Jackie Lynn had just finished eating her dinner the next evening when the telephone rang. She presumed it was Flora, calling to report on Mary Julia's first day at her house. Instead, it was Long Wolf.

"Hi. How are you?" he pleasantly began.

"Alright. How about yourself?" she politely inquired. Then she questioned with a chuckle, "Do you realize, other than last night, you have called me every night this week?" Secretly, Jackie Lynn was pleased to hear his voice.

"Yes, I do. One might think I was more than slightly interested," Long Wolf affirmed. Then he jovially added, "Actually, I have called you *every* night. You hadn't gotten home from picking up Mary Julia last night, and I didn't leave a message. How did everything go? Did Mary Julia settle in okay at Flora's?"

Jackie Lynn was impressed that Long Wolf remembered not only where she had gone the preceding night, but also both her friends' names. However, she had spoken a lot about both of them. It was unbelievably easy for her to converse with this man.

"It all went fine. I'm supposed to go to a movie one night this weekend with the girls," she confessed without thinking.

"Oh! Does that mean you've been freed from your busy legal schedule? If so, I'd love to spend a few hours with you as well. The weather is predicted to be ideal. I could bring you to my cabin, and we could go for a walk together and share a picnic lunch," Long Wolf proposed.

Jackie Lynn wanted to kick herself. She had told Long Wolf she was too busy to be with him this weekend. Now, she had disclosed that she had time for a movie with the girls.

"Um...well...I figured my support was vital to Mary Julia right now, so I had to clear some time for her," Jackie Lynn tried to cover. "I'll be busy the remainder of the weekend. May I have a rain check? The grounds surrounding your cabin are impressive. I wouldn't mind visiting them again. But not this weekend."

"Okay. I don't want to pressure you," Long Wolf considerately surrendered. "I guess I'll have to continue to call and talk to you each night until you agree to see me again."

"You're quite persistent, aren't you?" she accused with a good-natured, amused laugh.

"When I desire something, yes," he proclaimed without hesitation. "Spending time with you is *definitely* something I desire. But I'll settle for speaking to you on the phone. For a while. You're interesting to talk to."

"You must be a glutton for punishment," Jackie Lynn commented. "Practically all I've talked about are my friends' problems. Then again, I suppose they are rather interesting. Tragic, but interesting nevertheless."

"Listening to you reveal your friends' ordeals shows me what a truly caring woman you are. It makes me long to get to know you better," Long Wolf confessed. "What finer way to get better acquainted with a person than talking to them? The telephone shall be my best buddy until I'm able to delight in your company again."

Before Jackie Lynn could reply, her call-waiting alerted her. "Could you hold on a second, Long Wolf? I have another call," she stated and placed him on hold. Flora was on the other connection.

"Hi, Flora. I have Long Wolf on hold. Hang on a minute and I'll let him go."

"No. Don't do that," Flora protested.

She did not wish to provide Jackie Lynn any excuse to stop speaking with her intriguing Indian man. "I was calling to tell you Mary Julia has settled in fine. How's Saturday night sound for that movie?"

"That sounds terrific. What time?" Jackie Lynn asked.

"Come for dinner around 5:00. We'll study the paper and decide what looks good," she suggested. "I'll let you go. Enjoy talking to Long Wolf."

"Alright, bye," Jackie Lynn said with a chuckle.

Flora would love to pair her with Long Wolf. Jackie Lynn clicked him back on the line. "Long Wolf, that's Flora on the other line. She needs to speak to me regarding Mary Julia," she untruthfully recounted. Jackie Lynn intended to end this discourse. Long Wolf seemed to be getting way too personal.

"Oh, okay. I'll talk to you tomorrow," he concluded. "Have a pleasant chat with your friend. Sweet dreams. You'll be in my thoughts."

You'll be in mine too, she conceived, but of course did not verbalize. Jackie Lynn lowered the receiver with relief. Nevertheless, part of her was already looking forward to hearing from Long Wolf again.

* * * *

As promised, Long Wolf called Thursday evening. He was apparently determined to keep firmly planted in Jackie Lynn's consciousness each and every day. He was succeeding.

"What did Flora have to say about Mary Julia? Was everything okay?" he considerately explored, seeming to innately pick right up on where their conversation had abruptly ended the previous night.

"She is settling in fine," Jackie Lynn answered, feeling guilty for purposely cutting him off yesterday. "How was your day?"

"I had a wonderful day. Greathouse Construction won the bid for another, somewhat large, construction job downtown, so I'm delighted," he happily disclosed. "How about your day? Are you swamped with work for your big legal case? Who is your client? Is this a business matter or an individual?"

Since she was not swamped by any particular case, Jackie Lynn had to think fast to come up with yet another lie to cover for her creative story. She could not chance being in Long Wolf's presence so soon. The fact that she was enjoying speaking to him each night on the phone significantly concerned her.

"Um…it's a private matter. I can't go into details. You know, client/lawyer confidentially," she evasively stated, sidestepping the whole issue.

"Oh, that's right," he surrendered. "Do you go out for lunch? Or do you work straight through?"

"I work straight through," Jackie Lynn answered.

This was not a total lie. She had not been going out. Since Mary Julia had been hospitalized, Jackie Lynn had fallen into the habit of eating at her desk. If she went out alone, she was prone to reflect on missing her friends. It was easier to eat at her desk and continue working.

"I catch lunch whenever and wherever I'm able," Long Wolf confessed. "It's usually in between meetings, or a sandwich at the construction site. I relate to working lunches. But in light of the fact that we are both downtown, if we both get a free moment in the near future, we should get together for lunch. That would mean I'd see you for a bit. An hour is better than not at all."

"I can't imagine that happening anytime soon. But sure, I would join you if I was completely free," she cautiously promised.

Oh, I'd love to meet you. We could sneak off to a nearby hotel, and I'd discover if you are as delicious as you look and smell! Cool it, Jackie Lynn! Time to get off this telephone. This gentleman is plainly able to cast some sort of weird spell over you.

"Sorry, Long Wolf. I need to go," she told him. "I brought a few legal briefs home with me that it's necessary I start going through tonight."

Lie, lie, lie. Unfortunately, I'm getting better and better at this with this man. Why don't I tell this guy to get lost? That would surely simplify things. I'm not telling Long Wolf to get lost, because I don't wish that at all, Jackie Lynn truthfully recognized. *It's essential I make sure things don't get out of hand.*

"Okay, I don't want to tie up your time," Long Wolf thoughtfully declared. "I'll talk to you tomorrow. Have a good night. Don't work too hard."

They hung up, and Jackie Lynn urgently wished she had something to work on – anything to take her mind off of this alluring man. How could he have such a profound effect over her from a few simple telephone conversations? How could she so desire hearing the sound of his voice each evening? Was she going through some type of midlife crisis?

No; I have control over this situation, she tried to convince herself. But, for the first time in her life, Jackie Lynn was not at all certain she believed this.

* * * *

Friday, after a morning in court, Jackie Lynn headed back to her office. Engrossed in her own thoughts, she opened her office door. She strolled inside and nearly ran straight into Long Wolf.

"Long Wolf?! What in the world are *you* doing here?!" she demanded in shock and dismay.

I planned so carefully, so I didn't have to see this guy for a while. Yet here he is standing right in front of me. He looks strikingly mouth-watering and that unforgettable, solely masculine smell!

Long Wolf smiled at her, and Jackie Lynn's insides melted. He brought his arms from behind his back and proudly presented her with a picnic basket. "I realize you are busy. But you have to eat. So I thought, considering I had an hour or so available, I would bring us *both* something to eat. Shall we?" he invited, motioning to her conference table.

Long Wolf had draped a red and white, checkered tablecloth over the conference table. "I swear I won't keep you long. I'll only stay long enough for us to get a bite to eat together. Please don't cast me out hungry."

How'd he get past the receptionist? I'll have to have a word with that girl about this! she planned.

Jackie Lynn warily made her way to a chair at the table and sat down. *How can I possibly send him on his way?*

With a wide, satisfied grin, Long Wolf proceeded to join her at the table. He sat down in the chair across from her. He immediately began to unpack the picnic basket. He produced a small feast: fried chicken, coleslaw, mashed potatoes, corn, and even dessert buckets.

"Gourmet meal courtesy of Kentucky Fried Chicken," he announced with an amused snicker. "It was quick and right on the way."

This information made Jackie Lynn laugh heartily. "I assumed you had cooked this meal for me with your own two hands," she lightheartedly kidded.

"Not today, but I'd love to cook for you at some point," Long Wolf affirmed. He reached across the table to uninvitingly slide one of Jackie Lynn's hands into his. "Hopefully, you will have a break in your punishing schedule before long, and I'll entice you to my cabin. I'll cook you one of the best meals you've ever had. For now, it's fast food, and a chance to share a brief interlude together. I'll take whatever I may get."

Gazing into his attentive, sensitive eyes, Jackie Lynn's body stirred with yearning. *I certainly have an appetite all of the sudden, but it isn't for the food.*

She slipped her hand from his unsettling grasp, and intentionally lowered her eyes. *Concentrate on eating! Eating quickly!* she sternly warned herself. She extracted a breast from the box of chicken.

"Do you like butter on your corn?" Long Wolf asked, as he raised a steaming ear from another container. "I'd be happy to butter it for you, so you don't risk burning those pretty, delicate hands."

"No thanks," Jackie Lynn politely declined, briefly glancing at him.

I'd like to burn my hands alright. Running them all over your hot body. And you may burn the rest of my body with your hands and mouth, she uncontrollably fantasized. *This is why I didn't desire to be with this man so soon. I'm much too attracted!*

"This is too much food. I'll stick to this piece of chicken and some slaw. If I eat much more, I may feel like lying down and taking a nap afterwards. I can't chance that," Jackie Lynn endeavored to make normal dialogue. She picked up her soft drink and took a couple of large drinks of the cooling liquid.

"That's fine. Whatever we don't eat will get eaten at the construction site by hungry workers," Long Wolf stated with an agreeable grin.

Before he set to the task of preparing his own plate, he stood and took his suit jacket off, hanging it on the back of his chair. Jackie Lynn was surprised to observe Long Wolf loosen his tie and unbutton the top button of his flattering, blue striped, dress shirt. He also unbuttoned and rolled up both his sleeves.

Long Wolf noticed Jackie Lynn curiously watching him and explained with the most engaging glint in his eyes, "I'm a jeans and T-shirt man. I have to wear these monkey suits day in and day out, but I try to make myself as relaxed as possible whenever I get the opportunity. You look nice in your attractive feminine suits, by the way. I have yet to discover you in anything that didn't seem to compliment you. Perhaps that's because you are a lovely lady."

For a second, Jackie Lynn was unable to catch her breath. She had the most insane urge to spring from her seat, throw her arms around Long Wolf's robust body, and smother those scrumptious lips with her longing mouth.

"Th…thank you," she said in a shaky voice and averted her eyes. She took a large bite of chicken.

Long Wolf sat back down across from her and filled his own plate with food. It was not what he dreamed to do. He actually desired to go to Jackie Lynn, pull her to her feet, and plentifully feast on her. He had glimpsed an unmistakable mirror of his own fierce desire in her eyes. He marveled at why she fought her attraction to him so excessively.

Patience, Long Wolf! She'll be worth the wait. Long Wolf did not understand why, but he was convinced of this.

"You have a nice office here," he commented, giving it a hasty perusal. There was a large mahogany desk, and there were several bookshelves, jam-packed with law books, along the walls. The best feature of the office was the large picture window, which looked out over a glorious view of the city skyline.

"I expect my office is small in comparison to yours, Mr. Greathouse Construction President," Jackie Lynn joked, endeavoring to lighten her frustrated mood.

"Yes, well, I'm only in *that* office when I absolutely have to be. Most of the time, when I'm not in negotiations in someone else's boardroom, I'm in my tiny, dirty, construction site office. Like my jeans and T-shirts, I'm much more comfortable in that environment," he said. "I have a feeling that's where we may vastly differ. I bet you love this cushy office, don't you? Being dressed professionally? And your in-the-heart-of-the-city apartment?"

"That's not exactly true," she disagreed. "I'm comfortable being dressed professionally, but I'm as comfortable dressed down. As to the other, yeah, I enjoy having a big office and living right in the heart of the city. But I enjoyed being in the country too, walking the grounds around your cabin."

Truthfully, the companionship I shared probably was the main reason for me enjoying the country considerably this past week. She preferred to be in the city. Most of the time Jackie Lynn found the country overly quiet and lifeless.

"I'm glad to learn that. I hope there'll be numerous opportunities for me to derive joy from walking in the woods around my cabin with you right by my side. I'd be content to participate in your city life with you also," he suggested. Long Wolf gave her another mischievous, boyish, half grin and resolutely locking eyes with her.

He had to struggle to keep from making some sort of bodily contact with Jackie Lynn - *merely holding her hand* - because he discerned his touch caused her discomfort. Truthfully, each time he touched Jackie Lynn, it prompted Long Wolf to explore touching more of her. As he focused with iniquity on her tantalizing full lips and the fork gliding between them, a familiar throbbing in his lower region overtook him.

Long Wolf picked up his soda and slurped a large amount of the fluid through the straw. He actually sat the icy cup in his lap to significantly cool his indecent response to simply being in this woman's presence.

"When does your case go to trial?" he inquired. He shoved mashed potatoes into his mouth to hide the huskiness that had crept into his voice.

Get a grip, Long Wolf! You are a grown man, not a teenager! he confidentially chastised himself, speedily drinking more of his Pepsi.

"Um…middle of next month," she replied.

Jackie Lynn had a case going to trial during that interval. Hence, she was not technically lying. It was not a case that tied up her lunches and weekends though.

Nonetheless, she was unquestionably convinced keeping up her clever business charade was a necessity. She had noticed Long Wolf's longing stare and the breathless way his last question had been uttered. This proved to Jackie Lynn he wanted her every bit as much as, if not greater than, she did him.

Oh, yes! It's vital I distance myself from this guy! Or I might end up allowing something to happen I'd undoubtedly regret.

"I'll be *very* busy until then," she stressed.

"Thank heavens for the trusty old telephone," Long Wolf proclaimed with an encouraging grin. "Just think, with all the talking we'll be doing, we should learn quite a lot about each other by the middle of next month. This sounds like a winning plan to me. In between, I'll welcome whatever stolen moments, such as this lunch, we're capable of having together."

Against his better judgment, he reached across the table. He carefully gathered Jackie Lynn's hand into his own, pulling it toward him. He leaned forward and dangerously permitted his hot, needful lips to kiss the soft skin on the palm of her hand. He left them lingering there for a few long moments.

Long Wolf's seductive, amazing lips actually touching her skin easily aroused the very core of Jackie Lynn. She let out a soft sigh. Then, as she realized what she had done, Jackie Lynn began to stammer, "L...Long Wolf...I...I need to finish eating...and...and...g...get back to work."

She was severely shaken by her overwhelming desires. Tears wrought from frustration actually threatened. She lacked the strength to retract her hand. It was taking every ounce of strength that Jackie Lynn was capable of mustering just to remain safely in her seat. Her very being was pleading for her to leap from that chair and lunge at Long Wolf completely unrestrained, permitting her staggering passion to entirely overtake her.

"I'm sorry," he apologized. He withdrew his eager lips and released her hand, much to Jackie Lynn's immense relief.

Painful longing was plainly written across Jackie Lynn's face.

She's obviously decided to deny herself such pleasure for whatever strange reason. The last thing Long Wolf wished to do was to hurt her in any way.

He picked up his soft drink cup, popped the lid off. He swiftly poured a mouthful, ice cubes and all, into his fiery mouth. The ice melted almost instantaneously. "You're right. I should be going. I only planned to stay a little while. I didn't intend to cut into your work time. I merely had to see you. I'll phone you later at home."

After speedily cleaning up their mess and removing the checkered tablecloth from her conference table, Long Wolf left. Instead of walking him to the door, Jackie Lynn made her way to her desk and wearily sat down. She watched him depart with very mixed emotions. She was severely shaken from the intense want Long Wolf effortlessly aroused in her, with simply an innocent kiss of her hand.

It was innocent, right?

Stranger still, and horribly unsettling, Jackie Lynn instantly missed Long Wolf as soon as her office door shut and he was out of sight. *What is happening to me?!* she contemplated in agony. *It seems I'm head over heels in love with this guy. But that's impossible! I barely know him.*

Jackie Lynn was exceedingly confused. Part of her wanted to refuse to see or talk to Long Wolf ever again. Another part of her longed to scurry out the door, entice him back into her office and spend every waking moment with him.

I'll see the girls tomorrow night. Talking to them might help me grow strong again. It's because I miss them and feel lonely that this man has any hold over me. I'll be alright, she strove to convince herself. She picked up the telephone and listened to her voice messages, unsuccessfully endeavoring to drive Long Wolf from her thoughts.

CHAPTER ELEVEN

CHALLENGES

Dinner, at Flora's, with the girls Saturday went well. As they sat in the dining room and were finishing their luscious, chocolate mousse dessert following dinner, Mary Julia revealed how impressed she was by Flora's new lifestyle. "Practically her every move is attended to by someone. It's as if I'm living with royalty," she recounted with a grateful smile. "I told Flora I'm delighted her life has turned out so well. I'd like to speak with that handsome husband of hers and inform him how pleased I am by the life he's given her."

Jackie Lynn and Flora exchanged a silent, knowing look. "Yeah. I'd like to tell Jacob exactly what I think of the way he's changed Flora's life too," Jackie Lynn admitted too gruffly.

Noticing Flora's fierce disapproving eyes, Jackie Lynn abruptly covered her displeasure with a forced grin. *When I'm certain Mary Julia is significantly healthy, I'll divulge the truth to her.*

"Speaking of the men in our lives," Flora spoke up, intentionally changing the subject. "How are things going with Long Wolf? Did you see him last night?"

"I saw him yesterday for lunch," Jackie Lynn disclosed.

She needed to talk to the girls regarding the peculiar intensity of her relationship with Long Wolf. Their support would enable Jackie Lynn to put circumstances in their proper perspective. "I hadn't planned to, but he popped into my office with a picnic basket. I had told him I was busy all weekend. This guy is not easily put off. He's persistent as hell. That should be a major turn off for me. But, for some strange reason, I'm unable to push him out of my life."

"Wonderful!" Flora approved. "Can you believe it, Mary Julia? Jackie Lynn might have the possibility to fall in love. Or has she already!?"

"Oh, come on, Flora, don't get carried away!" Jackie Lynn strongly objected. "Yes, I find Long Wolf interesting. And yes, I'm attracted to him. But that's as far as it goes. That's as far as it is going to go!"

"The lady does protest much too much! What do you think, Mary Julia?" Flora kidded, conspiring with their other friend against Jackie Lynn, like old times.

"You are definitely right, Flora," Mary Julia agreed, sharing a hearty laugh with her. "You should see the way your eyes are lighting up merely discussing him, Jackie Lynn. He must be special."

"He's different," Jackie Lynn pensively admitted. "There's something about him. I can't explain what. I mean, yes, he's handsome. But it's not simply his looks that draw me. Maybe it's because he's an excellent listener, and I have missed having the two of you in my life so much."

"You're making excuses, so you don't have to admit you are *very* interested in this fellow," Flora argued. "It's about time. What would be so awful about allowing yourself to fall in love? Sure, you've been hurt in the past. Who hasn't? That's no excuse to thoroughly shut yourself down. If Long Wolf is good to you and you are drawn to this guy, enable him to share your life. What have you got to lose?"

Only my sanity, Jackie Lynn contemplated.

When she realized what had run through her mind, she physically stiffened and declared in a harsh voice, "I don't need a man in my life, Flora. I've been getting along okay by myself. I'm highly capable of keeping right on getting along alright."

"I'll bet Flora could have claimed the same thing before she met and married Jacob," Mary Julia ignorantly joined the discussion. "But look how well that has turned out for her. I'm grateful to you, Jackie Lynn, since you were honest with me concerning my life and talked me into going into the hospital. I wish total happiness for you too. The right man can positively, greatly enhance a woman's life. Perhaps Long Wolf is that man for you. You'll never know if you won't give him a shot. You waste more time pushing men away than you do developing relationships with them."

And the wrong man can destroy a life, Jackie Lynn knowingly considered, glancing at Flora's painfully averted eyes.

"Look, I realize you both love me and desire happiness for me, so I'll tell you what. I promise not to deliberately push Long Wolf aside. As long as I'm finding his company enjoyable, I'll keep spending time with him. We'll see where that leads. Will that satisfy the two of you?"

"It's a start," Flora remarked and Mary Julia nodded her head in encouraging agreement.

"Terrific. Could we please change the subject?" she proposed with exasperation. "Do you have a newspaper, Flora? We should be deciding what movie we might like to see."

"Yeah. It's in the library. If we are finished eating, why don't we go look it over?" Flora suggested. She drank the remainder of her iced tea and arose from the table. The others followed her lead, anxious to get on with their excursion.

* * * *

The women picked a comedy and were luxuriously escorted to the movie theater in Flora's limousine. Mary Julia was impressed once more. "Do you drive yourself anywhere anymore?" she explored with an envious grin.

"No. Jacob won't hear of it," Flora confessed. She did not add that her limo transportation was yet another way for Jacob to totally control her life.

Flora was positive the driver reported each trip to Jacob. She took a sobering second to accept that, subsequent to tonight's disclosure from their driver, she would have to justify to Jacob why Mary Julia was staying at the house. Flora prayed this knowledge did not enrage him so much that he canceled the rest of his trip and came home. She needed more time, and she would have her escape plan from her hellish life entirely worked out. If he came home before planned, it could ruin everything.

"Flora? Are you okay?" Mary Julia scrutinized with concern, noticing an odd expression on her face.

"Yes. I'm fine," she assured her. She reassuringly placed a hand on top of one of Mary Julia's and flashed her a convincing smile. "I was thinking about Jacob."

"Oh, I'm sorry. I shouldn't keep talking about him," Mary Julia contritely apologized. "I'm sure you miss him terribly."

"That's why I'm thrilled to have you as my houseguest. It gets lonely in that big place when Jacob is away," Flora conceded.

Of course, it's a relief to be lonely, rather than have to put up with Jacob's unpredictable violent tirades when he is home.

"I'm sure happy to be there. And grateful. It seems the two of you are giving me a whole new life. I'll find some way to repay you both," Mary Julia pledged, fondly glancing from one esteemed friend's face to the other.

"Seeing you *truly* happy will be all the repayment necessary," Jackie Lynn acclaimed. She placed her hand on top of the other two ladies' hands. "Let's cut out this sweet talk, or you'll cause me to cry. I'm overly sentimental tonight for some reason. I hope this movie is funny, because I could use a few good laughs."

"We all could," Flora concurred, stabilizing her own haphazard emotions with a forced chuckle. She was delighted to finally be assisting with her friend's recovery. Mary Julia's gratitude touched her very heart.

They arrived at the theater shortly thereafter. They were met by many curious stares as they emerged one by one from the limo and walked toward the lobby to purchase their tickets. Mary Julia purposely walked between her two friends, close by their sides. She fought the impulse to grab both their hands, like a frightened child being shielded by her parents.

She strove to ignore the multitude of strange unsettling eyes admiring her, *especially those of the males.* The simple slacks and sweater she wore felt transparent. The men appeared to be able to peer right through them and observe her stark naked. All at once, Mary Julia felt very unsure of herself.

I shouldn't be out. I must have left the sanitarium much too soon, she fearfully concluded. She kept her head bashfully bowed so she could not view the intrusive eyes she felt upon her.

No. You're alright! She recalled what the doctor had told her prior to her departure from the hospital. "Remember, Mary Julia, reentering the *real* world shall be difficult. But you are strong. You are capable of handling it."

Yes. I can handle this, she reassured herself.

As she joined the ticket line with her friends, Mary Julia bravely raised her head and began to glance around her. She was instantaneously regretful that she had. Walking straight toward them and smiling the most radiant smile was one of the most gorgeous men she had ever laid eyes upon.

This man was darkly tanned, slightly over six-foot tall, and had a slim, but nicely muscular, body. He had short, jet black, curly hair and the most exquisite baby blue eyes she had ever had the painful pleasure to gaze into. Mary Julia's legs went weak and buckled, her head started spinning, and her stomach violently tumbled.

I'm either going to faint or be ill, she feared. *I'm not strong enough to be faced with this man!* Her eyes desperately searched to discover which was closer – the bathroom or the exit door.

"Flora!" the man's voice happily acknowledged, and Mary Julia looked in his direction to find him clutching her friend in a familiar bear hug.

Oh, to have those splendid arms around my body! She indecently fantasized, her mouth practically watering.

"How are you? You look beautiful! My old man's absence must be agreeing with you. I heard he had gone to Europe for a few weeks. I apologize for not having been by the house recently. Is everything going well for you?" the handsome man continued to speak to Flora.

"It's going terrific, Jonathan," Flora stated with a friendly convincing grin. "Jonathan Roberts, my stepson, permit me to introduce you to my two dearest friends. Jackie Lynn Forrester and Mary Julia Walters. Mary Julia is staying at the house with me while your father is away."

"It's nice to meet you both," Jonathan greeted, offering a handshake to Jackie Lynn and then to Mary Julia.

When his fingers touched Mary Julia's, it was more than she could possibly take. She sheepishly turned her head from his stirring magnetic eyes. She rudely retracted her hand, twirled, and dashed toward the woman's restroom, instantly in tears.

"I'll check on her," Jackie Lynn volunteered. "Nice meeting you, Jonathan." she politely uttered as she rushed away.

Jonathan's eyes displayed total confusion as they met Flora's. "It's not you, Jonathan," she swore. "Mary Julia hasn't been well. This is her first time out in a while. She's shy around strangers right now."

"Oh, I'm sorry," he apologized, peering toward the restroom where both women had disappeared. "If I had known, I wouldn't have approached you. You could certainly use a few hours out amongst your friends. I hope I haven't spoiled things for you."

"No. Don't you worry about that. You've been great. Thanks to your assistance, I may soon have a happy life," Flora quietly recounted with obvious appreciation. She gave Jonathan a bittersweet smile.

"Why don't you go be with your friends? I'll stand in line and buy tickets for the three of you," he offered. Stepping into the ticket line, he gently shoved Flora in the direction of the restrooms.

"Thanks. But I'm unsure if we will be staying," Flora informed him. "You're bound to have a date here somewhere. She'll be getting restless."

"Aw, Flora. You know me much too well," Jonathan revealed with a devilish grin. "I came out to buy popcorn and soft drinks for the two of us, so my lady friend will basically think I'm stuck in line. Which isn't far from the truth. I'm much more concerned about your lady friend. Try to persuade her to stay. You both could use a night out. Which movie are the three of you planning to see?"

"That comedy *Misunderstood*," she answered.

Flora realized there was no sense arguing. Her stepson was a determined, persistent, young man. Flora thanked God he was. Jonathan was the key to her ending her marriage to his dad.

When he had unexpectedly stopped by the house, following one of Jacob's worse beatings, Jonathan had unwaveringly contended he knew his father had beaten her. It was then that Flora had discovered that Jonathan unquestionably believed his father had killed his mom. He insisted he would not stand by and watch him inflict the same fate on her. They had been conspiring together ever since to get her safely apart from Jacob.

When Flora entered the women's bathroom, she found Jackie Lynn standing in a remote corner with her arm around a sobbing distraught Mary Julia. "Forgive me, Flora," Mary Julia whined when she spied her. "I'm evidently a nutcase. I didn't intend to embarrass you in front of your stepson. It was just…I basically…I'm incapable of being around a man yet. Maybe I can't *ever* be around a man like that. Oh God, how can I be normal?! How could I have presumed I'd be capable of leading a normal life! I'm a total fool!"

"No, you aren't!" Both Jackie Lynn and Flora disagreed almost in unison.

"Mary Julia, you have to remember what the doctor told you. He said there were bound to be setbacks. This is your first time out, and Jonathan is quite handsome. He's a born playboy, so it's natural for you to react fearfully. But you'll be okay. We're both here for you," Flora reassured her. She also placed a supportive arm around her.

"It might be too soon. Perhaps I should still be in the sanitarium. What if the doctor was wrong to release me?" Mary Julia anxiously rambled, tears coursing from her eyes.

"Mary Julia, do you trust me?" Flora quizzed in a level voice. She gently placed a hand under Mary Julia's chin and positioned her face so that they had direct eye contact.

"Of course," she affirmed without hesitation.

"Do you trust Jackie Lynn?"

"Of course I do," she firmly proclaimed. Her hysteria was being rapidly replaced by bewilderment by Flora's line of questioning.

"Then trust me when I insist you *are* ready. We *aren't* going to let you fail," she soundly professed. "You're similar to a baby taking its first unsteady step with the aid of her parents' able hands. You might wobble, but we won't enable you to fall. Soon your legs will be strong enough that you shall not only walk by yourself. You'll run. But there's no way around it. You have to take that first step. I truly believe tonight is the night for that. Trust us. Permit us to assist you in taking that first step."

Mary Julia apprehensively stared into both her friends' expectant, caring faces. *They have complete faith in me. They are confident I am capable of living a normal life. That I can conquer my obsession with perversion. I have to try, not only in gratitude to them for their staunch support, but for myself. Undoubtedly, I long to be free of my horrible addiction.*

"O...okay," she said in a shaky voice. She fished a tissue out of her purse to wipe the remnants of her hysterical tears away. "I'll go back out with you both, and I'll attempt acting like a sane person. But…Flora, could you please keep *him* away? I'm not ready to carry on a conversation, even brief and casual, with such a man."

"Of course," Flora concurred. "Freshen your face. Jonathan is buying our tickets. When we go out, I'll get them from him. We'll go into the theater, have a seat, and enjoy the movie. You won't have to talk to him."

Supportively linking her arm through Mary Julia's, Flora led her to a mirror to fix her makeup. When Mary Julia had finished, the trio of women slowly emerged from the bathroom moving into the bright, loud, crowded lobby. Mary Julia worried about what Flora might have revealed to Jonathan regarding her obviously bizarre behavior.

She was tempted to glance around and search for him. Nevertheless, she fixed her eyes on Flora and Jackie Lynn, who protectively walked close, one on each side of her. Mary Julia humorously considered that they almost appeared to be her bodyguards.

"There he is," Flora told her other two friends. Jonathan was only a short distance away. He smiled and waved three tickets in the air. "You stay here with Jackie Lynn, Mary Julia. I'll be right back."

Mary Julia stopped dead in her tracks. She sensed Jonathan was nearby. Her heart raced uncontrollably. She foolishly raised her eyes and confirmed her suspicions. He was only a few steps beyond. Jonathan was looking directly at her with those gorgeous, ocean blue eyes.

His eyes did not hold pity, as Mary Julia presumed they might. Instead they seemed extremely interested. Her stomach tumbled and her legs shook. *No! I'm okay!* she maintained, grateful when she felt Jackie Lynn securely holding her arm.

Look away! Mary Julia commanded herself. Nevertheless, she could not help attentively studying Jonathan's becoming profile.

Jonathan's attention was fully focused on Flora now. He handed her their tickets and said a few final parting words. Mary Julia's breath painfully caught in her throat, as Jonathan glanced her way again. He comfortably flashed a friendly breathtaking grin, and politely waved goodbye to her and Jackie Lynn.

"It's okay," Jackie Lynn guaranteed. She gave Mary Julia's arm a reassuring squeeze. They watched Jonathan turn and walk away.

"Mary Julia, are you okay? You're very pale," Flora observed with concern as she rejoined the two of them.

"Y…Yeah," she stuttered, relieved, and at the same instant oddly disappointed, as she lost sight of Jonathan. He had quickly blended into the large crowd. "Could we go in the theater and sit down though. My legs are really weak."

"Sure," Flora conceded. She grabbed Mary Julia's other arm and led her forward. "You're doing great. It's going to be alright. Remember, one step at a time."

One step at a time, indeed! Mary Julia accepted. *How can I fail with the support Flora and Jackie Lynn are unconditionally providing?*

As the doctor had advised, she would draw from their strengths to make her own self healthy. *I* will *make it!* Mary Julia convincingly maintained for the first time since her startling encounter with Jonathan.

CHAPTER TWELVE

COURAGE

Jackie Lynn was relaxing on her couch the next morning, reading Sunday's newspaper, eating a piece of toast with jelly, and leisurely drinking a cup of coffee when her doorbell unexpectedly rang.

Who can that be? I'm not expecting anyone, she thought with annoyance, unhurriedly rising and walking to the door.

When she looked through the peephole and discovered it was Long Wolf, she was flabbergasted. *What in the world is he doing here?* she wondered in surprise. She self-consciously noted the thin silky nightshirt she was wearing.

As Long Wolf softly knocked and rang the bell a second time, Jackie Lynn hesitantly unlocked the door. However, she left the chain on so the door only opened a couple of inches. "Long Wolf! What in the world are you doing here?" she scrutinized.

Jackie Lynn kept her scantily clad body concealed behind the door. She bewilderingly peeped through the open crack. Long Wolf glimpsed Jackie Lynn's mostly bare leg and the bottom of her short nightshirt. She was still dressed for bed, which was understandable considering it was rather early.

"I'm sorry," he apologized, wishing he could observe more of her. "I didn't wake you, did I?"

"No," she answered. Jackie Lynn bashfully pulled her leg back, as she noticed Long Wolf's interested appraisal. "I was basically lazing around, reading the paper and drinking coffee, taking my time waking up this morning. What brings you here? I certainly wasn't expecting you."

"I realize you weren't expecting visitors. I had to go into the office this morning and pick something up. Since I was in the neighborhood and I could tell it's going to be a gorgeous day, I decided to stop by and attempt to twist your arm into accompanying me to the cabin for a bit. You've been working so hard recently and occupying most of your other time helping your friends; you could use the break. How about it? Might I entice you to spare me a few precious hours? I'd prefer to have the whole day, but I'll settle for whatever stretch you're able to set aside. Come on! Don't say no. It will revitalize you. You'll work that much faster," he argued, his appetizing lips curling into the most radiant smile.

Jackie Lynn could not refrain from smiling at Long Wolf's persistence. She remembered her promise to her friends the previous evening to give a relationship with Long Wolf a fair shot. *What could relaxing a few hours in the country with this guy hurt? I'll no doubt find it enjoyable.*

"Okay," she conceded. Jackie Lynn unlatched the chain and opened the door the rest of the way. Still partially concealing her body, Jackie Lynn instructed, "Have a seat on the sofa while I go put some clothes on. If you'd like, you can pour yourself a cup of coffee. The mugs are in the first cabinet by the stove."

As she turned her back on him and hurried toward the bedroom, Long Wolf could not resist the temptation to watch her. *What a sexy attractive lady!* he could not help but longingly conclude. He loved the way Jackie Lynn moved across the room and how her nightshirt nicely clung to her shapely figure.

Long Wolf hated it when she stepped into the bedroom and shut the door. Nonetheless, he was delighted he had persuaded Jackie Lynn to spare some time for him. He took a seat on the couch and patiently waited.

* * * *

Flora had just finished her breakfast Sunday when she received an unanticipated call from Jacob. Their driver *had* divulged that Mary Julia was staying in his home for an undetermined interval and that Jackie Lynn had visited. Predictably, Jacob was not at all happy about any of this. He revealed his heated displeasure through a heated telephone conversation with Flora.

Several tense moments later, she was relieved when the abusive discourse ended. Jacob was being summoned to make one of the many speeches he was scheduled to deliver in his lengthy overseas tour. Flora was distressed about what Jacob's next course of action might be. If he chose to conduct his lectures for today and then fly home, she feared for not only her own life but that of Mary Julia's.

Jacob regarded his wife's kindness to her friends a careless and blatant betrayal. If this enraged him enough, without a doubt, Jacob was capable of killing in retribution. Flora could not take the chance of this occurring. She had not only herself to protect, but Mary Julia as well.

She picked up the phone and placed an urgent call to Jonathan. She was mollified when he answered. Flora had been afraid he would not be home, and she desperately needed to talk to him.

"Hi, Jonathan. It's Flora," she revealed, attempting to sound carefree, although this was very difficult. They had agreed to impart nothing unusual when they talked, as somebody could always be listening in and reporting their discourse back to Jacob.

"Hi, Flora. How are you? I couldn't believe we ran into each other at the movies last night. Did you enjoy the show?" Jonathan carried on a casual, friendly dialogue, even though he secretly assumed something must be wrong. He patiently waited for Flora to somehow convey what that might be.

"Yeah. So did the girls," she curtly replied and then inquired, "I hate to ask this but if you aren't overly busy, could you stop by later? This is kind of awkward. My friend Mary Julia needs to get used to being around people again and she seemed to like you. I'm not setting up a date or anything. I'd appreciate it if you would come over and we could all spend a little time together. Your father telephoned. He'd rather Mary Julia wasn't here when he returns because he'll want to be alone with me. It's vital I make certain she is ready to be on her own and part of that is learning to be around people again. And who knows. You're aware of how your father is; he's likely to come home early, so the sooner I build Mary Julia's confidence the better."

"Did my dad say he was coming home sooner than planned?" Jonathan probed. He purposely kept alarm out of his voice, despite knowing, if his father returned, it would be a setback to every one of their plans to shrewdly remove Flora from her tormented life with Jacob.

"No. But just in case, it's necessary that I have Mary Julia ready to move as soon as possible. You might be able to help," Flora disclosed. She wanted Jonathan to come right away. She could ensure they had privacy and inform him of everything that had transpired with Jacob.

"I'm always glad to help," he assured her. "I'll see you soon."

"Thank you, Jonathan," Flora gratefully uttered, and the two hung up. She would talk to her helpful stepson regarding her fears. He would know what to do.

It's going to be okay, Flora told herself with greater confidence than she felt.

* * * *

Jackie Lynn dressed comfortably for her adventure in the country with Long Wolf. She put on belted shorts, a lightweight, multi-colored, cotton blouse, and her leather walking shoes. She swept her hair off her neck and pulled it back in a neat ponytail, realizing it would be much cooler this way. As usual, Long Wolf found her quite attractive.

During the car ride to his cabin, typically, they engaged in easy conversation. Long Wolf privately noted, *This is the most relaxed I've seen Jackie Lynn. Being with her friends must have been good for her. For me as well. She seems content to be with me, rather than nervous like usual.*

At the cabin, he proposed they take a leisurely walk through the woods. Without hesitation, Jackie Lynn agreed. It was the ideal day for it. The sun was shining brightly. The sky was a heavenly clear blue, with only a few white puffy clouds riding high. The temperature was in the high seventies at most.

It was a rare treat for Jackie Lynn to be able to enjoy being outside in such weather. Plus, she was happy with the companionship. *Flora and Mary Julia are right. I basically need to relax and welcome this man's company*, she recognized and flashed Long Wolf a warm and inviting smile.

He joined her side, and they started down the path through the impressive foliage. They had only been walking for a short period when Long Wolf unexpectedly encircled Jackie Lynn's waist with his able hands. He brought her body to an abrupt halt, whispering in her ear, "Shh. Look."

Jackie Lynn stared expectantly through the trees in front of her. She saw a doe and her baby carefully scrutinizing them, as they cautiously made their way through the forest. "Aren't they pretty?" Jackie Lynn quietly commented.

She liked the delightful touch of Long Wolf's hands on her waist. She did not tense. Instead, when the deer were out of sight, she deliberately swiveled her body to face Long Wolf. They were standing dangerously near and he held her, but Jackie Lynn did not pull away.

"Thank you," she murmured a little breathlessly, happily smiling at his sumptuous face. "I've never seen live deer in the wilderness before. It's really something to see."

"Boy, you genuinely are a city girl, aren't you?" Long Wolf kidded with an amused snicker. Turning sideways, he slid one arm affectionately behind her back and urged her forward.

Long Wolf had intensely longed to kiss Jackie Lynn, and for the first time, he had sensed she would not have resisted. Nonetheless, Jackie Lynn was more open to him than she had ever been, and Long Wolf did not plan to risk scaring her back into her protective shell. "Didn't your parents take you camping?"

"Ha. That's a good one. I can visualize my mother camping," Jackie Lynn sarcastically revealed. "She wouldn't have had the foggiest notion how to take joy from a beautiful day such as this. She would have stayed inside with the drapes shut. Preserving her dark little world. The same one she expected me and every one of my stepfathers to exist in."

Long Wolf was surprised by the hostility Jackie Lynn's voice beheld in regard to her mom. *I've guessed right. Jackie Lynn apparently doesn't get along with her parents, or her mother anyway.*

Observing the shocked look on Long Wolf's face and realizing what she had haphazardly divulged, Jackie Lynn wisely changed the subject. She asked with a deceptive laugh, "What else do you have planned to show me, Mr. Country Boy? There aren't any bears in these here woods, are there?"

She definitely doesn't wish to discuss her relationship with her parents, Long Wolf gathered. *That's okay. There's time for me to learn more about her later. She'll eventually grow to trust me enough to disclose everything. There's no rush.*

It was strange. Long Wolf had never yearned to know so much about a woman, but he sensed it was important he be patient. "Would you like for me to show you a bear? No, there aren't any in these woods, but I could take you to a spot where there are. Name your pleasure, my lady. I'll make sure it comes about," he pledged, displaying a mischievous grin.

"For some reason, I don't doubt that," Jackie Lynn proclaimed, her eyes longingly holding with his. She further amazed and delighted him by saying, "Presently, my pleasure is being here with you."

"Marvelous! The feeling is *very* mutual," Long Wolf concurred with a wide satisfied smile. He squeezed her tighter to his side as they continued their pleasant stroll along the trail.

* * * *

Mary Julia was lying on a float, with her eyes closed, restfully sunning in a spacious pool. She suddenly had an odd sensation of being watched. She opened her eyes and was shocked to observe the male Adonis from the movie theatre the night before, lingering by the side of the pool. He was gawking down at her.

It startled Mary Julia so greatly that her entire body jerked and the raft abruptly flipped. Even though she was in the shallow end of the pool, she floundered helplessly for a second. She accidentally swallowed a mouthful of water, and came up gasping and choking.

"Hey, are you okay?!" Jonathan called with alarm. He ran to the stairs and helpfully extended his hand to Mary Julia.

Before she contemplated her actions, she took his capable hand and allowed him to help her up the concrete steps and out of the pool. Jonathan placed a supportive arm around Mary Julia's wet body and guided her to the closest lounge chair. He sat her on the side. Then he retrieved a few dry towels from the table where they were plentifully available for use. He went a step further to thoughtfully wrap one around Mary Julia's shoulders and hand her the other.

"I'm sorry. I didn't intend to startle you," he apologized. He squatted to eye level with her, as one might a frightened child.

Mary Julia gazed into his endearing, magnificent, blue eyes and contemplated the soft, yet strong, hand and arm that had touched her. She could not help but shudder with fear. *Oh God! How can I be faced with this man again?! This can't be happening!*

She wanted to spring to her feet and scurry away, but she was uncertain her legs would cooperate. *If I remain here....Oh God, I want to touch his adorable face so badly! Oh, to sample those full lips!* her brain had begun racing. Mary Julia could feel panic coming on.

"Jonathan," Flora's called. Mary Julia was relieved to discover her friend approaching.

Jonathan rose to his feet and faced Flora. Flora, however, was staring at Mary Julia's white, terrified face. "Mary Julia, are you okay?" she scrutinized. She protectively rushed to her friend's side.

"She's fine," Jonathan answered for her. "I frightened her when I came up. She fell off her float in the pool and swallowed a few mouthfuls of the splendid pool water. But she's alright. I hate that I disturbed her. She looked so peaceful lying on her float sunning herself."

She's a pretty lady, Jonathan also naturally observed. *She looks very becoming in that bright, hot pink bikini she's wearing.* It distressed him that she was clearly fearful of men. *I wouldn't mind getting a lot better acquainted with her, but will she humor me?*

"Is that iced tea over there on that table? Can I get you a glass?" he questioned Mary Julia.

He is being so kind, and I'm making a fool of myself, Mary Julia noted with frustration. She forced herself to look in his direction.

She could not go through the remainder of her life running from and avoiding every good-looking guy who crossed her path. She needed to deal with and conquer her foolish fear. What more suitable occasion to begin with than now?

"Y…yes. Th…thank you," Mary Julia shakily answered.

Flora was thrilled to watch Mary Julia speaking to Jonathan. Maybe inviting him over would accomplish dual purposes, her own and helping her friend. "Um..Jonathan, wait a second," Flora said, causing him to halt and turn back toward them in confusion. "Mary Julia, why don't you come to the table and we shall all sit and talk together. I'm sure Jonathan would welcome getting to know you better, and I'd like for you to get better acquainted with him as well. How about it?"

Flora would not force the woman, but she had to offer the initiative. Mary Julia looked uncertain and hesitant. "It will be okay," Flora whispered and offered her a helpful hand.

Flora is asking me to trust her. Mary Julia absolutely had to, no matter how hard it appeared. She hesitantly took Flora's outstretched hand and rose on wobbly legs, allowing herself to be led to the table. Flora sat her down and directed Jonathan to have a seat in the chair beside Mary Julia. She sat on the other side. Flora gave Mary Julia's hand a reassuring squeeze before releasing it.

Jonathan poured Mary Julia a glass of tea, as he had previously offered, and held it out to her. Mary Julia studied his perfect face. She was embarrassed when her hand shook as she accepted the glass. She abruptly sat it on the table in front of her, even though she understood she was being somewhat rude by not taking a drink. Mary Julia was scared she would drop the glass if she continued to hold it. She glanced at the table top, attempting unsuccessfully to settle her frayed nerves.

"I'm wondering if we could possibly start all over," Jonathan proposed, feeling badly for Mary Julia.

She was obviously struggling to overcome her shyness and uneasiness around men. He very much wished to help. He remembered how difficult it had been to conquer his own bashfulness and backwardness, cruelly enforced by his overbearing and controlling father.

"Hi. I'm Jonathan Roberts. Flora's stepson. Although she isn't old enough to truly be my mother, I regard her as a friend. I understand you are one of her dearest friends. I'm glad to meet you...um..."

Mary Julia bashfully raised her eyes and gazed into Jonathan's caring eyes. What a sweet, considerate fellow he seemed to be. *And very, very handsome! Speak, Mary Julia! He's furnished a lead in. Open your mouth and talk!*

"Um...I'm Mary...Mary Julia." she managed to mumble.

Jonathan encouragingly smiled, and Mary Julia's insides stirred. She purposely averted her eyes. "It's nice to meet you, Mary Julia. How long have you and Flora known each other?"

She forced herself to glance at him and slowly answered, "For years. We worked together before she married your dad."

It was a whole, concise sentence! Mary Julia could not believe it. She was actually conversing with this man. *Can I keep it up?!*

"Does that mean you are a lawyer?" Jonathan investigated with genuine interest.

"Yeah. I realize it's hard to conceive, but I am," Mary Julia revealed, compelling herself to look him in the face even longer.

There was a rather unsettling part of her that desperately yearned to suggest Jonathan step behind closed doors so she could have her way with him. *If Flora wasn't sitting next to me, how would I behave?* Mary Julia fearfully wondered.

"No, that's not hard for me to believe. Do I look like a pediatrician to you?" he asked. "Because that's my profession. I guess it's good that I doctor children, since I don't know if adults would take me seriously as their physician. Unlike my notable father, I don't run around looking like a stiff in a coffin, in my three piece suits and ties. I go into the office each day dressed similar to the way I currently am – shorts and a polo shirt seem appropriate to me for a doctor. What do you think?"

This caused Mary Julia to actually laugh. He appeared to be a rich playboy who had not worked a day in his life and who did not desire to. She undeniably had trouble picturing him as a doctor.

"You're laughing at me," he teased, pretending to be indignant. "Does this mean you wouldn't trust me with your child? I'm superb at what I do."

"I'll have to take your word for that in light of the fact I'm not married and unquestionably don't have any kids," Mary Julia remarked, realizing she was relaxing. This guy was easy to talk to. She bet he had a slew of women in his life.

Was he as good in bed? No sooner had the unwanted speculation irritatingly crossed Mary Julia's intellect than she tensed and glanced away for the first time in several minutes.

Thank God, he can't read my mind, she conceived.

"I tell you what. If I ever have a malpractice suit brought against me, God forbid, I shall hire you for my lawyer. I have faith in *you*," Jonathan playfully acclaimed with a snicker.

Mary Julia raised her head and smiled at him. So was Flora, from across the table. She was actually smiling at the sight of both of them. *What a cute couple they would make*, she could not help but ponder.

Nevertheless, Jonathan was a confirmed playboy and did not seem to have any subsequent plans to settle down with one special lady anytime soon. He was not a good choice for Mary Julia to have anything but a casual conversation with at present. *What a shame! They could possibly be good for one another,* Flora recognized.

Jonathan noticed Flora grinning at them. It was then he remembered he had come to help *her*. He had been spellbound by Mary Julia, so he had nearly forgotten Flora was at the table with them.

"Mary Julia, I'm happy I had this chance to talk with you. We originally got off on the wrong foot. First, I interrupted your private outing with the girls. Then, I practically drowned you today. I hope you feel more comfortable around me now," he said, as he rose from the table.

"I'd like to stay longer, but I stopped by merely to bring Flora some legal papers she is going to file for me," Jonathan briefly explained and then informed Flora, "I apologize. I left them in the car. Would you mind walking there with me?"

"Of course not," Flora consented, rising from the table. She noted the look of disappointment on Mary Julia's face.

"Goodbye, Jonathan. It was nice talking to you," Mary Julia admitted, attentively studying him.

I wish I could see you again, she accepted. She hated for him to leave. *Am I making progress?* Mary Julia hoped.

Jonathan waved at her and allowed his eyes to pleasurably linger a few seconds longer, before he forced himself to depart with Flora. *I might have to visit again*, he secretly considered. *After all, didn't Flora claim that Mary*

Julia needed to get used to speaking with people again? By that, I conclude she meant men, considering Mary Julia doesn't seem to be shy around women. I'd be doing both Flora and Mary Julia a favor by coming to visit and talking with Mary Julia. Yes, I'll positively have to do that!

Checking to make certain no one was within earshot, Jonathan turned his full attention to Flora and uneasily probed, "What's up? What did you need to discuss with me? Has my father somehow threatened you?"

"He always threatens me," Flora conceded. "The limo driver evidently reported to him that Mary Julia is staying here. Your father is enraged. He hung up on me earlier, and I'm afraid he might come home early in retaliation. We can't allow that to happen. It's critical that I somehow am aware of his plans. I have to get Mary Julia out of here if he intends to return home. I can't take the chance of him hurting her."

"He's not going to harm either one of you!" Jonathan assured her. "I'll contact the gentleman I have watching him and have the guy be on the lookout for him to change his plane tickets. I'll alert you immediately if Jacob plans to come home. Don't worry."

"Oh, Jonathan! You're such a wonderful person! I honestly don't know what I'd do without your support. I appreciate it so much!" Flora gushed, her voice choking with emotion.

Jonathan opened his car door and handed Flora a few papers, which were garbage, keeping up the clever charade of Flora helping him with legal issues. "It's the least I can do. That monster should have been locked up for life after he killed my mom, but he got away Scot free. I won't stand by and permit him to kill once more."

Jonathan gave Flora a brief caring hug, before he climbed into his automobile. She watched him drive off. Flora wished there was some magic way she could get Jonathan to settle down, because he seemed like the ideal man for Mary Julia to have in her life. Jonathan deserved a special lady in his life as well.

Oh well, if it's meant to be, it shall come to pass, she hoped. Flora turned and walked back toward the house.

* * * *

After relaxing for a spell on the dock by the pond, with Jackie Lynn by his side, Long Wolf suggested the two of them head back to his cabin. He also offered to fix them some lunch. Jackie Lynn was agreeable to this suggestion. She was beginning to get hungry, after only having toast for breakfast.

"I'm amazed you didn't suggest we catch a few fish from this pond for you to prepare," she joked, as he helped her to her feet and they started back.

"I bet you've never had fresh fish either," Long Wolf speculated. He placed his arm behind Jackie Lynn's back.

"No. And frankly, if I had to watch you chop one up, I wouldn't be able to eat it afterwards. Yes, I am a city girl through and through. And proud of it. Thank you very much," she bragged with a wide grin.

"Well, city girl, it's a good thing there are good ol' country boys such as me, or you would have no food to eat," he factually pointed out, although he was playing. It did not bother him that their worlds were so different. It made things more interesting as far as Long Wolf was concerned.

"Yes. That's undeniably true. And I'm grateful. So what do you plan to fix us to eat?" she explored.

His face unduly solemn, Long Wolf abruptly stopped walking and said in a soft voice, "Snake."

"That sounds nasty," Jackie Lynn managed to utter, before she was at once silenced by Long Wolf's hand. He had clamped it securely over her mouth, simultaneously immobilizing her by pulling her tightly against his body.

"Shh, Jackie Lynn. Be quiet and don't move an inch," he instructed in a serious, barely audible voice.

It was then that, out of the corner of her eye, Jackie Lynn saw something stir near her feet and she heard this horrible, bone chilling, hissing sound. *Oh, my God! There actually is a snake in front of me!* she realized with panic. She

167

was suddenly so terrified she was uncertain if she was breathing, much less moving.

Hours seemed to go by; even though in actuality it was merely a few minutes. Long Wolf removed his hand from her mouth. "It's okay," he affirmed, although he was being quiet. "It slithered off through the grass."

Jackie Lynn was paralyzed. She could not force herself to look. "Jackie Lynn, honey," Long Wolf addressed in a peaceful voice.

He slowly started around the side of her. She whimpered with remaining terror as he carefully rotated her body to face him. Long Wolf carefully slid Jackie Lynn into his comforting arms. "It's alright. It's gone. You're okay."

Jackie Lynn shivered, hesitantly peeking over his shoulder into the brush where the horrifying creature had supposedly disappeared. Thankfully, there was no sign of a snake or movement in the grass. All she desired was to get out of these woods, and she did not care to return. Regardless, Jackie Lynn remained where she was, being coddled in Long Wolf's hearty, reassuring arms for several more moments.

When she eventually drew back, she was shaken by the intense, caring look in Long Wolf's eyes. "I'm sorry, honey," he apologized. "I hate that you got frightened. I wanted you to enjoy today. I should have been watching more closely. Those snakes aren't aggressive, but I nearly allowed you to step on it. I'm glad it didn't harm you." *I shouldn't have forgotten my walking stick. Perhaps the Indian legend of it protecting us against all harm is true after all.*

Long Wolf pulled Jackie Lynn back against him and warmly and consolingly massaged her back. She was engulfed by a sensation of being totally safe. It was unbelievably gratifying to be held by this man. As much as Jackie Lynn yearned to get out of the forest, she hated to have to separate from Long Wolf's cozy body.

It was Long Wolf who pulled back this time, but he did not remove his secure arms. Instead, he gazed into her needful eyes. When he gently caressed one of Jackie Lynn's cheeks and the side of her neck, she could not help but sigh in contentment.

Long Wolf could not fight his desires for her any longer. He heatedly brought his lips to her cheek. Then he delicately kissed her neck, where his hand had fondly brushed. At long last, his mouth hungrily engulfed Jackie Lynn's mouth. She responded with insatiable passion. Their lips and tongues could not get enough of each other. Their mouths feasted plentifully on one another.

Several breathtaking minutes later, they reluctantly separated and stood silently staring at one another in stunned disbelief. Neither of them had ever been so moved from simply kissing. It was almost as if they had made love with only their mouths.

What just happened?! Jackie Lynn wondered with alarm and bewilderment. She staggered backwards, separating herself entirely from his arms.

Wow! Long Wolf was thinking as he gradually regained his senses. *This lady's kiss has indeed been worth the wait! If she shares that much passion with merely a kiss, what must it be like to have her in more intimate ways?*

The simple consideration had his manhood responsively struggling against his shorts. Long Wolf longed to take Jackie Lynn into his arms and begin to explore further. However, as he continued to absorb her gaze, he observed overwhelming fear replacing the initial shock of their revealing exchange.

She looks like that doe we saw earlier, warily scrutinizing me and prepared to scurry in a flash at the first sign of threat. He needed to say something to calm her enveloping fears.

"I apologize for that, Jackie Lynn," Long Wolf began. He instantly added, "Not because I regret it happened, because I definitely do not. You shouldn't either. What I'm sorry about is that it scares you so much. I don't want to scare you away. Since the first night I met you, I've been uncontrollably drawn to you. And you've been drawn to me in the same manor. You've continuously fought your deepest desires. I'm pleading with you, 'don't push me away.' I promise I'll take things slow. We are starting something special here. Don't you sense it? I know it!"

First, the most amazing kiss she had ever had and now, such heartwarming words. *Am I dreaming?* Jackie Lynn pondered for a few seconds.

No, Jackie Lynn! Don't get caught in some silly fantasy world! Keep your head on straight! It was the fright from seeing that snake that made being in his arms and that kiss so powerful, she strove to firmly convince herself. Nonetheless, deep down, Jackie Lynn honestly knew it was abundantly more.

"Jackie Lynn?" Long Wolf called, troubled by her continuing muteness. "Please say something. It's vital that I know how you feel."

"Hungry," she unexpectedly announced. She gave him a wide grin and rubbed her stomach, making light of all that had transpired and cleverly changing the subject.

We'll pretend the kiss *never happened. That's all that's necessary,* Jackie Lynn decided.

She started moving forward along the trail. Glancing over her shoulder at Long Wolf, she joked, "Well, come on slowpoke. You said you were going to fix me lunch. I'm practically starving."

Oh, I'm starving too! But it's not food I long to feast on, he accepted in exasperation.

Long Wolf followed Jackie Lynn's rapidly fleeing figure. It was obvious she was endeavoring to shut him out. Jackie Lynn was determined to keep her feelings completely shielded.

That's alright for now. I'll play by your rules, my lady. I fully intend to uncover every one of your secrets eventually. I shall succeed, no matter what it takes! I know without a doubt you are absolutely worth the effort, Long Wolf concluded. He fell into pace right beside Jackie Lynn.

CHAPTER THIRTEEN

ATTRACTIONS

Jackie Lynn had been at the office about an hour Monday when the receptionist walked in. She had a wide satisfied smile on her face. She enthusiastically presented Jackie Lynn with an enormous lead crystal vase. The vase was filled with two dozens of the prettiest, softest, light peach roses either of them had ever had the pleasure to lay eyes upon.

"Where would you prefer I sit these?" the receptionist investigated with an envious chuckle, quickly adding, "If you don't have a spot for them, they'd look quite nice on my desk."

"On my table is fine," Jackie Lynn instructed with a half grin, typical of her mixed emotions.

Partially aggravated, she rose from her desk to take a closer look. She was certain the delightful smelling, lovely arrangement was from Long Wolf. She did not want any extra romantic gestures to woo her, such as these flowers.

It had been impossible to get him off her mind since their wayward, torrid exchange yesterday at his cabin. Long Wolf had been a perfect gentleman afterwards. He had not even tried to kiss Jackie Lynn when he had taken her home. *But, oh, I had yearned for him to!*

"I hope you enjoy your beautiful flowers. Someone surely seems to be your admirer. It must be exciting," her receptionist declared. She reluctantly turned and vacated the office.

171

Jackie Lynn removed the card that was attached and hesitantly extracted it from its tiny envelope. The card read, "Jackie Lynn, you are constantly in my thoughts. Our day together was wonderful! Looking forward to sharing more time together soon. I'll call you tonight. Warmest wishes, Long Wolf." Despite herself, Jackie Lynn's heart leapt in delight. She foolishly considered bringing the card to her lips and gleefully kissing it.

That would be a poor substitute for what, or who, *I really long to kiss,* she indecently fantasized.

Her intellect betrayed her as she vividly pictured herself wrapped in a heated embrace with Long Wolf. She could envision herself feverishly devouring those scrumptious tasting, marvelous feeling lips again and again. *Damn! I was going to forget it happened. Forget how unquestionably amazing it was. I can't!*

On the contrary, it was something she would probably remember for the rest of her life. Jackie Lynn wondered if any other man's kisses could come close again. *Oh, this is maddening! I can't allow myself to desire this man so intensely. Or worse…start needing him.*

Jackie Lynn laid the card on the table by the vase and turned her back on the flowers. The soft, floral scent was already filling her office. *Okay, it* was *one hell of a kiss! That doesn't mean I have to act like a school girl who falls head over heels in love with the first boy I kiss. I need to make sure I don't lose control of the situation around him. There's no telling what might happen if I do,* she accepted. *I'm going to court in ten minutes. That shall take Long Wolf off my mind. I'll be alright. I'm simply blowing this thing way out of proportion.*

Jackie Lynn made her way to her desk, picked up her briefcase, and hurried for the door to go to court. She was determined to put her bothersome musings concerning Long Wolf behind her for a short while.

* * * *

Mary Julia and Flora had just finished dinner when they had an unanticipated visit from Jonathan. Both of their stomachs dropped in trepidation. Flora was frightened that Jonathan's presence again so soon meant he was bringing bad news regarding Jacob.

Could Jacob be headed home at this moment? Has Jonathan come to warn me so I can attempt to protect Mary Julia and myself? she fearfully contemplated.

Mary Julia was naturally filled with anxiety. Even though she had managed to conduct herself appropriately yesterday in this man's presence, she felt cruelly tested each occasion she was faced with his company. *What is he doing here? Why is he staring at me? Maybe he isn't. Perhaps I'm merely imagining it. After all, he's surely here to see Flora,* Mary Julia endeavored to reason.

She was frantically attempting to calm her erratic nerves, and she hastily lowering her eyes so she did not give Jonathan the wrong impression. Mary Julia did not wish him to think she had any greater interest in him than as a casual acquaintance, even though quite the opposite was true.

"Ladies," he greeted with an intriguing smile and approached the dining room table.

Their server came from the kitchen and promptly asked, "Mr. Roberts, may I get you something cold and refreshing to drink? Or something to snack on during your visit?"

"No thanks, Anita," he replied. Mary Julia's whole body tensed as he slid out the chair right next to her and sat down.

"Jonathan, what brings you here so soon?" Flora explored. She was trying to keep any sign of alarm out of her voice.

"Well, frankly, Flora, I stopped by to see Mary Julia," he disclosed.

Mary Julia looked into his startlingly good-looking, relaxed face in astonishment. "M...me?" she stuttered uncertainly.

She directed her gaze toward Flora to ascertain if she had planned this. Her friend was peering at Jonathan in surprise also. So it seemed that Flora had not arranged her stepson's social call.

"Yes, you," Jonathan acknowledged in a friendly, chipper voice.

He innocently touched the top of Mary Julia's hand to further demonstrate his point, but she defensively jerked it out of reach. He retrieved his hand, and she at once felt guilty, and remarkably silly, for having such an unnatural reaction to such a simple gesture.

I'm sorry, Jonathan. I can't have you touching me in any way. It's difficult enough for me to calmly sit here beside you. I'd prefer to take your hand and lead you to a private spot and...Oh, don't think such things, Mary Julia! she scolded herself. Her panicked eyes locked with Jonathan's, pleading for understanding.

"Um...Jonathan, could I speak to you in the library before you visit with Mary Julia?" Flora probed, rising from the table.

"Sure," he conceded. He anxiously wondered if some other critical issue had arisen. "Mary Julia, will you excuse me for a few seconds? When I return, could I talk you into taking a walk in the flower garden with me this evening? It's nice outside. I enjoyed talking to you yesterday and would like to learn more about you. What do you say?"

He wants to spend time with me outside, Mary Julia noted in utmost turmoil and uneasiness. *Alone! Simply the two of us! Can I trust myself?!*

"I'm begging you not to turn me down," Jonathan implored. He sensed she was diligently striving to come up with an excuse for not spending time with him. "I've had a rough day. If an attractive lady such as you rejects me, I know not what I might do. You wouldn't crush me like that, would you?" he pretended to pout.

Mary Julia realized he was kidding. He sincerely seemed to want to spend time with her. *Why? I've acted bizarre each time he's seen me. What on earth could he possibly desire from me?*

She pondered the appreciative way he had studied her in her revealing bikini the previous day. *What has Flora told him about me? Does he think I might be an easy lay? He'd certainly be right! I can't dare take the chance! If he comes on to me in any way out there, I might well lay with him behind the bushes.*

"Surely there is *at least* one other female you could be spending time with," Mary Julia verbalized, strangely irate all at once.

I won't allow myself to be taken advantage of by this oversexed gorgeous stud. He'd have it with me in the bushes and later, stick it to one of his numerous, slightly frigid, socialite girlfriends. Oh, yes! I know this type of guy too well! I have made one too many men similar to him quite happy in the past. No more! I undoubtedly have greater regard for myself now than to fall back into that disgusting trap!

Jonathan was puzzled by the angry edge to Mary Julia's voice all of the sudden. He studied her with confusion, as he slid his chair back and rose to follow Flora. "I have a healthy dating life if that's what you are getting at. That's not what I'm asking of you. I happen to respect Flora immensely and if you are a friend of hers, I'd like to consider you a friend of mine," he admitted.

Mary Julia felt foolish. *God! I'm paranoid on top of everything else. This guy is simply trying to be kind. I'm making him into some sort of pervert.*

"I'm sorry, Jonathan," she apologized and forced a smile. "I'd love to take a walk with you when you are through speaking to Flora. I'll wait for you in the great room."

I need to do this. I'm capable of being by myself with this man and not attacking him, Mary Julia told herself.

"Great! See you shortly," Jonathan happily affirmed. He grinned at her before he reluctantly spun to follow Flora, who was patiently waiting.

As soon as they were in the library behind a closed door, he asked in a quiet distressed voice, "What's up, Flora? Is something the matter?"

"What? Oh, no. I apologize, Jonathan. I didn't mean to distress you," she immediately dismissed his anxiety. "I wanted to talk to you about Mary Julia."

"What about her?" he scrutinized with a puzzled expression on his face.

"Well...I don't exactly know how to say this, so I guess I'll just come right out and tell you what I think," Flora cautiously began. "Mary Julia has been through a great deal. She's fragile. I have to protect her. And...well...you're somewhat of a playboy, Jonathan. Your motto seems to be 'love them and leave them'. I simply don't want you to get any ideas in regards to Mary Julia. She is in *no way* prepared for some romance. Especially a wham, bam, thank you ma'am."

"Ouch, Flora!" Jonathan responded with a disapproving grimace. "I've made a heck of an impression on you; haven't I?"

"Oh, I'm not putting you down, Jonathan. Please don't think that," she promptly and contritely established, patting his arm in retribution. "You are a wonderful caring man. It's merely...it's obvious you greatly enjoy the game of chasing and capturing beautiful women. I've observed the way you've admired Mary Julia. I don't wish her to become one of your conquests. She could assuredly use your male friendship, but nothing else. Okay?"

"Understood, Mother Hen," he remarked with a hearty amused snicker. "Friendship is all I am proposing. Mary Julia appears to be a sweet lady. I'd like to help her come out of her shell. But yes, I noticed she is very lovely. I'd have to be blind, or dead, not to notice that. I promise I won't take advantage of her."

"Alright, Jonathan. I hope you aren't angry with me for saying what I did. I had to know your intentions," Flora further explained.

"No, of course I'm not angry, Flora," he guaranteed. "What you said is partially true. I don't take my romantic relationships with women seriously. Although I'm slightly better than...what was it...wham, bam, thank you ma'am?"

"I shouldn't have been so crude," she pointed out with embarrassment. "It's just...I don't think I've seen you with the same woman twice. But you are certainly entitled to live your life any way you desire."

"But not with your friends," Jonathan joked with an entertained laugh.

"No. Not with my friends, you heartbreaker!" Flora teased back, sharing his carefree laugh. She affectionately squeezed his arm.

"Understood, stepmother. In light of the fact I've agreed to be a good boy, may I have that walk and talk with Mary Julia now?" he continued to banter.

"Yes. Thank you oh so much; for being an amazing, understanding stepson. Your stepmother does appreciate it," Flora attested. She gave him a playful shove toward the door.

Flora was delighted Jonathan had chosen to spend more of his time with Mary Julia. She had hated warning him about his behavior. Nevertheless, she could not take any chances where her cherished friend was concerned.

Jonathan had a clear problem with any kind of commitment. Although, she knew quite well he could be a good friend. Presently, having a male friend was exactly what Mary Julia needed.

* * * *

Long Wolf phoned later than usual that evening. He normally called shortly after Jackie Lynn got home from work. Jackie Lynn was irate, because she had been fitfully waiting, *and wishing*, for the telephone to ring.

Over an hour had passed since she had arrived home. Jackie Lynn had found it virtually impossible to concentrate on accomplishing anything else, such as reading or watching television – Both of which she had unsuccessfully tried.

It had been ages since she had been preoccupied with receiving a man's calls. Jackie Lynn was not comfortable with this fact. She especially disliked the way her breath excitedly caught in her throat and her heart fluttered when the phone finally did ring. She happily discovered the caller was Long Wolf.

"How is my lovely lady this evening?" he cheerfully asked.

"I'm terrific, Mr. Romantic. Thank you very much for the flowers. They're pretty," Jackie Lynn showed her gratitude.

She smiled in appreciation at the arrangement sitting prominently on her coffee table. She had been unable to leave them behind at her office. That would have been wiser though, because they brought to mind too much the gentleman who had sent them to her.

"They aren't half as pretty as the woman I sent them to," Long Wolf complimented.

"Okay. Enough with the buttering up," Jackie Lynn proclaimed with an embarrassed snicker. "What exactly are you after, Long Wolf?"

"Well, since you ask, I'd love to have your company tonight," he amazed her by saying.

"Oh sure. By the time you take two hours to drive into the city and figure in the two it will take you to drive back home, you are talking about a very, very late night for a weeknight," Jackie Lynn logically pointed out.

"I will have to figure in the two hour drive back home but not the drive into the city. You see, I'm in the city. I haven't gone home yet. I had to work later than usual," he recounted. "What do you say? Will you agree to spend time with me, before I have to make that *lonely*, long drive home? You'd be doing this weary, hardworking businessman an enormous favor."

"Well…when you put it that way, how can I refuse?" Jackie Lynn commented with a relaxed, agreeable laugh.

I should turn him down, she was pondering. *But he sent me these pretty flowers. What could it hurt to see him for a short while? I long to be with him!*

"May I take that as a yes?" he prodded, sounding thrilled.

"Yes," she conceded. Jackie Lynn decided to foolishly follow her heart's desires and squelch the objections the intelligent part of her brain was loudly sounding.

"I'll see you shortly," Long Wolf announced, ending their discourse.

I'll be waiting, Jackie Lynn giddily recognized. She headed for her bedroom to make herself look more presentable for his visit.

* * * *

Mary Julia nervously waited for Jonathan in the great room, second-guessing her decision to take a walk with him. *This isn't a good idea,* she decided.

Mary Julia's paralyzing fear was making ordinary breathing extremely difficult. *No! I can do this! I shall!* she stubbornly assured herself. She rose to pace back and forth and force her lungs to start breathing normally.

Regardless, Mary Julia jumped as she heard her name being called. She looked up to observe Jonathan standing in the entranceway to the great room. Flora was at his side. "Are you ready to take that walk with me?" he suggested with a friendly grin.

"S...sure," she answered insecurely. She slowly compelled her uncooperative legs to move in his direction.

What if my legs were to buckle and I was to fall in the bushes? Would I yank him down on top of me? No, Mary Julia! No such thoughts! she sensibly chastised herself.

"Flora, would you care to join us?" she inquired.

"No," Flora hesitantly replied, ignoring Mary Julia's scared pleading eyes.

She could not constantly be by the girl's side to protect her. *If Mary Julia is going to fully recover, she has to handle being by herself with males without reverting to her old ways. No matter how hard this might be for her.* "You guys enjoy your walk."

This is it. I have to handle being with this man totally on my own. And deal with my overwhelming attraction to him in an appropriate manor, Mary Julia continued to give herself pep talks.

But she was uncertain what behavior was suitable between a man and a woman who were simply friends. This would be the first time in her life that Mary Julia had attempted such a thing. Regardless, it was vitally important she discover how to deal with men on a far less personal level.

"Come on, Jonathan. The flower garden is a lovely spot to be when the weather is this nice," she remarked with feigned cheerfulness. She bravely linked an arm with him and began dragging him along.

I'm able to do this! she concluded over and over. She vigilantly attempted to ignore the stirring sensation of his muscular arm touching hers.

* * * *

When the doorbell rang at Jackie Lynn's apartment, she had barely finished freshening up for Long Wolf. As soon as she had gotten off the phone, like a whirlwind, she had rapidly changed clothes. She had discarded the ratty T-shirt and loose shorts she lounged around the apartment in. Instead, she had put on slacks and an attractive, melon, somewhat low cut blouse.

Jackie Lynn had also vigorously brushed her long black hair to bring out its natural glossy sheen, and she had touched up her makeup. She had finished by applying her favorite perfume to her neck, wrists, and appealing cleavage between her breasts.

All the while she was pondering, *I shouldn't be doing all this. I should have stayed the way I was. Maybe that gorgeous man wouldn't be attracted to me. Perhaps he wouldn't remain long.* However, deep down, Jackie Lynn wished him to be attracted to her and to stay and visit with her for as long as he wanted.

When she opened the door and let Long Wolf in, he stared at her strangely and smiled as they walked toward the sofa. Jackie Lynn self-consciously wondered if she had smeared her lipstick across her face, or something equally distasteful, in her haste.

"Why are you looking at me that way?" she asked with paranoia, as they had a seat side by side.

"Oh, it's merely that I didn't expect you to go to so much trouble for me to pop in unexpectedly," he stated. "As usual you look very, very nice. You surely don't relax around here looking so immaculate."

"Thanks for the compliment," she acknowledged with an amused giggle. "Are you telling me you'd rather I look like a slob for you?"

"You couldn't look like a slob if you tried," Long Wolf flattered with confidence.

He found he was incapable of fighting the urge to touch her, so he gently caressed the side of her face. Jackie Lynn's cardiovascular rate elevated rapidly with exhilaration. As the inside of his hand softly slid toward her mouth, her lips uncontrollably responded. She lightly kissed the center of Long Wolf's palm. He hesitantly retrieved it.

"You have the most extraordinary lips in the world," he hoarsely informed her. His exquisite dark brown eyes studied her lovely alluring green ones with fierce desire.

So do you! she conceived, but was wise enough not to reveal. "Uh...can I get you anything?" she inquired. "Would you care for something to drink?"

Oh, yes! I'd love to drink the moisture of your skin! he contemplated with lustful yearning. *She's telling you to cool down, Long Wolf,* he concluded.

"No thank you. I have everything I want right here," he professed, gently squeezing her hand. "Tell me about your day. Any interesting cases?"

The most interesting thing to happen to me is currently being in your presence. The most interesting and hands down, *the most exciting.*

"Nothing thrilling," Jackie Lynn replied.

She struggled to get a grip on her untamed libido, before she foolishly took this man's hand and led him unchastely into her bedroom. "What about you? You were the one who worked late. What kept you in town, Mr. Greathouse?"

"More wheeling and dealing on another large construction deal," he disclosed with little interest. "That, and I stayed around hoping I could persuade a special lady to spare some of her time."

"Oh…and she refused so you came here; right?" Jackie Lynn joked.

"No, fortunately she agreed to see me and I came *here*," he answered with blatant admiration. He brought her hand to his mouth and planted a brief, but affirming, kiss on the back of it.

"Do you have any idea how much I'd rather be kissing your magical lips?" The question came out without Long Wolf planning it, but he sincerely meant it.

My Lord! If those lips of his touch mine again…I can't permit that to happen! Jackie Lynn determined with reasonable panic. She pulled back from him.

"Long Wolf, maybe you coming here wasn't such a good idea," she told him in a weak unsure voice.

"Oh no. It was a very *good* idea," he proclaimed.

He eagerly bridged the distance she had placed between their bodies. To Jackie Lynn's further horror, he securely wrapped his powerful arms around her back, squeezing their bodies together. Their faces, and of greater importance, their lips, were less than an inch apart.

"Tell me you don't want me and I'll release you." Long Wolf promised. His hot breath was blowing on the enchanting mouth he longed to possess.

Jackie Lynn parted her lips to speak, but she was stunned to hear no words come out. She could not make her mouth utter the lie. She wanted him. Jackie Lynn wanted Long Wolf so badly her body ached deep within.

"Long Wolf," she finally breathlessly called.

"Yes, darling, I'm here. I want you too," he heatedly professed. He lavishly smothered her responsive mouth with his scorching, insistent lips.

* * * *

As darkness started to settle in, Flora was beginning to get worried. She wondered if she should go outside and check on Mary Julia. She felt foolish, considering she genuinely trusted Jonathan.

On the other hand, he is a man after all. What if Mary Julia has thoroughly lost control of herself? Can Jonathan resist as he should? Will he try? Of course he will, Flora. This is ridiculous for you to be so distressed.

It was about this time she heard laughter and the front door closing. *Oh good! They're coming in. Everything's alright*, she accepted with relief.

Flora pretended to be reading a book. She glanced up as the cute couple entered the great room. They were giggling and smiling at each other. "Have you two been in the garden all this time?" she could not help but nosily probe.

There were not any lights in the garden. Hence, she could not imagine what they might have been engaging in out there in the dark. *Or rather I can. This is what had me worried.*

"No. Jonathan talked me into going out for an ice cream cone," Mary Julia admitted. She gave him another easy smile and a reminiscent chuckle. "He's one of the sloppiest ice cream eaters I've met. I had to wipe his chin he had such a mess. The boy has no licker."

Oh, wouldn't I love to find out differently? No. No thoughts such as this! she commanded.

Mary Julia had constantly been chasing every related consideration away throughout her interlude with Jonathan. She was proud of herself for having successfully done so. She had simply enjoyed his company as a male friend. Mary Julia was amazed *and thrilled* she could pull this off.

"Hey, it was the hot chocolate topping they put on those dream cones. It melted the ice cream faster than anyone could possibly lick," Jonathan defensively argued, seeming embarrassed.

Flora was glad they were relaxing together. The only thing that remotely upset her was the way their eyes continuously met and held. It was apparent they were attracted to one another.

"It seems the two of you had a good time together. I'm glad," Flora stated.

"Yeah. I did," Mary Julia confessed, displaying a grateful smile. "Thank you, Jonathan."

"The pleasure was *obviously* mine," he teased, pointing to the ice cream stains on his shorts. "Seriously, I enjoyed my visit with you, Mary Julia. Perhaps we could get together again fairly soon. What do you say?"

She did not hesitate before she consented, "Yes. I'd like that."

"Great," Jonathan declared with a magnetic smile. "I'll let you ladies settle in for the night. I have to be at University Hospital by 5:00 a.m. as the pediatric authority in the emergency room, so I should be turning in early tonight. You ladies have a splendid night."

"You too," they both said almost in unison.

"I'll be seeing you both," he uttered a friendly goodbye. Nonetheless, Flora noticed his eyes lingered unduly long on Mary Julia before he turned to depart.

CHAPTER FOURTEEN

KINDLING

The alarm woke Jackie Lynn from the most delightful dream. She reached with her eyes closed and hit the snooze button. She wished to take a few additional minutes to happily recall her marvelous fantasy. It had starred Long Wolf.

He had been kissing her over and over, making her utterly delirious with longing. He had effortlessly swept her off her feet, into his able arms, and carried her from the living room directly into the bedroom. There, Long Wolf had adeptly proceeded to sexually fulfill her as no man had done before. Jackie Lynn smiled and sighed with peculiar contentment.

Suddenly, she could feel Long Wolf's incredible lips upon hers. It was not until he whispered a husky "Good morning, extraordinary lady" that she opened her eyes in shock and accepted he really *was* there, sharing her bed.

That same instant, she consciously realized she had not been dreaming at all. She had been vividly remembering what had actually occurred the previous night. This conclusion astounded her. *Had it truly been that amazing?*

Jackie Lynn did not have to wonder this for long. Long Wolf's supple mouth left her lips and erotically trailed down the side of her neck, and along her bare shoulder. His hands expertly caressed and touched other instantaneously aroused parts of her.

Oh yes! It had indeed *been wonderful!! Long Wolf has awakened me in ways I've never imagined. He's undeniably the greatest lover I've ever had.* Jackie Lynn would have happily permitted him to take her on another impassioned ride to heaven. But Long Wolf's unanticipated, and unwanted, proclamation abruptly shocked her back to her senses.

"Jackie Lynn, I love you!" Long Wolf avowed, as he prepared to eagerly make their two bodies one once more.

His words were being declared in the heat of passion. They could not be sincere. Nevertheless, Jackie Lynn could not simply ignore them. A definitive and alarming *'I don't want you to love me!'* kept pervasively flooding through her brain.

"Long Wolf, don't!" she surprisingly protested all at once. She placed a hand firmly on each of his shoulders and shoved their bodies apart.

"Jackie Lynn? What?!" he probed in terrible confusion. He struggled to part from her at the last second.

She wanted to scramble from the bed, but Long Wolf's arms securely held her. Jackie Lynn settled for rising to a sitting position against the headboard. She ridiculously shielded her nakedness with the sheet, even though Long Wolf had lavishly touched each part of her. He slowly slid into a sitting position beside her, where he could carefully study Jackie Lynn's face. He needed an answer, or at least a clue, for her current unusual behavior.

As Long Wolf gazed into her eyes, he was dumbfounded to discover the scared doe look in them. He had assumed Jackie Lynn's fears had been squelched by their tender and extremely compatible lovemaking. Evidently he had been mistaken.

"Tell me, baby. Tell me what's wrong," he lovingly pleaded.

"I'm not a baby, or most especially *your* baby," she more strangely snapped, sounding angry.

Yes! That's exactly what he wishes. He wants me to be as helpless as a baby so he can control my life, until he becomes tired of me. I won't have it! I am a strong independent woman. I don't need a man in my life to survive!

Jackie Lynn would not enable Long Wolf to make her think she did by confusing her mind with such words as love either.

"Look, Long Wolf. It's vital I get out of this bed and get ready for work," she professed, determinedly slipping from her bed.

Jackie Lynn's mind and heart were racing. She hastily started towards the bathroom to shower *and to hide*. Prior to disappearing behind the door, she spun toward Long Wolf. He was lying on his side, with his head propped up on his elbow, attentively studying her with a stern expression on his face.

"I need time alone to focus on what has happened here," she explained, swiftly adding, "We evidently got carried away with the moment. And…"

"I'm not believing this," he impolitely interrupted with exasperation. "Yes, I'd confess that we most assuredly got carried away with the moment. Because it was one hell of a moment! We've been fighting our desires for each other since nearly the first instant we laid eyes on one another. You desperately wanted me and I desperately wanted you. You were free and unrestrained. It was as it's supposed to be between a man and a woman. Between a man and a woman who care about one another, as I think we do. Am I wrong? Can you honestly tell me you don't regard what happened as being absolutely remarkable and unparalleled?"

"Yes, Long Wolf. Last night was remarkable!" Jackie Lynn breathlessly acclaimed. She was unable to keep from pleasurably replaying it in her mind. "I'm not saying I regret what happened. It's just…well…I don't want us to get carried away. After all, we are both adults. This love stuff doesn't have to be a part of our little affair. It's not necessary for you to profess your love for me to take pleasure from great sex…well at least good sex. No!…I must admit it was *great*. See, I'm capable of admitting that without feeling I have to proclaim 'I love you'. So let's not begin acting as if we were teenagers, and start this 'I love you' stuff each time we decide to share a bed together."

Long Wolf started to speak, but Jackie Lynn promptly held up her hand to silence him. "No argument! I've got to get ready for work or I'll be late. Unlike you, I have a boss to report to. I'll get into the shower first. While my hair is drying, I'll put coffee on for us. You lay there and relish the moment," she smugly suggested. She had a satisfied grin on her face, as if she had just won her first big case in court.

Jackie Lynn turned around, advanced into her bathroom, switched on her favorite station on the radio, and moved fluently into her morning routine. She was pretending Long Wolf was not even there. He lazily sat up contemplating, *Man, this lady is definitely going to be a challenge! But I'm not called 'Wolf' for nothing.*

Long Wolf got out of bed. Without asking, he opened the bathroom door. He ever so quietly slipped the shower door open and stepped within, before Jackie Lynn could protest. "I thought I should at least wash your back in exchange for the kindness you've showed me. You know exactly what I'm referring to, letting me sleep over and all. *Most importantly*, sharing your bed and your *delicious* body with me for that *great* sex you mentioned in your speech earlier."

Long Wolf could tell from the look on Jackie Lynn's face that she was fuming. He grabbed her forearm and carefully spun her around so her back was to him. While holding her stationary, Long Wolf proceeded to slide his hand from her thigh and over her firm buttocks. He gave one cheek a slight squeeze, before moving his hands to caress her shoulders. At that point, he let go of Jackie Lynn's arm and began to use both hands.

Jackie Lynn was so mad she could not think straight. However, she was nearly paralyzed by the extraordinary feel of Long Wolf's warm tender hands. He slid them up and over her wet shoulders, then down and across the soft, sweet flesh of her breasts.

As she felt his lips on her wet neck and his tongue licking behind her ears, Jackie Lynn's breath caught in her throat. Between short panting breaths, Jackie Lynn attempted to speak, gasping, "Oh, please, we must hurry, or we will both be late…be late for…"

She could not make herself complete the sentence. She eagerly spun to face this tall scrumptious man. Jackie Lynn aggressively slid her hands through his dark, soft, chest hairs. Long Wolf's chest heaved with heated breaths of anticipation of what would come next.

Suddenly, Jackie Lynn forced herself to come to her senses. She swung around and carefully shoved Long Wolf aside. "This has got to end!! I'm not going to be late for work because of your lack of willpower and sexual needs!" she swore. She opened the shower door and quickly stepped out onto the cold, rude awakening floor.

Excellent! she noted. *I needed something cold to jolt my brain back to reality.*

Jackie Lynn had not bargained on Long Wolf following her and tormenting her further. He hastily grabbed her bath towel, before she could get her hands on it. "Long Wolf!" she protested. She reached in exasperation to take it from him.

Similar to a bullfighter dodging a bull, he expertly yanked it from her grasp. "I only wish to make certain you dry off properly," Long Wolf clarified with a suggestive smile and leering eyes.

He stepped toward her and proceeded to painstakingly, and quite erotically, move the towel over Jackie Lynn's entire body. He started somewhat innocently with her shoulders and back. When he brought it around to the front, and lingered appreciatively over her breasts, Long Wolf also pulled her to him and yearningly kissed her.

"Long Wolf..." Jackie Lynn tried to protest. But she could not utter another word. She could not restrain her lips, or her body, from enthusiastically responding to him.

"Don't go, Jackie Lynn," he pleaded in a hoarse insistent voice. He provocatively moved the towel lower. "Stay here with me. I need you. I want you. I long to demonstrate over and over how *great* it can be for us. Permit me to show you." Long Wolf kissed the side of her neck. Then he persistently moved his scalding tongue toward Jackie Lynn's heaving, expectant, erect nipples.

Oh, I haven't taken a vacation day in a while. What could taking today off hurt? she mindlessly pondered. She was entirely losing herself to the sexual madness Long Wolf was so easily evoking in her.

"If you mean that, why don't you replace that towel with something more meaningful?" she murmured seductively with feverish eyes. She swayed uncontrollably against the towel he was lewdly rubbing between her legs.

"You'll not have to ask me twice," Long Wolf concurred. He effortlessly swept Jackie Lynn off the floor, into his arms. He impatiently carried her into the bedroom, heading directly for the bed.

* * * *

After making love that morning, Jackie Lynn called her office to let them know she would not be in. She could not separate Long Wolf. She had never yearned to spend the entire day with any other man so intensely.

After she hung up the phone, since they were famished from their vigorous, unhampered, physical exertion, Jackie Lynn fixed them an enormous breakfast. She cleverly made use of what she happened to have on hand. She prepared delicious omelets, plentifully stuffed with ham, cheese and green peppers. In addition, she fried bacon and squeezed fresh orange juice.

Long Wolf was close to Jackie Lynn's side the whole time. He helped her dice up the ingredients for the omelets, and he took over the frying of the bacon while she squeezed their juice. He appeared to be as comfortable in the kitchen as she was, and Jackie Lynn had to admit she liked having him there by her side.

We're basically two people enjoying each other's company for the day. I'm going to relax and relish this day. I'm not going to worry about anything. It's one day. I deserve to indulge myself in a little fantasy and have great male companionship for a brief while. Tomorrow, I shall go right back to my normal life, she convinced herself.

So when Long Wolf suggested they go to his cabin for a few hours, Jackie Lynn agreed. She felt safe and secure with him. Hence, she would even walk the trails again if that was what he desired.

* * * *

At Long Wolf's cabin, Long Wolf adequately showed Jackie Lynn he could perform as adeptly in his own bed as he had in hers. She did not resist his passions, because she wanted him as greatly as, if not greater than, he wanted her.

Afterwards, they took a leisurely stroll along the majestic footpaths once more, winding deep into the forest interior. This time Long Wolf was careful to take along his walking stick. He shared with Jackie Lynn the Indian legend behind carrying this piece of wood. He showed her the carving on the side, which looked like a face. He explained that this was a carving of the Wood Spirit's image. Carrying the stick with this image upon it kept the Wood Spirits happy, and thus protected the wielder from harm. Jackie Lynn gave him a very skeptical look, and she kept an alert eye out for any snakes that might venture across their path. The two chatted comfortably and flirtatiously the entire stretch.

When they reached the pond, Long Wolf indecently proposed they discard their clothes and take a swim. Jackie Lynn was initially hesitant. But Long Wolf began kissing her lips and neck, and he sneakily pulled her T-shirt upward. She allowed herself to be persuaded.

It was the first time she had skinny-dipped. It gave her the most silly, delightful sensation of freedom. This man was introducing her to many new and marvelous experiences. Jackie Lynn could not remember being so overwhelmingly content in ages.

Enjoy the moment, she warned herself, warding off fears that had arisen all at once. Jackie Lynn knew too well how fleeting happiness could be. She did not expect it to last.

After playfully swimming together for quite a spell, Long Wolf hoisted himself onto the dock. He helpfully extracted his beautiful companion from the water as well. Placing his wet arm supportively around Jackie Lynn's water pearled body, he eagerly led her to the grassy plain where they had left their clothes haphazardly scattered.

After taking a seat on the lawn, Long Wolf intelligently proposed, "Come sit beside me. Let's permit the sun to dry our bodies a bit before we attempt to put our clothes back on." He patted the ground next to him, directing Jackie Lynn to also have a seat.

She willingly lowered herself to the ground, sprawled out on her side facing him, and propped her head up on an elbow. Grinning devilishly, she investigated, "Is drying off *all* you have in mind for us?"

"Well, truth be told, presently, I'm delighting in the view," Long Wolf confessed. He appreciatively surveyed her full breasts and her long, sleek, curvy body from head to toe. "You are *so* lovely."

His sweeping gaze in the bright illuminating sunshine caused Jackie Lynn discomfort, especially when she observed the look his eyes held. She fully expected to find lust there. Instead, his eyes were fixated on her as one would some sort of a treasure to be adored.

"Thanks for the compliment, but you know what they say. Actions speak *much* louder than words," she suggestively tantalized.

She endeavored to wholly divert Long Wolf's brain into regarding her only as a sexual object. Jackie Lynn obscenely reached to cup her hand around his observable erection. She lewdly commented, "It doesn't appear the cold water had any negative effects on you. You fit nicely into my hand as you always have. Makes me wonder if you'd feel the same everywhere else."

"My my! You don't give an Indian the opportunity to rest at all, do you?" he responded in a husky voice.

Long Wolf stretched out on his side beside Jackie Lynn. He slid her into his sturdy awaiting arms and savored her stimulating mouth. She yearningly rolled onto her back. She drew Long Wolf along with her and happily waited for him to take her to paradise. Jackie Lynn only intended to give herself to him this one day.

Tomorrow, she would put her guard back up and cool things down. Soon, Long Wolf, such as Jackie Lynn's other lovers, would move on to another woman. She knew the pattern too well, and it was fine. This way she never grew to need a man. Thus, she would not come close to repeating the mistakes of her mother.

* * * *

Jonathan called Flora Tuesday evening. He asked if she and Mary Julia might care to accompany him to dinner in the city Wednesday. He also asked if she had heard any more from his father.

"No. I haven't heard a word from him. This is odd, considering he usually calls a minimum of once a day." *To check up on me.*

"Oh, don't worry about him, Flora. Word from my doctor friends has it he has been very, very busy," Jonathan remarked, importantly adding, "He currently has no plans whatsoever to come home. Since you're temporarily abandoned, agree to have dinner with me tomorrow. Do you think Mary Julia will come?"

"I'll have to ask her. She hasn't been back to the city. It holds a lot of bad memories for her. But I think if she knows she'll be spending time with you, she will go. Thank, you, Jonathan, for what you're doing for her. She had a good time with you the other night. It's important she learns how to deal with being around men again," Flora confided.

Jonathan privately wondered what terrible thing had happened to Mary Julia. He started to interrogate Flora for more details, but he thought better of it. *I'd prefer to gain Mary Julia's trust and have her share it with me.*

"Give me a call after you find out. If she agrees, I'll plan to pick you both up around 5:00 tomorrow. If she doesn't feel up to it, the two of us could get together if you like."

193

Flora had to smile. It was obvious Jonathan did not wish to have dinner with *only* her. In fact, he would probably much rather have dinner exclusively with Mary Julia. Flora had been invited to dinner to make sure things were kept solely on a friendship basis between him and Mary Julia. Flora respected him for this.

"I'll talk to Mary Julia and I'll phone you later. Or I'll have her call you," she told him with a conspiratorial giggle.

"Fantastic. I'll be waiting to hear from one of you," Jonathan stated as the conversation ended.

* * * *

The next morning, Jackie Lynn woke up about a half an hour before her alarm was supposed to go off. She rolled over and stared with amazement into Long Wolf's serene slumbering face. *Why did I allow him to spend the night again?* she contemplated. *Because I didn't want our unbelievable rapture to end*, Jackie Lynn accepted, her body tingling with excitement at the mere thought of it.

As she fought the impulse to affectionately stroke Long Wolf's handsome appealing face, she decided, *It ends now! I'll send him away this morning. No matter what, I'll cool things off. He won't make me need him! Regardless of how extraordinary he might be in bed or how well we seem to get along otherwise! I have to make certain I keep my head on straight!*

With this resolve, Jackie Lynn rolled over so that her back was facing Long Wolf. However, before she could rise to a sitting position on her side of the bed, her movement awakened him. He immediately scooted against Jackie Lynn's backside and dropped his arm around her side. A second later, Long Wolf placed titillating kisses down the side of her neck and along her shoulder blade.

"Ah...It's early. We have awhile before we have to abandon this nice warm bed. What do you think we should do? I have a suggestion." he murmured. He ran his hand seductively up and down Jackie Lynn's side.

"Long Wolf," she protested in an excited pant. "We don't have time. I've got to get ready for work. I have to go in today. I can't be late."

"I know," he reluctantly conceded, her voice hoarse with longing. "I'll tell you what. If you will agree to have dinner with me after work, the possibility of what could happen later might hold me for a while. Otherwise, I'm not responsible for my actions at this moment. What do you say?"

"I say…yes," she gasped. Jackie Lynn struggled not to turn toward Long Wolf. He softly brushed the side of her heaving bosom, while he simultaneously tormented her with persistent kisses at the base of her neck.

Get out of this bed! Pronto! She knew full well, if she did not, she would not be able to resist him.

Jackie Lynn somehow found the strength, and she disengaged herself from Long Wolf's grasp *and those damned, powerfully persuasive lips.* She nearly leapt up to sprint toward the bathroom without looking back. "I'll be out shortly," she declared in a muffled voice. She disappeared behind the door and locked it. She climbed into the shower and blasted herself with frigid, revitalizing water.

CHAPTER FIFTEEN

SURPRISES

Long Wolf wanted to drive Jackie Lynn to work and pick her up afterwards for their dinner date. She told him it was necessary that she drive separately, because she had to visit clients during the day. He also required his automobile to conduct business, so he begrudgingly agreed they should take two different cars after all.

Jackie Lynn was relieved. She fully intended to cancel their date. There was absolutely no way she was going to get together with this dangerous man again so soon. Her hunger for him was unduly great. If she shared a meal with him, she would undoubtedly share her bed.

It's vital I nip this in the bud! No playing around! This thing, whatever it is, is getting overly serious! she warned herself.

Therefore, as soon as she reached her desk, the first thing Jackie Lynn did was phone Long Wolf's office. She knew full well he would not be there. He had disclosed he had a meeting that morning with a potential customer in the prospect's office building. It gave Jackie Lynn the perfect occasion to leave an apologetic, 'Sorry I'm unable to make it tonight' message on his answering machine, and so she did.

Okay. That's done, she proudly confirmed, as she lowered the receiver. Nonetheless, there was the strangest, yearning ache that occurred almost simultaneously. *Oh, for*

Peat's sake, Jackie Lynn! Yes, it was the most wonderful sexual experience of your life. That's no excuse for getting mopey over this guy! Get busy! Put him out of your mind!

Jackie Lynn attempted to study papers on her desk. She was having an awful time concentrating. She contemplated how unmistakably mouthwatering Long Wolf had looked that morning. He had come out of the bathroom in only a towel. Thankfully, she had just buttoned the last button of her blouse and was neatly tucking it into her skirt. Jackie Lynn had grabbed her suit jacket and scurried from the room.

Regardless, when Long Wolf had emerged from the bedroom fully clothed in his nice well-tailored suit, he had looked just as stunning and appealing. *Oh, and he had smelled delectable! I longed to eat him rather than having breakfast.*

"Good Lord!" Jackie Lynn exclaimed in frustration. She slammed the papers down on her desk. "I need to talk to someone about this before I lose my sanity. If I call Flora, I'll be able to put it in perspective and then get some work done."

She raised the receiver and dialed her friend's number. Naturally, the answering service responded. "May I speak to Mrs. Flora Roberts please? This is Betty Rogers calling in regard to her nail appointment," she ingeniously lied.

A few seconds later, Flora answered the telephone. "Yes, Ms. Rogers," she said with a chuckle, suspecting who it might really be.

"Yes, Mrs. Roberts. I was wondering if you'd like to try our newest fad? Black nails with white stars. The good witch look." Jackie Lynn proposed and giggled wildly.

"Of course," she concurred, sharing her friend's laughter. "After all, I must keep up with the other socialites."

They comfortably laughed for several seconds before Jackie Lynn scrutinized, "How is everything going?"

"It's going well," Flora happily disclosed. "I haven't heard from Jacob in a few days. Jonathan stopped by and took Mary Julia out for an ice cream cone the other day. Now, we are both supposed to go to dinner with him tonight. I couldn't be happier with her progress."

"Oh, that sounds marvelous!" she excitedly acknowledged. "I'm glad to hear that. If Mary Julia is able to be around that good-looking stepson of yours, she should be capable of being around practically any man. I'm so thrilled for her!"

"Yeah, me too. I tried to telephone you yesterday at the office. The receptionist informed me that you had taken a vacation day. Then I called your apartment, and you weren't there. So tell me, where were you?" Flora grilled. It was unlike Jackie Lynn to take a vacation day out of the blue, unless she had quite a good reason. "I hope this has something to do with our discussion about you pursuing your relationship with your Indian man."

"I pursued it alright," she admitted with noted aggravation. "We wound up in bed together Monday night. Not only did we end up in bed, but he spent the night. Then I spent yesterday with him, and he ended up spending the night again. Do you think I've significantly pursued it?"

"Oh, my goodness! This is beginning to sound serious. When was the last time you allowed a guy to spend two nights in a row with you? I'm not sure I remember," her friend pointed out.

"Flora, please don't tease me about this one," Jackie Lynn pitifully whined. "Things are moving way too fast with this man. I didn't intend to sleep with him. It turns out he is as giving and considerate in bed as he is out. I'm beginning to get scared."

"Don't start running, Jackie Lynn. He sounds fantastic," she advised. "Why don't you give yourself a break, relax and enjoy the affair. What's the worst that could happen?"

Jackie Lynn could not disclose what she believed the worst could be. It was the one thing she could *not* reveal to Flora *or anyone*. "I have no desire to *need* a man, Flora! He's the type of fellow a woman could easily lose control to if she permitted herself. I won't!" she proclaimed.

Jackie Lynn asked in a much quieter voice, "Did you say you and Mary Julia were going to dinner? May I join you? I could definitely stand a visit with you girls."

"Of course you can join us," Flora assured her. "How about we plan on picking you up at 6:30? I'll have Jonathan meet us there."

Flora clearly desired to spend one-on-one time with Jackie Lynn. *I have to attempt to talk sense into this woman. Her voice is light and airy each time she talks about Long Wolf. It's apparent she adores him. I won't permit her to push him away.* She believed the right man could make a woman's life complete, regardless of the fact that she had picked badly.

* * * *

Flora's limousine promptly arrived at 6:30 at Jackie Lynn's apartment. Jackie Lynn was delighted to see it. She had been pacing in the entranceway for about half an hour, impatiently awaiting her friends' arrival. She had not been able to endure being alone in her apartment any longer. She could swear Long Wolf's scent hung in the air.

Not only was there a message on Jackie Lynn's answering machine when she walked in the door, but Long Wolf had called again since then. Naturally, Jackie Lynn had not answered it. Hearing Long Wolf's voice, as he left yet another message, made her want to scream.

Long Wolf had also left numerous messages for her at the office. *He's truly trying to drive me insane!* Jackie Lynn noted in frustration. *It won't work. He won't conquer me. I'm a strong independent woman. No man is capable of destroying that. I won't think about him anymore tonight. I'll just enjoy being with my friends.*

Jackie Lynn raced out the door and toward the limousine. The chauffeur helped her into the limo. She plastered an exaggerated grin across her face as she joined her two best friends. "Hello, ladies. How are you?" she initiated pleasant chitchat.

She settled into the seat beside Mary Julia and directly across from Flora. The small, well equipped bar, within her reach, automatically caught her eye. Without asking, Jackie Lynn fixed herself a rather stiff bourbon and soda.

When she noticed Flora looking at her peculiarly, she suggested, "Can I fix you girls anything? I couldn't resist. I've always longed to have a drink in the back of a limo." In actuality, she greatly needed something to settle her raw nerves a bit.

"I'm going to wait until I get to the restaurant," Flora replied, a hint of disapproval in her voice.

"I'm not drinking," Mary Julia added. "I don't think it's wise for a while. Until I'm convinced I'm fully in charge of myself. Did something happen that upset you, Jackie Lynn. You snatched that drink too fast simply to be getting one for the hell of it. You seemed to especially need it. Trust me; I recognize the signs too well."

"I'm uncertain, but it might have something to do with the man in her life," Flora concluded with a knowing grin, not giving Jackie Lynn the possibility to answer.

"What about him?" Mary Julia curiously explored. She flashed Flora an eager smile, anxious for her to reveal whatever hidden information she possessed.

"Jackie Lynn has gotten very, *very* close to Long Wolf since we last talked to her," Flora betrayed. She knew Jackie Lynn never kept secrets from Mary Julia.

"Does she mean the two of you have slept together?" Mary Julia probed with shock, directing her full attention to Jackie Lynn.

"Thank you, Flora," Jackie Lynn hissed, her eyes displaying clear displeasure.

She took a few large gulps of her drink. Jackie Lynn made eye contact with Mary Julia and acknowledged, "Yes, Mary Julia. Long Wolf and I have slept together. I don't want to discuss that. I understand you have been spending time with Flora's stepson recently, and he is supposed to meet us tonight. That's wonderful. Are you aware of how well you are doing?"

"Yes," she brusquely replied. Then she curiously returned to her inquisition. "Why don't you wish to talk about Long Wolf? Was it a bad experience?"

"No. Quite the opposite," Flora aggravated Jackie Lynn by uninvitingly chiming in once more. "I'd venture to guess her experience with Long Wolf was one of the best Jackie Lynn has ever had. That's why she is afraid to share with us."

"I'm not afraid to share anything!" she defensively growled, slurping more of her drink. "I basically wanted to put him aside for tonight. He asked me to go to dinner with him. I chose to go with you two instead. I needed a night out with the girls."

"If he wished to have dinner with you, but you wanted to get together with us as well, why didn't you invite him also? We'd like to meet this guy," Flora pointed out with unveiled irritation. "You don't have to answer that. We both know you too well. When you claim you want to put him aside for tonight, you mean you want to put him aside *period*. So far, everything I've heard concerning this man leads me to conclude he should be a keeper. Why in the hell are you purposely trying to destroy things?"

Jackie Lynn emptied the remainder of her drink down her throat. Then she angrily answered, "You believed Jacob was a *keeper*! What if Long Wolf has deep hidden secrets I'm not aware of? I'm basically slowing things down, so I don't get hurt or involved in something that could ruin my life like you getting tied down with Jacob." The words automatically slid out of Jackie Lynn's mouth. She did not even stop to think about Mary Julia being in the car with them until it was too late.

"What's she talking about, Flora?" Mary Julia anxiously asked. "I got the impression the previous time we were all together there was some sort of tension between you and Jacob. I caught the worried looks that passed between you and Jackie Lynn when I mentioned him. What in the world could he have done to have ruined your life?"

Flora's eyes darkened with anger, disappointment and pain. She intently glared at Jackie Lynn. *Mary Julia isn't fit enough yet to be burdened by my unfathomable predicament. Jackie Lynn knows this.* It amazed Flora that Jackie Lynn had thoughtlessly aroused Mary Julia's suspicions. She did not have a clue what to say to their younger friend.

"Don't just sit there staring at one another as if somebody died," Mary Julia demanded, irritated by their continuing silence. "I get the feeling something horrible is going on here. I don't appreciate being left out of knowing what. You girls didn't used to keep things from me. Do you have so little regard for me, since you discovered my problems that you'll no longer share things with me? I can't stand this! I'm the same person you used to freely confide in. Or maybe a better person. I want you to tell me what's going on right this minute!"

"No, Mary Julia, of course we don't think less of you..." Flora denied.

"No, it's not that at all," Jackie Lynn seconded. She wrapped a reassuring arm around her shoulder and conveyed her apology to Flora with her eyes. "It's simply that you've been through so much yourself...well...Flora and I decided we'd wait to let you know…"

"Jackie Lynn, don't!" Flora interrupted in horrified disapproval. In a quivering voice she stated, "Mary Julia, I want you to concentrate on fully getting well. There isn't anything for you to concern yourself with me. Jacob and I have had some problems. I intend to solve things soon."

"Flora, I plan to focus on getting well," Mary Julia pledged. "But you are one of my dearest friends and if you are hurting it's essential that I know about it, so I can help if I'm able. Please tell me what's going on. What kind of problems have you and Jacob had?"

"Flora, I'm going to tell her," Jackie Lynn declared. She reached across to apologetically squeeze Flora's hand. "She has a right to know. She loves you too."

"There is nothing she can do," she argued in a feeble voice, fighting tears.

"Why not allow me to decide that?" Mary Julia stubbornly responded, looking toward Jackie Lynn for answers.

"There is no easy way to say this," Jackie Lynn somberly began. "Jacob has turned out to be a monster. He beats Flora."

"He...he...did you say, he beats her?!" Mary Julia gasped incredulously. She gawked from Jackie Lynn's to Flora's cringing face with shock and sympathy. "Then...why are you living with him, Flora?! We've got to get you out of his place!"

"Mary Julia, trust me when I say I'm working on that. I plan to depart at the same time you do," Flora sketchily disclosed. "That's all I'm able to divulge. That's all Jackie Lynn knows as well. She's not exaggerating when she calls him a monster. He's capable of killing, so I have to be very careful. It's not necessary for either of you to worry, because my plan is coming along well. I'll be out of Jacob's residence prior to his return, and he shall be out of my life for good. I love the two of you for being concerned and such amazing friends."

The three converged in a group hug, as Flora began to freely cry. Mary Julia started crying as well, weeping for her friend's sorrow and pain. "Oh, Flora, I feel terrible for you!" she lamented. "You have far too much on your mind already without being burdened with taking care of me. I should be staying with Jackie Lynn."

"No," Flora disagreed. She pulled back so she could look into her friend's caring eyes. "You being with me has been a Godsend. You keep my mind off how awful my life has become. You give my life meaning."

Besides, I want to spend as much time as possible with my friends during Jacob's absence. It might be a good spell before I have contact with them after I set my plan for freedom into full motion.

"Are you sure there isn't anything Jackie Lynn or I can do?" Mary Julia confirmed.

"I'm positive," Flora resolutely stated. "It's vital you keep your promise to me. I don't want you concentrating on my problems. I swear I have them under control. I want you focusing on yourself. You can make me happy by continuing to make yourself healthy. Okay?"

"Alright," Mary Julia assured her. She gave her a brief reassuring kiss on the cheek.

The trio separated and fell into a pensive silence. Jackie Lynn felt horrible about revealing Flora's secrets and upsetting her. Nevertheless, she was glad Mary Julia knew the truth. She had hated keeping things from her. It had been utterly unnatural, in light of the fact that the three had always openly shared everything. When Flora finally broke the silence, they all chatted about far less serious issues for the remainder of the ride to the restaurant.

* * * *

Jonathan was waiting for them just inside the door of the restaurant. Not so strangely, Flora and Mary Julia had chosen Cornucopia, one of their favorite restaurants. Nonetheless, tonight, it bothered Jackie Lynn terribly to be here. She and Long Wolf had dined in this restaurant twice, the last occasion being the previous night.

As soon as they were seated, coincidentally at a table near the one she had occupied the preceding evening, Jackie Lynn ordered a double vodka and tonic from the waitress. *I don't wish to start thinking about him*, she was desperately trying to convince herself. She absently twisted her cloth napkin in her lap. Flora painstakingly studied her friend's predictable behavior, pitying her but remaining silent.

Mary Julia was focusing her attention solely on Jonathan, and he on her. It was as if Flora and Jackie Lynn were not at the same table. She felt relaxed with him. It was like they had already become good friends, despite the fact they barely knew one another.

Jonathan asked her about her day. Even though Mary Julia had little to tell him, he listened attentively to her every spoken word, as if she was telling him a grand adventure story. Then he shared humorous tales concerning some of the children he had treated that day.

As they laughed together, Flora and Jackie Lynn exchanged an amused smile. "They make a cute couple. Don't you think?" Jackie Lynn whispered in Flora's ear.

Flora nodded and smiled wider. "You and Long Wolf probably do as well," she annoyingly added.

Jackie Lynn was relieved to observe the waitress approaching with her drink. She did not wait for the girl to sit it on the table. She practically snatched it from her hand. She hastily took a couple of hearty gulps. She hesitated and opted not to reply to Flora's observation. Noticing her friend's obvious distress, Flora wisely questioned her about work instead.

Jackie Lynn had just rapidly downed her second drink when Flora noticed her strangely gawking across the room. She detected something was plainly amiss when she beheld her friend's face turn a mortified shade of red. Long Wolf was walking right toward their table.

How?! How is it possible for this to be happening? How could he have found out where I am? How am I going to explain there are no clients...no business dinner?

Long Wolf stunned Jackie Lynn by saying, "Hello, darling." He walked up beside her, and he shocked her further by planting a brief kiss just to the side of her gaping mouth.

"I apologize for showing up out of the blue. I certainly didn't intend to interrupt your dinner with your clients, but I must confess I followed you here. I had just pulled in the parking lot of your apartment building to drop off your compact. You left it in my car last night. I was going to leave it in your mail slot," he remarked, taking it out of his pocket and holding it out to her. "I saw you rushing out and getting into that limousine, and I was curious about who you were meeting with and where you were going."

"You...you followed me? You shouldn't have done that, Long Wolf!" Jackie Lynn chastised in a low growl. A spark of angry resistance appeared in her captivating green eyes. *Who the hell does he think he is following me around?!*

"Long Wolf?" Flora impolitely interrupted with an approving smile. She extended a hand in his direction. "I'm glad to finally have the opportunity to meet you. I'm Flora Roberts, one of Jackie Lynn's best friends. I've heard many nice things about you. Permit me to introduce you to another of her very best friends, Mary Julia Walters, and my stepson, Jonathan Roberts. If you don't have any pertinent plans this evening, why not join us for dinner?"

Jackie Lynn glared somewhat hatefully at this backstabbing woman. Flora was zealously shaking Long Wolf's hand and grinning idiotically at him. *I can't believe this is happening!* she contemplated in horror. *For one thing, I'm supposed to be out with clients, as far as Long Wolf knew, and for another, I didn't want him having dinner with me tonight.*

"It's wonderful to meet you both and you also, Jonathan. I've heard a great deal about you ladies," Long Wolf admitted with a cheerful smile. Their waitress attentively hurried behind him. She investigated if they required another chair and place setting added to their table.

"Yes, please," Flora informed her. She slid her chair over and pointed to the space between her and Jackie Lynn. The waitress swiftly grabbed another chair. Jackie Lynn stood, in an almost drunken stupor, and rudely jerked her chair sideways to make room for Long Wolf.

A second later he was sitting right next to her. He took Jackie Lynn's hand into the both of his. "I'm sorry, sweetheart. I must have misunderstood. I thought you said you had a business dinner. I followed you here simply to find out what big shot you were representing that had arranged to have you picked up in a limo. I hadn't meant to intrude on your dinner. You appear to be upset with me. This deeply disturbs me. I don't know if I can stand that furious look much longer."

"Stop talking to me like that!" Jackie Lynn sharply slurred, in a hushed tone. She defiantly fought to remove her hand from his.

"Like what?" Long Wolf investigated in confusion. He tightened his grip around her soft hand.

"That sweet, mushy, darling and sweetheart crap. What's that about anyway? You don't have to put on a show for my friends," she critically accused.

"I'm not putting on a show," he vowed in a voice barely above a whisper. "Look, perhaps you could use some fresh air. Can we please go someplace private and discuss what could possibly be bothering you?"

"No," Jackie Lynn rigidly stated. "*We* cannot!"

She rose on shaky legs, nearly turning her chair over. She tapped Jonathan on his shoulder saying, "Come on, Jonathan. I love this song. Dance with me."

Having their personal discussion rudely interrupted, Mary Julia's eyes darted from Jonathan's alluring, attentive face to Jackie Lynn's hovering, unsteady form. She unconsciously was glaring at her with a perfect mixture of bafflement and anger. Before he acknowledged Jackie Lynn's strange request, Jonathan caught a glimpse of the transparent annoyance on Mary Julia's face.

Is that jealousy I'm observing? he wondered, an unforeseen satisfaction registering.

"Um…Jackie Lynn, I'd love to dance," he remarked with a radiant smile. He looked into Mary Julia's disappointed face, before he gently clasped one of her small, delicate, pretty hands. "But I promised the first dance to Mary Julia."

Mary Julia's face lit up. She rose to her feet beside Jonathan. The live band was playing a slow, romantic, popular song. Prior to eagerly leading Mary Julia across the restaurant toward the dance floor, Jonathan glanced over his shoulder and suggested to Jackie Lynn, "Long Wolf might welcome a dance with you."

Long Wolf had already risen to his feet. He possessively placed his arm around Jackie Lynn's shoulder. He squeezed her against him and confirmed, "Yes. I would love to dance with this beautiful woman." Glancing in Flora's direction, he pleaded, "Please excuse us for a minute, Flora."

Without waiting for Flora's response, Long Wolf stubbornly led Jackie Lynn towards the dance floor. "Long Wolf, let go of me!" She softly, yet viciously, demanded through gritted teeth.

"I will. But only if you will go outside with me and talk," he agreed.

"Alright," she hissed, struggling against his secure hold.

Long Wolf reluctantly released Jackie Lynn then. Lightheaded, she rushed towards the nearest door. In her irrational, drunken state, rather than going out the door to the parking lot, she ended up navigating them out the door leading into the garden. Jackie Lynn's stomach dropped as she spied the other various couples milling around there. It was the place for lovers to take a private moment together. Each couple appeared to be entirely lost in themselves. Some strolled side by side, with arms tightly intertwining around one another's bodies, and some sat on benches by the fountain, speaking with their faces quite close.

When she tried to turn back, Jackie Lynn lost her balance and fell straight into Long Wolf's outstretched and supportive arms. He instinctively tightened his grip and pulled her against his sturdy chest. He stared adoringly into her eyes and rubbed his hands soothingly down the small of her back. Jackie Lynn was overwhelmed. She felt like crying.

"Long Wolf, I'm begging you," she pleaded in a pitiful defeated voice. Her eyes filled with hot salty tears, which began trickling down both cheeks in a steady stream.

"I…I need…I can't…I basically need for you to leave me alone. You don't understand…this is too much…too fast!" At that point, she started sobbing uncontrollably on his shoulder.

"Jackie Lynn, I'd do almost anything for you. But leaving you alone is something I simply cannot do," Long Wolf quietly rebuffed. He placed his hand beneath her chin to raise her face, so he could gaze directly into her lovely, watery, emerald eyes.

Jackie Lynn looked into his gentle, comforting, deep brown eyes. Her lips impulsively parted ever so slightly. Long Wolf could not resist her luscious, warm, inviting mouth. He moved his own mouth to passionately devour hers. He could taste the salt from Jackie Lynn's tears on her lips.

As always, Jackie Lynn's headstrong, self-imposed restraint against this man was thoroughly lost. Rather than fighting him and shoving him away, she heartily reciprocated his advance. She smothered Long Wolf's mouth, outside and in, with her wet, eager, responsive lips and fiery, adept, teasing tongue. It was only after several breathtaking moments that Long Wolf gained the strength to remove his lips and disengage himself from this fascinating lady.

"Tell me you're completely immune to the absolute magical passion that exists between us," he gasped in a heated whisper. He stared into Jackie Lynn's dazed eyes with eyes which were noticeably desirous.

Not expecting her to reply, Long Wolf quickly continued, "The passion we share is rare, Jackie Lynn. Surely you must realize this. It's not merely normal sexual attraction. It's something much, much deeper. It's overpowering for me. It is for you as well. If it scares you, that's okay. It scares me too. But, please, don't run. Don't throw away the extraordinary pleasure we experience with one another. Permit me to freely bestow gratification. I need to do this more than anything I've done in my life. And you wish it as badly as I do. Please, darling," he pleaded. He drew her back against him. He further teased her by seductively running his hot, moist, scorching lips along the side of her neck.

"Okay," she urgently consented in a breathless voice. The very core of her was stirring in fluent response to Long Wolf's moving words and his gentle touch. "Take me home. Now!" Jackie Lynn demanded. She planted one conclusive, aggressive, lengthy, longing kiss on his scrumptious mouth.

"Let's go say goodbye to your friends," Long Wolf reluctantly proposed when they separated.

Going back into the restaurant and talking to Jackie Lynn's friends was not what he wanted to do. Long Wolf actually yearned to rush them to his car and speed away to Jackie Lynn's apartment and her awaiting bed. But he did not desire to be impolite to her friends or cause them distress if she disappeared without a word. So, the two hastily made their way back inside the restaurant and to their table.

Flora was at the table by herself. Mary Julia and Jonathan were still dancing. "Flora, thank you so much for inviting me to join you for dinner, but Jackie Lynn isn't feeling well, so I am going to take her home," Long Wolf spoke for both of them.

Jackie Lynn simply nodded her head. All she could focus on was isolating herself with this irresistible man. Her body was literally aching for him.

Flora smiled and nodded at Long Wolf. "Take excellent care of her, Long Wolf. She does look a bit feverish now that you mention it," she remarked with a wicked, knowing snicker.

"Don't worry. I intend to take *very* excellent care of this beautiful lady," Long Wolf assured Flora. His lips curved into a cozy attractive smile, as he hastily departed with Jackie Lynn close at his side.

Flora happily watched them exit, tightly clinging to one another. She shook her head and smiled. *To me, they obviously seem to be in love, even if that headstrong friend of mine can't bear to admit it.*

Flora wished Long Wolf could somehow tear down the impenetrable, protective wall Jackie Lynn kept staunchly in place. This wall prevented any man from truly receiving her love. *Jackie Lynn deserves to have the love of a good man, and so does Mary Julia.*

Flora turned around and patiently waited for her other friend and stepson to rejoin her at the table for a pleasant dinner.

* * * *

Mary Julia and Jonathan were strangely quiet subsequent to their return to the table. They seemed oddly uncomfortable around each other all at once. Both appeared to be lost in their own silent musings.

When their meal was over, Jonathan walked the two of them out to the limo. He bid a pleasant goodbye to each of them before going to his automobile. Settling into the limousine for the long ride home, Mary Julia seemed unexpectedly despondent.

"Mary Julia, what's the matter?" Flora investigated. She was distressed by her friend's peculiar silence and sudden unhappiness.

"I don't know, Flora. It's difficult being a freak," she declared, her eyes puddles of sadness.

"Why in the world are you saying that, Mary Julia?" her dear friend demanded. "You're doing wonderful!"

"Oh, yes. Marvelous!" she acknowledged with heavy sarcasm. "Why did my legs nearly crumble when I sensed Jonathan wanted to kiss me on the dance floor? I felt like a total fool. He instantly guided me off the floor and helped me back to our table. Did you notice he hardly looked at me or talked to me the rest of the night? Who could blame him? He's bound to be getting tired of my screwy behavior."

What Flora had observed was that *both* Jonathan and Mary Julia had looked upset upon their return to the table. Having a female friend was new for Jonathan. If he had wished to kiss Mary Julia, that meant he was attracted to her as Flora had assumed.

"Mary Julia, there is something you should know. I think I know why Jonathan acted the way he did. It may have been my fault."

"Your fault?" she repeated with puzzlement, her eyes intently studying Flora's.

"Yeah. You see, Jonathan has always been a big playboy. He collects women such as some men collect baseball cards. Only he trades them regularly, one for another. So I took him aside and told you were off limits. I made him promise he'd *only* be your friend. Nothing else. Hence, if he had the desire to kiss you, he probably didn't know how to handle it any greater than you did. He may have been as scared as you," Flora shared.

"That might explain the look I saw in his eyes before he led me back to the table," Mary Julia theorized, half to herself. "I figured he was merely confused by *me*. Maybe he was confused by his own emotions as well. I hope you're right, Flora."

"You really like Jonathan don't you, Mary Julia?" she dared to suggest.

"Yes. I do. I could definitely use his friendship. I have to confess, I longed for him to kiss me. But the mere thought of anything other than being friends with Jonathan scares me to death right now. Do you think he's capable of being my friend, or do you think he will run far away?" the confused woman wondered.

"I honestly don't know," Flora answered. "He's been a remarkable friend to me, but I'm his father's wife. That makes it easy for Jonathan to *merely* be my friend. On the other hand, him being a friend with an attractive *single* female is entirely another thing. I truly wish he'd continue to try and be your friend, Mary Julia. Because you could be good for one another."

"Me too," she remarked in quiet voice. She settled into a dejected silence.

Flora's heart ached for Mary Julia. Her younger friend clearly was interested in Jonathan. Mary Julia was distinctly contemplating more than friendship with him.

Will it be better for her if Jonathan does decide to keep his distance for a while, or will he continue to help Mary Julia heal if he keeps coming around?

Flora was uncertain of the answer. She became lost in her own deep, concerned, silent reflections for the remainder of the long ride back to the mansion.

* * * *

It was late when they arrived home, and they were both tired from the lengthy car ride. The two ladies headed upstairs to their bedrooms to retire for the night. Mary Julia's room was at the top of the stairs. Flora's was at the end of the extensive hallway. When they got to the top of the stairs, Flora took a moment to wish Mary Julia a good night's sleep, reassure her not to worry about Jonathan, and give her a brief, reassuring hug. Then she proceeded down the hall to her own room.

When Flora opened her bedroom door, she was unsettled to discover the light was on. *Perhaps I forgot to turn it off earlier*, she concluded, easing her concern.

She proceeded to the bed, sat on the side, and immediately kicked her high heels off. She pulled her silk blouse out from her skirt, slowly unbuttoned it, peeled it from her body, and laid it neatly on the bed beside her. She had just reached behind her to undo her bra when *his* familiar cutting laughter caused her to jump erratically.

Flora spun her head sideways to find Jacob emerging from the bathroom. His eyes were wickedly leering at her. Her heart leapt into her throat, threatening to choke Flora with each erratic beat.

How can this be possible? How could Jacob possibly be here?!

"Hello, my deceitful, disobedient wife. You *are* glad to see me, aren't you?" Jacob explored. He stumbled toward her. It was apparent he had been drinking. The overwhelming stench of the alcohol and his red face were clear signs he had been drinking a lot.

"J...Jacob. What...what are you doing home?" Flora questioned in shock. She released the clasp to her bra and left it in place. She desired to wrap her silk blouse back around her, but she knew Jacob would not allow that.

"Hmm...what am *I* doing home?" he parroted, plopping down on the bed and barely missing Flora's lap.

He grabbed a fistful of her hair, and he yanked her face very close to his. As Jacob began to talk, she recognized the overpowering odor of alcohol on his breath. "This is *my* home, isn't it?! I wasn't sure if you remembered that. I wasn't even sure if you remembered you had a husband. A husband who you made certain vows to. A husband who you made certain promises to. A husband who you disobeyed and lied to. That would be *me*; right?!" he questioned. He released her hair but tightly clutched her jaw. With his other hand, Jacob suggestively ran a finger down between Flora's breasts and began toying with the top of her bra.

Say something quickly to try and calm him! Flora silently ordered herself.

"Yes, Jacob. Of course, you are my husband," Flora replied and was quick to add, "And I am *very* glad to see you. I know you are upset about Mary Julia being here, and you have every right to be. I never meant to break my promise to you. But as I explained to you on the phone, she was only staying here while you were away. I'm terribly lovely when you're away for so long – please understand. Now that you have returned, naturally, I will tell Mary Julia that she must leave. I'll send her away first thing in the morning. Then you will have me all to yourself again, and all of my attention can be solely centered on you once more, as it should be. I always want to be a good wife to you, Jacob. That is what matters most to me. I am so sorry that I have upset you, my darling. Let me try and make it up to you."

"Well, aren't you just the perfect little wife!" Jacob sarcastically uttered. A small spray of disgusting spittle sprinkled Flora's check as he pronounced the 'p' in perfect.

Jacob was very inebriated, and Flora prayed that this would work to her advantage. She could tell that he wanted to hurtfully enact his revenge on her for disobeying his commands – *I had contact with my friends once more.*

"How I wish that it was true that I *was* the perfect wife, Jacob," Flora continued to carefully play along. "But obviously I'm far from perfect. As I was saying, I am so sorry that I have upset you. I'm begging you to let me try and make it up to you. Let me show you how much I've missed you while you've been gone," she pleaded. Flora deliberately placed her hand between Jacob's legs and began to persuasively stroke.

She felt sick to her stomach. Nevertheless, Flora understood that she had no option but to have sex with Jacob or be severely beaten. Of greater importance was how his unforeseen, unappreciated re-emergence would affect every one of her and Jonathan's carefully laid plans for her escape.

Flora could not believe Jacob had come home early. She had not felt this awful in ages. *Why hadn't Jonathan's informant called to warn him?*

Jacob reached behind Flora to roughly release her bra. He started cruelly clawing at her naked breasts. "Is this what you want, Flora? You want to freely give yourself to me? Your body has missed your husband? Is that what you are trying to tell me?"

"Yes, Jacob. I've missed you terribly. Please make love to me!" she begged. She undid his belt and unzipped his pants.

"If this is so, and you are in such a damn hurry to have me make love to you, then get that damn skirt and pantyhose off....now!" He snapped his fingers and ordered, as if she were a dog.

Flora immediately stood and unzipped her skirt and shoved it to the floor. She stepped out of it and pushed her pantyhose down as well. Jacob staggered to his feet, and shoved his pants to the floor. He shoved Flora back onto the bed and lay down on top of her. She numbly lay there to allow him to do as he liked.

Since Flora was in no way aroused, having sex with Jacob was very painful to her. What was fortunate, however, was that he was so overwhelmingly drunk that it was over within minutes. When Jacob rolled off of her and immediately fell into a heavy drunken slumber, Flora crept into the bathroom and repeatedly threw up.

She rose on unsteady legs, pulled a terry cloth robe off of a peg on the back of the bathroom door, and wrapped it tightly around herself to try and stop her violent shivers. She was plagued with despair. *I'll never get away from this man.* All hope appeared to be lost. Flora lowered herself back to the bathroom floor by the toilet and brokenheartedly cried herself to sleep.

CHAPTER SIXTEEN

ESCAPE

When the alarm awoke Jackie Lynn, she was mystified to discover herself alone in bed. *Where's Long Wolf gone?* she wondered. She slowly arose to a sitting position on the side of the mattress. *Perhaps he didn't spend the night this time. Maybe he sneaked out after I fell asleep.*

Part of her hoped this was true. It was too hard waking up in his arms each morning. *Sex. Great sex. That's all there is between us. That's all I want between us. So if he has left, then so much the better. I can keep my emotions out of it much easier this way,* Jackie Lynn convinced herself.

About this time, she could swear she smelled coffee and bacon. *Am I imagining that?* Jackie Lynn sluggishly climbed from the bed and curiously headed for the bedroom door.

She had not gotten far when the door opened. Long Wolf stood in the doorway in his sexy, form fitting, black boxers. He was holding a tray full of food. "Good morning, beautiful!" he greeted in a chipper voice, an attractive, satisfied smile on his face. "I was going to serve you breakfast in bed but I see you are already up."

Thoroughly and somewhat indecently scrutinizing Jackie Lynn's naked body from head to toe, he suggested, "I think you should put something on, or I might not be able to resist sampling you instead. Even though I am starving for food, looking at your lovely inviting body is whetting my appetite for something other than that."

Yes, I can certainly tell this is true. There is a significant bulge in his boxers that's impossible to miss. It makes me hungry for things other than food as well.

Knowing she needed to control her rampant impulses, Jackie Lynn abruptly turned and rushed across the room to her closet. She pulled a short, slinky, red, silk robe from a perfumed hanger and covered her nakedness with it.

When she turned around, Long Wolf had sat on the side of the mattress with the tray sitting beside him. He was clearly waiting for Jackie Lynn to join him. "How long have you been up?" she asked. She walked back over to the bed and sat down. The tray was between their bodies.

"Long enough," he answered, handing her one of the cups of coffee. "My stomach woke me. Or perhaps I was hearing yours rumbling. We never did take time to eat last night."

"Uh-huh," she briefly responded, with an automatic reminiscent smile. She took a cautious sip of her steaming coffee.

Jackie Lynn's only appetite the previous night had been for Long Wolf, and he for her. But, she had to admit she was starving now. "You should have waked me if you were hungry. You're my guest. I should be making your breakfast. Not the other way around."

"Personally I like it when we make breakfast together. I enjoy when we do *anything* together," Long Wolf confessed. He was unconsciously studying the movement of Jackie Lynn's mouth as she chewed a piece of bacon. He picked up another piece and placed it in his own salivating mouth. "Speaking of doing things together...I'm planning on visiting my mother at the Reservation this weekend, and I'd like for you to come with me. What do you say?"

"Your mother?" she repeated, sounding a bit on guard. "You want me to meet your mother?"

I know what it means when a man wants a woman to meet his mother. This sounds way too serious to me.

An amused smile appeared on Long Wolf's face, and as if reading Jackie Lynn's mind, he said, "I want for you to go away with me. I want for the two of us to have wonderful fun together, isolated from worry, business and otherwise. And, yes, I would like for you to meet my mother, as well as other members of my family, and even some of my friends. But, I can assure you this should be no cause for panic. I just think you will have a very good time, and it will be relaxing for us both. So please don't turn this idea down unless you have a very, very good reason. Don't use some big client or case as an excuse."

I really blew things when Long Wolf caught me at dinner last night with my friends. Now, he'll never believe my excuses of special clients or overly busy cases.

Quite strangely, however, the realization slowly dawned on Jackie Lynn that she did not want to make an excuse for not going away with this man. *I want to go*, she reluctantly allowed herself to accept. *It's been a rather long time since I've gone anywhere, and a trip to an Indian Reservation sounds like it might be fun.*

"Okay. I'll go with you," Jackie Lynn found herself too eagerly agreeing. She hastily picked up her plate of scrambled eggs and began to fill her mouth with them before she foolishly conceded to anything else.

She was amazed by how delicious her food tasted and decided to confide this to Long Wolf. "I can tell by the taste of this food you're adept in the kitchen as well," Jackie Lynn noted with a pretty appreciative smile, and naughty eyes.

"As well? As well as *where*?" Long Wolf mischievously teased with a playful chuckle, comfortably hooking an arm around her waist.

"You know too well where," she laughed. She demonstrated by glancing at the bed and then back at his face. "We don't have time for you to show me once more. So don't get any big ideas, Mr. Long Wolf. Fixing me breakfast is enough. I need to finish eating, take my shower, and get ready for work."

"Yeah, I know. That's why I got up early and fixed our breakfast. But, darling, you have to admit we would save time if we showered together," he proposed with twinkling, suggestive eyes. Long Wolf bent his head sideways to bestow a brief inviting kiss on the side of Jackie Lynn's neck.

"Of course," she concurred with a satisfied giggle and teased, "I suppose the least I can do, after you've been so wonderful as to fix me breakfast, is grant you the chance to prove yourself in each room of my apartment."

"Ah…wonderful! That still leaves the dining room and the living room," Long Wolf enthusiastically pointed out.

"Not this morning, it doesn't," Jackie Lynn rectified. She placed a firm hand on his broad dark-haired chest and fiercely pushed him away from her. Nevertheless, her face held the most radiant smile and her eyes literally gleamed with happiness.

I will get through to this woman somehow, Long Wolf secretly calculated, intently studying her. *She has feelings for me. I'm positive of that. I just need to figure out a way to help her reveal them.*

"Let's hurry and finish eating, so we can take that shower," he suggested. He handed Jackie Lynn her piece of toast, as he concentrated on finishing his own food.

* * * *

Mary Julia distantly heard her name being called. She sleepily opened her eyes, and was met by Jonathan's gorgeous, stunning, ocean blue eyes. She thought she must surely be having the most wonderful dream.

She discovered otherwise as she heard him say, "I'm sorry to wake you, Mary Julia, but I need for you to pack. I need to get you and Flora out of this house right now!"

"Wh…what?" she stuttered in confusion. She vigilantly tried to force her groggy brain to concentrate on Jonathan's alarming words. Pushing herself to a more attentive, sitting position, Mary Julia asked, "What do you mean, Jonathan, about needing to get us out of this house? What's wrong?"

"I don't have time to explain it all right now. Just please get dressed," he said. Jonathan allowed his eyes only a few seconds to linger appreciatively on the attractive way her silk nightshirt clung to her ample bosom. "And pack. Then wait here until I come and get you. I want you to lock the bedroom door when I leave too," he warned with a very serious tense face.

"Does this have something to do with your father? Is he coming home early?" She surprised him by asking.

"I take it Flora has told you what a monster he is?" Jonathan inquired.

When Mary Julia hesitantly nodded, he said, "Well, I'm sorry to inform you that he's home now. In fact, he returned home some time yesterday evening, while we were all out having dinner. There was a message on my answering machine last night when I got home telling me Jacob had left Europe. Then I called here and the answering service said he had turned in for the night and had requested that he not be disturbed. I hate to ask you this, Mary Julia, but are you a heavy sleeper? Could you have slept through screams and things being broken?"

"Oh, God, Jonathan! Do you think he's beaten Flora again?!" she asked in panicked terror. Mary Julia scrambled instantaneously from the bed and stood beside him. "We've got to go see if she's alright. I didn't hear anything last night, but what if he has done something terrible to her?!"

Unwisely, she started to race past him toward the door, but Jonathan grabbed her arm. He brought Mary Julia to an abrupt halt. "No!" he quietly, yet resolutely, spoke. "I'm going to check on Flora. You are *not*! You're staying right here, getting dressed, packing your stuff and waiting for me to come and get you. This is important, Mary Julia. I need to know that you are safe while I go and make sure Flora is also. Please promise me you'll remain locked in this room and get ready to leave this house."

Mary Julia studied Jonathan's extremely worried eyes. She realized the most essential thing was her dear friend's welfare, so she conceded to his wishes. "Okay, Jonathan. I'll stay here. Just please go take care of Flora. Hurry, please!!"

Jonathan despised the fear he now saw in Mary Julia's lovely eyes. He wanted to comfort Mary Julia, but he recognized that he did not have time right now. "I'll be back as soon as I can. Everything is going to be fine," he endeavored to assure her, with greater confidence than he actually felt.

He turned to depart, but as Jonathan stepped into the hall, he spun back around and motioned for Mary Julia to come and lock the door. She rushed to the door and hastened to turn the lock.

God, please let Flora be okay! Mary Julia prayed as she expeditiously turned to go and get dressed and begin packing her suitcase.

* * * *

Jonathan hastened down the hall to his father's room and quietly opened the door without knocking. Walking into the bedroom, he spied Jacob sprawled across the mattress, snoring loudly. He noted that Flora was not in the bed with him and wondered with concern where she might be.

He crept very gingerly across the room toward the bathroom. When he entered that room, he was shocked to find his stepmother lying on her side on the floor in front of the toilet. He raced to her side and was very relieved when he discovered she merely appeared to be sleeping. However, Flora's cheeks were chapped from the endless tears she had shed during the night. She had cried herself to sleep.

Damn! What horrible things did Jacob do to her prior to her taking tearful refuge in this bathroom? Jonathan angrily wondered.

Kneeling beside her, he very gently shook her shoulder. "Flora," he called in a persistent whisper. "Please wake up."

She stirred after a few seconds and looked up into his face with total bewilderment. She slowly rose to a sitting

221

position, pulling her terrycloth robe tightly around her to entirely cover her nakedness. "Jon... Jonathan? What…what are you doing here?" Flora asked with uncertainty. It took her a few more seconds to gain total consciousness and remember what *she* was doing there.

"Shh," he abruptly warned. Then he murmured in a deliberately quiet voice. "Jacob is still sleeping. Are you alright? Has he harmed you?"

"No, not physically," she answered in a whisper, her eyes full of hopelessness. "But our plans are blown, aren't they, Jonathan?" Flora very pitifully stated. "I'm never going to get away from him now."

"No, Flora, don't think like that. Our plans aren't blown. Just changed," he reassured her. "We need to start by you getting out of this room before that bastard wakes up."

Jonathan rose then and held out his hand to help pull her to her feet. Flora took hold of his hand and rose beside him on unsteady feet. He very quietly led her out of the bathroom.

Jonathan was relieved to observe that his dad was still soundly sleeping. He continued to lead Flora across the bedroom and to the precarious safety of the hall. He softly closed the door behind them.

"What now?" she asked in bewilderment.

Flora tightly tied her robe, since it was the only clothes she had on. She was grateful the robe was large and bulky and fully covered her from just below her neck to just below her knees. She still wished Jonathan had at least given her time to slip some undergarments on, but she understood the necessity of escaping the bedroom before Jacob awoke.

"Go down to breakfast," Jonathan instructed. "I'm going to get Mary Julia. Then we'll all eat together. I'll find a way to get Jacob out of the house. I already have Mary Julia packing. So once I've gotten rid of my father, you can throw a few things in a suitcase and I'll get you out of this house too."

"Out of the house?" Flora questioned in wonderment. "Where are you taking us?"

"You're coming to my house for the time being," he hesitantly disclosed.

Jonathan knew Flora was going to object. He had come up with this idea previously, and she had promptly rejected it. Flora did not want to put anyone in the line of danger from Jacob.

"It will only be temporary. I'll have you away from there before my father has any idea where you are," he promised, silencing Flora before she could speak. "Now please go downstairs, Flora, while I go get Mary Julia."

She decided not to argue with him. *This young man might be my only hope.* Flora could not stand being in this house with Jacob for another day. *If he doesn't physically kill me then, at the very minimum, I will lose my mind.*

Flora separated from Jonathan's side at Mary Julia's bedroom door. She proceeded to make her way down the stairs as Jonathan was knocking on her friend's door, softly announcing it was him. *I'll go downstairs and inform the cook that the three of us are ready to eat breakfast and I'll patiently wait and see what Jonathan's next move will be*, Flora concluded.

* * * *

Once Jonathan made sure Flora and Mary Julia were safely downstairs, he went into his father's study and called the hospital. He knew if Jacob was offered some interesting, challenging, surgical feat, the egomaniac would be out of bed and out of the house very quickly, for several hours. It would not matter whether he was suffering from a hangover or not. After all, it was not as if his father valued human life at all. If some physical impairment caused him to make a mistake that took a life, Jacob was always very shrewd about casting the blame onto some inexperienced nurse or young intern.

Luckily, the brilliant doctor very rarely loses a life. He truly is a very competent, talented surgeon. Even if he's operating at merely half his capacity, he's better than some surgeons are at their very best, Jonathan determined, counting on this. He would feel awful if he had his dad called in to operate and a patient lost their life.

223

Jonathan contacted one of his doctor friends at the hospital and had him check the surgical roster for that morning. Fortunately, there was a very complicated heart transplant taking place in a matter of hours. Jonathan cleverly informed his friend that his father had returned from Europe, and it plainly would be in the best interest for the hospital to call him in to assist.

Jonathan's friend enthusiastically agreed and said he would pass the information onto the surgical team immediately. Jonathan knew it would not be long before they would be calling the house for Jacob. Very satisfied with himself, he promptly went into the dining room to join the ladies for some breakfast while they impatiently waited for the call to come.

* * * *

As soon as Jackie Lynn got home Thursday evening, she tried to call Flora to inform her of her plans. She planned to take Friday off, so she and Long Wolf could start out very early that day on their trip to his Indian reservation. She was surprised to find herself excitedly looking forward to their trip together.

It had been a very long time since Jackie Lynn had gone away with a guy. Normally, she vacationed with her friends instead. Usually she would not allow a man to share as much of her life as she had Long Wolf.

I'm going to enjoy myself on this trip. And permit this fellow to grant me the pleasure he so wonderfully can, she eagerly resolved with a greedy smile. *After all, it's simply a few days. What could a few days alone with him possibly hurt?*

Given that they were leaving so early – *in addition to my more selfish reasons* – she had invited Long Wolf to spend the night. Jackie Lynn had been very surprised *and disappointed* when he had declined her offer. Long Wolf had claimed he needed to go home, and take care of some things there, before they headed out of town. He had told her he would see her bright and early the next morning to begin their trip.

Jackie Lynn felt uncomfortably alone. *Talking to Flora will help*, she attempted to convince herself as the service picked up the telephone. She cleverly lied and claimed to be some beauty consultant once more, Mrs. Johansen.

"I'm sorry, Mrs. Johansen," the man promptly said. "Mrs. Roberts is out of the house at the moment. Can I take a message for her?"

Darn! Jackie Lynn thought with frustration. She had really wanted to pass some time talking to her friend.

"Could you please tell Mrs. Roberts that I will be out of town until late Sunday, but that I will call her when I return?"

"Yes, very well," the man politely replied. "Thank you for calling, Mrs. Johansen. I will certainly see that Mrs. Roberts gets your message."

Jackie Lynn hoped Jacob's service really did pass on her message to Flora, because she did not expect to have access to a phone at the Indian reservation. Feeling oddly out of sorts, although not altogether sure why, she decided to go and take a long, hot, relaxing bath. She needed to get to sleep early anyway.

Jackie Lynn's mood lightened as she thought about Long Wolf coming to meet her in the wee hours of the morning and their impending trip. *Yes, that's it. I'll lazily relax in the tub for a while and then I'll go to bed. I'll be sure to fall asleep quickly that way, and then before I know it, I'll be seeing that irresistible Indian gentleman again, and we'll be going on an exciting adventure together.*

* * * *

Flora had wanted to call Jackie Lynn and inform her that she and Mary Julia were at Jonathan's. However, Jonathan had wisely talked her out of it. "I'm sorry, Flora," he apologized. "It's best if not even Jackie Lynn knows where you are right now."

Flora could most assuredly see the logic in Jonathan's argument, so she did not call her dear friend. *Pursuant to what's determined regarding my immediate future, Mary Julia may soon be joining Jackie Lynn anyway*, Flora sadly realized.

She had spent the rest of the day in serious discussions and planning with Jonathan concerning her impending future. By evening, she was so totally exhausted she decided to go to bed early. Prior to turning in for the night, Flora went into the den to say goodnight *and goodbye* to her beloved younger friend.

The dear girl had spent almost the entire day alone in this room, either reading or watching television. Jonathan had made it very clear that he wanted her to know absolutely none of the details of Flora's planned escape from his dad. Therefore, Mary Julia had no idea how permanent her friend's disappearance might be from their lives. Jonathan hated that he had to separate his stepmother from her cherished friends, who he realized were like family to her. Nevertheless, he knew of no other way to truly keep Flora safe from the terrible violence his deranged father so freely enjoyed inflicting on her.

"Mary Julia," Flora called in a soft voice.

Mary Julia looked up from the book she had been reading and gave Flora a sweet smile. She was glad to finally see her friend. "I'm going to bed," Flora told her in a weary voice.

A lump formed in Flora's throat and threatened to choke her as she asked, "Could you come here and let me hug you before I leave?"

Mary Julia noticed the extreme sadness in Flora's eyes. She sprang to her feet, rushed to the open doorway and into Flora's awaiting arms. Flora squeezed Mary Julia tightly against her and held her for a long while. "I love you, my friend. You're like the little sister I never had, and I want so much for you to have a happy life. You have to promise me you will take care of yourself. Can you do that for me, Mary Julia?" she said in a voice just above a whisper. Flora began to cry, despite her resolve not to become overly emotional.

"Flora, I would do anything for you. I love you dearly," she proclaimed, giving Flora's body a tighter squeeze. Heartsick tears began to fill her own eyes.

Flora is going away. Mary Julia knew this without having to hear anything that Flora and Jonathan had planned. *This makes perfect sense. Flora has to flee. It's the only way to prevent her monster of a husband from hurting her any further.*

Even though Mary Julia's heart was breaking at the thought of not having her friend in her life, she loved Flora enough to want her safety above all else. "When do you leave?" she dared to inquire.

"First thing tomorrow morning," Flora replied. She drew back a bit from her friend, to study her face. "I can't answer any more questions, Mary Julia, so please don't ask. The less you know the better. It's for both our safety."

"I understand," she assured her.

Mary Julia clutched both of Flora's hands in her own for a few more minutes. Finally releasing them, she said, "Goodnight, Flora. I'll be in to join you a bit later." Jonathan had thoughtfully vacated his king size bed for Flora and Mary Julia's shared use during their short stay.

Flora gave Mary Julia another brief hug and a loving kiss on the cheek. Then she sadly turned and headed for Jonathan's bedroom. Jonathan stood in the hall. He was looking sympathetically at Mary Julia. "Do you feel like company for a while?" he asked.

"Yeah. I could use some company right now," she confessed, brushing away a few stray tears that had escaped.

As Jonathan neared her, Mary Julia turned and walked across the room. She took a safe seat on the end of the love seat. *I'm very vulnerable right now. I can't afford to allow him to get too close. I need comfort, and it would be much too easy to take comfort as I always have, in the arms of a man, having sex with him. No! That isn't going to happen. I'll stay strong, not just for myself but also to keep my promise to Flora*, she resolved.

She watched as Jonathan took a seat against the arm at the opposite end of the short sofa. It was as if he not only innately sensed her need for some space but also respected it. It attracted Mary Julia even greater to him – not a purely sexual attraction but something altogether different. Something she was not at all certain she understood.

Naturally, she was drawn to Jonathan physically. *Any woman who isn't blind would be!* But it was the kindness Mary Julia so strongly perceived in him that captivated her. She did not want to be with him merely to have sex, but also to talk and to share emotions. Jonathan was the first man Mary Julia had ever been truly comfortable with. She was not this relaxed with her doctor from the sanitarium.

"Mary Julia, are you okay?" Jonathan asked with sincere concern.

He attentively scrutinized her lovely troubled face. He wanted so badly to scoot over beside her and hold her hand. However, Jonathan knew this would not bring solace to this woman.

Quite the opposite. Most likely, Mary Julia would bolt from the room, and that is the last thing I want to happen. Yet it's so hard not to touch her. That's because I want more with her than I usually do. She's breathtakingly beautiful, but she's not merely a conquest to me. Not just a play toy. I better watch my step! I could start to care about this one. That would not be a wise idea. She's been really hurt by some man or men, and she needs a man who isn't damaged goods. I can't be positive that some of my old man's craziness hasn't been inherited. She simply needs me to be a friend. So hands off! he warned himself. Jonathan wisely gripped the arm of the love seat to secure himself firmly in place, rather than moving closer.

"No, Jonathan. I'm not okay," Mary Julia replied. "I can't envision my life without Flora in it. It scares me and it breaks my heart. She and Jackie Lynn are the only two people in the world who I've felt truly loved me. They are my true family as far as I'm concerned. Gosh, it was hard enough when she moved away from us with your dad. At least then I knew I could still see her. I get the impression that won't still be the case. I get the feeling I may never see her again."

Her voice cracked and tears immediately started again. Mary Julia lowered her head in her hands and began to sob like a heartbroken child. It was more than Jonathan could bear. Within seconds, he had repositioned himself on the sofa, moving to sit hip-to-hip with Mary Julia, and pulling her into a tight embrace.

"Shhh. Mary Julia, it's going to be okay. I promise," he endeavored to reassure her. He tenderly stroked the back of her head and neck.

He was astonished by how acutely he wanted to discover some magical way to stop her deep suffering. Her happiness was crucial to him. *My God, Jonathan! What is this?!* he wondered. *No other woman's feelings have ever mattered this much. But I barely know this woman. It's not as if I could actually be falling in love or anything as crazy as that. I must just feel sorry for her. That has to be all it is!* he attempted to convince himself, slightly pulling back from her.

As Jonathan gazed into Mary Julia's anguished, tear streaked face, his heart twisted a little more. Before he could stop himself, he gently brought his lips to touch hers. It was merely another way of comforting this woman, of easing her overwhelming agony.

He did not anticipate Mary Julia's eager, and somewhat aggressive, response to his innocent kiss, or the perfect way their mouths and tongues heatedly entwined within moments. The fierce desire she so instantaneously arose in him was staggering. The thought indecently crossed Jonathan's mind that he would *very much* enjoy sprawling backwards across the sofa and pulling Mary Julia down on top of him. Instead, he reluctantly forced himself to separate from her, before things got out of hand. They both deliriously panted for breath, silently staring in awe at one another for several more minutes.

"My God, Jonathan! What just happened here?!" Mary Julia finally shrieked. The realization fully dawning on her that she would not have stopped if this man had not pulled away.

I would have had sex with him. I'm almost positive of that, she accepted. She was instantly disgusted and ashamed of herself.

"I'm sorry, Mary Julia," he apologized.

Jonathan placed a greater distance between their bodies. The staggering passion overtaking him, at this very moment, was so persistent it physically hurt. Nevertheless, he stubbornly refused to give in to his instinctive desires, even though this was totally out of character for him. Jonathan loved having his way with the ladies.

Not this time! Not with this woman! It wouldn't be right. Not for either one of us!

"I was only trying to comfort you. I never intended to take advantage of you," Jonathan tried to assure Mary Julia.

"It's not your fault, Jonathan," she admitted. "I thought I could merely be your friend. That's all I wanted. I thought I was doing it. But…oh…I was just being stupid. I don't know why I believed I could just be friends with a guy."

"Because we *are* friends," he hastened to argue. "But I have to be honest, Mary Julia. I've been attracted to you since the first time I laid eyes on you, and I believe you've felt the same way. So what transpired between the two of us was only natural. I'm not the slightest bit sorry it happened. But I know you've been fiercely hurt by someone and aren't looking to get into a sexual relationship. So I'm willing to back off – for *now*. That doesn't mean we can't continue to spend time together as friends, does it?"

The several minutes of silence which passed, while Mary Julia thoroughly contemplated what Jonathan had said, were agonizing. *What if she says she wants nothing further to do with me?* He was dumbfounded to ascertain that he truly feared this.

I don't want things to end between us. The relationship Jonathan had developed with Mary Julia, although it had only been a short while, meant more to him than any other relationship in his life. Of this, he was quite certain.

"What if I tell you I think we need to be in one another's lives? You make me want to be a better person, and I think I make you want to be one as well. I think we could be very good for one another," Jonathan was amazed he had admitted. He also realized he was not sorry he had said it, because he had truly meant every word.

"Jonathan, I'm sorry," Mary Julia spoke after another long pause. "This is all happening way too fast for me. I think I should sleep on it before I answer your question about us continuing our friendship or not. I'm not sure if it's possible after tonight. I don't want you to think it's on account of you. I think you are a very nice, wonderful man, but I'm very scared. And very weak. I can't get into a sexual relationship. And...and...well...presently, it's taking everything I have not to throw myself at you and finish what we started a few minutes ago. But it can't happen. There is way too much you don't know about me. If you did, you might not even want to be around me, much less be my friend."

"I think you are very wrong, Mary Julia. I can't imagine you telling me anything that would make me not want to still be your friend and spend time with you. We all make mistakes. God knows I have. There's a great deal you don't know about me either. That's why you're correct when you say we shouldn't rush into a sexual relationship. We need to spend time together filling in all of the blanks. Please promise you'll at least consider trusting me enough to share these things with me and permit me to share my past with you. Don't allow your fears get the best of you and cause you to run. Who knows? We could be starting something wonderful here. But we'll never know if you don't give *us* a chance," he argued.

Mary Julia was amazed to discover that Jonathan's kind, intelligent words had managed to somewhat calm her solely sexual urges. She now was thinking more about this man's feelings than anything physically concerning him. She definitely did not want to hurt him.

Now what I have to decide is what would hurt Jonathan greater. Trying to be his friend and possibly failing. Or giving up now, when he so evidently does not want me to. She did not have an answer. *I'll call my sponsor tonight and discuss all this with her. Perhaps she can help me come to some decision.*

Mary Julia watched as Jonathan stood and stepped toward her. He gallantly offered his hand. She hesitated for a moment, scared to touch him. She finally stretched out her own hand. Jonathan clutched it and began to pull upward.

"Come on. Why don't you go and join Flora and sleep on things. Things always have a way of looking better in the morning," he said. He gave Mary Julia an encouraging smile, which warmed her heart even more.

"Okay," she agreed in a slightly dreamy voice. She rose and walked by his side. A hopeful smile automatically appeared across her face. She realized how nice it felt to walk beside this man and have him do such a simple thing as hold her hand.

* * * *

Flora had fallen into a deep slumber almost as soon as her head had hit the pillow. Unfortunately, she had not slept long when she had been jarred awake by a terrible nightmare. A nightmare in which she plainly heard Jacob's voice asking in a low growl, "How could you possibly think you could ever leave me? How stupid did you think I was, Flora? What in the hell is wrong with you?!"

Jacob's voice had sounded so hateful and so very real that Flora had to force herself to open her eyes. When she did, she jumped in alarm as, through her sleep-clouded eyes, she could swear she saw the silhouette of a man sitting on the side of her bed. She quickly and tightly shut her eyes again and tried to convince herself, *What I am seeing is not real! It's only a bad dream.*

However, before Flora could open her eyes again, she had been pinned to the mattress by strong hands. Now she was certain she was not just having a bad dream.

Jacob was really there.

But how? Not again!

The sound of more angry words coming from his mouth positively confined it. "Once again, you have obviously forgotten the vows you made to me. Most specifically, *till death do we part*?! Because that's the one that really matters! The only way....the *only* way....you are ever going to leave me is through death. I thought you understood this!" he ranted, moving his hands to painfully encircle her neck. "I should snap your stupid little head off! But, no! You aren't escaping that easy. I won't permit you to win! My first wife got the better of me this way. Now I realize you are just like her, you good for nothing tramp! You want things to be over?! Fine! Let them be over for good!"

How'd Jacob find out where I was? How can he possibly be in Jonathan's house and bedroom in the middle of the night? Has Jacob done something terrible to Jonathan and Mary Julia? What are his plans for me now?

Panicked thoughts raced one after the other through Flora's muddled brain, as this maniac released his death hold on her neck. Instead, he grabbed handfuls of her hair and started brutally pulling her upright in the bed.

"Help!" she somehow managed to briefly bellow.

Jacob tightly cupped a hand over her mouth, wrenched her to her feet, and started dragging her toward the open window across the room. "Shut up, bitch!" he ordered through gritted teeth, in a gravelly voice barely audible.

I don't think he's harmed Jonathan or Mary Julia, Flora concluded with massive relief, both for herself and her friends. *Otherwise, why would Jacob be concerned someone might hear me? Oh, God! Please let them be alright. Please help me!*

All at once, the bedroom door was sent flying open, and the ceiling light illuminated the room. Mary Julia desperately rushed into the room. "Let her go!" she shouted. She charged at Jacob full steam and forcefully pounded, with both fists, on the arm which tightly held her friend.

Jacob intelligently decided that he was too inhibited by his heavy alcohol consumption to take on two very resistant women at the same time. So, he fiercely slung Flora sideways into his son's chest-of-drawers, causing her to lose her balance and fall to the floor. He viciously centered his concentration on her interfering friend instead.

"You whore! You need to be taught to keep your nose out of married people's business!" he yelled loudly, rapidly jerking his arm away from her assault. In the next instant, Jacob's hand so savagely struck the side of Mary Julia's face she feared she might lose consciousness. Willpower was unable to keep her on her feet. She crumpled to the floor.

"No, Jacob! Please don't hurt her!" Flora was screaming. She forced herself to stand and stumble back to his opposite side. "I'll do anything you want. Just please leave her alone!"

"Leave them both alone!" Jacob heard Jonathan's voice shouting, as he appeared in the doorway. His eyes frantically swept from Mary Julia's struggling form to his father and Flora. *I wish I had walked Mary Julia all the way to the bedroom and not just out of the den.*

Jacob, at once, hooked Flora's neck into a stranglehold and pulled her staunchly against him, slightly choking her for effect. Walking unstably backwards towards the window, he advised his son, "See to your whore, and stay out of my business! You've interfered too much! Did you sleep with your stepmother? Is that why she came with you? Maybe you slept with the two of them at the same time. Nothing would surprise me with you! I know that you were over at the house several times while I was gone. Did you really think I would believe Flora was visiting some friend in the city? Don't you think I found it a little odd that you were there for breakfast this morning, Jonathan? Did you ever think that I might have Flora followed? You've always been one giant disappointment to me! Your mother babied you too much and had too great of a negative influence before I removed her from our lives. Now I've got to do the same with Flora. I know that now. No more! Till death do us part, Flora. You are going to get your wish!"

Jonathan glanced at Mary Julia. She was staring right at him. Her eyes urgently pleaded with him to do something, even though she said not a word. He could not stand by and permit his father to do this again. He had not been able to save his mom, but he would not allow Jacob to harm Flora.

While Jonathan watched the fool stumble sideways through his tall, open, bedroom window, he spied the broken lock at the top and guessed how his dad must have gotten into his condo. He must have climbed up the fire escape, to his fourth floor balcony, dismantled the lock on the window and hid in the bedroom to wait for Flora.

Jacob should have been miles away, in the city, at Mary Julia's apartment looking for her there. After all, that was the decoy he had so carefully set up to lead Jacob astray. But their plan had gone miserably awry, and things could get much, much worse if he did not do something very quickly. He had no time to waste. Jonathan dashed across the room, determined to put an end to his father's demented attack on Flora.

He bound effortlessly through the open window and plowed so powerfully into his dad's side that Jacob reflexively released the unstable grip he had on his wife. Both Flora and Jonathan took instantaneous advantage of the short reprieve. Flora raced away from Jacob, and Jonathan grabbed her arm and pushed her safely behind him.

"No more, you sick son on a bitch!" Jonathan spat in anger. He charged his father's staggering figure with astonishing force, slamming his dad's back against the short balcony rail. Had Jacob not been so drunk, his son might have broken his lower back.

"So the pussy ass does have a little backbone! Perhaps you'll turn out to be a chip off the old block after all," Jacob provoked with an amused smile on his face, shoving Jonathan backwards. "Well, come on, show me what else you have," he further challenged.

Jacob swung an unsteady fist at Jonathan's head, which his son easily managed to dodge. He managed to catch Jonathan in the stomach with his other strong fist. This prompted Jonathan to bend slightly in response. Jacob wasted no time landing another effective blow. He caught Jonathan with an upward jab to the chin, causing his son to stagger backwards several steps. Jonathan stumbled helplessly into Flora and almost knocked her through the open window into the bedroom floor.

The brief support of Flora's body provided Jonathan a second to regain his balance and unleash his full rage. He pummeled into his father, wildly swinging both fists, landing blow after powerful blow to his dad's head and lower body.

The whole time Jonathan was pushing his stunned and overwhelmed father closer and closer to the balcony railing.

As Jonathan successfully landed another series of stinging blows, he watched his dad sway helplessly backwards, clawing strangely in the air above. Then he simultaneously heard two terrible screams. One was that of his father as he unexpectedly disappeared from Jonathan's sight, plunging backward over the balcony and falling toward the concrete sidewalk four stories below.

As Jonathan slowly turned and caught sight of Flora's horrified face, he instinctively knew that the other scream had come from her. It was only then that it fully dawned on him that he might have just killed his father.

CHAPTER SEVENTEEN

NEW HOPE

Mary Julia thought about calling Jackie Lynn to recount the terrible occurrence at Jonathan's condo, but she never got a chance that night. The police arrived right after Jacob had fallen. Mary Julia had called them when Jonathan had pursued his father out of the window.

An ambulance had shown up about fifteen minutes later. While Jacob was whisked from the accident scene to the closest hospital, Mary Julia, Flora and Jonathan were all escorted to the nearby police station for questioning. After all, Jacob was a well known, respected, brilliant surgeon in the community, and he had not merely fallen four stories by accident. The police naturally had to consider that there might have been foul play involved.

The police separated Mary Julia, Jonathan and Flora. They placed each of them in their own tiny interrogation room, as if they were criminals. A very seasoned homicide investigator, Kenny Best, was chosen to interrogate all three. He started with Jacob's son, since he was the one who had propelled his dad from the condo's balcony.

"Okay, Mr. Roberts, can you tell me precisely what happened tonight at your condo?" Kenny began the interrogation.

"The best I can tell, my father climbed up the fire escape, broke the lock on the window and came into my home uninvited," Jonathan began to explain. "He came there to harm my stepmother. I think he planned to kill her."

"What exactly would give you that idea?" Kenny furthered questioned.

Jonathan shared that as a boy he had witnessed his dad repeatedly beating his mom until she had ultimately died of a cerebral hemorrhage. He told Detective Best that he had started helping his stepmother devise a plan of escape from his father after he had stopped by his father's house unexpectedly one day and found Flora battered.

"Flora was covered from head to toe with bruises and cuts," he disclosed. "She was to leave my house tomorrow morning. I have contacts you can check with who work for the abused women network. They were going to take Flora away tomorrow and hide her, so my dad couldn't find her. But he discovered she was at my place tonight and came to get her. He had knocked Mary Julia to the ground and was dragging my stepmother in a stranglehold toward the open window when I came into the room. I didn't intend to push him off that balcony. I wasn't trying to kill him. He just kept fighting me and egging me on...I've never been out of control like that," Jonathan commented almost to himself, frustrated tears coming to his eyes.

He had hurt – *or probably killed* – his father tonight in a fit of anger. *My God! What if there is some of his violent nature in me? He became this way because my grandfather was the same way. I have to break the cycle! I can't be like them.*

Detective Best poured Jonathan a glass of water and left him alone in the room, providing him some time to compose himself. Kenny thought Jonathan seemed genuinely shaken about what had transpired, and Detective Best had a great deal of experience in judging what was genuine and what was not. He headed into the next interrogation room to begin questioning the women, one by one.

When Detective Best questioned Mary Julia, she collaborated what Jonathan had told him concerning Jacob knocking her to the floor. Mary Julia's cheek was badly swollen and beginning to bruise where Jacob had struck her. She also told him that when she had come into the bedroom Jacob had been threatening Flora and was pulling her by her hair. She told the detective that when she had charged Jacob and demanded he release Flora, he had tossed Flora sideways into the chest of drawers. Detective Best thanked Mary Julia for her testimony and left her to go and question Flora.

Flora openly admitted that she had feared for her life many times, but never as much as she had tonight. "I truly believe he would have killed me tonight if it hadn't been for Jonathan," she relayed, sounding slightly numb. Her eyes stared vacantly away from Detective Best and her body uncontrollably shuddered. The frightful images of Jacob's attack and Jonathan sending him flailing over the balcony were vividly running through her mind, like an instant replay video.

Even though Kenny thought all of their statements seemed truthful, he still had some skepticism, since the victim had such a respected reputation as a surgeon in the community. Therefore, he asked Flora if she had any proof of past injuries. She told him that Lolita, their housemaid, had seen Jacob hit her a time or two, and she was confident other members of the staff had heard or saw some of the violent attacks as well. As far as physical proof – doctor's statements – she shared that she had only been to see another doctor once, since Jacob usually treated her injuries at home.

However, this particular time, Jacob had knocked her down the steps. Since he genuinely feared that she might die from internal bleeding he could not detect at home, he had taken Flora to the hospital. Flora gave Detective Best the hospital physician's name. She had remembered it well, since he had been so overly kind and attentive.

Kenny left her alone in the interrogation room, promptly proceeding to his desk to make a call to the hospital. Luckily this physician was not only on duty but he recalled treating Mrs. Roberts the night of her alleged abuse from Jacob. The doctor candidly conveyed to Kenny that he had found definite signs of ongoing abuse and had noted this in Flora's medical file. He told Kenny that it was only as a 'courtesy' to an esteemed medical associate that he had not reported Flora's injuries as possible abuse to the proper authorities. The doctor further elaborated that he had taken Doctor Roberts aside and made it clear that if Flora had any more 'accidents' he would be forced to report it. He sounded truly remorseful, as he apologized to Kenny for not reporting it that day.

The evidence was mounting that Jacob Roberts was unmistakably a man who abused his wife. This being the case, along with the suspect's convincing statements regarding what had occurred tonight, Kenny rapidly concluded Dr. Jacob Roberts' injuries were the direct result of self defense on Jonathan's part – justifiable homicide if Jacob Roberts should die. He immediately decided to close the investigation.

If there was one thing Kenny Best could not stand, it was a guy who would beat a woman. In his many years as a police officer, he had seen more than his fair share of such cases. They never got any easier for him to stomach.

Filled with pity, he re-entered the room in which Flora was still seated and sat in the chair beside her. "Mrs. Roberts, I spoke to the physician at the hospital," he began, placing a supportive hand on her shoulder. Flora raised her head and stared at him with frightened, somber eyes. "He confirmed everything you told me. Jacob's accident will be ruled self defense, and I'm very sorry for the anguish this guy has plainly caused you."

"Thank you," she quietly muttered, feeling very relieved.

Thank God! Flora silently thought. While she had waited for Detective Best to make his call to the doctor, it had nervously occurred to her that she and Jonathan could have to serve jail time for Jacob's injuries – or death – because they had no proof of how horrible he had been to her. The servants probably would be too fearful to confirm anything – especially Lolita, who was only in the United States because of a green card. If she lost her job, she could be shipped back to Cuba.

"I think it's completely despicable for a man to do what your husband did," Kenny shared. He endeavored to keep anger out of his voice and lightly squeezed her shoulder. "Mrs.

Roberts, I've seen these cases many times before. Outside scars aren't the only ones you will be left with. The mental scars are far worse and have more lasting effects. There are special support groups that can help."

With this, he held out a business card in Flora's direction. She took the card and glanced at it. On the card were Detective Best's name and number and the name and location of a local battered women's support group. When she raised her head to exhibit a small smile of gratitude to Detective Best, Flora noticed for the first time that he was a rather nice looking fellow.

Kenny's concerned eyes were a captivating, unique shade of bluish green, and his hair was a sandy blond, peppered with gray and thinning a bit on top. Flora guessed this man was most likely only in his mid-forties. She figured his difficult job as a police officer had probably taken its toll, and this caused him to look slightly older than he was.

"I'm sorry to have made things worse for you by having to pull you in here and question you like some sort of criminal," Kenny apologized, his attractive face showing sincere regret. He rose from his chair then and offered her a hand. "Why don't you come with me and we'll gather up your friends. Then I'll have an officer take all of you wherever you want to go."

Flora pushed her chair back, took Kenny's outstretched hand, and stood up beside him. Unlike Jacob, he was short and stocky, standing only as tall as she was. "Detective Best, you're with homicide. Does this mean Jacob is dead?" she asked, fearing the worst. As much as she had wanted this man out of her life, the thought that Jonathan might have actually killed him made her sick at her stomach.

"He was alive when the ambulance took him away, and I haven't gotten any calls to inform me of anything to the contrary. So I would assume he is still among the living," Kenny explained. He caught himself vindictively thinking her husband certainly deserved to die.

"Well, then I suppose you better instruct your officer to take us all to the hospital," Flora surprised him by saying.

He knew it was none of his business but he insisted, "Mrs. Roberts, don't allow him to suck you back in if he survives. None of what he did to you was your fault, regardless of what he's probably made you believe."

"Don't worry. I have no intention of going back to Jacob if he survives," she staunchly proclaimed. "But I need to know his fate to decide what my next move will be. If he survives, I may be going far away and living under an assumed name. If he should die, however, then I would like to return to the city and try to recapture my old life, the one I had before I got sucked into this man's madness."

Kenny's heart ached even more for this woman's fate. So many battered women ended up having to be the ones who had to change their whole lives, run and hide, and live in fear. He hated this fact. It was another, terribly wrong injustice in the legal system. He knew if Flora was to press charges against her husband and he was found guilty, Jacob would serve little or no time for his crime. It frustrated him a great deal.

"Your friends are in those two rooms over there," he told her, pointing to two closed doors a short distance away. "I'll get an officer to escort you all to the hospital." Kenny reached out and patting her arm. "Take care," he said, and then he turned and walked away.

* * * *

Due to the very serious, multiple injuries resulting from his fall, Jacob was in surgery for hours. Even though the surgical team, a lot of them personal friends of Jacob, did everything they could, they were devastated to discover that they were unable to save him. The fall had rendered entirely too much damage to repair, despite their most vigilant efforts.

After the head surgeon had sadly delivered the news to them and had been on his way, Jonathan surprised Flora by saying in an unemotional voice, "It's over then, Flora."

Could it be true? Is Jacob reign of terror over me really over? Can I really go back to the city and try to start my life over? "Jonathan, I can't express how grateful I am to you for all your help. But I'm sorry your dad had to die," Flora sympathetically told him.

"Well, I wish I could say I was sorry," Jonathan quietly responded with slight bitterness. "I am glad you are finally safe and can go on with your life now."

I only hope I haven't inherited any of my father's or grandfather's madness, he meditated, anxiously noticing Mary Julia watching him. Jonathan could not get it out of his mind how easily he had met his father's violence tonight with violence of his own. *Yes, I saved Flora. But did I go overboard to do it?*

He had to have answers to these questions. His future depended on it. *A future I hope includes one very special lady.* Jonathan allowed his eyes to lock with Mary Julia's lovely, sapphire, admiring ones for a few seconds.

"Why don't we get out of here? I'll call us a cab. Flora, you and Mary Julia can go back to my father's house now. Even though it's already morning, perhaps you can try and get a few hours sleep, knowing you are truly safe now. Later today, the two of you can decide what your next steps will be. It will be awhile before Jacob's estate is settled, so you can continue to stay at the house. Or you and Mary Julia can go back to the city and start your lives there again."

I'll focus on what I need to in order to get my life back on track, he promised himself.

Jonathan knew of an excellent counselor, and he intended to begin seeing this individual on a regular basis right away. *I'll find out whether I'm worthy of you, Mary Julia, and if I am, then you'll be seeing much more of me. If not, then we'll have to remain apart.*

"That sounds like a winning plan to me," Flora hastened to agree, feeling very, very weary. Nonetheless, at the same time, she had more hope, all the sudden, than she had had in a very long time.

Jonathan left the two women standing there and headed toward the pay phones to call a taxi for them.

"Do you think he's okay?" Mary Julia asked Flora, when she was certain Jonathan was out of ear range.

"I think he will be," she said with a newfound sense of confidence. "In fact, I think we all will be, given a little time."

I hope so, her friend meditated, saying a brief prayer for all of them.

* * * *

Long Wolf rang Jackie Lynn's doorbell ten minutes earlier than expected, bright and early at 1:50 a.m. She was putting the final touches on her makeup. Before dashing for the door like an expectant schoolgirl, she checked herself in the mirror one last time and decided that she was satisfied with what she saw.

Jackie Lynn had chosen to leave her long hair down, rather than pulling it off her neck, because she knew Long Wolf preferred it this way. It was cascading naturally around the sides of her face. In light of the lengthy car ride, she had decided to dress comfortably in jeans, a nice pastel colored cotton T-shirt, and a pair of leather tennis shoes.

When she opened her apartment door to Long Wolf, she felt justified in her choice of clothing, since he was dressed in a similar way. *He is so good looking!* Jackie Lynn could not help but observe. She studied his neat shiny black hair, handsome face, and heartwarming smile. She also noted that Long Wolf's appealing muscular body was complimented by his T-shirt and jeans.

"Well, can I come in?" he asked after a few moments, with a slight chuckle. He appraised the way she was admiring him. *She's missed me*, Long Wolf concluded with satisfaction.

"Of course you can. I'm sorry," Jackie Lynn apologized, feeling a bit foolish. She backed up a step and ushered him forward into her apartment.

Shutting the door, she whipped around to face him, stuttering, "It's just…" Jackie Lynn hesitated for a moment in uncertainty, but decided to say it anyway, "I missed having you here last night. I missed feeling your arms around me."

"Is that so?" Long Wolf commented with a contented grin. He hurriedly closed the distance between them. "Well, I can certainly fix that," he assured her.

He enfolded Jackie Lynn in a secure, caring hug. He had missed holding her also. *This woman feels so perfect in my arms*, he could not help but conclude, softly stroking her back.

"Do we have to leave right this minute?" Jackie Lynn alluringly whispered in Long Wolf's ear, her yearning lips heatedly tantalizing the side of his neck.

It would be much too easy to succumb to the overwhelming sexual desire this special lady so easily arises in me every time I'm with her. Long Wolf could envision sweeping Jackie Lynn into his arms and carrying her to her bed. Nonetheless, unbeknownst to Jackie Lynn, he had made a secret pact with himself that he would not make love to this woman again until she could be honest regarding her feelings.

Long Wolf wanted to hear Jackie Lynn admit that she truly loved him. He sincerely believed this was true, but Jackie Lynn did everything she could to convince herself that their relationship was solely based on their sexual compatibility, and nothing deeper. Long Wolf intended to persuade her otherwise, and he had resolved to begin with their time away this weekend.

"Um...Jackie Lynn," he said, abruptly pulling from her arousing embrace. He left her with a dazed expression on her face. "Much as I would enjoy staying here with you, we have a very long drive ahead of us. So, yes, we really do need to leave at this moment. I'll get your bags," he volunteered. He headed across the room to where her travel cases were sitting. There was one medium-size suitcase and one shoulder travel bag.

"Is this all you have?" Long Wolf asked. He threw the strap for the bag over his shoulder and hoisted the suitcase in his other hand, swiftly moving toward the door.

"Uh...yeah," she answered. Jackie Lynn watched him oddly for a few more minutes.

Long Wolf stood in the open doorway. He was obviously waiting for Jackie Lynn to exit the apartment. Jackie Lynn went to retrieve her purse and walked through the open door. *Something's definitely up. He wanted to get out of my apartment way too fast.*

This was the first time since they had become intimate that Long Wolf had deliberately turned down an opportunity for the two of them to brazenly be together as lovers. Jackie Lynn was not sure she liked this new twist.

Or maybe I missed him so much and wanted him so severely I'm making a mountain out of a molehill, she hastened to reconsider. *No. I'm not going to analyze everything. This weekend is going to be a fun time away with a guy I'm comfortable spending time with. Let happen what may.* With this new resolve in mind, Jackie Lynn followed Long Wolf out of the building, enthusiastically anticipating their weekend adventure.

* * * *

After five hours of carefree traveling, Jackie Lynn and Long Wolf stopped for breakfast at a truck stop restaurant. They had another five hours of driving ahead of them. By getting such an early start, they would still have half a day to enjoy life at the Reservation. So far, Jackie Lynn felt very relaxed being with this guy. Nevertheless, for some unknown, probably totally unfounded reason, she had a terribly uneasy feeling about her friends.

As the waitress was leaving their table after taking their breakfast orders, Jackie Lynn was surprised to hear Long Wolf inquire, "What's wrong, honey?"

"Why do you ask that?" she questioned. Her eyes were studying him inquisitively, and there was a look of confusion plainly on her face.

He can't possibly sense my worry over the girls, she doubted.

"I don't know. It's something I see in your eyes. They darken a bit when you're worrying about something. I noticed it in the car a while ago and I see the same thing in them now," Long Wolf shared. "I didn't say something to upset you, did I?" They had been talking almost constantly, discussing everything under the sun, ever since they had left her apartment that morning.

"You must be the most observant man I've ever met," Jackie Lynn said with a slightly nervous chuckle.

She did not know whether she liked this guy being able to read her facial expressions so well. It made Jackie Lynn more than a little apprehensive to realize that he paid such close attention to her mannerisms. *Could be the actions of a man head over heels in love,* her mind betrayed her by taking into account.

"So does that mean I'm right?" He continued to question. "What's up?"

"It's not anything you did or said," she assured him, as the waitress came back with their cups of coffee.

Jackie Lynn prepared her coffee for drinking, stirring in cream and sugar. Then she looked up at Long Wolf, admitting with slight embarrassment, "It's crazy really. For some bizarre reason, I have this weird feeling that something is wrong with Flora and Mary Julia. It's most likely because I left without talking to either of them. Or due to the fact that I'm used to one or both of them being the ones to travel with me."

"If you truly feel that way, then you should call them before we go any farther," he surprised her by saying. "We could always turn around and head home if anything is wrong. If not, then at least you'll have peace of mind. You can use my cell phone in the car when we leave, or I can go and get it for you right now if you want."

Long Wolf's sincere concern for her friends' well-being, and his unselfish offer to return home if they weren't okay, touched Jackie Lynn's heart despite her resolve to keep him at arm's length. He was assuredly the most caring and giving man she had ever met. She studied his charming, honest face, and struggled to keep from rising from her chair, affectionately cradling that face in her hands, and bestowing an extensive and appreciative kiss on his mouth.

What she did not know was, while Long Wolf faithfully watched her eyes change from worry to gratitude and longing, he also wanted to vacate his chair and take Jackie

247

Lynn in his arms. He wished more than anything that the two of them had made love prior to departing that morning. Long Wolf now seriously questioned his decision not to be with her in this way.

Maybe I was being foolish. Her eyes tell me so very much. They are gleaming brightly with love for me no matter how many times this headstrong woman tries to convince me otherwise with her false words. Jackie Lynn can deny it all she wants with her mouth, but it's impossible for her to hide the truth in her eyes. As far as Long Wolf was concerned, the eyes were a mirror to a person's very soul.

He was about to indecently suggest that the two of them go to the car for something other than making a telephone call, when their waitress returned. She roughly clattered a bottle of Catsup and some syrup in the middle of their table and unemotionally announced, "Your breakfast will be out in a minute." She turned and rushed away without so much as making eye contact with either of them. She had instantly broken the magical spell Jackie Lynn and Long Wolf had been silently casting over one another.

The few second reprieve was all Jackie Lynn needed to regain her practiced restraint. Long Wolf noticed the change in her almost immediately. She looked away from him. Rather than drinking her coffee, she picked up the small glass of ice water, rapidly consuming the entire glass in seconds.

Long Wolf could not help but smile in amusement. *She's cooling herself down and very carefully reigning in her emotions. Yes, my original decision was right!*

It was quite apparent if he resumed a sexual relationship with this woman, Jackie Lynn would use it against the two of them developing a lasting relationship. She would continue to proclaim, over and over, "All we have between us is a wonderful sexual compatibility" – forever denying the deep love he was certain she had for him.

Long Wolf fully intended to prove to Jackie Lynn that they had much more going on between them then just *great sex*. He would somehow get her to admit the love she had for him. When this eventually happened, he knew it would surely be one of the happiest days of his life. Fortunately, Long Wolf had long since learned that anything worth having was definitely worth waiting for. He could wait however long, and do whatever it took, to win over this special lady's heart.

"So would you like for me to go and get the phone?" he inquired, breaking the extended silence which had developed.

"No. I appreciate the offer, but I'm positive that Flora and Mary Julia are fine. Because they are like sisters to me, I have a tendency to worry about the two of them a bit too much sometimes. We're only going to be gone a few days, so I'm setting my mind that these dear friends of mine are a-okay. I'm going to completely concentrate on having a relaxing, good time with you instead. Sound good?" she asked, flashing Long Wolf a convincing smile.

"Sounds great! And I'll do you one better. I promise to do everything I can to see that we have a wonderful time this weekend," he pledged. He reached to briefly squeeze one of Jackie Lynn's hands in assurance and because he wanted to touch her so badly.

"Terrific, I'll hold you to that Mr. Long Wolf," she teased with a silly giggle. Her eyes locked with his for a brief instant, before the waitress appeared holding a tray with their breakfast dishes on them.

Long Wolf released Jackie Lynn's hand, and they sat back in their chairs, waiting in anticipation for her to sit the food in front of them. They began to eat and talk casually about their everyday lives, each sincerely interested in what the other had to say.

* * * *

They reached the reservation around 1:00 that afternoon and were warmly welcomed by Long Wolf's family and friends. His mother kissed and embraced her son and held him for a very long time, tenderly patting his back and jabbering animatedly to him in a language strange to Jackie Lynn. She was a short rounded woman, with long gray hair, which she had braided down her back.

When Long Wolf introduced Jackie Lynn to his mom, his mother's deeply wrinkled face folded into the sweetest smile and she enthusiastically hugged and kissed Jackie Lynn also, saying in broken English, "Weecom! Weecom!" It was not everyday that she spoke English, so she had to struggle to remember the words.

"She's delighted you have come with me," Long Wolf told Jackie Lynn, giving his mom a warm, cheerful smile.

It was quite plain that Long Wolf adored his mother, and she him. She went to her son, fondly stroked the side of his face, said more strange words to him, and then started away. She looked expectantly over her should at the two of them.

"She wants me to show you around," he explained, gallantly holding out a hooked arm for Jackie Lynn to latch onto.

She took Long Wolf's arm, happy for the bodily contact with him and they walked on. The incredible view at the Reservation was almost breathtaking. There were miles of trails among wooded acres. They seemed never-ending. Jackie Lynn would soon learn from Long Wolf that the Indians used these trails mostly for hunting, hiking and horseback riding. Nearby, to the west, was an unspoiled stream. As you turned to the east, all you could see, or so it seemed, were miles of beautiful mountains.

Jackie Lynn was anxious to see the in and outs of a real Indian Reservation, and she was enjoying having Long Wolf proudly share it with her. *I'm not even going to let the way his mother keeps staring at me, as if she were trying to decide if I would make the perfect match for her son, bother me.*

* * * *

After dark, a few of the younger Indian girls, giggling wildly, tried to entice Jackie Lynn into joining in a *rather erotic* circling dance around a roaring campfire. With a sinister grin, Long Wolf tried to prod her into joining in the dance too. She stubbornly refused.

SISSY MARLYN

Jackie Lynn soon understood why Long Wolf had wanted her to dance. The girls were obviously dancing to arouse the attention of a male they were interested in. Before the dancing was finished, the male companion of each young girl's choice had eagerly accompanied her. They danced together then, going around and around the fire several times, in very intimate embraces, before the couples each took turns leaving the crowd.

"Now what happens? Are they going off to share a bed?" Jackie Lynn whispered in Long Wolf's ear. Then she added with a wide wicked smile, "If that's the case, then perhaps I should have danced for you."

"Ah, my dear, what you just witnessed was indeed an Indian mating ritual," he explained with a knowing chuckle. "However, should these couples choose to share the same cot tonight, they are intentionally telling everyone they have chosen one another as life partners. An Indian wedding celebration will, of course, then follow. It's still not too late. If you would like to dance now and then accompany me in my tent for the night...*well*..." Long Wolf invitingly teased. He encircling Jackie Lynn's waist with his arm and pulling her against his body.

"Dream on, Indian man!" she staunchly declared with laughter. She lightly elbowed him in his ribcage to loosen his possessive grip. She did not squirm completely free from Long Wolf's grasp though.

It was evident that the two of them would not be sleeping together tonight, so Jackie Lynn was happy for whatever contact she was allowed to have with this man. In actuality, she would have liked to warmly kiss Long Wolf's curved smiling lips. *A kiss to show him I'm glad I've come here, that I'm enjoying myself, that I haven't been this relaxed in such a very long time.*

Jackie Lynn wisely realized this probably would not be a good idea. A kiss such as she wanted to share with Long Wolf would most likely signify something special to the people she was amidst. She assuredly did not want to give them the wrong impression. They plainly had no conception of lovers in strictly the sexually sense.

Jackie Lynn gathered that if she openly demonstrated any affection toward Long Wolf, other than the most basic, then his tribe would assume the two of them were deeply in love and deemed to be life partners. As she glanced around and noticed the many eyes closely watching them, it made her more nervous and cautious.

With this in mind, Jackie Lynn reluctantly said, "Long Wolf, we've had a pretty long day. Especially with the long drive and all. Don't you think it's about time we went our separate ways and turned in for the night?"

Jackie Lynn had been careful to add the part concerning *going their separate ways.* She had even purposely raised her voice a bit when she had said it, even though several of Long Wolf's people did not appear to understand English.

"Yes. That's probably a good idea," she was slightly surprised to hear Long Wolf agree. He spoke in a strange tongue to some young teenage girls, who were sitting nearby and intently watching them. They scrambled to their feet, rushed over to pick up lanterns, and came over to the two of them. "These girls will take you to your teepee. Rest peacefully. Dream freely. I'll see you in the morning."

He slipped his arm from around her body, and Jackie Lynn scurried to her feet. She could not take the chance that Long Wolf might endeavor to impart a goodnight kiss. "You have a good night's sleep too. See you tomorrow," she rattled and hastened to turn and walk away between the two young Indian women.

The girls were avidly chattering in their foreign tongue. Jackie Lynn got the distinct impression their whole conversation was centered around her. She soon discovered that she had been right.

The Indians still mostly lived in securely constructed teepees. The girls took Jackie Lynn to theirs. One lifted the flap and went inside with her lantern. Then, another of them led Jackie Lynn inside and over to a cot. The girl sat down and enthusiastically motioned for Jackie to take a seat beside her.

Jackie Lynn sat next to the smiling, friendly girl, as indicated. Following her gaze, she inquisitively watched while the other young woman retrieved some items from a small nearby, wooden table. She turned and headed in Jackie Lynn's direction. Taking a seat on the other side of her, the girls soon began to talk and giggle amongst themselves. One started tenderly combing Jackie Lynn's long hair, and the other began decoratively adorning it with the fresh flowers.

Jackie Lynn curiously wondered if this was some sort of bizarre bedtime ritual that the Indian women engaged in with guests. She found it even stranger when the teenagers began to color her cheeks and forehead with some strange, red and yellow paint. With a mixture of amusement and some trepidation, she could not help but wonder, *What have they got in store for me?*

Suddenly, as if reading her thoughts, the girls abruptly rose to their feet. They stared down at Jackie Lynn with proud expressions on their faces. While the one girl took the items back to the table from whence they had come, the other offered Jackie Lynn her hand. She obviously wanted her to stand. Jackie Lynn promptly stood, continuing to play along with their playful charade.

After all, they appear to be enjoying themselves so much, and all of Long Wolf's people have been so nice to me since I've arrived. I certainly don't want to do anything that would offend them. For some reason, Jackie Lynn believed she could trust these young ladies not to do anything that would cause her any real harm.

Before they eagerly led her from the tent, they draped a long colorful piece of material around her shoulders. It was soft, almost like flannel, and it had brilliant colors, of red, blue and yellow, splashed all along it. They crossed the ends down the front of her t-shirt and secured them by tying a shorter piece of the soft, vibrant material tightly around the waist of her jeans. The girls then hastened to lead Jackie Lynn across the dark surroundings and to another tent. There was already light inside this teepee.

Maybe this is where I'm really supposed to sleep, Jackie Lynn mused, thinking once more that the girls had just completed some bedtime ritual for her.

So when one of the young ladies obscurely opened the flap to the teepee and the other anxiously pushed Jackie Lynn forward, she did not hesitate to enter. The girls, on the other hand, began to laugh and sprinted away. When Jackie Lynn turned her full attention to the interior of the teepee, she at last understood the girls' seemingly bizarre behavior. Long Wolf sat on the side of a cot in nothing but his underwear.

"Long Wolf! Did you put those poor girls up to this?!" Jackie Lynn asked with distinct irritation.

How could he take advantage of young innocent girls that way? she was wondering with aggravation.

"No. I most certainly did not!" he affirmed. He nervously sprang from his sitting position on the cot and slid his pants on. "You need to get out of here! Remember what I told you earlier. A woman is not allowed to accompany a fellow into his cot."

Taking Jackie Lynn by the arm, he hastily led her out of his teepee. Once she was safely outside, Long Wolf widely held open the flap for a few seconds so that the light from within shone brightly upon her. He wanted a second to appreciatively study the attractive way the girls had prepared this woman for her visit to him.

"I remember what you told me about your Indian custom 'share a cot and share a life together'. I didn't plan this. Those teenage girls brought me here," Jackie Lynn stated, twirling to face him. "Is that what those girls intended? Were they trying to betroth me to you? Is that why they fixed me up like this?" she rapidly questioned. Noticing for the first time how he was approvingly admiring her, Jackie Lynn swiftly turned her back on Long Wolf. She deliberately stepped a few more paces beyond.

"I would say yes," he replied, reluctantly letting the teepee flap drop from his grasp. He rushed to join Jackie Lynn's side. "They apparently like you and think the two of us appear to belong together. I can't say I disagree with them.

254

But they shouldn't be tricking you like they did. I better walk you back to your teepee."

"Do you suppose they will let me in?" she asked with growing irritation.

"I'll talk to their mother and see that the girls stop playing tricks," he promised her. "I do have to say they did a beautiful job. You look very pretty with your flower decorated hair and painted Indian face. This Indian man could almost have been convinced to permit you to remain in his teepee," he confessed in a husky inviting voice. He draped an arm around her body and pulled her to his side. "You would make a very fitting Indian wife."

"Get that out of your mind, savage!" she warned in a half teasing tone. She lightly slapped Long Wolf's arm and purposefully put a little distance between them. "This may be your Reservation, but don't get any wild-haired ideas about making me a permanent resident. Cause it isn't going to happen."

He knew this was very true. Jackie Lynn could not trust him enough to declare her love for him, much less think about ever becoming his wife. *I'll never give up!* Long Wolf resolved. He reached to take her hand.

I'll show you, Jackie Lynn. You can trust me with your heart. Perhaps some day, we can *be together as husband and wife*, he secretly schemed and dreamed. *For now, I'll take her to be with the women for the night, and go to my teepee alone to dream of other nights when I can freely share my bed and my body with this beloved woman.*

* * * *

Long Wolf took Jackie Lynn to one of the older women's tents and told her about the girls' prank. The older women said a few foreign words to Long Wolf, and they smiled and laughed together. He seemed to be agreeing with whatever she had said.

When the woman turned to her, Jackie Lynn was surprised when she relayed in English, "I'm sorry if my daughters embarrassed you, Miss. As I was explaining to Long Wolf, they meant no harm. They couldn't help beholding how in love you and Long Wolf are, so they wanted to help the two of you get together. But you and Long Wolf are adults, so it is up to the two of you to decide. If you choose to be together as life partners, that will be of your own hearts. The girls had no right to try and trick you into it. I will speak to them and have them apologize. You have my word they will trick you no more."

"It's okay," Jackie Lynn quickly responded. "I understand. Really I do. I was a teenager once myself. I realize, at that age, every relationship between a man and a woman looks like *true love*. You think in terms of people pairing up and being together always. Actually, it's sweet. So please don't get after them. I'd just like to go to the tent and go to sleep for the night. I am extremely tired."

A look of confusion suddenly appeared on the Indian woman's face and she silently studied this strange foreign lady for a few tense moments before she hesitantly noted, "Forgive me for saying so, Miss, but you sound as if you have a very hardened view of love. I hope I have misunderstood and that you aren't saying that only the very young believe in lasting love between two people. It would be a shame to see you throw away happiness and fulfillment. I know these special relationships can and do exist, because I have witnessed many such lasting unions among my people. Not the least of which was my own pairing with my dear departed Indian husband. Everyone has a soul mate, a true love. To find that person, the gods must truly smile upon you, as they did me."

"I'm sorry," Jackie Lynn was swift to reply. She was not only sympathetic for the sorrow this widow must be feeling, but she remembered how terribly Flora had grieved when she had lost her first husband.

Yes, some people are capable of loving very deeply and having relationships that lasted. I don't believe I'm one of those people. But there is no way I can explain this to this persistent Indian woman. Nor do I have any intention of trying.

Thankfully, Long Wolf came to her rescue. "I think Jackie Lynn is just very tired, Little Willow. I think she needs to be shown to a cot for the night and not be disturbed."

"As you wish, Long Wolf," Little Willow said, sounding like she was obeying an order. "Come," she said to Jackie Lynn and hastened out of the teepee, obviously expecting her to follow. "I will take you to my daughters' teepee. I promise you they will not bother you once they have helped you wash the love colors from your cheeks and gently untangled the flowers from your hair."

"I'll see you in the morning," Long Wolf said. He stepped from the teepee behind Jackie Lynn. He did not attempt to follow as she headed away with Little Willow.

To follow me is probably to break some other sacred Indian ritual, Jackie Lynn silently accepted. *Their lives are so simple and uncomplicated it's no wonder they easily have faith in everyone finding one lasting love, their soul mate.*

The peaceful lifestyle of these people was overwhelming to believe. There was only tranquility. In a way, Jackie Lynn envied Long Wolf's people. Her own life had proved to be so much the opposite, and there was not anything she could do to change that. *That is, except carefully guard my heart. That I will do*, she staunchly vowed, silently walking side by side with Little Willow to her teepee for the night.

* * * *

They left around 3:00 p.m. the following day, with plans to stop at a hotel for the night after driving about halfway. After Long Wolf's mom had finished giving her son an enduring goodbye hug, she turned her full attention to Jackie Lynn.

She engulfed her in a tight embrace and whispered in an emotional, quivering, pleading voice, "Loo..ve, bea..u..tiful cloo..sed floo..er... Let Long Wolf's li..ight of loo..ve for you... and yoo..urs for him... oo..pen up your pee..tals. It is by the hands of naa..ture... that a floo..er will bloo..om. It is by

257

the will of the gods…that loo..ve too will fu..lly bloo..om."
She had obviously struggled to say so many words in English,
but it was clear to Jackie Lynn that it had been very important
to this woman to impart these closing words to her.

Jackie Lynn could not help but feel shaken by the old
woman's caring parting words. Part of her wanted to pledge to
Long Wolf's mother that she would try to do what she had
asked. The other part of her vitally needed to keep life simple
– and overall logical. She could never allow her emotions to
overcome her logic.

Sound reasoning clearly told her, *Opening up my heart
to a man, even Long Wolf, could be opening myself up to pain,
sadness and disaster. I won't permit that to happen. Not even
if I do feel as if I'm breaking a sweet old Indian woman's heart.
Not even if, deep down, I know I'm not being genuinely true to
my own heart's desire.*

This unwanted revelation passed through her head
instantaneously, and totally without warning. Jackie Lynn
found herself reflexively pulling out of Long Wolf's mother's
arms, as if this woman had somehow planted some evil thought
into her unwitting brain. She backed up a few steps and stared
with bewilderment at the elderly, warm, caring, smiling woman
that faced her.

Feeling foolish for her silly suspicions, she reached out
and lightly patted Long Wolf's mother's arm politely saying,
"It was very nice meeting you and spending time here. Please
take care of yourself. Thank you and your people for sharing
their lives with me."

She hastily turned, taking long hurried strides toward
the car, not looking to see if Long Wolf was even following. *I
need to get away from this place. Apparently, being
surrounded by these people, with their simple fairytale views of
love, has gotten to me. That's all it is! Once I'm away, these
silly ideas will stop plaguing me.*

Minutes later, inside the automobile, she sighed with
relief as Long Wolf sent the vehicle bumping down the dirt
road, and the Reservation faded from view.

CHAPTER EIGHTEEN

HONESTY

Five hours later, Long Wolf pulled off the freeway and into the parking lot of a nearby Holiday Inn, intent on stopping for a good night's rest. Jackie Lynn had other things in mind. Ever since they had left the Reservation, she had been luridly looking forward to stopping for the night. Without the restrictions of the Reservation, nothing was stopping her and the man she had been longing for all weekend from being together as consensual sexual partners.

I can deny that I love this guy. But I can never deny that our wondrous sexual encounters are some of the most fulfilling experiences I've ever known. These past few days of imposed celibacy have only served to radically intensify my most intimate desires for Long Wolf.

Jackie Lynn stepped into their hotel room. She waited impatiently for Long Wolf to shut the door and free his hands of their suitcases. Then she threw her arms around his neck and pulled him into a tight, inviting embrace.

Jackie Lynn immediately engulfed his warm seductive mouth with her own hot yearning lips and tongue. Almost instantly, Long Wolf's body betrayed him. His shorts significantly tightened in the front below his waist, and his mind joined the prompt surrender. The words – *I can't possibly deny this woman's needs* – freely coursed through his muddled mind.

Long Wolf found himself returning her hungry kisses and allowing Jackie Lynn to push him backwards toward the nearest bed. He had purposely requested a room with two double beds, because he had planned on the two of them sleeping separately.

Weak with passion, he collapsed on the end of the bed, and mindlessly allowed this seductive woman to undo his belt, discard his T-shirt, and begin to shower his bare neck and shoulders with alluring kisses. Long Wolf knew he needed to protest their lovemaking at this very instant, or he would never be capable of stopping himself. Nevertheless, when he opened his mouth and called, "Jackie Lynn", the words came out hoarse and seductive, rather than halting.

"Yes, Long Wolf!" she gasped in response.

She pulled back, but only so she could hastily remove her own shirt and bra. The beautiful sight of her full breasts, and overly inviting erect nipples, was a greater temptation than this mere mortal man could withstand. He pulled Jackie Lynn against him, burying his head amidst her breasts. He delightfully suckled one and then the other.

There will be no more thought of not making love to this woman. At least not now. But we'll talk afterward. Long Wolf was determined that this must happen.

Right now, he surrendered to the overwhelming passion that this woman he so desperately loved arose in him.

* * * *

Because Jackie Lynn had so suddenly, significantly aroused Long Wolf, their first encounter was over fairly quickly. He was always considerate to his lover's needs as well as his own, so he continued to hold Jackie Lynn and stroke different areas of her body until he hardened in response once more. He surrendered to her once more, with heated passion, but much slower this time.

When their second coupling had ended, Long Wolf took delight in gazing at Jackie Lynn's glowing eyes and blissful, smiling, satisfied face. She was ready to curl up in his warm embrace and fall asleep, but there was no better time than this moment to endeavor to talk to this lovely lady about their strong feelings for one another.

He began on a light note, saying, "So tell me, Jackie Lynn. If I weren't in your life, can you imagine any other man pleasing you as much as I do?"

She smiled wider and gleefully confessed, "Truthfully, you've made me wonder this very same thing. I think you very well may have spoiled my sexual experiences for life, Mr. Long Wolf. I can't help but think of that old Carly Simon song *Nobody Does It Better.*"

"Do you think I enjoy making and seeing you happy?" he further questioned.

"You seem to very much," she answered without hesitation and gave him a grateful peck on the lips.

"Do you have any idea why that is?" he asked, tenderly massaging her shoulders to keep her relaxed.

"I think it's because you're one of the most kind, considerate men I have ever met," Jackie Lynn shared.

She ran her fingers through the soft, black hair on his chest, wanting to touch him since he was touching her. *And because of all of the wonderful touching he has already rendered.*

"There's a reason why I go out of my way to be considerate to you, and there is a reason why our lovemaking is so magnificent. That reason is this – I'm out of my mind in love with you. I truly believe you feel the same way about me. So why can't you trust me a bit more and admit your feelings? It could be so much more wonderful!"

"Oh, Long Wolf!" she wailed in defiant protest. Jackie Lynn pulled her hands away and rolled out of his arms. "What's between us has nothing to do with love! We have been wonderfully, sexually attracted to one another since we first set eyes upon each other."

"I know," he acknowledged. "I *was* attracted to you then…in so very many ways…not just sexually. But it's gone far beyond mere attraction. I love you now. If you would only be true to your feelings we could grow to love one another more and more."

"I'm very glad I came with you this weekend. I understand, since seeing your people at the Reservation, why you have this fairytale belief of love everlasting, this soul mate you're certain everyone has. Your people may be able to sustain such love. Apart from the Reservation, in my world at least, it's quite different. I've seen firsthand what *supposedly true love* can do to people, especially to the woman in the relationship. I'm sorry. I'm not interested," Jackie Lynn declared, her eyes taking on a hard and saddened look. "Why can't you settle for what we have? What's so wrong with being so wonderfully, sexually compatible? Can't we just focus on making one another happy in this way for as long as we are both content doing it?"

"It doesn't matter to you at all that I love you?" Long Wolf quietly asked. He wanted to wrap his arms around her. He wanted to somehow take away the devastating anguish that had caused Jackie Lynn to stop believing in love. It was so sad to him.

"Long Wolf, I don't want to hurt you, but regardless of how you feel about me, I can't return those feelings. So if you can settle for what I'm capable of giving, then I'm willing to keep seeing you. Otherwise, we might as well say a final goodbye when you take me home tomorrow," she explained in a quavering voice.

Her heart had all of the sudden lodged in her throat. *Am I afraid of what he's going to say next?* Jackie Lynn questioned. *If he says he no longer wants to see me, then it's for the best*, she tried to persuade herself.

Long Wolf rolled closer and pulled her into his arms. He squeezed her affectionately against him, and he said, "That's just it. You don't understand what love is. It isn't walking away when everything isn't precisely as you might wish it to be. Love means sticking by the other person no matter what. That's exactly what I intend to do." *I'll stick by you. I'll find out what has hurt you so badly, and I'll show you that it can be different. Then, you will profess the love I know you have for me.*

Oh God! Jackie Lynn's panicked mind wailed. *A man that truly believes in sticking by someone no matter what. Can Long Wolf sincerely mean this? Surely not. He must be caught up in 'being in love'. I know all about such fantasies. Gosh, how many times did I see my mother have men 'in love' with her? How many times did I see them walk...no, not walk...run out of our lives? Yet, as long as I'm careful to keep my guard up, could there be any real harm in continuing to see this guy? After all, if nothing else, I can be supremely sexually satisfied. I wasn't lying when I told him I have doubts that I would ever find another man who could please me as much.*

"Hey, sweetie," Long Wolf said, interrupting her private scrutiny. He pulled back slightly so he could look into Jackie Lynn's bewildered eyes. He tenderly rubbed one side of her face, and he added, "Don't be upset. Someday, maybe you'll trust me enough to confide to me what has soured you so on love. But not tonight. Tonight, I want you to fall asleep and wake up in my arms. Do you think you can do that?"

Jackie Lynn *was* tired, and she had been thinking of doing this very thing prior to Long Wolf's *profession of love* speech. Now, she could not help but wonder, *Will my mind quiet down enough to allow it?*

As if reading her thoughts, Long Wolf began to softly massage both of her temples. "Shh, don't work that brain of yours so hard, baby. You have plenty of time to decide about me. Because I intend to remain in your life for a long, long time. Close your eyes, and focus on my arms being around you. Entirely relax and go to sleep. I'll be here tomorrow for you, like I always will be. Tomorrow, the day after and the day after that."

My Lord! He truly sounds like a man in love. What in the world have I gotten myself into? How did I allow this happen? Why does it bother me so much all of the sudden to think of him getting hurt by being involved with me? God, you have to keep me strong! You can't permit me to get caught up in this 'love' nonsense.

Even though Jackie Lynn wanted to keep her thoughts racing – to determine her best plan of defense – she could not resist relaxing in this man's comforting arms. Nor could she fight his soothing, massaging fingers. It was not long before she fell into a deep and contented sleep, despite herself.

* * * *

They arrived at Jackie Lynn's apartment around noon the following day. As soon as she walked in, she noticed the message light flashing on her answering machine. She pushed the button to listen to her messages. Jackie Lynn was shocked when she heard of Jacob's catastrophe.

She was also *pleasantly* surprised to learn that Flora and Mary Julia's had returned to the city to live in Mary Julia's apartment. *How could so much happen in the short period of time that I've been gone?* she wondered. She thought about the eerie premonition she had had about her friends the day she and Long Wolf left for their trip.

Jackie Lynn immediately called Mary Julia's apartment and talked to her friends. Long Wolf had a seat on the couch and waited patiently. He wanted to be there in case she was upset when the conversation ended.

However, when Jackie Lynn hung up the telephone, she seemed happy. "Flora sounded more relaxed then she has since marrying Jacob," she relayed. "It's a terrible thing to say. I can't help but be glad that Jacob is out of her life, even if it ended the way it did. He deserved what happened to him. Do I sound like a horrible person?"

"Not hardly," Long Wolf assured her. He rose to his feet and gave Jackie Lynn a confirming hug. "I'm glad that Flora is free from him too. I know how much you love those friends of yours. You *all* deserve to be happy."

She knew what Long Wolf was getting at. She wondered when he would revisit their discussion from the previous night. He had not mentioned his undying love for her yet today, and she had been pleased that he had not.

"Well, I should be going. I still have the drive to my cabin to consider," he said. He pulled back from her a little and studied her eyes.

Is he hinting for me to ask him to stay here in the city? She could not help but wonder. The scary part was Jackie Lynn was tempted to invite him to stay. Nonetheless, she knew that this would not be wise. She needed some time alone to think. *To gather up my defenses.*

"I'll walk you to the door," Jackie Lynn said. She started moving in that direction. "Thanks for asking me to go to the Reservation with you this weekend. I enjoyed meeting your family and spending time with your people."

"Is that all you enjoyed?" Long Wolf playfully asked. He lingered in the open door.

"You know very well that it wasn't," she revealed, flashing him a reminiscent smile.

"You enjoy the rest of your day. Just remember that I love you from the bottom of my heart," Long Wolf asserted.

Denying Jackie Lynn the opportunity to say anything in retort, he eagerly brought his mouth to hers and gave her a prolonged, stirring kiss. When the kiss finally ended, it took Jackie Lynn a second to regain her composure. When she did, she said, "Long Wolf, I wish you wouldn't say that."

"I'm sorry. On the other hand, I wish you *would* say that," he admitted.

Then, thinking he better lighten the mood, with a chuckle he added, "That's okay. Banish a fellow to his lonely cabin in the woods without warming his heart with professions of love. That's alright. I can light a fire in the fireplace to try and keep myself warm. It's not like there won't be other chances for you to say it to me. I'll call you later, and perhaps then you will have changed your mind. If not, there will be many more opportunities."

"Long Wolf!" Jackie Lynn halfway growled, not enjoying his teasing. She knew, deep down, he was still trying to convince her to take a chance on love.

"I'll see you soon, beautiful," he said and gave her another lengthy kiss.

It was apparent he did not want to go, and the more Long Wolf touched her, the more Jackie Lynn did not want him to go. So, when the kiss ended this time, she stepped back several paces to wedge some much needed distance between them.

"Have a safe trip home," she said a little breathily.

Long Wolf nodded and gave her one last heart-melting smile. Then he turned and walked away. Jackie Lynn closed the door. Even though she was tired, she decided she should go and visit the girls for a while.

I don't want to be by myself. I'm missing Long Wolf and I certainly don't want to be alone with my thoughts of him.

* * * *

As she was headed home from work the next day, Jackie Lynn heard a shocking announcement on her car radio. Her attention riveted to the announcer's words, she turned the radio louder and listened with all her might.

"The accident occurred at the Greathouse Construction site of the new Lincoln Office Park complex. A support beam somehow broke loose from a crane high in the air. There are at least two fatalities. We will, of course, be reporting as we learn more details. Stay tuned."

Her stomach dropped to her toes. *Fatalities? Who?!*

Long Wolf had been so excited about his company landing the Lincoln Office Park deal. He had said on the phone last night that he would definitely be at this construction site today. He had aggravated her by playfully stressing, "If you should absolutely need to divulge *something* that can't wait until the next time we're together, you can call me at the Lincoln Office Park site anytime tomorrow."

Jackie Lynn had known he had been devilishly referring to her professing her love for him. It was obvious he did not intend to give up on this crazy notion. *So what if he was at the construction site? He's usually in the office, isn't he? There are so many construction workers on the grounds. Surely the accident couldn't have involved him.*

266

Jackie Lynn realized that she would not rest until she knew for sure that Long Wolf was okay. She made a rather reckless U-turn and speeded back toward downtown, where the construction site was located. As Jackie Lynn neared the scene of the catastrophe, she saw many police automobiles and ambulances. She felt queasy.

Calm down! It's terrible that this accident has occurred, but it has nothing to do with Long Wolf. If he's here though, knowing how caring he is, he's no doubt very upset. So me being here is a good thing, because I can at least try to bring him some comfort, she planned.

Jackie Lynn parked her car as close as she could get to the site and jumped out. She pushed and shoved her way through the somewhat large, curious crowd that had gathered to view the tragedy. After what seemed an excruciatingly long time, she forced her way up to the police barricade. This barricade was preventing the masses from advancing any further onto the site. Jackie Lynn broke out in a cold sweat when she saw two body bags not far away.

"Officer!" she yelled in a loud, rather panicked voice. She stretched over the barricade, endeavoring to clutch his nearby arm. "Wh…who…who was killed? Can you tell me?"

"Not for sure," he answered rather brusquely and started away.

Jackie Lynn simply had to know. On weak, shaky legs, she crawled under the barrier. She fearfully began making her way toward the covered bodies.

"Ma'am! You can't be in here!" the same cop declared. He grabbed her arm and pulled her toward the barricades.

"I have to know!" she insanely shouted in his face. "I know the owner of this company. Long..um…Abraham Greathouse. I need to see him to..to..make…um..I have to know that…." Jackie Lynn could not make herself say what her mind was screaming, *I have to make sure he wasn't one of those so tragically killed!*

"Okay, lady," the officer said. "Let me see what I can find out for you. But you have to remain here. Even if you open one of those body bags, chances are you wouldn't know for sure who the person was. That support beam really did a number on those two. Stay put, and I'll be right back!"

Severely shaken and nauseated, Jackie Lynn scanned the faces of the men walking around by the bodies. *I'll see Long Wolf in a minute*, she told herself.

She searched and searched; yet Jackie Lynn did not see anyone she recognized. *Oh, where is that damn cop?!* she wondered.

Jackie Lynn turned around and scrutinized the faces in the horde of people on the safe side of the barricade. *Maybe Long Wolf's left the site for some reason and is trying to fight his way through that crowd*, she mused. She saw no sign of him there either.

Just then, she felt a large hand on her shoulder. She swirled around with a relieved smile plastered on her face. She expected to discover Long Wolf standing there, after playfully sneaking up on her. Instead, it was the cop, along with a stranger in a hard hat.

"Hello. I'm Abraham Greathouse's assistant, Samuel Lewis. This officer said you were asking about him. May I ask who you are?"

"I'm Jackie Lynn Forrester," she proclaimed. "I..."

"Oh, *you're* Jackie Lynn," Samuel responded, before she had the opportunity to say anything further. He sounded somewhat shocked. "Abraham has talked about you a great deal." The man's face was much too serious for Jackie Lynn's sense of security. "Jackie Lynn, why don't you come with me to Abraham's office and we'll talk."

"Where is Long..um..Abraham?" she inquired, beginning to get panicky. "Is he coming here? Does he know about the accident?"

Samuel's eerie silence and his sudden reluctance to look her in the eyes had Jackie Lynn's stomach doing nervous flip-flops. Her heart fearfully raced and her head started to throb. What was worse was he glanced toward the body bags and grew very pale, before he said in a very quiet voice, "I'm so sorry, Jackie Lynn. Abraham evidently was trying to push one of our workers out of harm's way. He failed in his attempt, and neither of them was able to escape the support beam."

Jackie Lynn's legs became like jelly beneath her, and she suddenly could not breathe. *No!* her mind avidly denied. *I didn't hear right, or there's been some horrible mistake!*

Jackie Lynn charged forward toward the dead, mangled bodies. It took both Samuel and the policeman to stop her determined advance. It took her several, completely dazed minutes to realize she was screaming at the top of her lungs.

* * * *

It took a rather powerful sedative from one of the paramedics to calm Jackie Lynn's traumatized tirade. Samuel offered to drive her home, given that she was no longer in any condition to be behind the wheel. He asked for the keys to her automobile and had another construction worker follow in a company truck, since he would need to return to the site as soon as possible.

Once they were on their way, Jackie Lynn gathered the courage to ask, "How…how..how do you…? It *could not* have been Long Wolf!" she exclaimed and burst into remorseful tears, despite the drug's helpful numbness.

"Trust me, Jackie Lynn, I wish it hadn't been. Abraham has been one of my best friends for years. I can tell you that he loved you dearly, because he talked about you all the time. It unmistakably *was* him. They found his hard hat not far from one of the bodies.

"His..his..ha…hard hat?!" Jackie Lynn doubtfully repeated. "That's what you're basing him being killed on?" She laughed somewhat hysterically then, even though she was still crying at the same time. Her emotions were totally haywire.

"No. It wasn't just that," Samuel sadly revealed, tears welling up in his own eyes. "His wallet is still in his top desk drawer in the office. He always keeps it there when he's on site. One of the deceased didn't have any wallet on him. Abraham was nowhere else to be found on site. I think you know him well enough, Jackie Lynn, to understand that if he hadn't been killed, he would have been right in the middle of the action talking to police and trying to comfort the families of the victims. One of the people killed *was* Abraham, Jackie Lynn, as much as I hate to believe it myself. I'll miss him terribly. In my opinion, there aren't many men who were as fine as he was."

Samuel's words cruelly squelched Jackie Lynn's last hopes. She had never experienced suffering like she did at this very moment. Her very soul ached. She felt as if Samuel had taken a large machete and slashed her chest open, whacking her heart into a thousand, sharp, painful pieces. She wanted to crawl up in a ball somewhere and die.

* * * *

Samuel walked Jackie Lynn up to her apartment and made sure she got inside okay. He asked if there was someone he could call to come and be with her, but Jackie Lynn told him she wanted to be alone for a while. She could not possibly talk to anyone about what she was feeling at this very moment, not even Flora or Mary Julia. It was too awful for her to possibly put into words.

She thanked Samuel for bringing her home and told him she would most likely go to bed, claiming she was totally exhausted. Samuel reluctantly left. Jackie Lynn wearily collapsed on the couch and stared absently into space.

She kept hearing Samuel's last words, "There aren't very many men who were as fine as he was."

Jackie Lynn knew it was undeniably true. She had never been with a man who had been as loving and doting as Long Wolf.

"He loved you dearly," Samuel had also said with surety.

Evidently Long Wolf had openly and happily shared his strong feelings for her with his friends. *Why on earth didn't I? Why in the world did Long Wolf love me so? I never gave him what he wanted*, she regretted, disgusted with herself. *Why didn't I tell him I loved him? I couldn't be this heartbroken by his death and not have loved him from the bottom of my heart too. How could I have been so stupid?!* This dreadful, belated realization had her wildly beating the couch with her fists and hysterically screaming and sobbing.

Due to her stubborn foolishness and fears, she and Long Wolf had spent precious hours apart. *I should have told him I loved him the other night in our hotel room when he practically begged me to. Because I did, and deep down, I knew this,* she allowed herself to truthfully accept for the first time. *If I had been honest with him in regard to my true feelings, we probably would have been inseparable from almost the very beginning.*

Jackie Lynn was furious with herself. *How could I have been such a fool and not have savored every moment I had with this wonderful man, rather than spending so much of our* cherished *time fighting to hide* my *emotions?*

She curled up in an embryonic ball and rolled back and forth, sobbing and wailing with heartrending remorse until she had totally exhausted herself. Then she fell into a tormented sleep.

* * * *

Jackie Lynn woke with a fearful start early the next morning, telling herself, *It was a terrible nightmare. It had to have been.*

She sluggishly walked to the door and retrieved her paper. A second later, Jackie Lynn dropped the paper on the floor and gagging, scurrying to the bathroom. The headline in giant black, bold print read, 'Greathouse Construction President, Abraham Lincoln Greathouse, Killed in Freak Mishap at Lincoln Office Park Site'. Underneath the headline was a handsome picture of Long Wolf in a business suit.

Jackie Lynn shook uncontrollably. Although her stomach was empty and there was not anything to expel, she heaved and heaved over the toilet. In actuality, she was attempting to somehow expel the gut-wrenching pain which had intensely gripped her.

Too weak to depart from the room, Jackie Lynn laid sideways in the floor in front of the toilet for some time. The ringing of her telephone roused her from her coma-like state, yet she could not force herself to rise to answer it.

It might be Mary Julia or Flora, she thought. *They have most likely seen the newspaper as well. But there's nothing they can do. They'll probably tell me how sorry they are, and I'm not up to hearing those useless words from them right now.* The telephone eventually stopped ringing.

Several minutes later, Jackie Lynn struggled off the floor. She wandered aimlessly into the living room. *I should call work*, she thought, *and notify them that I won't be in.*

But Jackie Lynn did not care if they knew that or not. *Nothing really matters to me*, she realized, feeling numb.

Listless, she sat on the couch. The phone started to ring endlessly once more. After it had quit for the second time, Jackie Lynn took it off the hook. She curled into a catatonic ball and rocked herself, attempting to do the impossible – diminish the never-ending agony.

About ten minutes later, the doorbell rang, and there was persistent banging on her door. "Go away," she weakly mumbled under her breath, trying to ignore it.

The knock sounded much too rough for Mary Julia or Flora. *But who else?*

Then Jackie Lynn heard the voice. *I know that voice. I know it very well.*

She struggled to rise on her weak, practically useless legs, listening even harder. *I must surely be losing my mind*, she thought. Yet she ran to the door, bursting with hope.

Jackie Lynn fumbled helplessly with the lock for a few moments, because she was so anxious to get the door open. When she finally pulled it open, she almost fainted. If it had not been for Long Wolf's strong arms, which promptly reached in to catch Jackie Lynn, she most definitely would have fallen. Her legs had totally buckled beneath her from shock.

"Oh, dear God!" she exclaimed.

Jackie Lynn raised her hands to frame Long Wolf's face and steadfastly caressed his cheeks, forehead and hair. "It's you! It's really you!"

Through broken sobs, she showered Long Wolf with grateful kisses. "Oh, God! I love you so much! Please tell me you are really here and I'm not just dreaming this! They…they told…they told me…you were…dead!"

"Shh," Long Wolf soothed, pulling Jackie Lynn into a comforting embrace.

Her body was still violently trembling. He rapidly led her to the couch and sat them both down. "My poor darling! I tried repeatedly to call you when I saw the paper this morning. But you weren't answering the telephone, and then your phone was busy. I then called Samuel to see what in the world had happened. Needless to say, he was shocked to be hearing from me too. He told me that you had come to the site yesterday and what you had been told. I'm so sorry you had to go through this, Jackie Lynn."

"But...where were you?! Samuel said your wallet was still in your desk drawer at the site, and they found your hard hat near one of the dead men, and you were nowhere to be found, so it had to be you," Jackie Lynn rambled on. She was still showering him with kisses and touching and staring at him, proving to herself that he was real.

"Shh," Long Wolf said again, gently kissing the tears from her face.

With remorse, he told her, "I feel terrible that you've had to suffer like this. I wasn't at the site long yesterday morning when I got a call from the Reservation. My mom had a heart attack. I left the site immediately and headed to the airport to have a pilot friend of mine fly me out to the Reservation. In my rush, I left my wallet in my desk drawer. As for my hard hat, the only thing I can figure is that the guy who was killed somehow grabbed it by mistake. I just got back this morning, so I knew nothing about that terrible tragedy or my assumed demise until I saw my death in the headlines. I still don't know who it was that was killed. I'll have to somehow find out today."

"Is your mother alright?" Jackie Lynn asked with obvious concern.

"She's fine. It was only a very mild heart attack. I'm more concerned about you at the moment," Long Wolf shared, hugging her tightly to him. "You're still shaking."

"Having your arms around me is all I need," she assured him with a relieved smile.

Jackie Lynn pulled her head off his shoulder so she could gaze into Long Wolf's intent, brown, devoted eyes. She truthfully affirmed, "I want you to know something, Long Wolf. I want you to hear the words coming from my mouth and know that I mean them from the bottom of my heart. I love you, Long Wolf. I'm sorry I've been such a fool by hiding my feelings from you for so long. I promise you I won't do that anymore. I love you, and I want you in my life. I'm giving you my whole heart and soul. I have total faith that you will take good care of them."

Her honest, long awaited words touched Long Wolf so profoundly they almost brought tears to his eyes. "Jackie Lynn, my love," he declared, tenderly kissing her forehead and briefly savoring her salty lips. "I've wanted to hear you say that for so long. I have never cared as deeply about anyone in my entire life as I do you. I promise I will take wonderful care of your heart and soul, and I know you'll do the same with mine. I'm sorry it has taken such terrible circumstances to get you to finally trust in our love."

"I was sorry too. When I thought I had lost you, all I could think about was how much time I have wasted being so foolish. But no more. In fact, I think you should move in with me, so we can spend as much time together as possible," she proposed without hesitation.

Long Wolf was more than a little surprised, and slightly worried. He was quite certain her offer had to still be linked to the overwhelming shock of thinking he had been killed. Seeing the obvious confusion etched on his face, Jackie Lynn asked, "Don't you want to move in so we can spend more time together?"

"Oh, it isn't that at all. I treasure every moment I spend with you," he reassured her, affectionately stroking Jackie Lynn's too pale cheek. "I just don't want you to move too fast, because of the trauma you have suffered. Only yesterday, you weren't even capable of admitting that you loved me. Now you are suddenly suggesting we move in together. I want you to be completely secure with one thing before we move on to another."

"I'm secure," she told him, touched by his caring analysis. "You're sweet. But I think you may be worrying about me a bit too much. The trauma, as you call it, forced me to face up to what I truly want. What I truly want is *you*," she proclaimed and hugged Long Wolf tightly, warmly kissing the side of his neck. "I wish you would take me in the other room and make love to me. I want to touch every part of you I possibly can to convince myself that you are really still here."

"Oh, I'm here. I wouldn't want to be any other place," he avowed, squeezing her tighter.

Long Wolf stood, gently scooped Jackie Lynn into his strong arms, carried her to the bedroom, and very tenderly tried to love away all of her lingering terror.

CHAPTER NINETEEN

NEW LIFE

Although Long Wolf moved into Jackie Lynn's apartment with her, they spent nearly every weekend in the country at his cabin. Jackie Lynn was surprised to learn that she liked this arrangement very much. She discovered it was very restful to spend her weekends there, subsequent to her hectic work weeks in the city.

Jackie Lynn found it to be the perfect romantic hideaway as well. Sometimes the immense love she felt for Long Wolf, and now openly acknowledged, was still frightening to her. However, now, when these deep seeded fears arose, she willfully fought them. She refused to give them power over her anymore. She would not allow them to separate her from her true love. She was amazed by how happy and content she was now.

Jackie Lynn was also elated to be working with her dear friends again. Mary Julia had returned to her old position and seemed to be doing well. Fortunately, there had been an opening for another partner at their firm, so naturally Jackie Lynn had recommended Flora. Simon Grayson was delighted to have her join their team. When she had been in practice previously, at an opposing law firm, Grayson & Associates had lost enough cases to Flora to recognize what a fine lawyer she was.

Even though Mary Julia and Flora were getting their professional lives back on track, their personal lives were a whole different story. A month had passed since Jacob's death, yet Mary Julia had not heard from Jonathan once. She had left him several phone messages. He had not returned a single one. This profoundly hurt her. She had thought *at the very least* they had developed a friendship. She could not understand why Jonathan would no longer want to talk to her.

Flora suggested to Mary Julia that she back off and give Jonathan a little space and time. After all, he was bound to be upset by the way his violent altercation with his father had ended. Flora believed this young man to very kindhearted and wise.

I can't imagine that Jonathan would just blow Mary Julia off. Mary Julia will surely hear from Jonathan when he has his head together. If this was the case, then Flora could certainly respect him for keeping his distance for a while.

As far as her own life was concerned, Flora could not seem to stop having terrible nightmares about Jacob. He was still alive and trying to kill her in each horrible dream. She could hear his awful voice over and over, waking her numerous times during the night. "I'll never divorce you, you bitch! Do you hear me! I'll see you dead first! Remember it's until death do us part!"

It was getting to the point where Flora was afraid to go to sleep at night. *I think I need help. It's been a month, and things aren't getting any better.*

She recalled the detective's thoughtful words, the night Jacob had died, in regard to having scars that did not show. Rifling through her purse, Flora located the business card that Detective Kenneth Best had provided. Without another moment's hesitation, she picked up the nearby telephone and called the number on the card.

"22nd Precinct," a female voice answered.

Flora nervously considered hanging up for a second, but thought better of it. Instead, she inquired, "May I speak to Detective Best please?"

"May I ask who's calling?" the woman asked.

"It's Flora Roberts," she responded, thinking, *That detective probably handles so many cases he'll most likely have no idea who I am.*

"One second, ma'am, and I'll see if Detective Best is available," the receptionist politely responded. She placed Flora's call on hold.

Okay, I still have a chance to hang up. Perhaps I'm being foolish. This detective probably has far more crucial things to deal with then a woman who has terrible nightmares. He'll most likely tell me to get a grip.

Flora decided to hang up and forget about tying up Detective Best's time with her frivolous problems. She was pulling the phone from her ear when she heard his kind voice calling to her. "Flora? Flora, is everything alright?"

He called me by my first name. Does that mean he still remembers me? she could not help but wonder.

Flora put the telephone up to her mouth and said, "Hello, Detective Best. This is Flora Roberts. I'm not sure if you remember me or not…"

"Yes, I do," he interrupted her by saying. "So what's up, Flora? Are you calling regarding the group I mentioned?"

How could he possibly know this? she wondered. She was amazed that he still remembered her.

"Yes. I am," she hesitantly admitted. "I can't seem to put the horror Jacob put me through aside. I have such awful nightmares. They are so real. It's like Jacob is haunting me. I need to find a way to put all this out of my head, so I can get on with my life and eliminate Jacob from it for good. Do you think I'm crazy?"

"Of course not," he assured her. "What you are going through is not unusual in cases of abuse such as you have suffered at this man's vicious hands."

Kenny would never cease to detest men, like Jacob Roberts, who so thoughtlessly enjoyed beating up women. The mental anguish the women in these terrible situations were forced to endure was such a reprehensible shame. Kenny was often frustrated that he could not do more legally to assist them.

That was one reason he was so happy to help out with the support groups.

"Flora, I wish you would come to the group sometimes. I think you would discover that having the support of women who have been through the same thing as you would help. Your support may help someone else as well," Kenny explained.

"Well, when you put it like that, how can I refuse?" she responded. She felt better that she had made this call. "When is the next meeting?"

"Tomorrow night at 8:00 p.m. It's in the parish hall of St. Bartholomew's Catholic Church. Know where that is?" he asked, prepared to provide her with directions. *She's a great deal stronger than many of the women who participant in the group. She'll get help by helping those who are weaker.*

"Well, considering that was my parish, I think I might recall how to get there. Even though I haven't gone to Mass there since my first husband, Anthony, died," she confessed. "But I'll come to the meeting tomorrow night. Thanks for inviting me."

"It will be a pleasure having you there," he surprised her by saying.

Is he going to be there? Flora wondered. "Well, I suppose I should let you get back to your job. Thanks so much for your time and the information concerning the group."

"No problem. I'm glad you called. I'll see you tomorrow."

"Okay, bye," she replied, lowering the receiver.

So he is going to be there tomorrow. Wonder why? Flora pondered. *I guess I'll find out soon enough.*

* * * *

Flora went to the battered women's support group the following evening, as she had promised Detective Best. She was greeted by this very man as she was walking in the door. "Hi, Flora. I'm glad you decided to join us," he said, stopping her in the doorway.

"Hello, Detective Best. I thought I understood you to say you would be here tonight. What exactly is your role in all this?" she asked. Her eyes displayed slight bewilderment.

"I mediate for the group," he explained. "I make sure everyone who wants to has the opportunity to talk, and things like that. Why don't you come with me and I'll introduce you to everyone. Since this is your first time, you don't have to discuss your own situation if you don't want to. You can listen to the others. Or feel free to share. The main thing I'd like for us to accomplish tonight is making sure you feel comfortable being here."

"I already do. Thanks, Detective Best," Flora replied with a warm smile. She wondered how in the world this police detective got involved in mediating a battered women's group.

"Flora, it's Kenny here. Not Detective Best. I'm off duty. Alright?" he pointed out, returning her smile.

"Okay, Kenny. Lead the way."

With this, Flora walked beside him toward a group of women and a large circle of chairs. Some of the women where beginning to settle in these chairs. Others were standing off to the side, drinking sodas, eating snacks and chatting. Flora was pleased that Kenny was here tonight. Something about him gave her a feeling of security, and it made being here a bit easier. Flora hoped joining this group could help her put all of her demons dealing with Jacob behind her.

* * * *

Jackie Lynn had been spending so much time exclusively with Long Wolf that she felt as if she was losing touch with her friends. She suggested they all go out to dinner after work one night, so they could relax together. She also wanted to fully touch base with what was happening in each of their lives. Naturally, Flora and Mary Julia agreed. They, of course, went to Cornucopia, their favorite restaurant.

They had just ordered when Mary Julia confided that she had desperately gone to Jonathan's house that past weekend. Her intention had been to force him to talk to her.

"He told me to stay away from him," she dejectedly told her two friends. "He said he doesn't want to see me. I don't understand. What did I do?!" she wailed in painful confusion.

"I think Jonathan is truly afraid he might turn out to be like his dad," Flora told Jackie Lynn and Mary Julia.

"He's not anything like his father!" Mary Julia asserted. "He's very sweet and loving. I was hoping maybe we could have some sort of serious relationship."

"Jacob was very sweet and loving when I first fell in love with him too," Flora pointed out. "I've heard that sometimes children who grow up with abusive parents also become abusive. Perhaps it's wise if you let Jonathan go, Mary Julia."

"I was abused as a child too, Flora. And I certainly would *never* become abusive. I don't believe that Jonathan would either," Mary Julia argued.

"You most certainly may be right, Mary Julia. But until Jonathan is sure of that…and I don't think that he is…I don't want to see you go through the same terrible ordeal I went through with Jacob. Jonathan may be doing you a favor. What do you think, Jackie Lynn?"

The waiter brought them all their small house salads. As he sat Jackie Lynn's in front of her, the smell of it made her nauseous all the sudden. *Damn stomach flu!* Her stomach had been upset for days.

"Are you okay, Jackie Lynn?" Mary Julia inquired, noticing her friend was staring oddly at her food.

"I'm sorry," she apologized. She drank a little of her sprite, in hopes it would settle her stomach. "We haven't been out like this in so long that I hated to cancel tonight. But perhaps I should have. I'm just getting over the stomach flu, so the sight and smell of food isn't too appealing to me. I enjoy spending so much time with Long Wolf, but I think all the running back and forth from my place to his is causing my system to go berserk. My monthly cycle is totally screwed up, and now I've had this stomach thing. You know I'm usually regular as clockwork and hardly ever catch these dumb bugs that go around. I guess I better start trying to get more sleep."

Jackie Lynn smiled rather sinfully at her last sentence. Long Wolf had not tired of filling her nights with anything but sleep, and neither had she. It still seemed as if neither of them could get enough of one another in this way.

Flora and Mary Julia exchanged a strange look. "What is that all about?" Jackie Lynn suspiciously asked.

"Well…" Flora dared to question, "You don't think you could be pregnant, do you?"

Jackie Lynn choked on her soft drink. Mary Julia patted her on the back. "That…That's not funny!" she declared.

"I wasn't trying to be funny," Flora responded. "That could be feasible, couldn't it?"

"No. No. Of course not!" Jackie Lynn vehemently refused. "I'm forty years old, for goodness sakes! If anything, I'm most likely starting to go through The Change. My mother was only forty five when that happened to her."

"And the upset stomach?" Flora continued.

"It's a bug!" she disputed with certainty.

"Well, I haven't noticed a lot of people sick at work with *this bug*?" Mary Julia chipped in, to Jackie Lynn's further aggravation.

"Look, Mary Julia, we were discussing you and Jonathan," Jackie Lynn said, hurriedly changing the subject.

There hasn't been anyone else sick that I've been around. Her friends *had* to be wrong.

She and Long Wolf had always used protection. After all, she was on the pill. Yet there had been that one weekend when she had forgotten to take her birth control pills along with her to his cabin. They had skinny-dipped in the pond, and then romantically made love under the beautiful, starry, moonlit sky.

But, Long Wolf had pulled out before…*darn it! Why are my friends making me worry about something so bizarre as being pregnant? It isn't possible! I'm positive of that.* Although, suddenly she had this cold shiver running up and down her spine.

"Jackie Lynn," Mary Julia called, lightly patting her arm to get her attention. "So what do you think about Jonathan? Do you think I should give up on him?"

Forcing her mind to focus on her friend's dilemma and put aside their absurd assumptions concerning her, she answered, "I don't know, Mary Julia. You're doing so wonderful. The last thing you need in your life is a messed up man. If you think there might be some sort of dark side to Jonathan, then I have to agree with Flora. Let him go."

Mary Julia realized that her friends had a valid point. *But I can't help remembering the way he so tenderly kissed me previous to his father's accidental death, or his kind words.*

And she had seen his pained expression when his dad had accused him of being 'a chip off the old block'. *I can't believe that Jonathan could be a monster like his father.* Mary Julia thought with heartache.

"So Flora, what's happening between you and your helpful policeman?" Jackie Lynn inquired with a hopeful smile. "Anything in the line of a romance?"

"It's not a romance," she promptly corrected. "He's the mediator for my battered women's support group. But he seems like a very nice fellow, and it makes me feel good to talk with him and have coffee with him occasionally following the meetings."

"Can you believe that question came from Jackie Lynn?" Mary Julia said to Flora with a slight chuckle.

"What's that supposed to mean?" Jackie Lynn asked with bewilderment.

"Before Long Wolf, you were Miss *no such thing as romance*. Now, it's obvious you wish Flora and Kenny were romantically involved. My, doesn't love work in mysterious ways? You really are head over heels for Long Wolf! Will we be hearing wedding bells?"

"You know the answer to that all too well," she replied a bit too defensively. "You know I don't believe in marriage. I'm very happy living with Long Wolf and he's happy with me. As long as things remain that way, I intend to thoroughly enjoy it. But if they ever fall apart, we *won't* have to go through some messy divorce. Lord knows I saw enough of that from my mother. No, not for me. Not ever!"

"Okay," Mary Julia conceded, throwing her hands up in surrender. "I'm sorry I mentioned it. I'm delighted that you've finally found someone to love, and I hope it lasts you a lifetime."

I do too, Jackie Lynn secretly thought.

She did not know how she would bear it if Long Wolf ceased to be a part of her life, but Jackie Lynn knew this could still happen. Like she told her friends, however, she deeply loved this man and he felt the same way in regard to her. Jackie Lynn had wisely resolved to live for the moment. She would not allow herself to worry about her future with this man.

* * * *

"Jackie Lynn Forrester," the nurse called.

She rose from her seat in the waiting room of her doctor's office and walked directly toward the nurse. She had decided to make an appointment, after still feeling severely nauseated for a few more days. Her insinuating friends had her a little rattled about what might be going on.

The doctor will give me something to settle my stomach for good and probably relate that I'm about to go through The Change, she convinced herself. *I'll prove how silly my friends' theories concerning my sickness truly are. The extra stress of worrying over something as stupid as possibly being pregnant will mess up my monthly cycles even more if I allow this to continue.* She smiled knowingly to herself as she followed the nurse down the hall to an examination room. *When I leave here today I'll feel so much better.*

* * * *

When Long Wolf got home from work that day, he was instantly alarmed when he beheld the serious, dejected look on Jackie Lynn's face. She also made no attempt to rise from the couch. This was unusual. She usually greeted him with a cheerful smile and a warm hug.

"Jackie Lynn, what's wrong, sweetheart," he inquired with caring concern, sitting beside her on the sofa. When he reached for her hand, she pushed his arm away.

"Don't touch me!" Jackie Lynn snapped. She seemed very close to angry tears.

"Okay. What did I do?" Long Wolf questioned in confusion. He fought not to touch her, despite her strong request.

"What did you do?!" Jackie Lynn repeated, as she sprang to her feet. "Oh, I'll tell you what you did! Or rather what *we* did?! Why in the hell I got so caught up in this love thing that I could have been so stupid, I'll never know!"

"What are you talking about?" he asked. He stood up next to her, grabbed her arm, and turned her to face him. Everything had been so wonderful between them, so he could not imagine what had gotten Jackie Lynn so upset with him.

"I let you get me pregnant! That's what I'm talking about!" she furiously blurted out. "I'd say it was the night you were supposed to have pulled out prior to the deciding moment. Evidently your timing was slightly off! What the hell was I thinking?…well, obviously I wasn't thinking!"

Long Wolf's mouth dropped open in shock. "Did…did you say you're pregnant?" he asked in bewilderment, knowing the answer.

"Don't ask me to repeat it!" she snapped, irate, frustrated tears automatically springing to her eyes. She struggled to free herself from Long Wolf's firm grasp.

Rather than release her, he pulled her into a secure embrace, "Shh. It's okay, baby. You being pregnant is *not* something terrible. You are forgetting one very important thing. I love you and I know you love me. I can't imagine anyone I would rather have a child with than you. We have plenty of time to plan our marriage and where we want to live. I'll sell my cabin and we'll move to a house in the suburbs…"

"St…stop!" she shouted, interrupting his cheerful planning. She pushed herself out of his convincing arms.

"You don't understand. I don't want any kids! And I *certainly* don't want to get married. Both are out of the question!"

"Jackie Lynn," he called in a soothing voice. "I understand that you are scared. You were terrified to admit that you loved me; yet look how well that has turned out. You just need to get used to the fact that you are going to have my baby. We're practically married now, so going through with a formal ceremony isn't going to change anything. Other than to make me more committed to you."

"Oh, yeah! Being in love with you has turned out to be grand!" she said sarcastically, hurting him a little. "It made me careless enough to get pregnant. Let me tell you precisely what I think of marriage. I lost count of how many stepfathers I had. I *will not* do that to a kid. I'm sorry you are so damn happy about this, Long Wolf, because I can't go through with this pregnancy."

His face suddenly turned very somber. "I hope you aren't alluding to what I think you are," he said in a saddened voice. "You wouldn't…you're not talking about having an abortion, are you?"

Jackie Lynn placed her hands over her face to hide her eyes from his disappointed ones. *Why does he have to love me so? The mere mention of me carrying his child has lit his face up in happiness. It most likely wouldn't have been long before he would have been suggesting marriage anyway. Why do things have to be so complicated with this guy? Why am I suddenly feeling very guilty about considering terminating this pregnancy?*

"Yes. That's precisely what I plan to do," she replied in a shaky voice. She averted her eyes from Long Wolf's.

There was an eerie silence for a few moments before he said, "I've got to think, 'you can't be serious!' But I know you well enough to realize that you are. So I guess the next question I need to ask is how can I possibly talk you out of this?"

Jackie Lynn's heart twisted as she gazed into this man's sorrowful eyes. *Stop it!* she silently scolded herself. *You can't start having second thoughts! You've never wanted children! So why would you now?*

"There's not anything you can do or say to talk me out of this," she admitted, glancing away again.

"Then why in the world did you tell me? Why not just sneak away, get rid of the baby, and come back all loving...like nothing ever happened?" Long Wolf demanded in frustration, a tinge of anger evident in his voice.

It was a good question. Jackie Lynn was not at all positive of the answer. She had been furious about the news. *So is that why I so inconsiderately blurted it out? What response had I been expecting? I sure hadn't expected Long Wolf to be so happy in regard to this pregnancy.* In fact, she had not thought about what his reaction might be. She was overcome with guilt by this realization.

"Look, I didn't expect you to be so damn thrilled about this, okay?" she defensively fired back. She forced herself to look at his solemn face. "You never said anything about wanting kids."

"The subject never came up. In actuality, I never anticipated having any children, because I never expected to have a woman in my life who I would love enough to want to make a child with. Then you came along," he confessed, drawing closer.

Jackie Lynn backed farther away. She was determined she would not permit him to put his arms around her. He was too adept at convincing her of things when he had those strong, assuring arms wrapped so tightly about her. Long Wolf stopped his forward gait. "This wasn't planned, but now that it's happened, how can you even think about killing our child?"

Why did he have to say that? I don't want to regard this foreign thing which has invaded my body as a person. I certainly don't want to think about it being a part of Long Wolf.

"Stop it!" she wailed in protest. "I can't have a child and that's all there is to it!"

"So to hell with my feelings then!" he challenged, rushing forward and grabbing her arms a bit too forcefully for comfort. "Well, alright. Then you explain to me exactly how I'm supposed to deal with knowing you killed our child after it's over and done?! How do I look into those beautiful green eyes without feeling this sadness...this loss?"

Jackie Lynn was terribly confused and torn. She had never planned on having kids. Regardless, she was pregnant. Worse yet, the deed had been rendered by a man who truly loved her and who she loved so profoundly her heart ached when they were apart.

All I know for sure is this is happening way too fast. I need time alone to think...to get this taken care of somehow...I'm not ready to deal with Long Wolf's feelings!

"Long Wolf, I want you to leave! Let go of my arms, and leave *now*!" she cried in agony. "I have to be by myself to think! You...you're making me crazy! I'm not ready for all of this! Please go away and leave me alone! I need time to myself!!"

She began to cry and sob brokenheartedly, holding the sides of her head as if it were splitting. The last thing Long Wolf wanted to do was leave her. Nevertheless, he knew this woman well enough to wisely realize that she probably did need some time by herself to sort out her massive bewilderment and torment. He picked up his jacket, slung it over his shoulder, and started toward the door.

Jackie Lynn helplessly watched him walk away and realized he really was leaving her. In crazed desperation and fear, she darted up behind Long Wolf and wrapped her arms possessively around his waist. When he started to turn though, she loudly and resistantly protested, "No! Please don't turn around. I can't stand for you to look at me with that awful sadness in your eyes. It will break my heart in two. Please try and understand, Long Wolf...I just...I can't do this!"

Jackie Lynn reluctantly released her hold on him. Long Wolf slowly opened the door, stepped out, and shut it softly. He did not look back. Jackie Lynn numbly stared at the closed door for a few moments. Then she meandered over to the sofa and sank into it, continuing to weep for a while.

My emotions are severely messed up by this pregnancy, she tried to reason. She knew it was much more than this. *Why does Long Wolf have to want this baby so badly?* He truly was tearing her apart.

I'm the one who has worked so hard to make myself a capable, self-reliant woman. I never figured kids into this equation, but I surely never figured loving a man as completely as I do Long Wolf either. Can our relationship survive if I abort this baby? She kept seeing his disappointed, angry eyes and thinking, *how would he be able to forgive me?*

* * * *

Jackie Lynn nervously awaited Long Wolf's return. The evening hours seemed to last forever. As it got later and later, she could not help but erratically worry, *Has he walked out of my life for good?*

Jackie Lynn changed into a nightgown and climbed into bed. She was restless, and she shivered from the cold aloneness that engulfed her. *But I'm not alone. I have Long Wolf's baby growing inside of me. No! Stop that!* she chastised herself. *I can't allow myself to think of this pregnancy that way! This isn't a person yet!*

Hours later, Jackie Lynn eventually fell into a fitful sleep. In her dream, she could see Long Wolf's eyes so clearly. He was calling to her through a thick fog. His voice sounded quite strange. She made her way closer, and she saw a small boy.

"Mommy," the child cried, but he was running from her.

When the child looked back, Jackie Lynn could see it was his eyes she had seen through the fog. The boy had Long Wolf's eyes. All the sudden, Jackie Lynn could see the child was headed straight for a cliff. She reached to grab him, but instead her hands ended up roughly shoving his back.

The child tumbled over the cliff. Jackie Lynn was screaming and clutching wildly at the space where the boy had been. Then when she turned, Long Wolf was standing behind her. "You killed him," he said in a pain-filled, disgusted voice. "You killed our child."

"*No!!*" Jackie Lynn attempted to shout. Long Wolf disappeared into thin air, and she had this dreadful sense that he was gone from her life for good. *Oh, what have I done?* she regretfully agonized.

Jackie Lynn bolted upright in bed, awakening to find herself drenched in sweat. She rapidly climbed from the bed and stumbled the short distance to the bathroom. Turning on the light, she looked in the mirror at her horrified face. She firmly resolved, *Tomorrow, I'm going to see a doctor. This has got to end! I can't go on like this! I'll lose my mind!*

She wet a washcloth with cold water and ran it across her sweaty face and neck. She turned off the bathroom light and went into the bedroom, lying down in bed. It was then that she sadly realized that Long Wolf had not returned for the night. Her body physically ached as if she had been battered. She missed him severely. She rolled over on her side in a protective curled up position and tried not to start crying again.

* * * *

Daybreak came with Jackie Lynn shutting her eyes again. She had not been able to go back to sleep. She had been awake since 3:00 a.m., and she had not gone to sleep until almost midnight. *This is going to be a very long day*, she concluded, knowing fully well what she must do.

Jackie Lynn lethargically reached for the bedside phone and called in sick for the day. She was not being untruthful. She did feel terrible.

She wearily rose from the bed to go and take a shower, hoping this might revitalize her. After this was done, Jackie Lynn dressed. She threw on a pair of slacks and a rather sloppy, overly large sweater, which she usually lounged around the apartment in. In Jackie Lynn's mind, she believed people could tell she was pregnant just by looking at her. In reality, she was not nearly far enough along for people to suspect a thing.

She went into the kitchen, retrieved her Yellow Pages from a drawer, sat at the table, and attentively scanned names of abortion clinics. Jackie Lynn looked for a clinic which was away from downtown, as if someone she knew might see her going there. She picked a place without an ad.

The address of this clinic was on the other side of town. Jackie Lynn realized it was not in the nicest area, but she did not care. The important thing to her right now was that no one would dare recognize her there. She picked up the telephone and dialed the number listed. Jackie Lynn was told she could be seen for a consultation early that afternoon.

She nervously moped around the apartment, turning the television and the radio on to make some noise to distract her troubled mind. *Surely Long Wolf will walk through the door any minute*, she half wished. *Oh, he's most likely at work. Is he capable of concentrating on work, or is he having as hellish of a day as I am?*

When noon came and still no one had shown up, Jackie Lynn left for the clinic. Her stomach felt sick, even though she had eaten neither breakfast nor lunch. She had had no appetite for either. To disguise herself further, Jackie Lynn put on dark sunglasses and a hat. After driving across town, about twenty minutes, although it seemed to take much longer, Jackie Lynn pulled into the parking lot of the tiny clinic.

As soon as she stepped inside, she could tell it was a virtual hell hole. The chairs were a dinghy gray with stains on every one of them – a mixture of spilled food and drink and past dirty bodies. The carpet was well worn and very soiled. Cigarette burns were visible in certain places.

Walking across the waiting room to sign in at the receptionist desk, she forced herself not to think about how things looked. She supplied her name as Anita Jones. It did not matter what name she furnished. She was not planning on running the bills for this *procedure* through her medical insurance. She would pay cash for her visits. Jackie Lynn clearly did not intend to provide her real name to these people.

It seemed like forever before the name 'Anita Jones' was called. She followed a tired looking old woman into an examining room. There, she was handed a yellow colored sheet and told, "Take off everything from the waist down. The doctor will be with you in a moment."

Jackie Lynn removed her slacks and underwear and had a seat on the exam table. She was getting sicker by the minute. The slight headache, she had awakened with, had become more like a migraine, and her heart was pounding so hard that she could feel it in her temples.

Just as Jackie Lynn exhaustedly lowered her head in her hands, the door opened and this mostly bald, old man, with stooped shoulders, a days worth of growth to his beard, and sour cigarette smoke breath, entered the room. He spoke very slowly, asking her to slide to the end of the examining room table, and then he roughly jammed Jackie Lynn's feet in the stirrups. She trembled and tears sprung to her eyes while he roughly began to stick his fingers into her body. It felt like he was rummaging for something that he had lost and could not quite find.

He stopped, after what seemed an eternity, freed her feet from the stirrups and told her she could sit up. Jackie Lynn rapidly scrambled to a sitting position, securely wrapping the sheet around her lower half. She waited for the appalling old man to recount to her what she so desperately wanted to hear, *"It's all a mistake, ma'am. You're not pregnant."*

Instead, the doctor's words were like a hot knife cutting through her soft flesh, "Ms. Jones, we can perform an abortion by the end of the week. Put your clothes on and see the receptionist for the exact time and instructions for the night before. You do realize that this is a cash only clinic, don't you? No checks. No credit cards. Just cash. We'll get the deed done for you."

With these cold words, he promptly turned and left the room, not even remotely interested in what her response might have been. She sat there for a second, glancing around her at her grotesque surroundings – a stack of dirty yellow sheets, the big light overhead, and a tray of well worn instruments pushed over to the side. It sadly and fearfully dawned on her that this was probably also the room where they preformed the abortions. She almost choked to keep from screaming out loud.

Putting on her panties and slacks, she flung the door open and literally ran past the woman at the front desk. As she rushed through the door, she could hear her calling, "Ms. Jones, you forgot your paperwork, honey."

By the time she got to the street, she was totally out of control, bawling her eyes out and shaking all over. She collapsed on the curb by her car and laid her face in her hands.

Oh, God! she thought. *I need to know there really is a God right now. I need some sort of miracle to get me through this. I can't possibly permit these people to do an abortion for me. Oh, God, if you are there,* please *help me!*

* * * *

By the time she got home, Jackie Lynn had managed to slightly calm herself. Nonetheless, every time she recalled the awful place she had been, she could not help but shed a few more disturbed tears. She was exceedingly grateful when she at last stood before the door to her apartment, turning the lock with her key. She wanted to go inside and hide from the terrible world outside.

"Jackie Lynn?" she heard Long Wolf's voice say as she walked in.

She looked up to see him coming from the kitchen. A mixture of emotions instantly washed over her at seeing him in her apartment again. Since he had not returned the previous night, Jackie Lynn had assumed that he had decided he was through with her for good. Part of Jackie Lynn was so happy to see Long Wolf that she wanted to run and confine him in her arms and never let him go. The other part of her was still so horribly confused she did not want him there at all. Dazed tears started freely streaming down her cheeks.

How in the world can this be possible? I've cried so much these last two days; I don't see how I can be capable of producing any more tears.

Long Wolf hastened to her side. "I want to hold you so badly. Can I?" Jackie Lynn was surprised to hear him ask.

Without thinking, she nodded her head, and through her tears sobbed, "Yes…I need..I need you..to..to hold me."

He gathered Jackie Lynn in his robust secure arms, soothingly rubbing her back and the back of her head. He kissed her forehead and her cheeks, and said, "I'm sorry. I shouldn't have gotten so angry with you yesterday. I spent all night thinking and thinking. I know finding out you were pregnant was horrible for you, and I made the whole thing worse by the things I said. It's just..I love you so much."

"Oh..I know! I love you too!" Jackie Lynn wailed, kissing him back. "I didn't want to do anything to hurt you. I just…"

"Shh! I know. You told me you couldn't go through with it," Long Wolf silenced her, placing his finger on top of her lips. "You don't have to explain to me. I know you weren't at work today, and I saw the clinic numbers by the telephone. We'll get past this. We have to. Love like we have doesn't come around every day, as you well know. We'll pretend this whole thing never happened. I'll never mention it, I promise."

Long Wolf is such a sweet, caring man. He thinks I've had the abortion. Regardless of how greatly he wanted our child, he's willing to put his own feelings totally aside for me. Jackie Lynn thought her heart was positively going to explode it was so overflowing with love for this man.

"I didn't do it," she quietly told him, pulling her head off Long Wolf's shoulder so she could gaze into his warm, devoted eyes.

"You…you didn't?" he asked in bewilderment, studying Jackie Lynn's face with confusion. He chose his next words very carefully. "So..have you got an appointment to have one done?" Long Wolf looked as if he was holding his breath. He was awaiting Jackie Lynn's answer in agony.

"No," she stated. She could see the relief in his eyes, although he was striving so hard to remain neutral. "You'll be delighted to hear that I can't go through with it. I guess what I'm basically saying is…we *are* going to have a baby."

Despite his resolve, Long Wolf lost all restraint then. He was so thrilled that he lifted Jackie Lynn over his head, widely smiling up at her. When he lowered her to her feet, he smothered her with a lengthy kiss. "Jackie Lynn, I promise you, you won't regret having this child. I'll do everything in my power to see to it that you are both *so* happy. You'll see; this is all going to work out!"

For the first time since she had found out she was pregnant, for some unexplained reason, Jackie Lynn was beginning to believe Long Wolf. He had never failed her before.

Is he the miracle that God sent me?
Jackie Lynn sincerely hoped so.

CHAPTER TWENTY

THE SETBACK

I might truly be free from Jacob Roberts for good. This realization made Flora ecstatic.

The support group she was attending each week made it possible for Flora to encounter peace. Flora had been going to these meetings for about three and a half months now. She no longer blamed herself, in any way, for Jacob's death. Nor did she experience guilt over being glad that this man was deceased. Her terrible nightmares regarding Jacob had also finally ceased.

Spending time with Kenny also brought Flora happiness. She had been seeing this man one night a week for quite a while now, and they had developed a wonderful friendship. Her time with him was very innocent, since she only saw him at the battered women's support group meetings at the church.

Flora was very grateful to this man for his wise suggestion that she begin attending these meetings. Sharing her terrible ordeal with other women, who had suffered the same or much, much worse, had served to strengthen Flora considerably. She honestly believed she was helping some of them by being there, and this left her with a good feeling about the whole thing.

* * * *

Mary Julia had decided once and for all that she had taken all the torment she was willing to where Jonathan was concerned. It had been almost four months, since she had last talked to Jonathan. She headed to his condo to confront him one last time.

Flora is beginning to show signs of moving on with her life. Jackie Lynn is going to have a child with the man of her dreams and hopefully will agree to marry him soon, so I'm tired of living my own life in limbo. I need to know once and for all if there is any prospect of a future for Jonathan and myself. So I'm going to his condo one last time, and I'm going to force him to provide some explanation for totally shutting me out, after leading me to believe he wanted some type of relationship, she resolved.

Mary Julia rang Jonathan's doorbell. She deceptively placed her hand over the peephole, so he could not see her and refuse to answer the door. Jonathan barely opened the door, and Mary Julia stubbornly pushed her way inside his home.

"Mary Julia, what are you doing here? Didn't I tell you I didn't want to see you?" he asked with exasperation. He turned and walked away from her.

"I don't care," she argued, making her way farther into his condo. "*I* want to see *you*! We are going to talk, and I'm not leaving here until you explain to me precisely why you can't, or *won't*, see me anymore."

Mary Julia waltzed past Jonathan into the living room. She was intent on taking a seat on the sofa and remaining there until he supplied her with some decent explanations for all her questions. However, just as she sat down, a woman's voice called to Jonathan from the hallway.

The same hallway that leads to Jonathan's bedroom, Mary Julia's mind painfully registered.

Looking slightly uncomfortable, Jonathan responded, "Just a second, Kate, an old friend of mine has unexpectedly dropped by. Can you give me a few seconds, and then I'll meet you in the den?"

Mary Julia's eyes began to well with tears. *How could I have been so stupid? Of course, that's it! He's involved with*

INTIMACIES

another woman. Why shouldn't he be? It's not as if I ever really meant anything to him. All of his mushy talk the last time we were together must have merely been romantic lines he was feeding me.

As quickly as she had sat down, Mary Julia sprang to her feet. She rushed for the door. Defiant tears streamed freely down her cheeks. As she got to the door, she heard Jonathan calling, "Mary Julia, where are you going? You're right. I do owe you some sort of explanation."

She turned for a brief moment, facing him, as he hastened to come up the hallway toward her. Mary Julia said in a hoarse voice, "Jonathan, why didn't you tell me the truth? I would have left you alone. I am so stupid...so blind! I can't believe I honestly thought you cared about me!"

That being said, Mary Julia turned, pulled the front door open, and rushed from Jonathan's home, without waiting for his reply. Jonathan scurried from the condo in hot pursuit, stopping just outside his door and yelling for Mary Julia to stop. Nevertheless, Mary Julia dashed down the four flights of stairs, scrambled along the sidewalk in front of the building, clambered safely into her car, and locked the doors. Jonathan hurried from the building, but Mary Julia ignored his final pleading shouts that she stay. Instead, she started the automobile, slammed it into reverse, and raced away.

I won't allow myself to be hurt by any more of Jonathan's creative lies. I heard the other woman's voice calling to him with my own ears, Mary Julia justified her actions.

Excessively confused by Mary Julia's tears and her bewildering behavior, Jonathan slowly re-entered the building. He climbed the steps to his condo in defeat. The woman, whose voice Mary Julia had heard, was standing in his doorway, curiously awaiting his return.

"What in the world was wrong with that young lady?" she inquired with a puzzled look.

Kate Anderson, or Dr. Anderson as Jonathan more familiarly knew her, had been one of Jonathan's mother's dearest friends. She had helped him come to terms with his

298

grief over losing his mom when he was a boy. She specialized in family psychiatry.

Jonathan had called Dr. Anderson the day after his father's tragic demise and asked if she would be willing to counsel him. She had agreed and had been coming to his home for private therapy sessions twice a week ever since. Her role this time was to assure Jonathan that he could properly deal with his anger without hurting someone else, most especially any woman he might care about. Jonathan had intended to keep his distance from Mary Julia until he was completely certain he would not harm her.

Mary Julia's unanticipated appearance at his home this evening, demanding answers from him as to his unexplained alienation, made Jonathan realize that he was hurting Mary Julia already by keeping her in the dark about his therapy. Jonathan was going to share with her exactly what was transpiring in his life, if she had not rushed away in tears.

What could that have been about? Jonathan could not help but wonder in a tormented quandary. *Something evidently upset her. It couldn't have been anything I said, because I never got a chance to open my mouth. Other than saying something to Kate. Oh, no! Surely Mary Julia didn't...could she have thought Kate was my lover? Did she think that she was coming from my bedroom, instead of the bathroom in the hall?*

Jonathan recalled the intense pain he had seen in Mary Julia's eyes and her strange accusing words, asking why he had not told her *the truth*. He shared his unsettling observation with Kate.

"So that was Mary Julia," the doctor noted. She helpfully added, "Jonathan, you do realize that a woman doesn't react the way she did unless she truly cares about a man? You are very plainly upset that this lady was hurt as well. Do you honestly believe that, if you are this upset by the sight of merely her tears, you could ever physically harm this woman? Think about it, Jonathan. Getting therapy was a wise idea to help deal with your father's death, and I've been happy to help you with that. But, as to inheriting his violent nature, do you honestly think you could be anything like him? You need to go and find this young woman and explain things to her. Stop letting your fears control your life and start a new one with someone who so obviously wants to share one with you."

"I think you are right," Jonathan surprised her by admitting. "I'm the one that's been a fool. I've got to go after Mary Julia and tell her all that's happened, the truth. Thank you for all your help."

"My pleasure. You know my number, should you ever feel you need me for any reason," Dr. Anderson said with a warm smile. She was a friend that cared as well as a therapist.

Jonathan led her back inside the condo, so she could gather her belongings. Then they left his home together. He planned to pursue Mary Julia. He hoped perhaps she might go to her apartment. He knew Flora was living there now, so if Mary Julia did not go directly home, he thought maybe Flora would permit him to wait with her there. He was not going to put off talking to Mary Julia any longer. He hated that he had upset her so. He was determined that he would soon make everything right.

* * * *

Mary Julia was very upset. She felt like a total idiot. *Why in the world did I think Jonathan would be any different! All men are monsters! Didn't I learn that early enough, when my adored daddy started molesting me? Then my stepfather did even worse to me. Why can't I learn?! I must be incredibly stupid!*

It was then that she beheld a man in sexy tights jogging by the side of the road. She honked the horn, hurriedly pulling the auto up to the curb beside him. Jogging in place next to her car, the somewhat handsome man inquired, "Can I help you, Miss?" He evidently thought she was going to ask him for directions.

"Well, if you would be so kind as to get in my car, maybe we can help each other," Mary Julia told him in a slow, seductive voice. She flashed him an inviting smile and promptly unbuttoned her blouse to shamelessly flaunt her ample cleavage to this stranger.

If he turns me down, I'll solicit someone else, she concluded. *Sex is all men are good for anyway. I'm tired of trying to fight the obvious. It's gotten me nowhere, and I'm horny as hell!*

The jogger nervously laughed and questioned, "You're kidding, right? Who put you up to this?"

Mary Julia was quick to unbutton her entire blouse and unhook her bra. She exposed her bare breasts to this stranger's stunned eyes. "Do I seriously appear to be kidding?" she asked, "Please get in the car. We'll go someplace *quickly*!"

The jogger stopped running in place. He glanced all around him, as if expecting someone to be watching. Then he enthusiastically climbed into the automobile with a wide, expectant, pleased smile. Mary Julia raced away.

* * * *

Mary Julia had expected to feel better after picking up the stranger from the street, taking him to a hotel room, and unshamelessly having sex with him over and over. Nevertheless, driving home afterwards, she discovered she felt very empty and disgusting. Like a drug addict, she knew the only way to overcome this terrible feeling was to get another fix, another strange sexual encounter.

No! she resisted. *I'm not going to go nuts. I won't permit this to happen over once a day. But, I'm not going without anymore. There is no point. All men are scum! Jonathan included!* She focused all her attention on the road and hurried home. Mary Julia hoped Flora was not too concerned about her.

* * * *

It was after midnight when Mary Julia finally got home. As soon as Mary Julia unlocked the door to her apartment, she was practically overrun by Flora and Jonathan before she could barely make an entrance.

"Thank God you're alright, Mary Julia!" Flora exclaimed. "Jonathan and I have been so worried. We were about to call the police and hospitals. Where in the world have you been?"

Jonathan scooped Mary Julia into a relieved embrace. She was overwhelmed with uncertainty. *What is* he *doing here? Why does he care if I'm alright or not? He has another woman in his life now. Why isn't he with her?*

She squirmed out of his arms. "Jonathan, what are you doing here?" Mary Julia asked, looking at his face with hardened eyes.

"I came here looking for you after you rushed out of my condo earlier. I've been waiting here with Flora for hours. Where have you been? Do you have any idea how worried we have been about you?" Jonathan questioned. He gratefully caressed one of Mary Julia's checks.

She pulled away from his touch and defiantly turned her back on him, walking several paces apart. Mary Julia wanted to tear into Jonathan, to exclaim what scum she thought he was. She somehow managed to contain herself and control her tongue.

She's definitely angry with me, and I think I understand why, Jonathan mused. *I have to clear up the silly misunderstanding that stands between us.*

"Mary Julia," he said in a quiet voice, pursuing her. "We need to talk. Flora, can you give me a second alone with her?"

"Of course," Flora agreed. She headed for her bedroom, so they would have the living room all to themselves.

She and Jonathan had talked for hours while they awaited Mary Julia's return. Flora was more convinced than ever that this young man truly cared for her friend. Jonathan merely needed to convince Mary Julia of this. Flora would grant them all the time and privacy they needed.

"Jonathan, I don't have time for this nonsense!" Mary Julia snarled through gritted teeth. Turning to face him, she rather adamantly pleaded, "Go away and leave me alone! Why don't you go and spend some more time with whoever you were with at your house earlier?"

"That's precisely what I want to talk to you about," he said. He grabbed her by one arm and stubbornly pulled her with him. "Come and sit with me on the sofa for a while and let me try and explain."

"It's too late, Jonathan!" Mary Julia argued. She attempted to pull away from him. "I understand now. Although I don't understand why you couldn't have told me you had moved on. It would have been a lot kinder. But I know now, so we have nothing else we need to say to one another."

"That's where you are very, very wrong, Mary Julia," he declared. Jonathan released his hold on her arm, because she was so vehemently fighting him. "The woman who was at my house earlier wasn't my girlfriend. She is a family friend…"

"Oh, please, Jonathan!" Mary Julia screamed. "You may think I'm an idiot, but I am not. I won't stand here and listen to you lie to me. Don't give me this crap about that woman just being a friend of yours! How naïve do you think I am?"

"Mary Julia, you are making me crazy!" Jonathan acclaimed. He grabbed her and spun her around so that her back was facing him. He placed one of his hands over the top of her mouth to silence her so he could finish.

Mary Julia squirmed and struggled against Jonathan's tight arm and hand. She was mumbling incoherently. He briskly added, "She *is* a family friend, but she is *also* an excellent therapist. I've been privately seeing her at my house. I needed to be convinced that I wasn't going to turn out like my father or grandfather and harm women. It's a cycle in my family that I *can't* be a part of. I couldn't take that risk if you and I are going to have the relationship I hope we can have."

Mary Julia slowly stopped struggling as the fact 'Jonathan is not seeing someone else' entirely sank in. She experienced a very brief moment of happiness. Then, suddenly, an image of the jogger she had picked up on the street clearly sprang to mind.

As Mary Julia felt Jonathan relax his hold, she turned to face him. Her face spontaneously turned a bright shade of red. She lowered her head and concealed her face in her hands. She felt lightheaded, like she was going to throw up.

Mumbling into her hands, Mary Julia began to vaguely confess, "Oh my God! I was so positive...I was so hurt! I thought you were so cruel...I'm *so* sorry!"

Jonathan gathered Mary Julia in his arms. He placed a hand under her chin and gently raised her head. When Mary Julia hesitantly slid her hands away from her face, Jonathan began unabashedly showering her flushed face with healing kisses.

"It's okay, Mary Julia. If anyone should be apologizing, it's me. I'm sorry I kept you away for so long, and I shouldn't have allowed you to leave this evening without explaining what was going on. Will you forgive me for hurting you?"

Mary Julia was shocked and a little sickened to hear Jonathan ask this. "Jonathan, stop!" he was extremely surprised to hear her exclaim. Mary Julia pushed herself from his comforting arms and away from his kind kisses. She was crying once more. "I can't bear to hear you apologize to me. You don't realize what I've done...You're not the one that's screwed up. I am!"

"What in the world are you talking about?" he asked in confusion. He reached for her again, but Mary Julia managed to escape his arms this time. She went scurrying away. She dashed into her bedroom, slammed the door, and locked it.

Hearing the door slam, Flora opened her own bedroom door and peered out. She saw Jonathan still standing in the middle of the living room. He was staring toward Mary Julia's closed door with utmost bewilderment. It was obvious he was befuddled as to what he should do next.

Flora vacated her room and approached him. "Jonathan, I think it might be best if you left Mary Julia alone for a while," Flora told him. "She's apparently very upset about something, and she'll need a little time by herself. Trust me, I know her."

"I let her go from my house earlier today when she was upset, and it seems I've hurt her even greater. I don't want to make that mistake again." Jonathan debated, looking very pained.

"Look, it's very late. Why don't you go home? Let me try to talk to Mary Julia," Flora attempted to persuade. "In the state she's in, she won't listen to you. Perhaps she'll be more receptive tomorrow."

Jonathan knew what Flora was saying was true; yet it was hard for him to stand back and do nothing. "Will you let me know what you find out?" he asked in reluctant surrender.

"I'll let you know what I can," she professed.

Flora led Jonathan to the door then. She said goodnight to him and thanked him for waiting with her for Mary Julia's return. She promised Jonathan she would do everything she could to talk Mary Julia into calling him the following day.

Going to her friend's bedroom door, Flora softly knocked and called, "Mary Julia. What's going on? I sent Jonathan home. Could you please permit me to come in, so we can discuss why you are so upset?"

A second later, Flora heard Mary Julia turning the lock on the door. "Oh, Flora!" she whined.

Mary Julia threw her arms around her friend as soon as she walked through the door. In hysterics, she began wailing, "I am such a nutcase! Why are you friends with me? I keep right on screwing up my life."

"What has happened?" Flora questioned very seriously. She pushed her friend away, so she could study her distraught face. "Does this have anything to do with where you were all those hours you were missing tonight?"

"Yes. I thought Jonathan had cheated on me, so I got even tonight with some stranger I found on the street. Sound familiar? All that hospital time genuinely did me a great deal of good! I'm hopeless! Now, Jonathan claims he wants to have a relationship with me. He deserves better," she dejectedly rambled.

"Mary Julia, have you told Jonathan about your illness? About what happened to you as a child?" Flora inquired with concern.

"No, of course not! That's what I should do though. Then maybe he'd realize I am hopeless and give up on me," she concluded.

"Jonathan should know about the abuse you suffered as a child and the illness it caused you to have," Flora told her. "Not so he'll think you are hopeless. So he might understand anything you've done as an adult. Even this last slip. It's understandable why you would have thought the worst of him, and why you reverted to old ways to deal with things."

"It's understandable to you, because you are one of my dearest friends," Mary Julia started to logically argue.

"And I love you. Jonathan may as well," she noted. "You need to at least give him the opportunity to understand. You need to divulge everything to him, Mary Julia. A relationship needs to be based on total honesty anyway. Be truthful with him and see if you have a chance for a relationship or not. If he cares about you the way I think he does, then he will accept your past. If not, then it's time you moved on."

Flora grabbed Mary Julia and held her tightly. "You need to call your sponsor and tell her exactly what happened tonight. She will help you to gather strength and get back on track again. You can't let yourself be dragged down, Mary Julia. Regardless of your setback tonight, neither I nor Jackie Lynn will permit you to go back down that road. We've seen how far you've come. Don't allow your addiction to overcome you," Flora pleaded, her voice becoming choked with emotion. *Jonathan had better be the man I think he is and accept Mary Julia as she is – whatever her faults. Jackie Lynn and I can't let her begin to self-destruct.*

Mary Julia allowed Flora to hold her. She needed to feel her friend's strength. *Do I have the strength to tell Jonathan everything? Will he accept me as I am?* Mary Julia had no clear answers to the endless questions which flooded her brain. *The only way I'll ever know is to take a risk and talk to*

Jonathan. If he rejects me, then I'll have to accept that. Flora is right. I can't allow myself to be pulled down. I won't.

CHAPTER TWENTY ONE

PROGRESSIONS

Flora called Jackie Lynn early the next morning, even though it was Saturday and her friend often slept in later on the weekends. Jackie Lynn's pregnancy kept her more tired. Flora needed to talk to Jackie Lynn regarding what had transpired with Mary Julia the previous night, and in Flora's opinion, this warranted possibly waking her friend. Fortunately Jackie Lynn and Long Wolf were already awake.

Jackie Lynn told her, "Long Wolf surprised me by bringing me breakfast in bed this morning. Right now, we're sitting here reading the paper together in bed."

Her friend sounded so peaceful that Flora hated to confide to Jackie Lynn what she had called about. Yet, Flora knew she sorely needed Jackie Lynn's advice, so she proceeded to inform her all about what had occurred between Jonathan and Mary Julia and about Mary Julia's sad backslide.

Following a lengthy conversation, Jackie Lynn promised Flora that she would do all she could to help Mary Julia get back on track and remain there. After she hung up the telephone, she turned to Long Wolf woefully sharing, "I am so worried about those two."

Long Wolf assumed she meant Flora and Mary Julia. "You love them a lot. I'm positive they will be fine," he assured her.

Jackie Lynn gazed at him with the sweetest eyes, and then with a short laugh, corrected, "Not the girls. I'm concerned for them too. I was actually talking about Jonathan and Mary Julia. It sounds as if he genuinely loves her, and she loves him. I can't figure out why they are ripping each other apart like they are."

Long Wolf placed his arm around her shoulder and gently stroked her hair. "Hmm...seems I vaguely remember two people that were doing some of the same things a short time ago." He laughed. Then with sincere mirth, he added, "Now, of course, they are the happiest, and luckiest, two people I have ever known."

Jackie Lynn knew Long Wolf was referring to the two of them. She cherished his cheerful, romantic, true-life storytelling. It made their courtship and love seem even more like a fairytale come true. Jackie Lynn gave Long Wolf a wider smile and tenderly squeezed his hand.

Quite suddenly, Jackie Lynn gasped and grasped her tummy. "Oh my!" she shrieked with a touch of surprise.

Instantly alarmed, Long Wolf panicked. "What! What is it?!"

Jackie Lynn chuckled gleefully and replied, "I'm sorry, I didn't intend to scare you. I think I felt the baby move. Here...right here. Put your hand right here on my tummy!"

Long Wolf enthusiastically laid his hand over her lower abdomen, and sure enough, there was this miraculous little flutter beneath it. "Wow! That...that's wonderful!" he exclaimed, delighted to feel the movement of his child for the first time.

Long Wolf got so excited he grabbed Jackie Lynn, squeezing her against him with joy. *I knew I was going to be a father. This makes it more real, and what makes it more perfect is how thrilled Jackie Lynn obviously is about it as well now.*

"Jackie Lynn, I love you," he crooned, and then warmly kissed her lips. "I know you are still concerned about your friends, but can we have a little talk."

"Oh, oh," Jackie Lynn responded, slightly tensing. "I hate it when you get serious like this. I think I should go take my shower."

"Oh, no you don't," Long Wolf protested with a playful grin. He securely held her in place. "I plan on taking that shower with you. We'll have plenty of time after we've talked."

"What do we need to talk about?" she asked.

"Well, for one thing, I heard what you said to Flora…how it would be good for Mary Julia to talk to Jonathan about her childhood, because it affects who she is now. I think the advisor should take her own advice. It's crucial that we discuss what made you who you are. Then perhaps we can talk about going forward."

"Going forward? I think we are going forward just fine," Jackie Lynn replied. She gave him a smile and patted her tummy.

"No, we aren't," he disagreed. "I felt my child move for the first time a few moments ago, and that was wonderful. But I want my child to have my name, and you still refuse to so much as discuss marriage. I have a pretty good idea this has to do with your childhood. I need to know what you need to overcome to have faith in us. The two of us together *forever*."

"For…ever?" she repeated very slowly. "Seems like I've heard that before somewhere," she revealed with somewhat of a faraway look. Looking Long Wolf squarely in the eyes, she told him with a forced smile, "I'm only going to say this one time, and one time only. I had a decent life as a kid. I had one dad who had a wonderful career in law. Since I loved what he did for a living so very much, I followed in his footsteps. I also had several stepfathers, five to be exact, but they were decent human beings, none of them abusive."

"So were you close to any of these stepfathers?" he continued to interrogate, in spite of the fact that he could tell Jackie Lynn was definitely ill at ease discussing these matters. Long Wolf believed he absolutely had to know the details of her past. It was imperative to their future relationship.

"Long Wolf, that was such a long time ago. I dealt with those demons. I don't want to talk about my childhood. It wasn't all rosy like yours," she vaguely admitted, sounding a bit defensive.

"Okay, if you dealt with all those demons, then what's wrong with marriage?" he inquired.

"Nothing's wrong with marriage. It's just not something I particularly want to do. We don't have to get married to put your last name on the birth certificate if that's all you're concerned about," Jackie Lynn pointed out.

"If you were close to your stepfathers, then it must have genuinely hurt each time one of them left," Long Wolf proceeded to theorize. "Kind of makes you think, no matter how much you love someone or they do you, the relationship will eventually end, doesn't it?"

"That may have been what I used to believe. That was before I met...and fell deeply in love, with you," she proclaimed, warmly gazing into his eyes for a few moments. Glancing away, she added, in a monologue, "Missing my stepfathers when they left didn't take away the good things they left me with. I gathered most of the strength I have now from some of these caring men. I learned I had a choice – either go on to become a better person or go on to be just like my parents. I agree with Jonathan when he says he wants to be sure he doesn't become like his dad. I want to be certain I'm not going to turn out like *her*."

Long Wolf listened attentively, allowing her to entirely finish before he clarified, "Like *her*? You mean your mother?"

"Yes," Jackie Lynn said a little sadly. Then she added, "She wasn't a bad person. Just a woman that was never content with any one man. Each man she'd get involved with would last about two or three years, at the most, and then she was off and running again. She was so sure that the next one would be the right one. She would latch on, marry the guy and strive to make the relationship work out...it never did. So off to the attorney for the paperwork to be drawn up, and D I V O R C E here we go once more!"

"So this is why you've fought me every step of the way, and you're still fighting me. You're still keeping part of yourself buried. It's a reserve...just in case," he told her.

Affectionately rubbing Jackie Lynn's shoulder, Long Wolf professed, "You don't need to hide anything from me, Jackie Lynn. In fact, I want to know it all. I'd wager to say I've managed to learn more about you than any man in your past, and I'll bet if you really think about it, you've never felt so in love in your life. I'm not being egotistical here – just stating the facts the way I see them. If you give in and decide to share a married life with me, maybe you'll be amazed to discover that it's possible to love me even more."

Jackie Lynn seductively climbed into Long Wolf's lap, took his hands into hers, and gazed into his eyes. "How could I possibly love you any more than I already do?! You're on my mind every minute of every hour of every day. I look at the paper and something there reminds of you. I look at a menu, and I see something you'd like. I can't begin to imagine loving someone more than I love you. Dredging up old, sad and ugly memories will not bring us closer. Trust me, I know this. I have put all the *demons* behind me, and that is why I *can* love you...please try and understand this."

Without another word, she began kissing Long Wolf all over his face and down his neck. Jackie Lynn wanted Long Wolf to make love to her so fiercely she could taste it. *This is going to be the end of this conversation!* she resolved.

Long Wolf could not resist. He knew she was trying to avoid finishing their conversation. Nevertheless, he swiftly decided he would permit Jackie Lynn to think she had caused him to forget, just so he could have her before they were off and running for the day.

I will eventually get Jackie Lynn to divulge everything I need to know. Of this, I'm determined.

* * * *

Jackie Lynn lay contented, with her head over Long Wolf's heart. She rose up and their eyes met and said *'I love you'* without any words passing. She softly ran her fingers through his dark, plentiful, chest hair and smiled happily at him.

312

This man is crazy, she thought. *There is no possible way I can ever love him any more than I already do.*

Jackie Lynn had never felt so wonderful in her entire life. She wanted to suggest they go take a shower. But she loved lingering in Long Wolf's arms after they made love, so she remained cuddling with him for over an hour.

* * * *

Jonathan arose late the next morning. He had had a terrible time sleeping. He could not get Mary Julia off his mind no matter how hard he tried.

Flora said she needed time alone. Okay, I've given her the whole night and part of this morning. I'm going to her apartment, and we are going to finish our discussion. I have to find out why she was so upset last night. It was more than the fact that I kept us apart for so long. Something else happened. I have to know exactly what that was.

So Jonathan showered, dressed and headed for Mary Julia's place. He did not even take the time to eat some breakfast. His entire focus was on Mary Julia and somehow resolving things between the two of them.

* * * *

"Mary Julia, can we please talk?" Jonathan pleaded in a soft voice, attentively studying her remorseful eyes.

She was standing in the doorway of her apartment, having just answered the door to him. She was still in her gown and robe, although it was almost noon, and she looked as if she had not slept much the previous night either. There were dark puffy circles under Mary Julia's eyes. Her wavy hair was unruly, pieces haphazardly sticking out in all directions.

"I greatly need you in my life, especially right now. It was a terrible mistake to push you away like I did," Jonathan said.

Mary Julia looked up into this man's wanting eyes. "You need someone, Jonathan," she told him, her voice cracking with emotion. "I don't think it's me. I'm too messed up for any man."

"Why don't we have a long talk, and you allow me to decide if you are worth my trouble," he suggested. He waited patiently for her to invite him inside. "Please let me come inside."

"Okay," Mary Julia agreed. She stepped back and ushered him into the apartment. "This shouldn't take long. Once you hear what an awful person I am, you probably won't want to see me again. But I think you're right. You should know. Then perhaps you'll find someone who is worthy of your love."

I think I have, Jonathan kept to himself. He could not imagine anything this woman could confide that would make him totally turn his back on her. He had never cared so greatly for a woman in his entire life.

Flora was coming toward him as he entered. "Jonathan, I'm glad you're here," she said. "I heard what you said to Mary Julia about the two of you having a long talk. I think that is precisely what the two of you need to do. I need to go do some shopping, so you'll have the place all to yourselves."

She had her purse over her shoulder and was swiftly heading for the door. "Mary Julia, if you need me for *anything*, call me on my cell phone. Otherwise, I'll see you later. You guys have a nice talk." Flora scurried out the door then. She did not give either of them the opportunity to protest. She barely even left them time to say goodbye.

Jonathan felt badly about forcing Flora out of her own home, but he was grateful to her for granting him and Mary Julia the privacy they needed. *She's truly a good person. I'm glad my father is no longer capable of terrorizing her. She deserves much better.*

Jonathan walked to the sofa and sat down, expecting Mary Julia to do the same. She refused to sit. Instead, she nervously paced back and forth.

Can I do this? Can I tell Jonathan what I've so thoughtlessly done? Tell him what a horrible person I am? Yes! I have to. He has a right to know!

Jonathan wanted to gather Mary Julia in his arms and assure her, '*Whatever it is that has upset you so – anything you might have done – it doesn't matter. I'll still love you no matter what.*'

As the thought crossed his mind, he sincerely realized that this was exactly how he felt. *I do love her. I'm not letting her get away. No matter what.*

"Jonathan," Mary Julia began at last, studying the floor as she continued to pace.

She would not look at him. *I can't look into his beautiful understanding eyes and tell him what I need to.*

"You think you know me, but you don't. I am a basket case. I'm that way because of two men in my life whom I truly adored and trusted. The first was my daddy who...who touched me in ways a dad should never touch his daughter. As if that wasn't terrible enough, next came my stepfather who loved me very much. When I say he loved me, I mean he *really* loved me. So much so, he elected to show me every night from the time I turned thirteen until my mom finally divorced him."

She paused and merely glanced at Jonathan. When Mary Julia saw the mixture of disgust and pity, she averted her eyes. "Anyway, when an adult does that to a child, it makes the kid feel really...really worthless. I thought I was bad. That I had done something to make my father and stepfather want to do these horrible things to me. When I tried to tell my mother, she slapped me and told me I was a filthy little liar. I certainly felt the filthy part. I endeavored several times to convince her, but all I got was ridiculed, beaten and punished."

She hesitated once more, and Jonathan struggled to remain seated. *I should be holding Mary Julia and reassuring her*, he mentally grappled. Nevertheless, he sensed that Mary Julia did not want to be touched. Therefore, he forced himself to stay where he was and closely listen to anything and everything she might have to add.

Mary Julia eventually began once more, "My mother ended up divorcing my stepfather two years later, but it didn't erase what he had done to me. By then, I was secretly sleeping with some boys at school. I got quite a reputation in high school. Let's just say all the guys knew who to come see if they positively wanted to score. After I graduated from college and went on to law school, I decided I needed to be a bit more discreet. By the time I got my law degree, went on to work at the firm, and met Jackie Lynn and Flora, I thought I had my secret life well under control. But, whenever the pressures got too great or I felt too badly about myself, I dealt with it through finding a man, and I mean *any* man."

Without looking up to see if he was still listening, Mary Julia painfully concluded her litany, "I thought I had put all this behind me after getting out of that loony bin sanitarium and meeting you. But when I saw that...that woman...I thought...well, you know what I thought. I snapped Jonathan. I went right back to the same old destructive ways. I picked up a jogger in your neighborhood, and we went to a hotel together. So do you see, you can *not* trust me! I can't trust myself! You deserve someone much better than I'll ever be!"

Jonathan was silent for what seemed like an eternity. In reality, it was only a few, very long moments. Rising from his couch, he walked to stand directly in front of Mary Julia. He gently tilted her chin up, so he could look into her eyes.

As Jonathan gazed into Mary Julia's eyes, she was shocked to behold not only sadness but a look of intense caring. *Could it be love? No, surely not! Especially after what I've just told him.*

The tears Mary Julia had held back for so long began to trickle down her cheeks. Jonathan spoke then, very softly, very unhurriedly, and with such warmth and compassion the words were causing Mary Julia's legs to grow weak.

Or is it that he is so near, the smell of his soft musk cologne and his warm breath against my cheek?

The words Jonathan uttered next caused Mary Julia's heart to leap in her chest. "Mary Julia, I love you! Please listen to every word I have to say and carefully consider them before you make any rash decisions...I can forgive whatever it is you have done in the past."

She opened her mouth to speak, but Jonathan hurriedly placed his finger on Mary Julia's lips and quieted her. "I'm not finished. I will not permit you to throw away the chance for the two of us to be happy. I know for a fact you love me too. I've also done some stupid things in the past, and I'll tell you about them. I have this place in my heart that's aching. Without your love, there will never be any hope of this anguish going away. I won't allow you to walk away because of sad things that happened in your past...*past* meaning anything previous to *today*. I want to be there to help you heal the wounds that were given to you as a child...and proceeded to deepen as you matured into an adult. I think you can do the same for me," he admitted.

By now, Mary Julia was not merely crying. Her sobs had become so intense, her chest was heaving frantically. Jonathan pulled her into his comforting arms, warmly cradling her against his chest. Mary Julia felt all of her resistance fade, and she collapsed into Jonathan's body. He kissed one wet cheek, moved across her forehead, and down the other wet cheek. Mary Julia was totally overcome by his caring words and the safety of his arms and body.

Perhaps what Jonathan said is true, and he can help me heal. I believe, with Jonathan, I can at last have faith in a man, learn to trust a man...even openly love a man, at least this man. Mary Julia all at once realized that she did not want to live her life *even one more day* without this wonderful man by her side. Her heart seemed to be bursting with love for Jonathan.

"I love you, Jonathan. I love you so much!" Mary Julia gushed. She kissed his forehead and cheeks, as he had done hers. Then she ended with a very passionate kiss on his lips.

When Jonathan pulled back, he had the most glorious smile across his face. "Mary Julia, you are going to be just fine! *We* are *both* going to be just fine! I feel like life has just begun! And what a wonderful life it will be!"

His enthusiasm had Mary Julia smiling and laughing as well. She felt as if a heavy weight had been lifted. She had never felt more wonderful in her entire life.

"Go take a shower and get dressed!" Jonathan excitedly directed. "I want us to go out and spend the rest of the day together."

"Where are we going?" she asked.

"That's for me to know and you to find out. Now scoot!" he said, releasing her and giving her a tiny shove toward the bathroom.

"Can I have another kiss before I go?" she teased, drawing closer to him once more.

"No," he surprised her by saying. He held out his arms to hold her at a distance. "Your kisses are like the sweetest candy. They make me want more and more, and I don't want to end up in the shower with you...at least not yet. Just go shower and get dressed. I'll be waiting right here for you. I'm not going anywhere."

Mary Julia watched as Jonathan took a seat on the couch. "Go!" he ordered with the most handsome grin.

"Okay," Mary Julia agreed and started away.

She could hardly wait to get cleaned up and be back in this man's company. Her life had hope and the promise of true love for the first time, and Mary Julia could not wait for it to get started.

CHAPTER TWENTY TWO

CONFESSIONS

When Long Wolf came from the bedroom the next morning, Jackie Lynn had just hung up the telephone in the living room. She was crying. He rushed to be near her and to find out what was wrong.

"Darling, what's the matter?" he asked very seriously, plopping down beside her on the couch.

"Oh, Long Wolf," Jackie Lynn wailed, throwing her arms around his neck.

He pulled her into a comforting embrace, anxiously waiting for her to continue. Long Wolf braced himself to hear something awful. He was dumbfounded when Jackie Lynn suddenly pulled back and had an enormous smile on her face, amidst her tears.

"That was Flora. Mary Julia spent a very romantic and revitalizing day with Jonathan yesterday. She told him everything about her past, and Jonathan convinced her it didn't matter whatsoever. Flora said he is deeply in love with Mary Julia and she is with him too. For the first time in her life, Mary Julia truly believes she is lovable and can begin to put her past behind her. Isn't that wonderful?! I'm *so* thrilled for her!"

"Yes, it *is* wonderful, and I'm very happy for Mary Julia. But you scared me to death when I saw you crying," Long Wolf confessed with a relieved smile. He teasingly kissed the tip of Jackie Lynn's nose.

"Oh, I'm sorry," she said with a wide grin. She gave him a soft, appreciative kiss for caring so much. "I was just so glad to hear that Mary Julia is going to find happiness after all this time, and so much agony, that my emotions got the best of me."

"So, wouldn't you like to make Flora and Mary Julia as happy?" Long Wolf cleverly inquired.

"What's that supposed to mean?" Jackie Lynn suspiciously, withdrawing half her smile.

"Well, it's just that...I think your friends would be in delighted tears if you would invite them to our wedding," he suggested with a rather mischievous smile.

"You never give up, do you?" she somewhat playfully scolded, laughing at Long Wolf's stubborn persistence.

"I promise you with all my heart that I will *never* give up when it comes to our relationship. I would *never* give up on our marriage either. No matter what," Long Wolf pledged, his eyes becoming very serious.

Jackie Lynn hated it when he got so intense, even though his words always ended up profoundly touching her heart. Long Wolf weakened her resolve never to marry a bit more each time, and Jackie Lynn was quite certain that he knew this was the case. That was why he kept raising the issue over and over. The bad thing was the only thing Long Wolf seemed to ask from her was marriage. The rest of the time, it seemed like he was always so generously giving of himself.

Oh, that booger! He knows I'm overemotional right now. That's why he is bringing this up at this particular moment. Jackie Lynn concluded. She tried unsuccessfully to squirm free from Long Wolf's strong convincing arms before he got her to agree to something she might regret.

* * * *

That afternoon, Long Wolf eagerly went with Jackie Lynn for her ultrasound. The baby was big enough now – twenty weeks – that the doctor inquired, "Would you like to know the sex of the baby?"

Jackie Lynn excitedly gazed at Long Wolf. He was still intently watching the small monitor and the images of their child as the baby moved to and fro inside of Jackie Lynn's womb. When Long Wolf finally looked over at Jackie Lynn with an enormous, delighted smile and warm adoring eyes, she asked him, "Well, do you want to know what sex the baby is?"

"I don't know," he answered. "It doesn't matter to me. I just hope if it's a girl she looks exactly like her beautiful mother. Or on second thought, maybe I don't. If I have a daughter and she looks like you, then I'll have to beat the boys off with a stick."

Jackie Lynn contentedly smiled at Long Wolf, squeezed his hand, and then turned her head to look at the doctor, "I think I'd rather it be a surprise," she answered.

"Okay," the doctor agreed, concluding the examination. "Everything looks great. I think you can count on having a very healthy baby."

Jackie Lynn and Long Wolf left the doctor's office feeling very pleased. Seeing her baby on that monitor proved to Jackie Lynn she really was going to have a baby. Sometimes she still found it very hard to believe.

* * * *

They were in the car on their way home when Jackie Lynn said, "Long Wolf, maybe we should have found out the sex of this baby. We haven't even started to decide what to name this kid yet."

"We'll just have to pick out one girl's name and one boy's name," he suggested with a delighted grin. He lovingly place his hand on her abdomen. "So what do you think little guy or gal? What would be a suitable name for you?"

Jackie Lynn loved it when Long Wolf touched her stomach and talked to the baby. She had never had any idea how bonded she would feel to him, as he happily stood by her side through this pregnancy. It was hard for her to conceive that she had ever considered abortion. *Thank God I wasn't so foolish.*

"Wait a minute. Something just occurred to me," she said. "Will this baby have two names like you? Do we give it its Indian name or does the chief of your tribe have to do that?"

Long Wolf looked slightly troubled by this particular question. He removed his hand from Jackie Lynn's stomach and stared out the windshield for a pensive second. "The baby won't have an Indian name," he hesitantly told her. "Normally the chief would name the child as you thought. But I can't take this baby to the Reservation. The chief would demand we go through an Indian wedding ceremony first. It's custom. Otherwise, I have shamed you by not marrying you but getting you pregnant. I can't tell my mother about this child. It would break her heart."

"You're kidding?!" Jackie Lynn asked in shock. But she knew he was not joking. She could tell by the firm set of his jaw.

"It doesn't matter," he said, striving to make light of it as he started the car.

Jackie Lynn was aware of how important his Indian heritage was to him, and that it did *indeed* matter, *quite a lot.*

"So that explains why you have wanted to get married so badly. Why didn't you tell me this?" she questioned a bit too defensively. Jackie Lynn touched Long Wolf's arm to make sure she had his attention.

"Because that has absolutely nothing to do with why I want to marry you. I want you to marry me because I love you with all my heart. I want to spend the rest of my life committed only to you, making you completely happy. Until you honestly have faith I will do that, I don't want you to say yes," he declared. He gave her hand a reassuring squeeze. Then he turned his full attention back to the road.

They fell into a rather uncomfortable silence for the rest of the trip home. Jackie Lynn could not help but contemplate what Long Wolf had revealed to her. She held the key to their child knowing his Indian heritage. She had the power to keep Long Wolf from sharing a grandchild with his mother. Jackie Lynn knew in her heart she could do neither. Long Wolf had remained silent in regard to these important facts because he did not want her to feel she *had* to marry him.

Now that I know, what option do I have but to do this very thing? She loved Long Wolf so severely she could not allow him to make so great an unselfish sacrifice for her.

"Long Wolf, let's get married," Jackie Lynn blurted out all at once. The words sounded very funny and unnatural coming from her mouth.

Long Wolf's head responsively jerked and he looked at Jackie Lynn in shock for a second, before he turned away. He responded in a disappointed voice, "No. I know why you are saying that. I can't permit you to marry me due to the fact that you feel you have to. If we marry, I want you to want it as badly as I do."

Jackie Lynn was astonished to hear Long Wolf turn down her proposal. She had thought this man would jump at any opportunity to get her to walk down that long aisle with him and recite those familiar vows to one another.

"You've wanted this for months. Why don't we just do it? I'll get used to the idea eventually," she endeavored to persuade him.

Jackie Lynn was still trying to adjust to the fact that she had actually proposed. No one would have convinced her she would have ever done anything like this in a million years. Nonetheless, Long Wolf was constantly causing her to do things she had never expected to do, such as have a child. Hopefully, he was correct about them being able to sustain a life-long bond as well.

"I don't want you to merely *get used to the idea.* If we marry, I want you to be deliriously happy about the decision. I want you to believe in us with your whole heart and soul. I think you still have very grave doubts we could make a marriage work. I don't care if we don't marry until we are very old, if it takes that long for you to fully believe we will always be together no matter what," Long Wolf stressed.

He was staring at her with such adoration that Jackie Lynn honestly believed her heart was melting. The only thing standing between the two of them was her foolish doubts.

How on earth do I get rid of them? she wondered. She did not have the slightest idea.

"Then how do I get to the point of believing in us with my whole heart and soul?" Jackie Lynn was amazed to hear herself ask out loud.

"Well, I've told you my opinion before. I think you need to do as Mary Julia and share all the details of your childhood with me. I think once you talk about things you might be capable of exorcising the demons that plague you. Perhaps I'm wrong. There's only one way to find out – you share everything with me," Long Wolf answered with absolute conviction, his eyes stern.

"I've told you essentially all the details," Jackie Lynn began to argue.

"It's not the details that matter. It's the emotions that go along with those details. That's what I need for you to open up to me. Your deepest emotions. The ones you still have locked in an impenetrable vault. You guard them tightly. The only emotion you don't hide from me anymore is your love for me. That I have no doubt of," Long Wolf said with a slight agreeable smile. He tenderly squeezed Jackie Lynn's hand.

For the first time, Jackie Lynn realized how Mary Julia must have felt when she had confronted her about her sexual addiction. *No wonder she fought me so fiercely. It's scary to try and face your darkest childhood fears. Can I do that? Can I bring all of those painful, forgotten memories to the surface once more? What if Long Wolf's wrong, and this serves no purpose where our relationship is concerned? Is it worth the risk? Long Wolf is worth any risk, and it's him I have to think of now.*

It was imperative that she strive to do whatever she could to come face to face with conquering her long held insecurities. "Okay," Jackie Lynn slowly conceded. "When we get home, I'll start with my earliest childhood memory, and I'll try to share all of the emotions of the events of my childhood. Have you got your degree in Psychology, Dr. Long Wolf?" she teased, striving to lighten the mood a little. Jackie Lynn was fiercely dreading their impending, revealing conversation.

* * * *

When they walked in the door, Jackie Lynn was very surprised when Long Wolf pulled her into his arms and began passionately kissing her.

"Long Wolf," she said breathlessly a few minutes later. "I thought you wanted to talk."

"After," he said, kissing her neck and unbuttoning her blouse.

Fine by me, Jackie Lynn mused.

She never tired of the two of them making love, although it was getting more difficult as the baby continued to grow. Long Wolf did not seem to mind though, and he was creative about trying to find comfortable and fulfilling positions.

* * * *

After they had made love and rolled lazily onto their sides, facing one another, Long Wolf ran his warm fingers through the sides of Jackie Lynn's long hair and tenderly caressed her cheek. He gazed adoringly into her eyes and told her, "I love you with all my heart and soul. That will *never* change. No matter what. On his death bed, my dad told my mom he would love her through eternity. I pledge the same to you. So, married or not, you will *always* have me by your side, and you will always have my never-ending love."

Jackie Lynn was extremely moved by Long Wolf's honest pronouncement. He not only made love to her with his body, but his words touched her deep inside. "Long Wolf, I have never loved a man the way I love you," she responded, reaching to touch his face as well. She outlined his wonderful, pleasurable lips with her fingers. "I don't want to imagine my life without you in it. You make my life so complete."

"The only other thing I wish for you is total peace of mind. Will you permit me to help you there as well? Will you confide to me all about Jackie Lynn long before I met her?" he questioned. He kissed the palm of her hand which had been toying with his lips.

"Yes," Jackie Lynn agreed. "Where do you want me to start?"

Long Wolf had her begin by talking about when her mom and dad had separated. She told him she had been only six years old. "That was my mother's longest marriage, and I think it only lasted as long as it did because of me. They fought a lot, but my father didn't want to leave. He adored me, and I adored him. I'll never forget the day he left. He hugged and kissed me, told me it was for the best that he left, picked up two suitcases and walked out the door. I sat there in our living room, watching him go and bawling my eyes out. That was one of the worst days of my life."

So she began slowly sharing her turbulent childhood. "My mother remarried only six months after the divorce from my father was final. My stepfather had worked with my father. My mother had evidently been having an affair with him before the divorce. He was a decent man, but I wouldn't allow myself to get close to him. That would have been a betrayal to my dad. So since my mother was so preoccupied with my stepfather, when I wasn't at my dad's house, I spent most of my time alone. Thus, I started to learn how to be independent."

"A six year old that had to learn to be independent. That sounds very lonely and confusing," Long Wolf commented, grasping Jackie Lynn's hand.

"It was, but soon, my mom was going through divorce number two, and I got to meet my soon to be second stepfather. This time mom decided to capture the judge who had presided over both of her divorces. So my second stepfather could have been my grandfather as well. He was a very sweet, older man, and he did everything in his power to try and win my good graces. I liked him the best of all of them."

"How old were you then?" he questioned.

"I was eight when they married, and I was ten when they divorced. Enter, lickity-split, step dad number three."

Long Wolf beheld a very faraway look in Jackie Lynn's eyes, and he could hear the bitterness start to enter her voice.

"Stepfather number three was a politician. He was busy campaigning the whole time my mother and him were married. I was clearly in the way, other than to be in charming, happy, family photographs with him and my mom. He wasn't totally useless to my life though. He taught me how to perfect the flawless fakey smile for the camera, and I can still put that smile on in court when I have to. Behind closed doors though, my mom had some of the worst fights with him. She would get him so furious I'm amazed he didn't strike her. Instead, he would break things. I can still hear the crashing when I think about it."

"Wow, that must have been scary for a girl your age. What did you do when these loud fights were going on?" he dared to inquire, massaging her shoulders.

"The first time it happened, they woke me up with their loud shouting and the crash of something breaking. I ran to my mother's defense. I thought some mad man had broken into the house or something. I'll never forget that night," she admitted. Her voice slightly cracked, despite her resolve not to cry.

Long Wolf pulled her closer. His loving touch made Jackie Lynn even more emotional, so she did begin to weep. "Don't fight it, honey," he told her in a quiet voice, gently kissing her forehead. "You've held these emotions back far too long. It's okay. You can let them all out with me."

In a somewhat garbled voice, she grudgingly continued, "My stepfather was the one who was concerned about me. My mom was too angry to stop her tirade. She was up in his face screaming at him and beating on his shoulders with her hands. She was accusing him of – I quote, 'fucking everything in a short skirt'. When he told her I was in the room, she turned and shouted, 'get your nosey little ass back in your bed. This is private!'. I turned and ran. I put the pillow over my head when I climbed into bed. Later, my stepfather came into the room. I remember him taking the pillow off and telling me everything would be alright. That my mom had not meant to yell at me the way she had. My mother never even came to check on me."

"I'm sorry, baby," Long Wolf sympathized. He kissed her wet cheeks and caressing her shaking shoulders.

Jackie Lynn was amazed she was crying over this. She thought she had put it all behind her long ago.

"So how old were you when your mother hooked up with stepfather number four?" he asked. Jackie Lynn was beginning to open up to him, and Long Wolf was not about to allow her to shut down.

"I'm sure she hooked up with my next step dad before the divorce to number three was final. But she didn't marry again until I was twelve. I didn't care. I wasn't in the house much then anyway. I spent a lot of nights at my best friend's house. I really envied her. Her parents must have had a marriage like yours did. They seemed to love each other a great deal as well as my friend Nicole. They were very good to me," she recalled with nostalgia, her tears subsiding for a short while. "Nicole's family moved away a year later, so I was left alone once more. That hurt worse than losing most of my stepfathers, because I had gotten close to her and her family."

"Where was your father during all of this? Were you still spending time with him?" Long Wolf probed.

"Not as much, no. You see, my father remarried, moved across the country and started another family, so they took up a great deal of his time. I never was very close to my stepbrother and stepsister, so I kind of felt like an outsider there as well. Soon after, my dad dropped out of my life altogether. He died a few years ago, but I didn't go to the funeral," she confessed, feeling as if she were going to start crying again.

This is getting ridiculous. What good is dredging up all of this old pain doing?

"Don't stop," Long Wolf encouraged. He tipped Jackie Lynn's head up and gazed with genuine interest into her sad eyes. "You're doing great. I fully understand now why you fight so hard to remain independent. You got used to that. If you stand alone, then you won't get hurt."

"I got hurt plenty," Jackie Lynn was surprised to hear herself admit. "Yeah. I guess it did make me a bit hard. But hard is good in this world. There are too many women out there like my mother, who have to cling to someone to survive, no matter who they make miserable."

"Including their daughter? You think she made your childhood miserable, don't you?" Long Wolf added, supportively hugging her.

"Yeah. I suppose so," she revealed. She wanted desperately to stop this painful stroll down memory lane. "So I think you get the general idea. Like I told you before, my childhood wasn't all rosy like yours. Far from it."

"No, no," Long Wolf protested, feeling Jackie Lynn's body stiffen in his arms. "You said you would divulge everything. What about your other stepfathers. I don't want you to stop until you are through."

"Is there some reason you want to hurt me?" she surprised him by asking. She was trying to stay tough. Yet, it was beginning to feel like the very softest side of her was being exposed.

"No, sweetheart. I never want to hurt you. I'm not the one who has. That was part of your past, and you need to come face-to-face with that actuality and *really* put it behind you. Now what was stepfather number four like?" he persisted, softly rubbing her back.

"He was a very wealthy businessman. My mom traveled a lot during this marriage. Seems like I read about her in the paper more than I saw her for the next three years," Jackie Lynn continued, not wanting to.

Now that Long Wolf had gotten her started, it seemed she could not stop. Maybe secretly she had always wanted to talk about all of this with someone she could thoroughly trust. *I do thoroughly trust Long Wolf*, she accepted.

"So who in the world did you stay with while your mother was doing all of this traveling?" Long Wolf inquired.

"Mostly alone," she relayed.

"Your mother left a twelve-year-old all alone?" Long Wolf gasped in shock and dismay.

"You forget I had been learning how to take care of myself for most of my life. I was a pretty mature twelve-year-old," she somewhat proudly proclaimed.

"Weren't you scared at night?" Long Wolf asked with pity.

"You get used to it after a while," she claimed, but Long Wolf could see in her eyes that Jackie Lynn had not particularly liked it. "Anyway, I had other friends, and I spent the night at their houses a lot, especially on the weekends. My mom wasn't gone for weeks on end or anything. I made it sound worse than it was."

Long Wolf doubted that. Jackie Lynn was covering again. "So this lasted until you were what...fifteen?"

"Yep. Hit the nail on the nose. Enter stepfather number five, another lawyer. He was a very sweet and caring man. My mother was jealous of all the attention he gave me. He even taught me how to drive," she divulged, a slight smile appearing on her face. "So you see, the three men I most adored as a kid had careers in law. Thus my logical choice of career also. Even though everything I've told you sounds pretty bad, it made me into a strong independent person, and I'm happy about that."

"Me too," Long Wolf agreed, bestowing a warm kiss on her lips. "I love your independent streak, and I would never do anything to try and break that. But you have to understand that being independent doesn't mean putting up walls and not letting anyone help you. Anyone meaning *me* specifically."

"I'm content to put aside those walls for you," she conceded, giving him another, more lengthy kiss.

"Thank you for sharing all that with me," Long Wolf said. He securely cradled Jackie Lynn in his arms. "I understand so much more about you now. You've never seen a relationship that actually worked. No wonder you are so afraid of commitment. But you aren't your mother, and because of the experiences she put you through, you never could be, even if you tried," he assured her, kissing her cheek and then the side of her neck. His reassuring words and his bodily strength made Jackie Lynn feel so totally secure that she found it hard not to believe him.

"Long Wolf. Make love to me again. *Please*," she hoarsely whispered in his ear.

Jackie Lynn wanted, *no, needed*, to be intimately joined with this man once more. Making love with Long Wolf would help her to forget again, to put the past back where it belonged – *in the past.*

CHAPTER TWENTY THREE

TOTAL TRUTH

After her and Long Wolf's never-ending journey of unending passion the night before, Jackie Lynn had soon fallen into a thoroughly relaxed slumber. She awoke alone in bed the next morning feeling fairly well.

I suppose Long Wolf must have awoken and left me here to finish sleeping. He is such a good man. Some day I'll feel completely safe with him. Not that I don't now.

Nevertheless, for whatever reason, every time the word *marriage* came up, Jackie Lynn's stomach tied in nervous knots. As hard as she tried, she could not stop that harrowing feeling of doom. She did love Long Wolf with all her heart and soul. However, starting a marriage, that, in a very short period of time, could end as quickly as it had begun, was something Jackie Lynn did not want to do.

Nonetheless, she could not help but ask the same, tired, old questions. *How does living together make it so different? We can break up just as easily, only it wouldn't involve any special paperwork to get on with our lives. But, then again, yes it would now, since we are going to be bringing this other little person into the relationship.*

Jackie Lynn's mind began to race with one after the other very scary, negative thought. She was so startled by her thoughts that she opened her eyes and sat upright in bed. *I have to plan for the baby,* my *baby,* not *our* baby. *Well in reality, it* is *mine...that is, if anything happened and we didn't remain together.*

All at once, for no logical reason, Jackie Lynn was beginning to panic. She fearfully contemplated, *I need to have a legally binding document that states Long Wolf, even though he is the father, could not take this baby away from me if something happened and we didn't stay together, not that anything is going to happen.* She countered in frustration, *I have got to stop thinking like this! I am, we are, and we will be fine.*

Long Wolf came into the room and noticed Jackie Lynn nodding her head, up and down, then back and forth. "Hey sweetie, what are you doing? Having a private conversation with that little bundle in your tummy?" he asked, coming up behind her and wrapping his sturdy arms around her waist.

Jackie Lynn jumped erratically as soon as he touched her. She had been so deeply self-absorbed by her troubled thoughts she had not heard Long Wolf come into the room. She pulled away enough to turn around and face him.

With a bit of irritation in her voice, she said, "I wish you wouldn't sneak up on me like that. Some day you are going to frighten me right into labor!" Jackie Lynn rather roughly pushed Long Wolf aside and started across the room to get dressed.

"Not so fast there, little miss. You can't scold me like that and then walk away. I have the right to put up a fight," he teased, laughing and striving to lighten things up.

Long Wolf thought Jackie Lynn was just annoyed because he had unintentionally scared her. She was not amused by his humor. Instead, she was overcome by defensive and angry feelings toward him. Jackie Lynn was not sure why she was feeling this way.

All at once, she had this awful, unanticipated flashback. She was seven years old, and she was locked in a very small, dark room, where she could hear only muffled sounds. The sounds were her mother having sex with a boyfriend, and the room was a walk-in closet where her mom had hidden Jackie

Lynn until the man either left to go home or went to sleep in her mother's bed.

Long Wolf noticed a major change in her expression. It alarmed him. Jackie Lynn looked as if she was being frightened by something, or someone. He rushed to her and gently touched her arm. She flinched.

"Oh, my darling, I am so sorry. I didn't intend to scare you."

Jackie Lynn's expression turned from terror to anger. She glared at Long Wolf and snapped, "Why couldn't you have left me alone?!"

Tears automatically began to form in Jackie Lynn's eyes, and her facial expression immediately changed to extreme sadness. She broke down and started to sob, placing her hands securely over her eyes. She was trying to block out the terrible, uninvited images that were now vividly flooding her mind.

Long Wolf pulled Jackie Lynn into his arms and held her against his chest, "It's okay. Everything is okay. I would never purposely scare you or hurt you. I'm so sorry for whatever I've done to make you cry. I adore you. I only want to love you and take care of you. Won't you please permit me to do that for a little while, at least until the baby gets here?"

His words, intended to bring comfort, instead had Jackie Lynn resistantly pushing away from him. "Right! This is all because I am having your baby! If I wasn't pregnant, where would you be right now? In that quiet cabin of yours, peacefully reading some article or book and relaxing after a long day at the office?"

Long Wolf studied Jackie Lynn very carefully with deep concern. Today was Saturday. No one had been to an office, and he was very relaxed right here with her in her apartment. *They* were supposed to be going to the cabin later today, however.

"Jackie Lynn, honey, it's Saturday morning; I haven't been to work today. Are you alright?" he asked with obvious alarm.

She slowly sat on the edge of the bed and stared at Long Wolf in bewilderment for several moments, "I told you this talking about my childhood, all this sharing of myself, would bring back terrible memories. Why didn't you listen to me and leave well enough alone?" Her eyes began to fill with tears once more.

Long Wolf did not fully understand what Jackie Lynn meant. The talks they had had yesterday were not regarding some horrible childhood, just a sad case of one woman not knowing what she truly wanted out of a relationship and forcing her child to live through her trials of trying to find it.

Something is definitely wrong with this picture! "Jackie Lynn, I don't remember any *really* terrible things in the stories you told me last night. I understand it might be harder for you though since you were living the story. I could only imagine it as you told it. Is there still something you haven't told me?"

Jackie Lynn could understand Long Wolf's confusion. She *had* purposely omitted some of the most painful things that occurred during those years. She had believed that this would spare her the appalling feelings of recalling them herself. Her plan had miserably failed. It was suddenly all there once more, *so clearly*, as if it had happened only yesterday, rather than years ago.

"I didn't tell you everything," she hesitantly revealed in agony. "I left out some of the details. I thought if I didn't talk about them, they would go away. They almost had, you know. I buried them along with my mother."

Stunned by her admission that her mother was dead – *I always assumed she was still alive* – Long Wolf took Jackie Lynn's hands into his own.

"I'm so sorry. I didn't know your mom was dead. I certainly didn't intend to cause you all this anguish. I just wanted to know you completely. I thought, if I knew all there was to know about you, I could eventually teach you to trust me enough to marry me. How long has your mother been deceased?"

"She died ages ago," Jackie Lynn rather numbly answered.

With tears streaming down her cheeks, she slowly began to fill in the traumatic blanks of the story of her childhood. Jackie Lynn knew there was no sense trying to hold anything back now. "I was about seven the first time she tried it...to commit suicide, that is. She slashed her wrists on a sunny afternoon. I had been outside playing in the yard when I heard her wailing. I ran into the house to discover her lying in the bathroom in a pool of blood. I grabbed two pillowcases from the linen closet and tied one around each of her wrists, and then I called 9 1 1. They were so kind. They remained on the phone with me until the ambulance arrived. That night, at the hospital, the doctors kept telling me I was a hero. That I had saved my mom's life. Only problem was, when I was left alone with her, she told me I had had no right to save her. She said she knew exactly what she was doing, and I had ruined everything. My stepfather took me home, and when my mother was well – *at least they thought she was* – he brought her home too. It took many years before I realized what she meant in regard to me ruining everything. She had planned on *him* finding her. Then he would have known how much she needed him, and he would have stayed. But he was late coming home, and I found her instead. That's how I ruined everything. Only if I hadn't come in when I did, she would have died."

Long Wolf was trying to understand. "But, honey, you said she was dead, or did I misunderstand you?"

Jackie Lynn's tears had mysteriously stopped and she was very eerily calm. In a somewhat unemotional voice and with a distant glaze over her eyes, she clarified, "Well, she *is* dead now. It took several attempts...until she...she succeeded. After each marriage went bad, she would try the same thing. It never worked, but she kept right on trying. First, by her wrists being slashed. Then she took an overdose of sleeping pills twice. Another time she tried to hang herself. And then, she ultimately succeeded the night of my senior prom. She got very drunk that night, and I guess since the wrist slashing had come the closest to working of all her attempts, she tried it again. My stepfather had left a few days before that, never to return. She had apparently changed her mind and attempted to call for help, but she had waited too long this time. So when I got home with my date, we found her laying in the living room in a pool of blood...everything was soaked...everything was red. She was pronounced dead at the scene."

"Dear God!" Long Wolf exclaimed in shock. He pulled Jackie Lynn's strangely limp body securely against his own. "How awful! My poor darling! No wonder you didn't want to talk about your childhood. I'm *so* sorry! I had no idea. I thought you were just hiding the pain of having so many stepfathers."

"I told you my stepfathers weren't the problem," she mumbled almost incoherently.

In a whisper, Jackie Lynn further confessed, "Even the strange men she slept with to get even with my stepfathers didn't do me any harm. They were never aware I was there. I was tucked safely away in the hall closet while she had sex with them."

Jackie Lynn shivered then, and Long Wolf truly thought his heart would break. "You know what the worst part of her committing suicide was? I wished her dead more times then I can count. But I never really meant it. The night...I found her...de..dead..I felt like I was the one who had slashed her wrists. Or perhaps I wished it was me who was lying there instead."

"No. Don't ever say anything like that!" Long Wolf protested.

He pushed Jackie Lynn back a small distance, so he could gaze at her pained face. He told her, "Your mom was very ill. That wasn't your fault, and it was totally natural for you to be angry with her, thus you thinking you wished her dead...although you really didn't. Damn! I want to take away all of your suffering somehow. Seeing you hurt like this is tearing my heart in two."

"Don't!" Jackie Lynn surprisingly screamed. She shoved herself totally away from Long Wolf. "I don't want your pity. I don't want *any* man's pity! I can handle this on my own. I have for so long, and I can keep right on. I don't need anyone to survive!"

Her last sentence stuck in Long Wolf's mind like a bright, flashing, neon sign. *'She doesn't need anyone to survive!' Of course! She's frightened to death of becoming exactly like her mother, not just in being clingy and noncommittal. Her real fear is of growing ill like her mother. And now she is going to have a child. No wonder she was so disturbed when she found out she was pregnant. She didn't want to put a kid through the same hell she had suffered through.*

"Jackie Lynn, honey, it's okay to be scared," Long Wolf assured her. He drew closer to her. "We're all scared of something."

"I'm not scared of anything!" she vehemently denied. She was shaking her head back and forth in denial, scooting farther apart from him.

"Yes, you are," Long Wolf firmly stated. He grabbed Jackie Lynn's arms and pulled her toward him. She struggled against his grasp, but he would not let go. "You're scared to death if you totally let down your guard, the same sickness that claimed your mom's life will take its grip on you. I'll pledge to you that I won't allow that to happen."

"You can't stop something like that. No one can," Jackie Lynn argued. Tears reactively started yet again. "Don't you think I would have stopped it for my mother if I could have?"

Jackie Lynn was sobbing now, her whole body vigorously shaking. At the same time, she still endeavored to push Long Wolf away. Regardless, Long Wolf slid her into a tight, soothing embrace.

"Shh, Jackie Lynn. It's okay, sweetheart. I'm here. I'm always going to be here. There's a vow that's made during the marriage ceremony where you swear to stand by the person in sickness and in health. *If*, and that's a big *if*, you ever were seized by violent depression, then I would move heaven and earth to get you the help you needed to overcome it. Depression is highly treatable if the suffering person seeks help. Your mother never did. In my opinion, none of your stepfathers loved her enough to try and see that she got the help she needed. Yes, one of them might have carted her off to some mental institution, but he still didn't bother to stay around afterwards to support her through recovery. He probably took her there to ease his own conscience, so he could hit the road guilt free," Long Wolf attempted to convince her.

He held Jackie Lynn in his arms for a very long while. Soon, her sobbing subsided, but she remained silent. Nevertheless, Long Wolf knew her mind was not idle.

She's thinking over everything that transpired this morning. All of her confessions and the strong emotions that have resurfaced after so long. Lord, help her come to terms with them, he prayed.

"What are you thinking?" Long Wolf dared to ask. He was tenderly massaging the back of Jackie Lynn's neck.

"I'm thinking that I've never been so scared in my entire life. I feel like a knight that's been stripped of all his armor. I have nothing to protect me now."

Long Wolf was astonished to hear Jackie Lynn admit this.

"You feel my arms around you, don't you?" he asked. He pulled back slightly, to convincingly gaze into Jackie Lynn's frightened eyes. "Let me be your coat of armor. No person, place or thing will ever pull me away. Our love for one another will keep us both strong."

"Well, if you are my coat of armor, then that means you will have to cover my body continuously," she began to tease, smiling for the first time.

"I'll cover and protect every part of you. Especially that heart of yours," Long Wolf vowed. He pulled her close to him and slowly caressed her face, neck and shoulders with soft, adoring kisses. "You can trust me, Jackie Lynn. No matter what."

He lowered the two of them until they were lying on their sides on the mattress, facing one another. He pulled the covers up to Jackie Lynn's neck, and then Long Wolf locked his arms behind her back.

"Close your eyes, beautiful. I want you to take a little nap, all warm and cozy in my arms. When you wake up, you'll find I'm still right here, holding you. I want you to feel what it's like to be totally secure, and positively believe you can always feel that way with me."

After all of the gut wrenching, emotional confessions and the tears she had shed, Jackie Lynn did feel exhausted. And as always, it did feel absolutely wonderful to lie in Long Wolf's strong, supportive arms. She shut her eyes as he requested.

Even if I don't sleep, I'll relax here for a while and let my emotions settle, she surrendered.

* * * *

When Jackie Lynn opened her eyes again, and glanced at the bedside clock, she was surprised to discover that an hour had passed. She had drifted off into a short nap. Long Wolf's arms were still securely locked behind her back, as promised, although he also appeared to be sleeping. She gazed happily at his handsome, slumbering face for a second. Then, with appreciation, she brought her lips to his scrumptious-looking mouth.

Long Wolf's lips automatically responded, and his mouth curved into a contented smile. Opening his eyes, he erotically ran one hand up and down her spinal column. His touch pleasurably awakened all the nerves throughout Jackie Lynn's body.

He definitely knows how to touch and please a woman, she mused. "You're such a wonderful man," Jackie Lynn professed. She stared deeply into Long Wolf's eyes with immense love and passion. "You must have had some terrific parents to have turned out to be such a caring, giving person."

"I did have wonderful parents, but you have much more to do with me being caring and giving. You mentioned my cabin earlier. You're right about me being there today if you had not come into my life. I would have been sitting in that cabin or walking in the woods alone, foolishly convincing myself I didn't need anyone to share my life with – that I was fine by myself. Sound familiar? You see, we *are* soul mates. We make the perfect couple," Long Wolf argued. He gave

Jackie Lynn another wide grin and sampled her wanting lips. "All I want out of my life now is to care for and give to you. If I can know I'm doing that, and you are happy, then I'll be one of the happiest fellows alive."

Not surprisingly, his words touched Jackie Lynn so greatly she felt like her heart was literally bursting with love. A startling revelation occurred to her all at once, "My gosh, Long Wolf! Do you realize that – as close as I've been to Flora and Mary Julia – I've never told them about my mother's suicide attempts, or especially about me finding her dead? I think you've become my very best friend, as well as my lover, today."

"I've never felt more privileged," Long Wolf admitted with a delighted smile. "Don't you feel much better now that you have shared that terrible burden with someone? It still hurts. It most likely always will. I can't make that totally stop. But I can share the pain with you, and I think that makes it a little less. Doesn't it?"

It certainly does. Jackie Lynn felt as if someone had lifted a ten ton weight from her mind and her spirit. Now that she had faced the terrible things she had lived through so long ago, they did not seem nearly as horrible anymore. She had made them worse all along by constantly suppressing the intense anguish associated with these atrocious events. "Okay. How'd you know I'd feel so much better afterwards? You kept trying to convince me, but I never would have believed you in a million years."

"I have a confession of my own to make. You asked me if I had my degree in Psychiatry. I majored in Business Administration, but my minor was Psychiatry," Long Wolf revealed with a slightly guilty smile.

"You pig," she playfully chastised.

Jackie Lynn lightly swatted Long Wolf's arm, even though it was impossible for her to be angry with him at this very moment. She felt as if she had been through an exorcism. "So I guess this means you have been constantly evaluating me all along."

"I never tire of evaluating every part of you," he lustfully divulged. He kissed the bend of her neck, as Jackie Lynn liked so very much. "You have to realize I can never truly be your Psychiatrist. A Psychiatrist has to remain emotionally uninvolved from his patient. That is never going to happen. But being your best friend and lover sounds absolutely wonderful to me."

"Well, we've taken care of the best friend part. So how about being my lover. Right now!" Jackie Lynn heatedly demanded. She obscenely ran her hands down the length of his chest and happily fondled his straining manhood.

"Hmm...I don't know. That's rather unethical. I could probably lose my license to practice," Long Wolf teased, grinning greedily in response to the glorious feel of Jackie Lynn's fingers.

"Just as long as you don't lose your *desire* to practice, I'll be happy," she declared, before hungrily feasting on his mouth.